Praise for Tiffany Clare's

## THE SURRENDER OF A LADY

"Tiffany Clare writes a swoon-worthy romance filled with rich details and vivid characters. Any readers wishing for a bold and sweeping historical romance need look no further—Tiffany Clare is a treasure of an author!"

—Lisa Kleypas,
*New York Times* bestselling author

"Exotic, bold, and captivating. Tiffany Clare's rich, sensual prose is delightful indulgence!"

—Alexandra Hawkins, author of
*Till Dawn with the Devil*

"Dazzling, daring, and different! Exotic and erotic! *The Surrender of a Lady* will have you turning the pages until you finish, no matter how late it gets. Tiffany Clare is a brilliant new talent in historical romance."

—Anna Campbell, author of
*My Reckless Surrender*

St. Martin's Paperbacks Titles
by Tiffany Clare

*The Surrender of a Lady*

*The Seduction of His Wife*

# *The Seduction of His Wife*

TIFFANY CLARE

St. Martin's Paperbacks

THE SEDUCTION OF HIS WIFE



Color cover illustration by Jim Griffin
Hand lettering by David Gatti



For information address St. Martin's Press, 175 Fifth Avenue, New York, NY 10010.

ISBN: 978-0-312-38183-7

Printed in the United States of America

St. Martin's Paperbacks edition / February 2011

St. Martin's Paperbacks are published by St. Martin's Press, 175 Fifth Avenue, New York, NY 10010.

10 9 8 7 6 5 4 3 2 1

*Because this is now written down forever and ever and*

*I love you, this one is all for you, Scotty-poo!*

# *Acknowledgments*

I couldn't have finished this book if not for my partner in crime (and your bazillion read-throughs), Elyssa Papa.

A special thank you for all my readers for this book and previous ones: Debbie Hajdukovic, Kristina, Maggie, Elena, Janga, and Santa. If I forgot anyone, it's 'cause I'm terrible at remembering these things until it's too late.

Helen, you always offer a bright light in my not-so-bright moments. Monique, thank you for sticking it through the really sucky, to the less sucky, and finally to the—I knew you could do this. Holly—I really don't know what I'd do if I couldn't harass you, sometimes on a daily basis!

And the biggest hug and kiss go to my friend, Alex Borovoy, for reminding me when it was tough that writing is about rewriting. Without that mantra I wouldn't have done what needed doing in this book that I will fondly remember as hell.

# *Chapter 1*

*You never write to me. I don't even know your whereabouts in the world.*

*1848 London*

"You can't go in there with me, Grace." Emma Hallaway-Mansfield, Countess of Asbury, tugged her sister's hand away from the latch on the carriage door.

Grace studied her with furrowed brows. "Emma, you asked me to come here with you. I won't abandon you in your time of greatest need."

"You have no choice." Emma had to go in there by herself. "If anyone should recognize us, our reputations will be in shambles. *You* can't risk that."

"I don't care. You're my sister. You would never ask me to go into such a place on my own."

"Think of Abby, Grace. If my reputation is completely ruined, I'll not be able to help find our sister a husband . . . you, on the other hand, will."

"You don't know the things that happen in such a place."

"And how would you know?"

Though Grace probably did know better than she, since her late husband had actually spent a great deal of time in her company. Which was more than Emma could say for her marriage. Emma refused to think about her marriage, or lack thereof, right now.

She'd been sitting here too long in indecisiveness—she was already running a few minutes late—and their nondescript carriage was drawing unwanted attention.

"Take the carriage around the square a few times. I won't spend more than twenty minutes inside."

"I ought to come with you. Waverly had no right in courting me, and then to turn around and do this to you."

"Believe me, I know." Emma sighed heavily and twirled her locket between her fingers as she tried to think of another solution. There was none. She was stalling at doing the inevitable. "But it can't be changed."

She had to find Waverly—the lying scoundrel—soundly reprimand him for his audacity, and then demand that her portrait be returned. A portrait she should have never painted. Or at least never have sold, since the subject in the nude was her.

With a deep breath, she tied a beaded velvet mask around her head to cover the top portion of her face. Not the greatest of disguises, but it would have to do.

"If you're not back in twenty minutes, I'll have no choice but to follow you in," Grace said.

Kissing her sister on the cheek, Emma said, "Twenty-five minutes, no more."

Emma turned up the latch on the carriage door. When her feet were on solid ground, her stomach turned into a jumble of nerves. She gave one last look in the dark window of the hack before turning away.

Night had fallen, but Haymarket was busy with foot traffic. She'd never been to this part of town. It was a place where gentlemen indulged in the sorts of wicked things a lady wasn't supposed to have knowledge of. Emma hadn't reached the ripe age of seven and twenty without discovering some of life's idiosyncrasies, particularly where men were concerned.

After a couple of deep breaths, her stomach steeled against her anxiety, and she moved grudgingly forward. Standing before a great wooden door with iron detail of a medieval design, Emma lifted the horned-devil knocker and rapped it once.

A small peephole slid open and was followed by the gruff voice of a man. "Pass."

"Balderdash," she answered.

The door creaked open, giving way to a beefy man with bare arms bigger than the width of her cinched waist. Goodness, he was a veritable giant. Emma barely resisted the urge to take a step back and flee to the safety of the carriage. Scars marred one side of his face; his blue eyes were like shards of ice cutting through her as he gave her a once-over.

She stood taller, showing her determination to enter a bawdy house, and met his rigid gaze with her resolute one. She would not be refused entry. Nothing would stand in the way of saving the loosening threads of her reputation.

"Ain't yer type o' place," the giant said.

"I'm sure it's not."

The giant took a step to the side, moving from the doorway with a firm scowl in place. "Don't usually have yer kinder flashies. But yer gots yer pass."

Emma looked around the amber-lit foyer. Rich Chinese silks and heavy Italian brocades hung on the walls in a conflicting mishmash of sheer and woven materials. Foreign perfume lingered in the air; it was so powerfully sweet, it burned her nostrils and had her holding her breath intermittently. The hallway was narrow and had no rooms on either side. A set of darkly stained wooden stairs loomed directly in front of her.

*Courage,* she told herself. She needed to pretend just for tonight that she had the courage to confront her nemesis. She couldn't imagine what Waverly thought to gain in blackmailing her here. His purpose was obvious; the whys were not. Ascending the steps quickly, she opened another, less forbidding door at the top of the stairs.

Emma's eyes went wide at the sight before her. The place was hot and crowded with at least fifty people—more people than she had expected. The room was wide and open, sporting high ceilings that did not dim the ruckus of everyone talking at the same time. Settees and deep couches were set around the room for patrons to repose on. The men in attendance all seemed to be of means if their pressed, finely cut suits were anything to go by.

Bawds mingled wantonly and freely amongst the crowd. Some were bare-chested while others wandered around without skirts and bodices to decently cover their unmentionables. Her hand clenched around her locket.

A small twinge of comfort enveloped her on noticing she wasn't the only one sporting a demi-masque. She wasn't the only one who needed to protect her identity.

On closer inspection of the debauched scene around her, patrons she thought were relaxing on the sofas were actually *in coitus.*

Eyes wide with that revelation, Emma reeled and nearly went back through the door to escape the scene unfolding around her. She stopped herself short of reaching that goal.

She couldn't leave. First, the direction on the letter

had been a firm demand that she attend this place. Second, her sister would have taken the carriage around and would arrive back in fifteen minutes at the most. Emma would not stand in the streets of Haymarket. It wasn't safe for a proper lady to do so.

Taking a deep breath to prepare herself for the scene behind her, Emma tried to act as if she'd been in a place like this before and held her chin up unashamedly as she turned back around.

A few naked women would not scare her away. She was no stranger to the female form, since she painted it on a regular basis. As for the men engaging in all sorts of wicked acts, she'd just have to pay them no mind.

Despite the low décolletage of Emma's pale cerulean evening gown, it was obvious she wore too many clothes *not* to be noticed by every man in the room. The other women of the upper echelon wore rich, dark tones, the gowns swept low off their shoulders. Emma was surprised their breasts didn't spill right out of their dresses.

Emma skirted toward the private rooms. Taking a deep breath, she pressed open the first darkly painted door to reveal a couple bent over a red velvet divan in the throes of passion. A fat, squat man heaving to and fro in some mockery of the primal dance held a fistful of yellow hair at the back of the woman's head.

Emma's breath faltered, her will to do this sinking faster than a rock thrown in water. She shut the door with a snap, hoping she didn't remember that horrible image for the rest of her days. Certainly married women didn't participate in such untamed, wanton things.

The letter had been clear that she was to find the *fourth* door on this floor. She wasn't thinking clearly when she most needed her wits about her.

Turning away from the line of doors, Emma looked about the room, hoping no one watched her. She hadn't thought it possible for her day to get worse, but it had. Her eyes locked upon a gentleman she wished she could forget as easily as he had forgotten her.

Putting her hand to her mouth, she hoped she didn't lose her meager dinner as she gazed at the man who had abandoned her a dozen years ago. He was like a predator lying in wait, all sleek and masculine where he lounged. Her heart stuttered in her chest at the sight of him. Swallowing past the lump in her throat was near impossible.

He wouldn't recognize her. Or would he? She'd never have recognized him except for the fact that he looked like a younger version of his father.

There was no mistaking that strong Roman nose of his, or the tussled waves of light brown hair that brushed the open collar of his shirt. His face was weatherworn and tanned, evidence he spent most of his days in the sun. The boy she'd known had grown into a distinguished gentleman.

How she wished it wasn't *him.*

But there lounged her husband—whom she hadn't seen in twelve years—with a bawd atop his lap.

What a farce this was.

# Chapter 2

*Words escape me. Why is it I'm helpless but to bleed ink onto paper, even if I never deliver the final version of this letter?*

Her husband. Emma wanted to scream.

A pained noise escaped her mouth before she could quell the hurt building in her chest. She dug her nails into her palm, hoping the physical pain would narrow her focus, erase the pain splintering her heart unbearably. It felt like the whole world was falling away from beneath her feet, ready to swallow her into a chasm of nothingness.

Unlike the other men milling about the room, at least *he* had the decency to keep his trousers done up. His head tilted back to the sofa, his eyes were closed. He watched no one, not even his ladybird. *She,* however, was not idle. Her hands massaged his chest. His shoulders.

Emma forced her feet to move back to the private rooms, but she couldn't keep her mind on the task she was supposed to be focused on. It was impossible to keep from turning back and staring at her husband.

She peeked around one of the supporting beams that shot through the floor before going into her appointed room. She trailed her eyes over his form one last time, absorbing every detail she could. He wore no necktie. His shirt gaped open where the buttons were released, revealing the hollow at his throat and the speckle of light brown hairs on his chest. A fresh dusting of hair stippled the lower portion his face.

How humiliating!

Her husband would rather have the company of a prostitute than spend any time with his wife. Hadn't it always been that way? He had never wanted her. Tears welled in her eyes, but she refused to let them fall.

Then his eyes snapped open; his dark brown gaze stared straight at her, nearly pinning her to the spot, sending a shock through her system. It was not the gaze of the young man she remembered, but of a man who had lived. *Really* lived. There was a knowing expression in that gaze.

Caught watching him, she turned hurriedly away. She was naught more than a well-dressed woman in a den of iniquity. He'd most certainly not recognize her after all their time apart.

Opening the door to find the private room empty, she stepped inside to shut out the image of her husband.

Emma leaned her back to the door and wedged her slippered foot tightly to the bottom to stop anyone from interrupting her moment of solitude. Her heart beat frantically at the fact that her husband had spied her.

For now, there were more pressing issues to deal with than one wayward husband. Wiping her sweaty palms down the side of her bodice, she reached behind her and clicked over the lock. There was a letter sitting atop the divan with her name scrolled on the outside.

She swallowed back her nervousness and sat heavily

on the couch as she unfolded the paper and read its contents. Waverly wanted her back in Bakewell in three days' time. Emma frowned. Why ask her to come here if he was only going to demand she be at her country estate?

Was it possible that he'd had a change of heart? Certainly, he didn't mean to reveal her portrait to the rest of the world without talking to her first?

She didn't know what to think or do. Knowing her sister wouldn't have made her way back around yet, Emma waited ten minutes before she slid out of the room to head back to the entrance of the harlots' den.

Suddenly an arm snaked around her waist and pulled her aside. She squealed out a protest and began to fight whoever had grabbed her.

When Emma looked up to the man who held her, she froze in his arms. Even her heart missed a beat at the realization that she'd been caught.

Her husband's expression was far from amused.

Swathed in blue silk and a felted black mask, Richard Mansfield, Earl of Asbury, could still make out the lady's high cheekbones, round eyes, and kissable pouting lower lip. She was like Aphrodite elevated above the disciples surrounding her, ripe for plucking and bedding.

There was no mistaking those luxurious blonde curls, or her tall, slender frame. He remembered her always being conscious of her height as a girl. Now she was cloaked in a confidence that had her standing tall and glaring back at him with rancor.

Why, of all places, was his wife in a whorehouse?

A wife he hadn't seen in more than a decade.

The moment she had come out of the private room, he had wrapped his arms around her waist to halt her.

Emma tried to squirm free, so he held her more

firmly. She was all soft, ripe curves pressed up against him, stirring his blood and awakening his body to a lust he'd never had for his wife before now.

*What in hell!*

"Unhand me, sir." Her voice was pitched low, like the sound of a woman well tumbled and unused to speaking. Did she hope to disguise the true timbre of her voice, or was she worried they would be overheard?

"I'm not fooled by your disguise."

Her gaze flickered to the open buttons of his shirt before veering off over his shoulder to the room beyond them as he forced her a step back and into the shadows.

Her lips parted, revealing the tip of her pink tongue; her pupils were dilated in a state of half euphoria. Maybe this type of jaunt onto the wilder, seedier side of life was a common occurrence. He was willing to show her just what kind of fun could be had in such a place.

What if she'd come here looking for some company of the male persuasion? Why else would she be here but for that reason alone? That thought set a trigger off in his mind and forced him into quick action.

Richard placed his arms on either side of her shoulders, his hands against the wall so she had no place to go, and stared into her green eyes.

What man wouldn't desire her?

He nearly growled at the thought.

Her slender form curved inward just the right amount at the waist. Her bosom was more than enough to fill a man's hand. His own flexed against the wall in anticipation of doing just that.

He leaned in closer, intent on figuring out her motives in coming here. Did she have an assignation tonight?

Fool of him to think she'd not found the comforting arms of another man over the years. So why did that thought sit so uncomfortably on his mind now?

With difficulty, he kept his hands pressed to the wall rather than somewhere else on her person. Like her breasts. He was helpless to stop his gaze from straying to the dip at her bosom. Though he liked what he saw, a little too much, he didn't appreciate the fact that every other man in the room had the same glimpse of what she had to offer. This possessiveness over a woman was unlike him. Women were a means to an end. A passing amusement when needed.

But Emma was his bloody wife. She belonged to him alone.

"Do you want to tell me what you are doing here, wife?"

"Leaving, if you don't mind."

Defiance was clear in her stance as she lifted her chin in a haughty manner and glared at him. Not the cowering miss he remembered her to be.

"What I mind is finding you here."

At least he blocked her from the view of other patrons. Her black-felted mask was a joke. How she thought to hide her true identity was anyone's guess. He lifted his hand, ignoring her annoyed huff of air as he fingered one of the curls that had fallen free of her pins. He wanted to feel her hair splayed over him as she worked herself above him.

She tried to duck under his arm, but he stepped closer to her. Her attempt to escape his hold was a wasted effort. He'd not let her leave until he was done talking to her. He wrapped one soft curl of her hair tightly around his forefinger, liking the silkiness against his rough hands.

Her skin would be soft to touch, too.

"I planned to come and go from this establishment quickly," she hissed under her breath.

"You cannot expect an answer like that to suffice. The last place I wanted or expected to find you was in a bawds' den." He kept his voice low, intimate. "I'll not have you traipsing around London looking for lovers."

Good God, how had she turned into such a beauty? She'd been pretty enough when they had married all those years ago, certainly not the nymph teasing him now with her demure glance. Would he have left for parts of the world unknown had they married when they were both more mature? He couldn't say. And would definitely never know.

"How dare you accuse me of any such thing. You've no right!"

"I have every right when my wife shows her face in a house for whores."

She cheeks flushed in anger.

What did she expect him to say? She dared to come to a place where any man had free license to approach her. He'd never desired her before—she'd been so young when they'd married. But now that she was in his arms, and quite grown up . . .

Couldn't he do everything running through his mind? It would be easy to push her up against the wall, nibble at the exposed bits of flesh: her neck, her shoulder, her breasts. So very tempting.

He blinked and shook his head to pull himself from the trance she'd put him in. What in hell had come over him? He had more important matters to look after while he was in London. And yet, he'd thought of nothing but bedding his wife since the moment he'd seen her.

Her seductive eyes stared back at him in question. He swallowed against the desire burning a firestorm through his body.

"How did you recognize me, Richard?"

With his free hand, he skimmed his fingers over the lacy edge of her décolletage. "Your lackluster choice in costume for a whorehouse was a clear enough indication you didn't belong." Actually, he never forgot a face, no matter that she had been a mere child of fifteen when they'd married.

She hissed in a breath at his crude language, or perhaps at his daring stroke. Wanting to know which had caused her reaction, he traced his finger lower. Her skin was as soft as he had imagined. He wanted to touch all of her. Massage every bit of feminine skin while he peeled back the layers of her modest dress. Pulling the curl he held around his finger straight down, he watched it unravel, then bounce back into place.

"I'm expected somewhere," she snapped and pushed at his shoulder.

She tried to sidle out from beneath his arm again. He didn't give her the opportunity to free herself just yet. He stepped even closer, so close their bodies touched from breast to thigh, and he did what he'd desired since getting her into this position. He ran his knuckles over the swell of her soft breast.

She hissed in a ragged breath. So, she was not completely unaffected by his touch. Good. Because he didn't know what in hell had come over him. He was supposed to be scaring her away from this establishment, not trying to seduce her into the nearest bed.

The problem was, he didn't want to let her go now that he'd caught her. Where the doxy had failed to amuse and arouse him, his wife had little problem. Interesting predicament this put him in.

He was definitely rising to the occasion.

Even so, this was not the right place or time for this kind of reaction. He didn't believe in coincidence. His wife's sudden appearance here, at the only brothel he ever visited in London when he needed a safe place to stay for a night or two, was some sort of trick.

Someone was trying to lure him into a madman's

game of life and death. Why they would include Emma was anyone's guess. He hadn't spoken to her or seen her in a dozen years.

He stared down at her. Up to this point she'd always meant nothing. And that had remained true until this very moment. Damn it. He didn't need any distractions right now.

With much reluctance, he dropped his hand from her breast to her tucked-in waist, and held on to the enticing curve of her hip. She was so small in his grasp. He wanted to cradle her protectively into his body, to take her out of this hellhole so no other man dared to lay eyes upon her.

He wasn't thinking clearly. Not at all.

Angrier with himself now than her, he snapped, "Your decorum is sorely lacking. Your boldness in finding a suitor leaves a bad taste in my mouth. Is it time I paid you a visit?"

Visiting her was not part of his agenda. On the other hand, he'd not let his wife traipse around London entering other places like this one. Or allow her to have an affair right under his nose.

Emma hissed in another breath and tilted her head back to regard him with nothing short of fury. "You've never seen fit to do so before."

She stepped away from him, back to the wall, so he'd have to reach for her if he wanted to touch her again. The little minx was challenging him. He jerked her back to him, aligning their bodies. She was warm and soft. Supple and exactly what his body wanted to sink into. But now was not the time to be led by his cock.

"Don't think we won't discuss this lapse in judgment, Emma."

This wasn't the safest place to speak of his planned whereabouts in the coming days. And he knew without doubt his plans now included a visit to their shared town house. Damn his wife for stepping foot in this place.

"So be it," she said, doubt lacing her voice.

Before she could push past him, he blocked her once again.

"I let you leave not because you will it, but because you should never have set foot in such a place."

"Your high-handedness falls on deaf ears. You cannot control me any more than I can control you, Richard."

He didn't know how else to act toward her. Not when he wanted to push her back into the room she'd come from and take every imaginable advantage he could. She took away his ability to think straight about the things that were most important right now.

Whatever happened to the meek girl she'd been when they'd courted?

"I will see you in due course." He stepped away from her and inclined his head.

She did not return the parting gesture with a curtsy. Instead, she left in a flounce of irritated skirts. She couldn't leave fast enough. Not once did she turn her head as she proceeded toward the stairs that led back outside.

Richard sagged against the wall, his strength finally giving out. A quick look about the room revealed no one watching their exchange or her hasty exit. Pressing his hand lightly to his side, his fingers came away slick.

Damnation.

He'd been doing fine until she'd shown herself. Exhaustion blanketed his mind, numbing his limbs at a rather alarming rate.

Dante, his longtime business partner and friend, was suddenly there, studying his bloodied side. "You need to take care of that."

Richard waved him off. "Follow the lady to her carriage. Make sure she's not accosted by anyone on the stairs or in the street."

With a scowl, Dante left to do as bid.

Glancing over the guests, Richard searched for the mistress of the house. When their eyes clashed, he called her over with a nod. She was putting him up as a favor tonight.

He'd be moving back to his town house tomorrow.

It was the perfect place to go. He needed to lay low for a few weeks, long enough for things to settle down in the East with his business dealings. Long enough for his and Dante's shipping empire to trade hands.

Dante had traveled with him to England after the attempt on Richard's life. He'd known the man for eight years, and Dante was the last business associate he could trust at this point. The man was loyal to a fault.

Marietta, the mistress of the house, was at his side, her ample bosom on display with ruched trimmings lined with a neat row of beads and feathers drawing the eye of any man within her vicinity. Her plump face, with her rouged lips and kohl-lined eyes, gave him a commanding expression.

"You shouldn't be up and about yet, your lordship. I'll not have you pulling out my fine stitchwork."

That had been the other reason he'd come to Madam Purforry's. She had a steady hand and didn't faint at the first sight of blood. She'd had him cleaned, his side sewn back together and patched up within an hour of his arrival.

"Stitches still feel tight. I've just stretched the skin." Cocking a grin at the mistress, he pushed slowly off the wall, impressed that he didn't fall over when he suddenly felt light-headed. "I'm embarrassed to say, I need your support."

Marietta put her shoulder under Richard's arm.

"No need to dally with the flashy types coming through here," she tsked. "I've got plenty of pretty innocent-looking girls if that's what you seek. They'll sit on your lap and do all the work."

Didn't he know that for the truth.

Marietta wrapped her arm around his middle, mindful of the blood-soaked patch on his shirt. Her voluptuous figure barely held his tall frame upright. "Juliet wasn't pleasing enough? I can send up another girl. Someone to take your mind from the pain."

"No company tonight."

He couldn't take her up on that offer now that he'd seen his wife. Emma looked the same . . . only grown up. As well as he could tell with that flimsy mask that did nothing to conceal her features. Her high cheekbones, her slightly freckled nose, those blonde curls of hers that looked and felt as smooth as the finest silk. He'd wanted to unravel her hair from all those pins and spread it out beneath him.

There his thoughts went again. Strange how he'd not spared his wife a thought since their wedding night and now his mind almost seemed consumed by her.

Arm tight around Marietta's shoulders, he made his way up to the third-floor landing out of view of the other patrons. Dante followed, having completed his task. The man wore a scowl that could kill. One that said, *I didn't save you for you to bleed out because of stupidity in a whorehouse.*

"I'm well enough, Dante. Just get me in my room so I can clean this up."

Dante hoisted him up with his shoulder, and Marietta retreated, promising to send up a repast. When he was finally sitting on the bed, he pulled his shirt off, hissing in a sharp breath.

Dante mumbled something that sounded a lot like "whore of a mother's son."

Taking the wet cloth from Dante's hand, Richard patted at the blood. "I've only pulled a stitch."

Dante retrieved a roll of linen, set in the room for the purpose of cleaning the deep slash in his side, and started ripping it into strips.

"We shouldn't be here. There are too many people here to notice our presence in London."

No, it wasn't an ideal place, not now that he figured someone had sent his wife here. Just so happened to be the last place in London he felt he could hide without drawing undue attention to himself. Seemed he was mistaken in that notion.

"We don't have a lot of options open to us. I can't really fight off anyone should they try to get the better of me right now. I'm pretty much useless like this. And until I'm on my feet again and at full strength, we have to stay to ground."

"Whores jumping about your lap is not a good way to do that," Dante grumbled.

"I wasn't about to slight the proprietress. She sent the girl, and I let the girl do what was asked of her." He held the strips of linen out to Dante. "The wound has to breathe. I don't want it turning septic."

Dante took the linens and set them out on the tall chest of drawers. "We should leave for your town house tomorrow."

"We will."

A light rapping of knuckles sounded at the door. Dante pulled a knife from somewhere on his person, a lethal-looking piece of curved metal that had to be ten inches long.

"Calm yourself. It's sure to be the meal Marietta promised."

Of course Dante never liked to be careless. He held the knife behind his back and cracked the door open enough to see who was on the other side. The door swung wide the next moment, and a servant came in carrying a covered tray.

She gave a pretty curtsy after setting down the tray on the round walnut server. Her cleavage spilled over the low-cut bodice, revealing her rouged areolas at the line of her gown.

"Will that be all, my lord?"

Another enticement. He would have laughed if it wouldn't have insulted the girl. Instead, he said, "Quite enough. Tell Marietta I do not wish to be disturbed until tomorrow."

"Yes, my lord."

When the door shut on her retreat, Dante threw the bolt in place and checked over the sandwiches neatly stacked on a plate. "Do you think she's poisoned it?"

"Marietta has no reason to be done with me. For the time being, our arrangement is mutually beneficial."

Leaning his head back to the wall, Richard closed his eyes and pictured his wife with her little mask and prim clothes.

"Who was the woman I followed down to the street?"

"My wife."

There was a pause.

"Was she looking for you?" Dante's expression was carefully absent of emotion, and his tone even.

No one could be more shocked by his wife's presence than Richard himself.

Cracking one eye open, he answered, "I doubt it." He'd not elaborate that she might have been here for an assignation. That was no one's business but his own.

Dante sat in the chair and picked up one of the sandwiches. "Curious that she happened to walk into this establishment as opposed to the thousands of others in this city. Someone knows we're here. We're being watched."

Richard nodded his agreement. "I'll talk with Marietta in the morning. I'm sure she's aware of the situation that brought my wife here." Probably knew who Emma was to meet with, too.

"We should leave tonight." Dante bit into the bread.

"Keeping out of sight will have to be enough. If someone wants me dead they'll have to get through Marietta's muscle. I wish them luck. I've never met a man who could get past them. Women, yes, but not just any man is going to get through those doors."

"We are like sitting geese."

"Whoever our foe is, they'll not get a noose around our necks." Richard let out a frustrated sigh. "Stop fussing and let me sleep. What we do will depend upon the information I get from Marietta. Once we start finalizing the deal with Heyworth, the waters will calm."

"Nothing has been easy in the sale of our business. I don't expect it to get any easier."

"Whoever is trying to make the deal fall through may get bored with this game of cat and mouse they've devised."

"I hope you are right," Dante mumbled.

Richard didn't respond. He hoped he was right, too. Or, despite all his careful planning, they might still end up dead before the deal could be finalized.

# Chapter 3

*Your father tries his best to keep my spirits up, knowing I long for word from you whenever a letter arrives. But there is never word for me*

Emma went directly to her painting room as soon as the sun had come up. She could spend most of her day painting. It let her think about nothing except the picture she was working on. Her marriage and Waverly were the farthest things from her mind. At least for now.

Setting her freshly cleaned paintbrush down on the lip of the easel, Emma stood back and studied her latest work.

The lighting was off. The position of the dark-haired woman sitting on a chair, holding nothing but a sheer orange scarf, did not evoke the erotic image that was clear in her mind. Her form, she supposed, was pleasing enough, the breasts high and overly generous in size, her waist narrow, her hips with the slightest flare. The dark-eyed beauty was missing a twinkle in her eye, something that promised naughty intentions. All in all, it wasn't bad. But it would need a great deal more tweaking before it was just right.

With a heavy sigh she plopped herself into the cushioned rocking chair.

A shame she'd not found a more lady-like hobby over the years. She'd once found a painting in the attic at her country estate of a woman erotically splayed across a bed. It had grasped onto her imagination like a lure reeling in a helpless fish. From that point forward, she couldn't rest until she had painted the female form just once.

That first painting had been her own form, since she had been too afraid to ask another woman to sit for her. Too afraid to share her secret with anyone at the time. She had sold it in a fit of anger on her twenty-third birthday. She'd been furious that her husband had ignored her for another year. That he had wanted nothing to do with her. It had been her only truly rebellious act against the unjust life she had been given.

She hadn't told her friend Nathan, the Duke of Vane, that the painting was a likeness of her. He was the only person aside from her sisters who knew of the erotic portrayals she spent so much time perfecting. In fact, he'd known about them before her sisters were privy to the information, as he was the one who sold the pieces for her.

She remembered the day she'd delivered the painting to him; a deal had been secured at that point. That had been the only time she'd ever seen Nathan angry. His words had been colorful as he'd reprimanded her for selling something no man had a right to see. But the deal had been struck and could not be undone. Nathan had made her promise never to paint another nude of herself. She'd agreed not because he'd exacted the promise from her, but because she wished she had thought long and hard about releasing that painting to the public.

With that thought, Waverly came to mind. He had been a friend to her and her sisters for the past year. Waverly would not get away with treating her so poorly. She'd make her feelings clear to the man. That she wanted her painting returned, and that none of the Hallaway women would have anything to do with him in the future. If that didn't work, she'd ask Nathan to retrieve the painting by other means.

Because if she didn't retrieve the painting, she feared Richard would find out about it. She wished she'd never set eyes on her husband. Wished he hadn't threatened to come home. Though she had a hard time believing he would come to the town house.

How long had he been in England? She knew he traveled the world extensively, was sure he had a house in India, too; that was the extent of her knowledge, since he'd never bothered to send his father word of his whereabouts. And it wasn't as though he'd write to her or, God forbid, pay her a visit when he was in England. Why should he visit her? He hadn't even come home for his father's funeral.

Fate was cruel, vicious.

She stood and untied her apron strings, trying to rid her mind of all the questions and worries plaguing her.

The drapes were drawn back, the sun warming the room quickly at this hour. Not only would she swelter in here midday from the midsummer heat, but she'd not be left in peace hiding in here past lunchtime. Her sisters would come looking for her soon if she didn't meet them for a walk, as was part of their usual morning ritual.

When she stepped outside, her sisters were sitting around the wrought-iron table in the small garden path, luncheon already set up.

Abby, the youngest sister, looked up from her book

and raised a conspiratorial brow. "See, I told you she'd be down before the noon hour. Guilt at abandoning us to our own devices has a tendency to gnaw at her."

"Couldn't you have stayed in your painting room for a while longer?" Grace asked.

"I'm sure you were minutes away from retrieving me. What did you lose, Grace?"

Grace sulked. "My pearl earrings."

"You really should know better than betting your odds against Abby." Emma rubbed her hand over Grace's arm in a soothing gesture. "I don't think you've ever won."

The footman standing by the serving cart pulled the cast-iron chair out for her. When she settled her skirts under the table, he dropped a serviette in her lap. A plate of fresh fruits and another with layers of sandwiches was set in front of her.

"Thank you. Take a break indoors," she told the man.

With a bow, he retreated. Today, private matters amongst sisters needed to be discussed, and Emma did not want to hear whisperings of it from the staff at a later date. They had pristine reputations to keep intact. Well, her two sisters did. Emma was merely tolerated in society. She'd long ago been scorned for her inability to keep her husband from wandering foreign lands, indulging in all sorts of trade. Then there was her longtime association with the Duke of Vane—the only person to ever befriend an awkward young woman whose husband had run off. Vane was also the embodiment of the word *wicked,* and a pleasure seeker in the most carnal of senses. It was no wonder so many thought she was having an affair with such a man: Many women couldn't resist him.

If word ever escaped that she painted erotic scenes that some of the richest lords owned, she'd be completely banished from polite society.

Emma had filled Grace in on everything that had

happened in the bawdy house when they'd gone up to bed the previous night. Abby probably knew all those details by now. Emma hadn't been able to bring herself to talk about the letter Waverly had written. She'd not be able to hide it much longer since he planned to visit her at Mansfield Hall.

Grace was the first to break the silence. "What are you going to do about Waverly?"

She leaned back into the cold support of the chair. "I don't know."

"Didn't he at least leave a note?" Abby's eyes widened when she didn't respond. "I knew it. Tell us what that rapscallion said."

"He said he would meet me at the country house. We will have to leave tomorrow."

"And what of your husband? What will you do if he comes here looking for you?" Grace asked.

The idea was so ludicrous that she laughed. "Richard will not come here. Not with the three of us in residence. I'm worried, yes, because I've made a mess of things. It was unwise of me to sell that portrait."

"Emma, you're being too hard on yourself. Your art is very exclusive and should have never found itself in the hands of that scoundrel."

"What am I going to do if Richard finds out?"

"How will he?" Grace said.

Emma did not want him to come home. Not with everything in her life upside down at the moment. Perhaps her sister was right. Perhaps her secrets were safe.

"Now, what do we do with Waverly?" Abby asked.

Emma cast her eyes toward her half-empty plate. "I'll figure him out when the time comes."

"I ought to pay the man a visit, give him a few choice words to swallow." Grace forked a mouthful of melon viciously.

"You can't. Let me handle Waverly my own way."

"I don't think you can reason with the man. It's obvious what he wants," Abby was quick to say.

"And what is that," Grace shot back.

"I may not have married, probably never will, seeing as I'm so long in the tooth, but I'll not play ignorant with my sisters. I know what happens in the marriage bed, and *outside* of it for that matter." Abby gave them both a piercing glare that dared them to ask more. "Don't you see what Waverly wants?"

Yes, she'd suspected Waverly's intentions in luring her to a house that catered to women with loose morals.

"Abigail Anne Hallaway, you will not say such things!" Grace admonished. "Some devil has taken hold of your tongue." Did Grace wish to shield Emma from this truth? It was pointless to do such a thing.

"I think the devil more or less ran away with it long ago." Abby grinned at them both, closed her book, set it on the table, and picked up a vine full of grapes.

Emma cut off a retort from Grace. "Leave Waverly to me."

Grace ripped off a chunk of bread from the center of the table and sat heavily in her chair, glaring at Abby.

"Why do you suppose he never showed?" Abby remarked, finger tapping her lip in thought as she focused on Emma again.

"I don't know. Maybe he saw Richard and decided to leave? Maybe he changed his mind? Maybe he's already revealed the truth."

"He hasn't. We would have heard something by now." Grace patted her hand in a comforting gesture. "We'll have to wait and see what happens when we return to Mansfield Hall."

All three sisters nodded their agreement.

"Come on," Emma suggested. "Let's go for a walk

and leave this mess behind us at least for the remainder of the day."

Grace nodded. Abby tied her straw bonnet under her chin before they were arm in arm venturing back through the house and toward the park.

"I still want to know what you'll do if your husband does come home?" Grace asked with a wistful sigh. Always the romantic.

"Do you really think he will?" Silly of her to ask, but the old hope of having him near, of having him come to see her as he used to when they courted so long ago, was taking root in her heart. "He never wanted a wife."

How it pained her to know that for the truth. Given half a chance, she knew she could have been a good wife to him. It seemed too late for such youthful fantasies.

"When men grow older, and you know I speak from experience," Grace said, "they want to settle down into a quieter life with their wives at their side."

"I daresay," Abby put in, laughing, "Asbury isn't so old as your husband was, Grace."

Grace and Emma both giggled with the assessment. Richard had turned thirty-one two months past. Grace's husband must have been in his sixth, almost seventh, decade when he'd passed away.

"True," Grace said. "But he probably wants children before he's too old. My husband already had children to take over his title and lands."

Did Emma want to be a mother? It seemed unlikely at this stage in her marriage. Especially after all the years she'd craved her husband's attention and received none. But the fact of the matter was, she was aging, and she wanted children very much.

When she was growing up, she'd always thought she'd have her own brood by the ripe age of twenty-seven.

She'd waited on her husband too long, wasted too

many years pining after something that wasn't meant to be. For the time being, she had her paintings to keep her time occupied. Not that she could share it with the world since they were mostly of an erotic nature. But it was something to keep her mind engaged.

They walked down the winding path of the Serpentine and sat on a bench to watch the ducks swim by.

Finally, Emma said, "Children would be a welcome distraction, and wouldn't be able to leave me so readily as my husband did."

Abby gave her a pensive look. "You were both so young that it's not fair to fault either of you in a failed marriage. We are surrounded by failed marriages. Most of our acquaintances will never have the security of wedded bliss." She scrunched up her nose. "Asbury should have known better than to keep running away from his life here. It's done neither of you any good. A shame really. And you are a fine woman, Em. Don't let that blackguard husband of yours make you think otherwise."

"I don't think otherwise."

"I'm glad to hear that." Abby tilted her head back, closed her eyes, and let the sun warm her face.

"You know things could change for the better if he does come home," Grace interjected. "You got on well enough when you were younger. People change over time."

Never could a statement be truer. She had changed a great deal over the years, mostly in the last three years since Richard's father had passed away. The man had been like a father to her. Her father-in-law had given her wings and set her free. He'd been a good man and was everything Richard apparently was not.

"I never spent any time with Richard outside the watchful eye of our chaperone. Someone was always five feet behind us making sure we acted appropriately. Most visits, we hardly had the opportunity to talk."

"Yet in those allotted times, he was always pleasant with you," Grace pointed out.

"I wonder if it was an act. Something to keep his father happy. I can't blame him for leaving; he was a young man bent on adventure. I was still a child in his eyes."

From the moment he'd entered her bedchamber on their wedding night, she'd started to cry. And she'd continued to cry for the remainder of the evening. She'd ruined a perfectly good wedding day by turning into a sniveling, whining young woman. He'd done his duty, and of course she'd let him. Without so much as a goodbye, he had left her that very night.

She shivered despite the warmth outside. She didn't like these memories resurfacing. It had taken her years to bury the happy and sad memories in the back of her mind. She wished she could banish Richard completely from her thoughts, but doubted he'd ever completely disappear from them.

# Chapter 4

*How can you miss that which you do not know?*

The housekeeper opened the door instead of the butler. The older woman stared at him in shock. Richard couldn't blame her. He'd not set foot in his town house since his father's death. The woman looked as though she'd faint from his presence.

"My lord," she said on stepping away from the doorway to admit him into the house.

"Is my wife in residence?"

That had been on his mind all morning. Had she stayed in Town, or had she left for Mansfield Hall at first light?

"Not at the moment, my lord." Richard had always been careful to avoid staying at the town house whenever Emma was in residence. He had no plans to avoid her this time. "She's gone for a walk with Lady Grace and Miss Abigail."

"Send your mistress into the parlor when she's back. And have the master bedroom set up for me. Mr. Lioni will occupy the guest room closest to the stairs."

"Right away, my lord."

The woman walked down the hall at a clipped pace to do as he bid. Dante came through the door the next moment.

"How long are we staying?"

"I haven't decided. We might travel north to my family estate." Much depended on his wife. He was looking forward to seeing her again. "If anyone knows I'm in London, there's nothing to stop them from calling on me. I can't see anyone with this obvious pain in my side. I won't reveal any weaknesses to potential enemies."

"We should consider leaving London immediately."

"I'm in too much pain to be jostled around in a carriage. We'll go in a few days." His wife was sure to flee for their country home after seeing him. "You'll have to book passage on the rail to Matlock. We'll take a carriage the rest of the way."

He hadn't been home to the estate since his wedding day. What would Emma think of his return? Strange that he'd not been able to rid his mind of his wife since last night. She was turning into a damnable nuisance. This desire to see her baffled him. His business took precedence. Always had. Or so it had always seemed in the past.

There was one important fact that remained: He wasn't a young man anymore. While his father had been alive, it hadn't much mattered whether or not Richard had stuck around. The title, the estate, all the entailments had been his for three years now, and he'd done nothing with them.

He'd meant to come home to England after his father's death, but he'd been caught up in the politics of his trade. Once his business was sold, he'd have a great deal more time to do his title justice, and fill the role properly as the Earl of Asbury. Part of that meant making peace with his wife and securing the family seat for future generations of Mansfields. And in securing his seat, he'd not be cuckolded by one of her lovers. Seeing her last night had proved that he couldn't leave her to her own devices any longer.

He'd not been completely deaf to the gossip surrounding her over the years. There were rumored affairs. Actually, one rumored affair, with a man known for his proclivities where the fairer sex was concerned.

Richard had settled into a wingback chair, a glass of lemonade in his hand to stave off the heat of midday, when he heard the commotion from the hallway. His wife rushed into the parlor with her hat in hand, gloves still on from her walk.

Emma tipped her head down in a curtsy. Her blonde curls were loose and spilled around her heart-shaped face. When she looked back at him, he was stunned to silence by her appearance.

He hadn't gotten a good impression of her in the dimly lit room last night. Under the full brunt of the sunlight coming in through the open windows, she was a remarkable woman. Her skin was speckled with the lightest of freckles over her thin nose and high cheekbones, which were rosy from her exertions outdoors. Wide, round eyes that were as green as raw jade stared back at him in silent astonishment.

Had he struck his wife speechless? She'd rendered him quite unable to find his tongue.

Her height lent her a litheness and agility that made him want to caress her as he would absently stroke a cat. Even her form was pleasing with its curves at the bosom and hips. She was more beautiful than any of the more exotic women he'd spent company with. More striking than he ever remembered or imagined possible.

He stood, remembering his manners too late. Damn her ability to make him speechless.

"Emma."

"What are you doing here?" she said in a rush, nibbling at her lower lip.

"This is my house." He didn't mean to bite out his words so harshly, but must she question his intentions?

"You never stay here when I'm in Town."

"It seems I need to look out for your welfare. Make sure you act as your position dictates." He meant it teasingly, but the words came out cross.

The color drained from her face. "What exactly does that mean?"

Damnation. He was making a bloody mess of this. "It means you are no longer allowed to venture out in the evening without telling me your whereabouts." There, that was said without an edge of anger.

"You have no right."

There was a fire about her that he hadn't expected. He was intrigued by this new contrast in her character. It was better than the meek obedient young woman she'd once been. Though that didn't mean he'd tolerate her traipsing around Town with a string of lovers in her wake.

"As your husband, I have every right." And he'd be damned if his wife ran wild, mingling with all sorts of degenerates. She was no longer free to do as she pleased if that was how she planned to go about her evenings.

"One could argue against the fact that you are any sort of husband. I'll continue doing as I've always done."

"No. You won't." He set his glass on the tall side table and took a step toward her. "It's within my rights to lock you in this house if it'll keep you from attending places not fit for a lady."

"I dare you to try."

He ignored her boldness. He would not be told no. "Don't tempt me."

She raised a brow and pursed her lips. "If you succeed in keeping me here, I will do everything in my power to make you regret coming home."

With that, she turned around and left the room, slamming the door behind her. He pinched the bridge of his nose and sighed. That was not the start he was hoping for.

Emma locked herself in her room the first chance she got. She didn't know what else to do. What else she could say.

Her husband had really come home. Had wasted no time in installing himself here after their first meeting in a dozen years. It all felt like some cruel joke on her. With the threat of Waverly revealing her art to the greater part of the world, why did Richard have to come home now?

He was mistaken if he thought he could walk back into her life. If he thought he could control her every move.

There was nothing to do but leave. Which she'd been planning to do regardless of his presence.

She needed familiar, comfortable surroundings right now. She knew Richard stayed in their London house on occasion when she was in the country. So whenever she was here, she always imagined his presence. Could even swear she felt him like some sort of ghost, even though he was flesh and blood. She'd never liked this house.

She opened her wardrobe and pulled out a few of the items she'd left at the beginning of the summer, tossing them on her bed. When she had nothing else to keep her hands busy, she sat in a heap of puffed-up skirts on the floor. She couldn't do this. She couldn't stay in the same house as Richard. She didn't know how to talk to him. Didn't know how she was supposed to act around him. Didn't like how he accused her of taking lovers.

What would she do if he followed her back to Mansfield Hall?

Why did he have to come back into her life now? When everything felt like it was falling apart. With Waverly threatening to expose her secrets.

A knock at the door had her heart pumping faster in her chest. What if it was Richard? She wasn't ready to see him again. Her nerves were on edge. Her emotions irrational. She felt light-headed, as though she'd faint if she stood. She couldn't move from where she sat on the floor wondering what she should do.

"Emma, love, let me in."

It was Grace.

Her shoulders slumped as she let out a long huff of air. She could deal with Grace. She could not deal with Richard. Never Richard. Unfolding her legs, she forced herself up to her feet and wobbled on shaky legs over to the door.

The moment the door shut behind Grace, Emma relocked it. Her hands shook so hard, she thought for a moment she wouldn't be able to turn the knob.

"What's happened?"

"He's here."

"I saw him sitting in the parlor as I came up." Her sister's arms should have been comforting as they came around her, but they didn't help with her shaking. "What has you in such a state?"

Emma shook her head. "I don't know what's wrong with me." Was she in some sort of shock after her confrontation with Richard? Too much had happened in the past few days. Too many changes were taking place in her life. She didn't like it at all.

"You've had a bit of a surprise running into him twice now. I'd feel the same way if my husband found me in a harlots' den."

"I thought . . . if he ever came home that I'd be happy. That he'd be like his father. Kind, loving. But he's nothing like I imagined. Nothing. He cares for no one but himself. And now with Waverly trying to ruin everything in my life . . ."

"Hush." Grace petted her hair, smoothing it away from her face. "Richard will warm to you. Everyone does. Men are strange beasts. He's no different from any of the men I've known. Give him time."

Emma stepped away from her sister and went to pull out the portmanteau from under her bed. "We have to leave. I can't stay here with him in this house. I'm not ready to face him yet."

"Do you want me to have Abby get ready? We can leave within the hour. Less if you like."

She nodded.

"I don't want to spoil your mood more, but you know he may follow us back."

"He won't."

*He can't,* she thought. She wasn't ready to have her husband in her life. Not when she'd spent so many years alone. Not when she needed to sort out this sudden mess with Waverly.

If Richard followed her, she didn't know what she'd do. How she'd hide what she'd done and made of herself over the years.

"I'll be back momentarily." Grace squeezed her hand and left Emma's bedchamber.

Emma felt silly running away. She felt like a young girl again. The one too shy to talk with him during their chaperoned courting. The girl too afraid to look him in the eye on their wedding day.

There were few good memories of Richard from her youth. She'd come to the conclusion that he hated her then as much as he seemed to dislike her now. Some things never changed.

Closing the latch on her bag, she waited for her sisters to join her.

Her pulse still raced. Her hands were clammy. The longer she waited, the worse she felt. Then her sisters were there, leading her down the back stairs and to a waiting carriage.

Abby sat across from her, worry narrowing her eyes. "You're as white as a sheet, Em."

"I'm fine," she said, even though it was a lie.

Would she be fine again? Would she adjust to her husband being in her life after she'd been independent and reliant on only herself for so long?

She closed her eyes and leaned her head against Grace's shoulder. The farther the carriage traveled, the calmer she felt. When she was home, she knew she'd feel like her old self again. There was no chance of him following her, she told herself. He'd never wanted anything to do with her before. He'd not start pursuing her now.

# Chapter 5

*Once, you said I had the kind of smile that made others reciprocate. I made sure you always saw my smile after that day. I never could figure out what I did wrong, because you rarely returned the gesture.*

"Madam," Brown said with a bow. "The Earl of Waverly."

Emma stood at the butler's entrance. Waverly ducked his head and ran his finger along the rim of his hat on entering the room.

When Brown shut the door, she sat without inviting Waverly to do so, and studied her unwanted guest with a look of dissatisfaction. His clothes were slightly rumpled, his necktie improperly knotted. His hair, normally slicked back with pomade, was in disarray.

He stepped toward her but stalled on seeing her scowl. "Emma, you must forgive me."

"You've lost the privilege of using my Christian name."

Which was a shame, because he'd been a constant companion to her and her sisters over the last two seasons. She had thought him a true friend. Had even been foolish enough to hope that he would ask for Grace's hand in marriage. How had she so thoroughly misjudged this man? She was usually a better judge of character.

"I understand your irritation. Please, hear me out."

"Hear you out? Hear you out!" The flat of her hand smacked against the arm of the chair. She took a deep breath to help rein in her rage. "You've as good as threatened my standing in society."

"I never meant to hurt you, Emma."

Did he honestly think he could waltz in here and be forgiven? There was nothing he could do to make this situation better. His name was blackened to her.

"I know Grace fancied herself smitten with me. I never meant for that to happen. Quite the opposite . . ."

Emma raised her hand and squeezed her eyes shut. A poor attempt to stop the words flowing out of his mouth. The man had no shame.

"I've always adored you. No one else," he finished.

"Please stop, Waverly."

"You have to forgive me, Emma." He was on his knees before her, clasping one of her hands between his own. When she tried to pull away, he locked his fingers tightly around her wrist.

"You must understand that I desired you long before I ever met you."

The painting. Because he had had the painting before he'd met her. She swallowed her disgust and tried to dislodge his hold on her wrist without success.

"You humiliated me and risked my reputation for selfish reasons."

"Emma, give me a chance to prove my worth and devotion to you."

He kissed her hand, lingering before he finally let her pull away. She stood from the settee, needing to put distance between them.

Waverly had never acted so brazen with her before. He'd never shown any interest in her before. Had never attempted to kiss or touch her in any way that was inappropriate.

"You can't do this. I'm a married woman." She rubbed at her wrist. He had hurt her when he'd grasped her so tightly. "I've counted you amongst my friends without realizing the depth of deception you were playing at."

Getting to his feet, he followed her retreating steps. Apprehension stiffened her body at his rapacious approach, but she refused to take another step away from him. She would not be bullied in her own home. Her heart pounded so hard, it felt as though it would leap right out of her chest. She was like a cornered rabbit, and she didn't like the feeling.

"I've adored you since the moment we were introduced. But knew I couldn't court you, so I courted your widowed sister to get closer to you."

There was only one thing left to determine: How had he figured out she was the painter? She was always careful with her signature.

"We could never have been more than friends, Waverly. Now we are nothing to each other."

His calm was lost with her pronouncement. His eyes were ablaze with deep loathing, the blue storming to a thundering gray. She'd not really noticed how haggard he was until now. His eyes were bloodshot where she could see the whites of them, and his skin was sallow. His clothes were not freshly pressed, his nails unbuffed.

"You're wrong. We are everything to each other, my dear." One side of his mouth kicked up in a depraved grin.

"Our friendship was at an end when I received your last letter. Leave, Waverly. Now."

She'd find another way to get her painting back. She was washing her hands of Waverly from this point forward.

She felt foolish for not keeping a servant in the room when her guest seemed likely to snap or strike out at her at any moment. The fire in his eyes told her his intention before he moved. Like a snake catching a mouse, his arms twisted around her waist and held tight. The stale smell of whiskey permeated him like a blanket of sour perfume. So suffocating. So wrong.

"We are far from done, my little lady. I need you."

She tried squirming free of his hold, but his arms would not budge. With a pained protest, he was given an unguarded opportunity to assault her lips. His cold tongue slithered into her mouth, causing her to gag. She renewed her struggle, trying desperately to free herself.

Pushing against his chest did nothing. Hitting him didn't help, either. Her attempts at release were futile. She did the next best thing she could think of under the circumstance—she kicked his shin.

More suddenly than she expected, he released her.

She'd been pushing so firmly against him that she landed hard on her rear, forcing the air out of her lungs. She gathered the last of her waning courage to face Waverly and stood with the help of the walnut table beside one of the chairs.

She pointed her finger to the door. "Get out!"

The pinprick of some profound antipathy remained in his gaze. She dared not blink or move. He stepped forward, ran his finger down the side of her face, and smiled. A snake's smile. A self-satisfied smile that told her he was far from done with her.

It took every ounce of resolve she had in her not to flinch away. She would not cower before this man.

"We have a great deal left unresolved between us. I

have something you value. I know all your secrets, sweet Emma. And I plan to use them to my benefit."

Clenching her teeth, she could do nothing more than stare at him with seething anger and newfound repulsion. She refused to speak. That would—she thought, strangely—give him some leverage over her. She didn't know how that was possible, but she was listening to instinct now.

He patted her cheek as if she were no more than a child and turned away. "I'll call on you in a week. That'll be enough time to prove my *friendship* to you. Enough time for you to come to your senses. Or I will hold a party in your honor—your attendance will not be needed, if you catch my meaning."

She did not like the slant of his voice as he spoke the word *friendship,* and dared not question her concern aloud about him revealing the painting to others. She'd find a way to stop him.

Turning up the door latch, he left. Emma's body immediately relaxed. A rush of air escaped her, and her shoulders dropped almost as if in defeat.

She could not let this get her down. Would it be possible for him to just disappear from her life? Something deep in her heart told her it wasn't going to be that easy. Her gut told her he would call again in a week's time, just as he had assured her.

A certain sentimentality washed over Richard as the carriage crossed the bridge, headed toward the manor, and rounded the main courtyard of the house. He'd always been indifferent to this place. It wasn't that he particularly hated his childhood home. He just hadn't liked everything it represented: the title, watching over the local residents, his seat in the House of Lords. Too much responsibility for a young man bent on doing something more thrilling with his life than whiling away in the country looking out for the good of others.

Not that he'd ever done anything for the greater good. Exploiting weaknesses in others in the hope of gained profit was not a respectable path. Though it had proved rather lucrative over the years. He'd been a man with a passion for adventure. He was done with adventure. Done with the unknown.

Perhaps the attempt on his life had been good for adjusting his moral compass. It had steered him in a less dangerous direction. One less likely to kill him prematurely.

He should have left the seedier side of trade years ago. Trading silks had seemed rather boring when he was younger, but would have been a better choice than having someone try to kill him at every turn dealing in opium these past few years.

He looked out the window to the striking presence of Mansfield Hall. Arched Gothic widows flanked the entrance. Ivy, clematis, and roses climbed the walls of the Tudor-style home, softening the cold white limestone backwash.

The footman opened the carriage door and set down the steps. Serving staff rushed forward to line up before his foot touched the ground, Dante following directly behind him.

The butler bowed before addressing him. "My lord. It is a pleasure to have you home."

"Have my things brought up to my room, Brown." At least he'd remembered the man's name. "I'll be staying for a while."

*To my wife's everlasting disappointment,* he added silently. She was rather put out by him when they last saw each other. He hoped he would fare much better today.

"Right away, my lord."

The man bowed again and took a step back. Richard wasn't interested in greeting his serving staff. All he wanted was to see his wife. She hadn't come forward. Did she plan to avoid him?

Before his thoughts turned more ill mannered and he cursed her to hell and back for cowardliness, she stepped through the door, an elegant yet stunning vision in white.

Richard had a great love for all things of beauty, and what a pretty creature she was. Thick golden locks of hair framed her pretty face under her straw bonnet. White leather walking boots peeked out briefly from the bottom hem of her white sprigged day dress. Emma's mossy green eyes were filled with astonishment she hadn't yet tempered. He was immediately arrested by her presence.

Strange that he'd been able to stay away from her all these years. Had he known she'd turned into such a lovely woman, he might have come home sooner. Even lower portions of his anatomy were reacting to the sight of her. This reaction was no stranger to him after their run-in a few nights ago. However, this was not a good time to be thinking lascivious thoughts about his wife.

"Emma." He tipped the rim of his hat at her, the corner of his mouth kicking up in a pleased grin. "I do believe you were expecting me."

The serving staff turned in unison to look at her. Her lush pink lips pursed and her nostrils flared, then quickly relaxed.

"One can never be sure of these things. I apologize for not having your room prepared in advance." With a clap of her hands, two chambermaids took their cue and left to prepare his room. "Which wing would you like your guest to reside in?"

Glancing over his shoulder, he saw Dante resting against the carriage in a carefree, nonchalant stance, completely belying the man's lethalness. "Next to the master chambers."

The thought of the bedchamber made him think about tumbling his wife in the drive. He needed to gather his wits and cool his ardor until a more opportune time arose. He'd definitely been without a woman for too long if this was the only direction his thoughts seemed to lead him in. Though he couldn't help but wonder what she wore under all those pleated layers of white muslin.

"My sister—"

"Is she staying on?" He wondered which one.

"We all stay in the same wing. We've made arrangements for the remainder of the season to find Abby a suitable husband."

All three Hallaway sisters. He should have them cleared out. Abby was a wily little thing, while Grace always found trouble for herself. Though he supposed they might have changed over the years.

"They will be comfortable in other rooms." Rancor tilted her words. This was not an auspicious start to their reunion if he'd already managed to anger her.

"I will have tea and a light repast prepared for you in the study. I assume you remember the way?"

"I do," he answered.

She'd grown more confident over the years. Or maybe it was the fact that she could look him in the eye without blushing and stammering childish nonsense. Time changed a lot of things. She was no longer the child bride he'd married but a full-fledged woman. A woman he could appreciate like a finely aged wine.

Had he been a different kind of man, he might have stayed on and lived up to his father's every expectation all those years ago. Maybe even made a good husband. The fact of the matter remained—he had not been a different man. Nor a *good* one, for that matter.

She looked at him for a long moment, as though undressing him where he stood. Richard crossed his arms over his chest and studied her in kind. Fascinating that his wife would assess him so blatantly. Before he could comment on her regard, she spun on her heel, her skirts twirling like a ballerina's before the heavy pleats settled around her legs.

Nothing more could be said between them. Not with all the servants standing on the limestone drive, curiosity and confusion coloring their expressions.

"Back to work," he ordered. Everyone took his cue and scurried off.

"You'll have to tell me why you've avoided that fine woman all these years."

He stared at Dante. "None of your business, my friend. I'll worry about my wife. You worry about watching my back until the ugly mess we left behind stays behind."

"I've known you for eight years, and you've never mentioned her."

"We've been married for more years than you've known me."

"Long time to stay away from a wife." Dante rubbed at his jaw. "Is she a veritable shrew?"

"More like a child I had nothing in common with." He shook his head, not wishing to dissect his marriage with anyone.

"Definitely not a child anymore." Dante chuckled and pushed his foot off the carriage to follow him into the house. "I hope she's stocked something stronger than tea in the study. It's been a long day."

Richard also hoped there was something stronger than tea to drink. He'd need something fortifying before facing his wife again.

# Chapter 6

*Why did you agree to marry me? For the life of me, I can make no sense of it.*

As soon as the door closed behind her, Emma put her hand to her chest and took a deep breath. That hadn't been as horrible as she had thought. When Brown had come out to say there was a nondescript carriage coming over the river, one without an emblem emblazoned on the side to identify the person within, she'd known without a doubt it was her husband.

She had watched from the window while the staff had lined up. Then Richard had stepped from the carriage, squinting at the sun before donning his hat. Directly behind him was another man. His shoulders were twice the width of her husband's, his height just as great. He was darker-skinned, and not in the sense that he spent a lot of time in the sun. She would guess him to be of Spanish or Italian decent.

She'd only given the other man a once-over. Her attention had been drawn immediately to Richard. What a formidable man he was. A foreign desire for something she didn't understand had unfurled in her lower stomach at the sight of him standing in the drive with a smug grin lighting his expression. Then she remembered how he'd treated her in London and squashed the unwelcome feelings.

He'd not get the better of her in her own domain.

She tipped her head back, the rim of her hat folded into her neck as she rested her head against the wall. How would she deal with all these conflicting feelings for a man she hardly knew? She had this desire to seek him out, find out why he'd come home. She wanted to learn everything she could of the man who had avoided her for so many years. On the other hand, she wanted to rage and scream at him for his thoughtlessness. Tell him he couldn't walk back into her life and demand whatever he pleased of her.

Not now. Not when everything with Waverly rested so uneasily. She'd also have to be more careful about her paintings with Richard home. He could never know the true nature of her art. She'd have to sneak around in the middle of the night, or early mornings, to paint her more erotic scenes.

Everything could be ruined by Richard's return.

Footsteps approached the front door. She made a quick decision to avoid Richard for the remainder of the afternoon and made her way out to the gardens, where her sisters sat in the shade of a great oak. On seeing her expression, they came to their feet. Grace had taken her hat off and swung it back and forth by the pink satin ribbon. Abby twirled a plucked daisy between her fingers.

"It's him, isn't it?" asked Abby.

She nodded, looking at Abby. "Come, we must find you new accommodations. Someone travels with him and that gentleman will reside in the room I assigned you."

"Why ever would you do such a thing? I love that room. It overlooks the mazes."

Because she hadn't thought to speak up on her sister's behalf. Instead she had held her tongue. She'd do as her husband pleased for the time being. Surely he wouldn't remain long.

"I had no choice in the matter," she said.

"You can stay with me," Grace chimed in.

"Absolutely not. We'll be bickering and ready to tear out each other's hair after a day." Abby turned back to Emma. "And I suppose I can't spend the night with you. Not now that your husband is here."

"No, you can't. I hardly believe this is happening." She shook her head and twisted her fingers together. "While he's in the study, we should oversee the room changes."

Abby leaned down to pick up her book. "I do hope he lets us stay on. I was looking forward to spending the summer with just the three of us."

"I see no reason for him to say otherwise."

Emma hoped he wouldn't send her sisters away. She didn't think she could stay in this house with him alone for company. She needed the support of her sisters. They'd help distract Richard if Waverly decided to make another appearance. It felt like her control over her world was tumbling down around her.

"Besides," Grace said, "I'm sure he'll let us spend at least a few weeks here. If he does ask us to leave, there is no reason for you not to join me at Winston Estate, Abby."

"That wouldn't be the three of us." Abby sighed.

They walked with their arms linked back up to the house. The study and adjoining library overlooked the gardens. Her husband stood in the window, watching them amble up the steps as the other man talked animatedly with his hands.

Richard's gaze was solely focused on her as she made her way up the path. That small something in her lower belly turned into a greater feeling. Goodness, she'd never had her wits about her when that man was around. His presence had always unsettled her.

Tearing her gaze away from Richard's, she headed indoors. How strange to have him here after so many years. How strange to still want something more from him even after he'd abandoned her without a care.

She could not forget the reason he was here, though. He thought her an unfaithful wife. To accuse her of something so disgraceful set her teeth on edge.

It was safe to say his wife was not happy to see him.

"Two sisters. You didn't tell me there were so many staying here. Perhaps this wasn't the best place to come."

"I didn't realize they were staying on."

Dante put his shoulder to the wall. "One of the sisters was sitting in the carriage outside of Madam Purforry's."

That was an interesting fact. The madam hadn't been able to enlighten him on who his wife was set to meet. If Emma had been there for an assignation, why would one of the sisters wait for her outside?

"No sense in worrying about their presence since we can't change it. It's unlikely anyone will come here looking for me. This is as safe a place as any. I'm sure your hide will be in as much danger as mine as the weeks unfold and the business is taken apart and sold off."

"No doubt. But you should do both of us a favor and send the other women away."

"My wife would not welcome the idea, and may decide to leave with them. I'll not tolerate that." This newfound possessiveness was rearing its ugly head when he least expected it.

"It'll be safer for her if she goes elsewhere. Safer for the three of them."

Walking over to the sideboard, Richard poured out two fingers of whiskey for them both. "I can look out for the welfare of my wife." The idea of sending Emma away irritated him. He wanted her close. "We both know this will settle down in a few weeks. A month at most. People will be after the next man who deals in opium and altogether forget our involvement."

Sitting behind the desk, he set his glass down and riffled through the drawers. There were stacks of old letters—business correspondence of his late father, he assumed. When Dante made to sit across from him, he stopped shuffling through the papers and looked up.

"Aren't you going to explore the house? There are more entrances and passageways here than I could name offhand. You may want to learn your way around."

"While we agreed that I'm better trained to handle any mercenaries, that does not make me your servant."

"I'll not spend my every waking moment in your company. I've had enough of it this week."

Dante let loose a deep chuckle. "Then I will find my way to my own room."

He stood slowly, glancing over to the glass-paned doors that led outdoors and the paneled wall with a brass latch that opened into the library, and then walked toward the entry they'd come through.

The only thing Richard wanted right now was some peace and quiet. A few hours to himself. They were safe enough. "If you follow the women's twittering, you should find your room without issue."

Dante inclined his head, then left.

Richard knew Dante was right. He should send the sisters away. He just couldn't bring himself to tell his wife to do so. She probably needed their comfort now that he'd reappeared.

He never expected her to welcome him with open arms. Not after his long absence. That would have to change. It wasn't as though he was going anywhere anytime soon. He'd have to learn to behave around her or she would never warm toward him.

The papers in his hand were twined together in tidy two-inch stacks with his father's bold handwriting on them. If he wasn't mistaken, they were letters written to his father's solicitor. There was a smaller stack of unaddressed lavender envelopes. His wife's, in all likelihood, and he'd not invade her privacy, though he wondered why they were in here with his father's things. He placed the feminine envelopes in the drawer and released the string holding his father's correspondence together.

He'd not remain idle while in Bakewell. He could sort through his father's effects and settle into his role as earl. How strange it felt to be leaving his old life behind. Did things inevitably change after a close dance with death? Or was this path of taking the straight and easy bound to happen as one aged?

Dante Lioni did exactly as Asbury suggested. He followed the voices of the women once he'd familiarized himself with the layout of the house. He hadn't expected a house quite so large as this one. It was as big as—if not slightly larger than—his estate just outside Milan. It took him a good twenty minutes to find the wing they would be taking chambers in.

Three sisters.

Asbury had a pretty wife; her hair was fair, as was one of the others, only hers held a slight tinge of red to it and she was smaller, shorter, thinner, and possibly younger than the other two. The third sister was darker in coloring, her hair a rich brown and lush with loose curls.

He wondered which one was the widow. He'd bet his life on the plump brunette.

A woman that pretty, that soft and feminine, couldn't stay out of the marriage market long. She was more desirable than the other two. Her breasts strained against the striped material wrapped about her. A button had loosened, third one down from her elegant neck. He couldn't see anything beneath but more white fabric. Her generous hips could not be hidden beneath all those frills and pleats on her skirts.

She stopped in the double doorway and told the maid in a soft voice what to do with the effects she held. When the maid took them, she rubbed her hand over the back of her neck. He scrubbed his hand over his hair-roughened jaw. He needed to shave; he must look frightening, like a half savage to a woman of her standing.

When the maid left to do her bidding, the brunette raised her eyes and stared directly at him. He tried to smile so he didn't seem as threatening, but for a man his size that was nearly impossible.

She didn't smile at him. Just returned his stare, dropped the hand that had been massaging the back of her neck, and took a small step back so she leaned against the door frame. She sucked in her lower lip. Her gaze never strayed from his eyes.

He should introduce himself. It was on the tip of his tongue, but didn't make it farther when she gave him an interested once-over from crotch to shoulder and then met his eyes again.

Yes, this one was certainly the widow. Hopefully of the lusty variety. He grinned and watched her sea-green eyes go wide. Perhaps she hadn't meant to look him over so thoroughly and pointedly. Now he wished she'd do it again, so she could see his definite interest below the waist.

It wasn't meant to be.

They were interrupted in the next moment. The strawberry-blonde woman came out of the room, calling to her sister, effectively breaking his connection to the brunette. The dark beauty was gone in the next moment.

A widow would make a good companion for the next few weeks in the country. Perhaps it was time to try some fine English stock. Better yet, he should start his hunt for a wife, since he was settling out of trade from the East and into a quieter life. A much less dangerous life. A life more suited to settling down with a family. The widow might not want anything with strings attached, so he'd play whatever game she was willing to give him.

Maybe having the sisters stay on wasn't such a bad idea, after all. Though he'd have to be careful to keep his plans to seduce Richard's sister-in-law to himself. He wasn't sure what his friend would think. But it would be the pretty brunette's choice as to how things unfolded from here on out.

Stacking the letters he'd gone through in the middle of the desk, Richard stood from the chair and stretched his back, careful not to put any strain on the stitches at his side. Damn thing was healing too slowly for his liking.

It was time he went up and talked to his wife. She needed to know what his objectives were. What he expected of her. He desired her and he had no intentions of denying it. He would convince her that that desire could be mutually beneficial.

As he walked through the house, he noticed it hadn't changed much. The pictures of distant relatives were all lined up in the same spot they'd always been while he was growing up. He wondered if she had changed anything in the old estate.

Rounding the stairs to the master bedchambers, he could hear the low voices of Emma and her sisters; not what they said, but it seemed to be a heated dispute.

He'd not eavesdrop like some old biddy. He leaned his shoulder against the door frame and waited for them to take notice of him. Abby saw him first since she faced the door. She tugged at Grace's belled sleeve, silencing her.

All three women stood on taking notice of him.

He'd not make them guess why he was here. He cleared his throat. "I'd like to speak to Emma privately before supper."

They made their curtsies, gave one last look toward Emma, and left the room. Once they walked past him, he stepped inside the sitting room of her apartment and shut the door—not all the way, just enough to give them a few moments of solitude.

It was a small room, a settee and one chair situated around the fireplace. The furniture had been updated in this room since he last set foot in it, when his mother was alive. There was a desk off to the right corner painted in a pale yellow, and heavy green-and-gold drapery outlining a wall of windows. The room was airy and light in decor. A door led off to her bedchamber on the left, and a dressing room on the right.

When his gaze roamed back toward her, she lifted her chin and stared him straight in the eye. "Is there something you wished to tell me that couldn't wait till later?"

"I wanted a moment alone with you." Was that so much to ask for?

She motioned to the chair across from where she stood. "Please. Won't you take a seat?"

He was afraid that if he sat, he might not be able to get back up now that a tingling sensation had started over his ribs.

He waved off the offer. "I'll be but a moment."

She inclined her head and made no move to sit, either.

Her hair was tied in a loose bun at the back of her head; a few strands had worked free of the knot and framed her face becomingly. She had more freckles than he'd originally thought, indicating she was an outdoorswoman. There was so much he didn't know about his wife. So much, he realized, he'd like to discover.

"What is it you wish to say?" Her question snapped him out of his observations.

"I plan to stay on for at least a month."

She nodded, seeming neither satisfied nor unsatisfied by his admission.

"Will you leave again after a month?"

"My business plans have been ever changing over the past year. One can never be sure what tomorrow will demand of me."

Her fingers twisted about a locket dangling over her breast. "Your father always said you'd eventually come home."

The old man had been right: There was no escaping his duty as the Earl of Asbury. He could travel to the farthest reaches of civilization, but he'd always come back to his roots. He'd never had an easy relationship with his father, and he certainly didn't want to think about him now.

"There are matters aside from my father that we

must discuss. Ones I could not mention in the company of others."

She seemed to stand straighter, firmer. Ah, she must understand what he wanted of her.

"You'll have to break off any relationships you're in. If I see another man here, it will not make for a pleasant stay for either of us. Also, I expect to resume my marital duties."

She visibly swallowed, then turned her head away from him. Her hands clenched the wooden inlay on the top edge of the settee.

"Do you think you can demand this of me on your arrival?" she asked quietly.

"I do. I'm your husband." And he'd be damned if she sought the arms of another now that he was home. "I'll resume my marital rights starting tonight."

Blotches of red covered her neck and cheeks. His wife embarrassed easily. Interesting, considering he'd caught her in a bawds' den only days ago.

"I'm to be given no time to adjust to your presence in this household?"

There wasn't time. He could be dead tomorrow if someone else were to strike out at him. "I think you've had enough time playing the countess without all that that truly entails."

"I retire early." She avoided his eyes. Her gaze darted from wall to window, object to object.

"Then so shall I." The golden fringe of her lashes lowered, making it impossible to read the emotions flitting in the green depths of her eyes. He gave her a nod, not that she took notice. "I will see you in an hour for dinner."

"Don't expect to follow me to my bedchamber once dinner has concluded."

Richard gave a heavy sigh. Some battles were worth

fighting, and some took persuasion and cunning. Cunning was not a word he could use to describe himself whenever he was in the presence of his wife. He didn't know how to treat a wife. Didn't know how to speak to her.

She stood in her sitting room, staring at nothing. A little dumbstruck by the conversation she'd had with her husband. That was the first real exchange of words between them since their wedding day. Did he really think he could demand she perform to his bidding?

She sat heavily on the settee, folded her hands in her lap, and took in a deep breath. She had one hour till dinner. She could find a way to ward him off. It was only fair to give her at least a few days, nay, a few weeks to become used to his presence. For heaven's sake, he hadn't said more than a few sentences to her in over ten years. What right did he have to come into her bedchamber without so much as asking how do you fare?

And to accuse her of adultery . . . the swine!

She'd had offers from gentlemen over the years. In fact, she had an open invitation with her dearest friend, the Duke of Vane. But she'd never taken him up on the offer, knowing that it would ruin a friendship much more valuable to her than the companionship he offered for a mere night or two.

Simply put, she wouldn't stand for Richard's demands. It was easy enough to lock the doors to her bedchamber.

First, he would learn to talk civilly to her. And he would learn quickly if he wanted an heir on her. Such a shame their wedding night hadn't been more fruitful. Not that she would have been ready for a child at fifteen. She'd learned a lot since those early days. Grown a lot.

The years she'd spent on her own had made her a stronger woman. There was no doubt in her mind that Richard would learn to be the gentleman. She would accept nothing less. Only when he could prove his worth would she leave the door to her chamber unlocked for his admittance.

A smile lifted her lips. With an anxiousness that had nothing to do with fear and everything to do with outsmarting her husband, Emma stood from the settee and walked over to the bell pull. Dinner would be an interesting affair with so many people in the house. It had been an age since company had come. She wasn't one to entertain. But this was different. This was her husband.

She always made the best out of a terrible situation, like when her husband had left after their wedding night. He hadn't thought it necessary to tell her he had no intention of living with her. Instead, he'd penned a note to his father explaining that he'd done his duty as future earl and had made use of his wife as was expected.

She'd read that letter outlining that private fact in amongst the stacks Richard's father kept locked in one of the desk drawers. At the time, it had been humiliating to realize Richard had never held her in any esteem. Humiliating to know he'd shared that private information with his father.

That letter no longer existed. It had been turned to ash long ago. But the memory of it burned clear in her mind to this day.

"Are the Mediterranean seas truly full of pirates?" Grace's expression was full of wonder as she gazed upon Richard in hope of a good story. A romantic story, by the wistful gleam in her eyes.

Emma hated that both her sisters seemed to adore Richard's company.

"There are. We were guarded on our trade routes, so I've met few in my travels."

"Such a shame," Abby said. "I had hoped to hear of a grand adventure."

Emma admitted she wanted to hear a story to highlight the reasons he'd stayed away for so long. She'd not voice that aloud. Not yet.

"I wanted a romance on the high seas." Grace stared back down at her food, picking through the green beans with her fork.

"I doubt Asbury has any decent tales for a lady's ears," Mr. Lioni said.

One would think that a decade of travel would have stored up its fair share of anecdotes. Emma looked down the long table to her husband. He was not smiling at Mr. Lioni's observation or laughing with her sisters who were in want of a good tale. He took a healthy gulp of his wine and another bite of the pheasant on his plate.

"Are there really no stories to impart after all these years, Richard?" Emma asked, truly curious.

"Maybe one."

"Do tell us," Grace chimed in, her dinner forgotten as she leaned forward on her elbows.

"It is a romance, but I'm afraid I'll have to edit out a great deal of the subject matter for the more delicate ears present." Richard placed his glass on the table and leaned in closer. "I met up with a friend of old some seven years back. He leads a very private life, so I'll not share his name."

"What if we promise not to tell a soul?" Abby pleaded.

"I'll still not reveal his name." Richard raised one brow, daring Abby to say more. For once, she didn't. "The story begins in China."

"China," all three Hallaways said at the same time.

Richard chuckled. "Yes, most of my travels sent me through the Orient."

Emma hadn't known that. How could she when her husband never wrote to tell her? A pang of something akin to jealousy had her tightening her grip on her fork. Her sisters would know as much about Richard as she. It simply wasn't fair.

Grace sat back with a sigh. Abby stared raptly at Richard. Mr. Lioni smiled as he ate another mouthful of the bird the cook had prepared.

"I was traveling along a common trade route and stopped at a familiar . . ." He hesitated, tapping at his chin. "Inn."

Probably not an inn at all, Emma thought, considering where they'd run into each other a few nights ago.

"He was ill. Had taken to a fever. Knowing the man, I couldn't leave him, so I took him back to my ship and brought on a doctor. It took a few months, but he finally made it back on his feet."

"What was wrong with him?" Abby's eyebrows creased in a frown.

"The cause of his condition is far more romantic than the underlying truth." Richard put his napkin on the table and lifted his wineglass between his hands. "He was in love with a beautiful Englishwoman. A lady of decent standing. He was so much in love with this woman that he couldn't think reasonably when she disappeared abroad."

Grace gasped and placed a hand over her heart. "What happened to her?"

"It matters not in this story."

"Did he find her again?" Emma asked.

How horrible for the woman to have found love only

to lose it so tragically. Not so much different from her own story. She'd been infatuated with Richard since they were both young. And she had been no more than a nuisance to him. His leaving had proved that. It had taken her five long years to figure out that she was unwanted by the one man she was meant for.

"Yes, and in a rather unlikely place." Richard stared back at her, eyes narrowed as though he could read her thoughts or at least interpret her pensive gaze, which was probably full of longing. She quickly looked down to her plate and busied herself with cutting off a piece of pheasant.

"She had married another in her youth," he continued. "He died tragically from what I hear and left her on her own in a country far different from ours. Because she was a woman, she could not speak for herself."

"Doesn't sound so different from England." Abby snorted. "It's not as if we have any rights."

"Oh, but you do. It did not matter that she was English. She had no protection. No man to speak for or defend her. She was sold into slavery."

Emma's fork chinked against her plate. Surely this story was false. Someone would have saved the woman from such a fate. Perhaps Richard embellished the story to make it more interesting.

"How is that possible?" Abby's voice wavered. "She must have had relatives who could come and take her away from such a horrible place."

"I'm inclined to believe the same thing," Emma added.

"Ah, but she had no relatives, and she was in terrible circumstances of her own."

"What happened to her?" Grace asked, her voice

breathless. It was as if this was the most enthralling story she'd ever heard.

"My friend found her in a harem and, unable to tolerate her enslavement, he finally purchased her from the prince who owned her."

"She didn't want to stay with the prince?" The timbre of Grace's voice was skeptical.

"The prince did not love her. He had countless women at his disposal. One wasn't so much a loss."

Emma doubted the story ended there. Actually, she doubted the story held any truth. Richard was paying her younger sisters with a kindness, so she'd say nothing on the matter. Let them have their fairy-tale endings. It didn't seem as if they happened in real life.

Emma suggested, "Shall we retire to the drawing room? I imagine the gentlemen would like to help themselves to some after-dinner refreshments and a cigar in the games room."

Richard turned to her with a mistrusting glare. Yes, she'd escape at the first opportunity, and he probably knew her intention. Had he given her more choice in the matter of begetting an heir, she might feel differently. Unlike the heroine in the story he'd spun, Emma planned to take destiny in her own two hands and mold it as she saw fit.

She had to hold her smile back. It thrilled her to get the better of him.

"An excellent plan. We will meet you in the drawing room in half an hour," Richard said.

She nodded and lowered her head enough that he wouldn't see the glint of victory reflected in her eyes. Everyone stood from the table; her sisters, bless their souls, came around to her end of the table, each taking an arm as the footman opened the door. A soft chuckle coming from the men's direction almost had her turning back. It was not her husband who laughed but Mr. Lioni.

When the door to the parlor was safely shut behind her and her sisters, Emma sighed and leaned against the white paneled wall with her hand still on the latch. "It has been a long day."

Abby raised one brow, looking from Emma's hand to her eyes. "You plan to escape your husband, don't you?" Abby made her way to her favorite chair. "He's not as dreadful as I thought."

"You should be thankful to have a husband who seems interested in you." Grace gave her a long assessing look. "He's handsome enough. Not at all frightful to look upon."

She would not tell her sister that the only thing Richard seemed interested in was producing an heir and then escaping the clutches of marriage once again. It was not for their ears. She could barely hold back the cringe of distaste when thinking about it. It only proved that he did not see her as a woman who could make her own decisions. A woman with feelings and needs of her own. Did he not understand that he hurt her by treating her so coldly?

Instead, Emma said, "He has been pleasant and has said more to me this evening than in our whole marriage. Unfortunately, a few pleasantries spoken doesn't mean he will stay." She turned the latch up behind her. "If you don't mind the absence of my company, I'll be feigning tiredness."

"You need to stand up to him," Abby said wryly. "Otherwise, he'll continue to take advantage of your kindness. It is my impression that men like to find ways to exploit our weaknesses. And he'll know you are hiding from him."

"I require time to adjust to his presence in my life. I

wouldn't be surprised if he was gone by morning." It wasn't fair that her sisters were sympathizing with her husband on this.

Grace, with her doe eyes and kindhearted expression, came forward and hugged her. "If you ever want to talk about your wedding night . . ."

Emma *didn't* want to talk about her wedding night. It had been humiliating. Hurtful.

"Thank you." Kissing Grace's cheek, she smiled at Abby still sitting over in the chair. "I'm off before he discovers my plan." She left the parlor before her sisters could keep her longer and headed to her room.

For tonight, she'd outsmarted her husband.

She took her time at her toilette, letting her maid brush out her curls and braid her hair back for bed. When that was done, she'd taken to pacing the floor. Counting down the seconds, she listened for her husband at the adjoining door. Not two hours later, he tried turning the handle up. She knew it wouldn't move. She'd checked it at least five times in the last hour to make sure it was locked.

"Emma, this is not what we agreed upon. Open the door." His voice was even. His temper had yet to rise at her defiance.

"You can't come into my life and act as if the last twelve years have meant nothing to you, then demand that I perform my duties as countess."

"You won't keep me locked out forever."

"Hopefully long enough for you to learn some manners."

There was a stretch of silence. She walked toward the door, wondering if he spoke quietly to himself. She heard him curse, then, "Emma. Enough of this; open this door."

She let out a long breath. Was she nothing more than a piece of property to him? She caressed the door with one finger, wondering if she should let him in. How would she respect herself if she opened the door for him?

"You always did have to have everything your way," she said in a whisper.

"Let me in, Emma." His voice was firmer. He was not happy with her. In fact, she was sure he was quite angry. Finally, an emotion she could fight against.

"I won't stand for your behavior. I'm older, smarter, and will not be cowed so easily as I was in my youth."

"I did not—"

"Choose your words carefully, Richard. You were the one to walk away from our marriage. I didn't even get a by-your-leave. Once, I would have adored your attention, any smidgen of attention you cared to dole out. No longer. I know how little you care for anyone aside from yourself."

Yet she still ached for him. Some small part of her still wished him in her life; wished he had never left.

She shook her head. She was better than that. She didn't ache for *him*; only for the companionship she had gone so long without.

"What can I do to get you to unlock the door?"

She huffed out an angry breath of air and shook her head. Putting her lips near the crack of the door, she whispered, "Good night, Richard. You are a stranger right now, and I'll not let a complete stranger into my private chambers."

"Emma, I can make this worth your while."

"I doubt that."

There was nothing left to be said. She didn't care what he grumbled about now. She walked away from the door, turned down her bedding, blew out the oil lamp set near her bedside, and put her head between two pillows so she couldn't hear his cursing. He would learn quickly that she could not be bullied.

# Chapter 7

*What is it you are trying to escape?*

Richard watched Emma toss pieces of bread into the pond. A gaggle of geese and two pairs of swans swam forward to grab them before they sank to the bottom. A breeze tickled at her hair, lifting it in its cool embrace. She pulled her lace shawl up around her shoulders and looked skyward. He did, too.

Storm clouds were rolling in. Fast. When she stood, the birds honked at her sudden movement and swam away. Emma still hadn't noticed him watching her, standing beside a large birch tree not more than a dozen feet away. Tying her wrapper at her breast, she gathered up the papers she'd been sketching on.

This morning as he'd shaved, he had come to the conclusion that he would court his wife. When they were younger, she had been captivated by his every word, alarming as that had been for a young man forced to spend company with a child-like girl. Surely, given time, she'd find him charming again.

Without a doubt, she was the type of woman to come

around once she could call someone a friend. He would make sure he filled that role.

Struggling with her hat, she finally let the wind have it. The straw rim was tugged clear off her head with a violent gust and lay wrapped about her neck still tied by the pink satin ribbon. Head back, she looked to the sky. The sun was quickly disappearing behind dark storm clouds. An electric charge hummed in the air as darkness enshrouded the countryside moments later, leaving them in an eerie aloneness.

He stepped forward, keeping one hand on the rim of his hat. The wind carried away the words he used to call to her attention, so he walked toward her and turned her around to face him. She let out a surprised squeal as he spun her around.

"We need to find shelter!" He had to yell the words so they weren't lost in the howl of the wind.

She turned away with a scowl. Clutching her elbow, he pulled her along the dirt path with him. She yanked free after a few steps.

"You're making me lose my things."

A pencil tumbled from between her papers, so he knelt down and picked it up, wiping the mud away on the sleeve of his coat.

"My only concern is getting us to shelter before the storm soaks us both through."

A crack of thunder boomed in the next instant and a downpour of rain let loose from the heavens. He looked skyward in pure exasperation. Someone *up there* was laughing at his paltry attempts to court his wife.

It was at least a half hour's walk to the manor in better weather. As it was, the dirt paths would fill with mud and be too slippery for his wife to transverse in her mass of skirts.

Grasping Emma's hand, threading their fingers together, he turned and yelled over the storm, "Pick up your skirts. We'll make a run for my father's old hunting cottage."

She didn't hesitate to follow his lead this time, all her art things tucked against her bosom and held by one arm.

Finally making the front porch of the cottage, he lifted the latch and pushed the door open. Both of them stood for a moment trying to catch their breath.

"Why are we stopping here?"

"Because it'll be a mudslide over the paths to the main house."

She looked at him, frustrated at having been caught in the rain—with him. It was an expression he was quickly getting used to seeing. He'd bet his finest cravat pin that she was annoyed that her plan to escape him this morning hadn't been successful.

She untied her shawl and shook some of the water from it in the open doorway with her free hand, not once meeting his gaze as she did so. "I suppose we'll only stay long enough to wait out the storm."

Taking his hat off, he wiped the water from the top and brim and set it on the worktable to dry.

"Come inside and close the door. I'll start a fire so we can dry out our clothes."

"The storm will leave as fast as it arrived. We'll be on our way shortly."

Her voice wavered. Was his wife nervous to be in his company alone? Interesting that she was shy now when she'd given him such bold words last night. He didn't want meek and timid. He wanted fiery and passionate.

Richard looked beyond the sodden, dripping frame of Emma to the roiling black clouds shot through with flashes of white lightning outdoors. It was not going to pass anytime soon. The weather had been building in this direction all morning.

He sighed out his frustration. "While we're here, we can discuss the course of last evening."

"I see no reason to discuss anything." Her chin tilted up, her eyes narrowed. There was the fire sparking there that he'd wanted to see so badly only moments ago.

He threw some peat into the old woodstove, struck a flint, and lit the moss.

The wind was picking up outdoors, sweeping away any warmth the fire gave off. "Come inside, Emma. We'll probably be here another hour."

"I certainly hope not."

He clenched his fists at his sides. Her penchant for disdain needed to stop. His company couldn't be *that* detestable.

"It won't be the end of the world to spend an hour in my company," he snapped.

She twirled around and finally looked at him. It was on the edge of his tongue to say she'd not escape him now and certainly not again this evening, but something held him back. They were stuck with each other for an indeterminate amount of time. He had no plans to spend that time fighting. He'd rather spend his time seducing and cajoling her into a better disposition.

Loose strands of wet hair ran over her temple and stuck to the sides of her cheeks. Her lips trembled from the cold and were tinged with a slight blue. She was shivering. Knowing she'd hesitate if he asked her to come closer, he walked toward her, relieved her of her art things, and set them on the table. When he turned back to her, he reached out and released the first few hidden eyelets on her bodice.

She smacked his hands away. He grasped her fingers

to stop her. They were so small in his hands, so soft against his roughness.

"I just want to keep you from getting a chill."

He released a few more of the tiny hooks before she stepped away from him, her hand slowly sliding away from his so she could cover the swell of her bosom. He raised a brow, shrugged out of his coat, and draped it over the back of the chair near the fire.

"Pass me your shawl." He held out his hand and waited for the scrap of material.

She didn't object, nor did her eyes meet his again. She stuck her arm out as far as she could—so she wouldn't have to come closer to him, he assumed.

He took the wet mass of lace and spread it out on top of his coat. Of course he didn't stop there. It wouldn't do for his wound to start festering beneath wet, chilly layers of material. His vest came off next. His gaze locked with hers for a few seconds, daring her to tell him to stop. She pinched her lips together and gave him her back, her arms folded over her front and her hands rubbing her arms to bring her some warmth.

"You can't undress here." Her voice was unsteady.

"Why not? It'll take less time to dry if you remove your clothes, too."

There was no mistaking his meaning. Yes, he wanted his wife naked. What sane man wouldn't? He was more than willing to do whatever was necessary to warm her, as well. The less they talked, the less they'd disagree on how the afternoon should unfold. And there were a great many things they could do that didn't involve talking.

"Absolutely not!"

He untied his neckcloth, trying to fight the smile

threatening to turn his lips up. He didn't think she'd appreciate him finding humor in this situation.

"Why not?"

"I'll not undress for you. To think you'd ask such a thing in the middle of the day when anyone can happen upon us."

"Have you never undressed for a lover during the day?" Stupid of him to ask. He didn't want to know the answer to that. The very idea of someone encroaching on his territory—with his wife—set his teeth on edge.

"How dare you assume such a thing!" She turned to him, her expression full of hurt. "I have no lover, Richard. Nor have I ever had the need for one."

How was it possible for anyone not to take a lover after twelve years? Hell, the rumor mill had made it all the way to the East with stories of his wife and the duke. There must be some truth to the whispers. Guilt for his many transgressions rose in his gut and put a bad taste in his mouth. No, she lied to save face. Lied to make him feel a cad for demanding access to her bed. Twelve years was too long to go without the touch of another.

The friends who had given him updates of her relationship with the duke would not lie to him. What purpose would that have served? Had they thought that the pleasure-seeking fiend of a duke chasing after his wife would goad Richard into coming home? It hadn't.

He stepped forward, not sure what he wanted to do. Prove that he desired her as much as any other man might?

"It's natural to assume that you would find companionship with another after our separation. That is the usual course of things for many young ladies, I'm sure." Not that he'd had the acquaintance of many ladies. "Emma, you're shivering and your lips are turning blue. Come over by the fire. I have no ulterior motives."

Which was a lie, but he didn't want her to stand half a room away trembling from the cold. As if to prove a point, he shoved his hands into the pockets of his trousers and waited.

After a short hesitation, she walked over to the fire, stuck her hands out close to it, and basked in the heat. His desire to touch her won out over his promise of no ulterior motives. He wrapped his arms around her, his chest to her back, and he worked quickly at releasing each of the clasps on her bodice. She was so cold against him that he rubbed his hands over her arms to help warm her faster.

As he looked over her shoulder, he could see the creamy white expanse of her chest. Gooseflesh rose over the exposed parts, the pink tips of her areolas showing through the wet chemise above the uppermost edge of the corset.

Good Lord, he wanted to taste her. As if against his will, he brushed the back of his hand over the swell of her bosom—they were as soft as they looked. She stepped back so she was pressed tightly against his front, her breast rising and falling faster with an increased tempo in her breathing.

Brushing the curls that were heavy with rainwater away from the side of her face, he leaned in closer, intent on nibbling the soft flesh between her shoulder and neck.

He thought about raising his other hand to peel the damp chemise aside, free her breast, and fill his hand with its softness. He did slide one hand around her front to splay possessively over her stomach. It was tempting to see what she'd do with his advances, but her posture was suddenly stiff, unwelcoming.

Forcing himself to take a step back so he wasn't tempted to do everything he was picturing to his half-naked wife, he dropped his hands to his sides but couldn't bring himself to move away from her just yet.

Willing his erection to subside seemed a hopeless venture when the blood pounding fiercely through his veins, and ringing loudly in his ears, demanded some sort of release.

She turned her head and whispered over her shoulder, "I shouldn't have come closer."

Longing filled her voice. Almost like an invitation to continue his advances despite her rigidity, despite her words.

"I will not have you catching cold." He had to clear his throat; his voice seemed to have lowered with his heightened arousal.

He left her by the fire and opened the door. Wringing out the bodice, he stood there, hoping the chilly wind would cool his rising passions. It didn't, of course. There was only one thing that could do that, and it involved his wife welcoming him into her arms.

He did have a few hours to try.

It was still black as night outdoors, the sky flashing periodically with lightning.

"You should take off your skirts. They're soaked right through."

"I'll be fine."

If she wasn't in danger of becoming ill from all the dampness, he'd have left her to her own devices. For God's sake, he was her husband. She needn't be modest in his presence.

"The weather isn't letting up any. Stop being stubborn, Emma, and take off your clothes."

Her mouth dropped open with his demand. Had she expected him to continue begging for something that was for her well-being? He was only angry because he couldn't have what he coveted most since coming back home. It wasn't fair for him to take out his frustrations on Emma.

He sat on the edge of the cot and pulled his boots off, then untucked his shirt. He wanted to strip his shirt off, but he wasn't about to show his wife the raw wound at his side or the erection straining against his smalls. He released the ties on his trousers and had to peel them from his skin.

She'd given him her back as soon as he started removing articles of clothing. Bitterness made him want to laugh. Made him want to toss his boots against the opposite wall.

Her arms were crossed over her chest, her pale fingers curled over each shoulder. The scoop at the back of the white chemise revealed pale skin. He wanted to push the scrap of linen off her shoulders and see what lay hidden beneath. He wanted. He wanted. He bloody well wanted. He was a greedy bastard is what he was. He stood from the cot and walked toward her.

He'd never wanted any woman so badly as he wanted her right now. He needed his wife out of his system. Out of his thoughts so he could focus on the business. There was only one way to accomplish that, and he would do his damnedest to pull her little claws out from his mind.

"The door is locked, and I've a craving to be filled."

Her fingers clutched tighter to her shoulder, the tips turning white with the pressure. He could see the outline of her sharp shoulder blades and was tempted to lick the droplet of water sliding down her spine. But he didn't touch her, knowing and hating that she would not welcome him.

He did, however, find the ties at the back of her skirt that held the material around her waist. He worked them loose and let the heavy mass of pleated material fall below her hips. The ties for the second layer were easier to loosen, and that, too, fell low enough for her to step out of the material.

His hands hovered just above her hips. What would she do if he grasped them, brought her back a step, and thrust his erection against her rear?

When she didn't respond or step out of the mass of skirts, he boldly suggested, "Take off your bindings." He'd be happy to help her unlace.

If she obeyed, he knew he'd not be able to keep his hands off her. What did it matter? They were alone and he did not like to be denied by the one woman who belonged to him. Women in general did not deny him. Damn his wife for being so difficult to win over.

Emma couldn't believe she'd allowed her husband this concession. To undress in his company—no, to have him undress her—was scandalous. She covered her breasts with her folded arms, because the corset and chemise were soaked right through, and she refused to remove her corset no matter how much it itched and stuck uncomfortably to her.

She'd not give in to him so easily. Not yet.

Sidestepping out of the material of her skirts, she pushed her slippers off her feet. They were covered in mud, so she kicked them toward the room's heat source. They hadn't been in the rain for more than five minutes but all the flounces in her skirts were soaked. At least the majority of her underclothes were dry.

She stepped closer to the fire, wrapping her arms tighter around herself, hoping the heat would infuse her body instead of seep out of it. She was so very cold and wanted Richard to wrap his warm body around her again. She shouldn't want that. But he'd been deliciously hot, encompassing her body when he'd released the clasps on her bodice.

Pride was an interesting thing. She'd not sink so low as to ask him for such an intimate favor when she'd been adamant about locking him out of her room.

She wished she could start their first encounter over again. Had he not met her unaware in a whorehouse, or again at the town house, perhaps they'd get along more amicably? No, it was better to have happened this way. She could not allow him back into her life so easily. Wouldn't allow her emotions to be entangled, either.

She glanced over her shoulder. "Were you out for a walk?"

Richard was spreading all their wet items out over chairs and tables close to the fire.

What did it say about her that she wished he'd dispense with his shirt so she could see the planes of his chest and trace the line of hair that trailed downward? She wanted to caress the length of his back so she knew what a man felt like, to memorize the contours, dips, and feel of sinew so she could paint them.

She turned and faced him, a breath held in her lungs.

She would not give in to temptation.

"I was looking for you," he said. "You avoided me this morning at the breakfast table."

"I generally take a walk in the morning." Though he'd been part of the reason she'd rushed out of the house with only an apple to tide her over till luncheon.

"Emma, you can't continue to keep me at arm's length."

She raised an inquiring brow.

"I realize I came across as the perfect cad yesterday, but I can be very agreeable under the right circumstances."

Agreeable? He thought demanding entry to her bedchamber agreeable? Absurd! Besides, she wasn't prepared for intimate relations with a man she barely knew. Given time, she might change her mind. It didn't matter that he fascinated her. He'd break her heart all over again if she let him get too close.

His brow creased heavily as he looked at her. "Do you wish to divorce?"

She was caught off guard by his frank question. He asked it like someone might ask her to pass the butter at the breakfast table. Did she want a legal, more permanent separation from him?

"I don't know. I've never put much thought into it."

He ran his hand through his hair and went down on his haunches near the fire to throw in more peat. He didn't take his eyes from her. The intensity shared in their gaze was like a bird ready to take its first dive off a cliff. Indescribable, exhilarating, a rush so fast she was left breathless.

He stood and walked over to the cot. "You're still shivering."

She was glad for the change in topic and exhaled a sigh of relief when the intensity shared in the stare completely snapped and brought her back to the present.

Shaking out a blanket, he came back to her and draped it around her shoulders. She clutched the edges and pulled it tighter around her. "Thank you."

He set two chairs next to her. "Here, sit down. You might want to take off your stockings and tuck your feet under you."

"I'll keep them if you don't mind. They aren't that wet." Not the truth, but she refused to take any more clothes off in his presence. She couldn't trust herself to not do something she'd regret later.

He shrugged and sat down as though nothing of

their current situation bothered him. How strange to be dressed so indecently, in the company of her husband. It roused her curiosity. She dared to look at him through lowered lashes, to see him at more than a passing glance.

His smalls stuck to his thighs, all the way down to the top of his knees, and outlined the muscled strength beneath. Her breath caught at the wholly improper sight she beheld. A sight she wasn't averse to. She trailed her gaze upward, forcing herself to exhale slowly so as not to reveal her shocked and somewhat aroused state. Staring at her husband in half dress made her heart flutter and her stomach flip in anticipation. She tamped down those desires and focused on him as though he were a mere subject of art.

His shirt was just as wet as his smalls, sticking to his strong arms and his chest. The shadows in the room played against the lines of his body. Her gaze trailed over the heavy pulse of the vein in his neck, the smirking expression tilting his lips, and then she was staring into his dark brown eyes. A flicker of amusement shone in their depths.

She inched toward him, putting their faces closer. They both smelled of the rain, but there was something masculine in the scent of his soap, enticing her to come closer.

Goodness, what was she about?

Did she plan to kiss him and make a fool of herself? It wouldn't be the first time she had made a fool of herself in his presence. She'd been doing that since she was fourteen.

Richard shifted in the chair next to her, hissing in a breath as though pained by something. When he leaned forward, putting his elbow to his knees, she pulled away from him and glanced over his form. His head was bowed down into his hands, his jaw clenched.

"Are you all right?"

"I'll be fine. Just ran too quickly to the cottage."

A stain of red bloomed at the side of his shirt. She was on her feet in seconds, the need for modesty lost as the blanket fell unheeded to the floor. Leaning forward, she reached carefully for his shirt, lifting it away from his side gently so she didn't hurt him more than necessary.

"I wouldn't if I were you. It's not a pretty sight."

She ignored him and pulled the shirt higher on his side. She didn't flinch away from the raw wound.

"I'm not going to let you bleed out here in the hunting cottage. You should have told me you were injured." There was a deep-looking slash across his ribs, puckered in an angry six-inch red line. Someone had stitched it closed and it wasn't swollen, so she didn't think it had any infection. "What happened?"

"Skirmish in the Mediterranean. It's normal in my line of work, so stop frowning."

Forgetting the blanket on the floor, she walked over to her clothes and tore a strip of linen from the upper portion of her skirts that wasn't covered in mud.

When she turned back to him, he rested easy in his chair watching her with his intense gaze so many people mistook for boredom when in fact it was far from it. Her husband was always assessing, she realized, calculating those around him.

She lifted her hands, holding out the strips of material. "Let me clean away the blood at the very least."

"The sight of blood doesn't make you ill?"

"No."

He gave a short, mirthless chuckle and started to pull his shirt over his head. Closing her eyes briefly, she tried to mentally prepare herself for seeing her husband's naked torso for the first time. Goodness gracious, how badly had she been savoring this moment and now she couldn't even watch it unfold inch by excruciating inch? Excruciating in the sense that she enjoyed this far too much when she should be focused on helping him.

"It'll be easier if I remove it," he explained, mistaking her expression for apprehension.

"I know."

She had to swallow against the nervousness that made it difficult to breathe. Before he could say anything, or she could change her mind, she pressed a strip of material against the bleeding portion of the stitchwork. The linen immediately soaked up the blood that had gathered atop the stitches. He didn't so much as flinch.

"Does it hurt?"

"I'm getting used to it."

"You've pulled one of these stitches in the middle." She put the tip of her finger where the knot had loosened. "Here."

She traced her finger along the hard lines of his ribs and stomach. Richard hissed in a breath, she was sure for an entirely different reason than the pain in his side.

"Hard not to notice when I did it. It's fine, Emma. I only strained it in our mad dash for the cottage. It'll stop bleeding soon."

Taking the longest strand of linen she'd torn from her skirts, she went to her knees at his side, wrapped it around his middle, and tied it off on his good side. His skin was warm where her fingers brushed his flesh. It brought a flush to her face.

Taking her time, she tucked in the ends, dipping her fingers beneath the linen, wanting to feel the warmth of his bare skin. His stomach muscles were taut beneath her curious touch. Her breathing grew ragged, her fingers trailing the lines of sinew on his good side.

His hand clamped around her upper arm and he pulled her off the floor. The heat of his naked chest teased her to come nearer. His breath stirred the tendrils of dry hair at her temple, tickling her.

"Continue that and we'll both be on the floor doing exactly what you are avoiding."

In the awkward position, she was forced to press her open palms to his knees to hold herself up. The intimate moment she thought she'd shared with him was gone with the harsh reality of his statement.

She stood, jerked her arm from his hold, and sat in the chair set too close for comfort beside him. "At least have the decency to clothe yourself now that I've patched you up."

For shame, she did not want him to dress. She could stare at his form all day, but she'd not make a fool of herself doing so.

He looked over her with a tilt to his head. Raked that penetrating gaze of his over her, studying her indecently clothed form with great interest. He raised a brow and asked, "Do you find me offensive?"

The answer frightened her. The problem was, she didn't find him the least bit offensive. She wanted to see what a man's body looked like without a stitch of clothing to cover it. She wanted to see the hard, thickened flesh he could not hide beneath his smalls. Feel it in her hand, on her body . . . between her legs.

Then, after she'd memorized the feel of him, she'd like to try her hand at painting the lithe grace he represented. With the shadows filtering through the cottage in half-light and the flickers of flame giving the room a romantic glow, he was a marvelous sight to regard.

A distressed sound escaped her and had Richard raising one dark brow. She felt hot all of a sudden and knew her cheeks had turned crimson.

"It's inappropriate while in my company. Please," she added.

He picked up his shirt from where it draped over his knee, slid his arms in, and buttoned it up.

"Emma, let me come to your bed this evening."

Was it better just to get their relations over with? Or make him wait a few more weeks? Then again, he probably wouldn't stay very long in either instance. Despite that harsh truth, she was still torn in her decision.

"I can't. I'm not ready."

She'd not be used for a means to an end. She'd not be treated as a piece of his property, all too soon forgotten when he found something more amusing to occupy his time.

His only response was a nod of understanding.

When the rain let up outdoors and the birds resumed chirping their afternoon songs, they dressed with quick efficiency. Emma was surprised when he accompanied her back to the manor, a silent presence at her side the whole way. She told herself she slowed her pace so she didn't turn an ankle. That it had nothing to do with keeping company with her silent and brooding husband. God, how she knew she lied to herself. She liked his company, even when he was being a bear.

"Your great passion in life is to draw?" Richard crossed the room and sat in the chair opposite his wife.

Emma wiped her fingers on a rag and set down her charcoal. "Drawing is the first step before putting anything on canvas."

She turned the page toward him. He sat forward in the chair and took the page from her hold. Two doves curled close together, necks entwined, beaks overlapped in an embrace where they were perched in a tree of myrtle.

Drawing was clearly not a passing amusement for

his wife. His assessment that it was her passion was spot-on. He lowered the sketch to his lap and stared back at Emma.

"It's astounding," he said. "I had no idea you had such a talent."

Not the best of compliments to serve his wife, but it coaxed a smile out of her. Wrapping her charcoals in the rag she held, she bundled her supplies up and set them on the table beside her chair.

"Did you need something?"

"You managed to escape me yesterday with your sisters. They are absent from the house today, so I'd like to persuade you to join me for the remainder of the morning."

"You wish . . ." She paused, and nibbled her lip in that curious way of hers.

"You asked me to court you, so that is exactly what I intend to do." It was no hardship on him to spend the morning with her. He rather looked forward to it.

She glared back at him distrustingly.

"What shall we do with ourselves, then?"

He pushed himself to his feet and held his hand out.

"Is it a secret?" she asked.

"You'll know soon enough." Would she refuse him? Though he hadn't gone to great lengths to pull together a little privacy for them, he was in wont of her company for at least part of the day.

He tucked her arm against his side and led her out of the parlor and to the front of the house. Matching blue roans were saddled in the drive. Hers was slightly smaller in stature than his gelding.

Emma didn't question him again as to their destination.

Richard waved away the attendant. He'd see to his wife's needs. Setting his hands around her waist, he lifted her up to the seat. She hooked her leg around the sidesaddle with the grace of any woman born to riding, even though she wasn't wearing a proper riding habit.

The allure of her legs so high up had him reflexively helping her settle her skirts, running his hands over her calf and dainty ankle. She did nothing more than raise an inquiring brow at his stolen liberties. Mounting his horse quickly with a grin on his face, he set their pace to a trot.

"Where are you taking me?"

"To the fishing pond. I had planned to spend the morning there with you yesterday. Would have, had the storm not washed through the county."

When they rounded a copse, Emma's breath caught and she pulled her horse to a stop.

"Richard . . ."

A blanket was spread out on the grass near the bench she'd sat on yesterday. A basket with a bottle of his finest white wine poked out of the lid and was situated atop the blanket. Dishes filled with treats, sweet and savory alike, were spread out in a feast for kings and queens.

Dismounting, he handed the reins of his horse over to the waiting footman and gave him instructions to take the horses back to the stable for two hours. That should give him plenty of time to win his wife over, at least in a small way.

He led her over to the picnic and helped her sit.

"So much food for only the two of us, Richard."

"I didn't know what you favored, so asked for a little of everything."

She glanced at him, her head tilted to the side as she studied him. He sat across from her and filled a plate with some cheese, bread, sliced ham, and fresh-picked raspberries, then made up his own plate.

"Is it not to your liking?" He noticed she only nibbled at her food.

"It is."

"You're quieter than normal."

She gave him a small smile. "Tell me more about your travels. Where you've gone, what you've seen."

"I've been everywhere on the Continent and through the northern tip of Africa. I had a house in India at one point, and have traveled to the farthest reaches in Asia. Which interests you most to know about?"

Emma wanted so many more details than he was providing. She wanted to know what had kept him in foreign lands. What had fascinated him so much that he'd never craved to come home?

Dare she ask those questions? It was her opportunity to understand her husband better. He'd set out to have this day with her. Away from prying eyes, away from familial interruptions.

"Did you prefer living abroad?"

Did he understand what she was really asking? If he preferred to live away from his home, his father, her.

Richard set his plate down and tossed the remainder of his bread into the pond for the ducks to eat.

"My father and I never saw eye-to-eye. I had great plans for adventure. He had great plans for me in Parliament."

"Your father showed me nothing but kindness." She couldn't comprehend why Richard would avoid his duty as earl.

"I don't expect you to understand. But my father and I never got on well. We fought incessantly. We disagreed just to disagree with each other. He wanted me to be like him. I was a disappointment when I turned out completely different from his choosing."

"He was always proud of you. He told me on many occasions."

Emma picked up a raspberry and rolled it between her fingers hard enough to color them with the juices. Him staying away had hurt her profoundly. Painting took away the sadness. Allowed her to focus on something different.

"I don't doubt your words. I will be the first to admit that I was acting no better than a child when I left. I hurt you in the process."

"Because you didn't want to marry me."

"My father had picked you as my bride before either of us could understand what that truly meant. When we married . . . I felt like I was being dragged into a life I wanted no part of. I craved travel. I craved carving my own path, making my own money, money not from the workers on my father's land." Richard leaned back on his elbows and tilted his head back, closing his eyes. He took a deep inhalation. "My father threatened to cut my allowance if I didn't wed you. He thought marriage would keep me here when I had expressed my interest in travel."

"Why did you marry me if you planned to leave?"

"Wholly selfish reasons. Rash reasons from a man who wasn't yet a man, but thought he could prove a point in doing one final thing to snub his father. The follies of youth sometimes haunt us eternally."

He had only been nineteen when they'd wed. A man who didn't understand that he was ruining a young woman's life.

"If you stayed away so long because of your father, why didn't you come home when he died?"

"It was three months after his death that I received that letter. It felt too late to come home, yet not soon enough. I was in the process of breaking down another part of my business and selling it off. Too busy to come rushing home to a wife I didn't know and hadn't bothered to ever try to know."

He stood suddenly, holding his hand down to her. "Would you like to walk? We can feed the remainder of the bread to the ducks."

She looked at his hand for a moment before taking it. He was done talking about the past, at least for now. She had to think on his words, on the small facets of his character he'd revealed to her over the course of their lunch.

She slid her gloved hand into his and let him pull her to her feet. He tucked her arm against his just as he gathered up the bread and handed her a few choice pieces to break up for the birds.

She was glad to have spent the day with her husband. To have learned a few small details of his past. To know why he'd run for so long.

Perhaps she'd never truly understood Richard's father. She might never understand why their relationship had been strained. The man had been another father to her. Maybe he'd done so out of fear she'd leave him, too.

# Chapter 8

*I feel like Sleeping Beauty, forever asleep, with the waking world continuing on without me fully aware. Only there is no prince to wake me from this slumber, this half-life.*

His fingers traced the edge of the envelope through his jacket. It appeared his wife was in regular correspondence with the Duke of Vane. When the letter had arrived, he'd had three options: He could open and read the missive himself to find out how close the duke was to his wife; he could take the envelope outside and set a match to it; or he could see his wife's reaction as he handed it over to her.

The last option would be the most revealing.

So here he stood outside her room, waiting. Always waiting for her. She had strung him along like a hapless dog over the past week since their impromptu picnic.

Richard didn't intend to spend half his morning finding her whereabouts, as he'd done yesterday, the day before, and the day before that. Pulling out his pocket watch, he checked the time. Half eight and Emma still hadn't come out of her room.

He was a patient man. He'd wait here until she was ready to face the day. The door pulled inward to reveal his wife. She looked elegant in a sun-yellow walking dress and straw bonnet with matching satin ties. The color added a spark of mischief to her eyes and a spot of pink to her cheeks.

Emma was like a night-blooming water lily, her beauty locked tightly away from the world, showing its true self only under the pale caress of moonlight. In an unguarded moment.

Not that he'd ever chanced to see her that way. Not yet. It was a matter of figuring out how to tear away the shield of modesty she wore like a chastity belt.

"Good morning, Emma."

She dipped her head on a curtsy.

He offered his arm. "Where do you escape to on this fine sunny morning?" It never hurt to charm a woman. He would win her over. He was a determined man.

That got a grin out of her, and her arm through his.

"I'm to meet with my sisters for an early-morning constitutional."

"Might I join you?"

She raised one blonde-winged brow. "I have no objection."

Perhaps throughout the morning he could charm his wife into a more agreeable mood—and her sisters while he was at it. If he had the other Hallaways on his side, this wooing—or whatever the hell he was doing—should unfold more smoothly.

Arm in arm, they met Grace and Abby in the back gardens. Both sisters frowned at his appearance. Ah, this was something the sisters did together. Emma had let him come along knowing her sisters would see his presence as an intrusion.

Abby scrunched up her brows in disdain. "Does Mr.

Lioni plan to join us in our outdoor excursion since we are making this an event for all?"

He gave the youngest sister his most charming smile. "I cannot say. He's an early riser, so there's always a chance he might catch up with us at some point."

Abby said nothing more; it was as though she were sulking at his interference. Grace, on the other hand, smiled and winked in his direction.

They walked down the great limestone slab path in twos. Rows of flowers lined the way, filling their morning with a multitude of colors and fresh, sweet scents. Candytufts to attract butterflies, red roses to add color, white delphiniums mixed in with the splotches of crimson.

His mother had kept this garden going when he was a child. Had spent hours at a time out here with him. He couldn't remember his father keeping up the gardens after she had died. This all must be his wife's doing. He glanced at her, but she focused straight ahead, hardly paying attention to him.

"The gardens are beautiful."

That got him a small smile. "Grace helped me when she started spending the summers here a few years ago."

"Beautiful. Regardless of how you accomplished it."

"Thank you."

His wife was more shy than normal. She was quiet. Contemplative.

Dante caught up with them ten minutes into their walk. It gave Richard the perfect opportunity to steal his wife away from her sisters.

Slowing his and Emma's steps so they could talk without being overheard, he said, "You've done a fine job in ignoring me this week, Emma."

"Have I?" She did not look at him when she answered. Instead, she kept her attention focused on her hand, where she brushed over the soft petals of a black-eyed Susan that stood tall in the path they walked along. Pinching the stem up high, he plucked one of the flowers for her.

He stopped and pressed a finger under her chin, angling her face toward him. He settled the flower so the stem was tucked behind her ear, the yellow petals just peeking out from beneath her bonnet.

"You've hardly said a word."

She studied his face, then turned away and gave him a tug to continue down the dirt path. "I had a restless night."

He looked her over. Sure enough, the whites of her eyes were lined in red, dark circles shadowed beneath. "Do you want to rest a moment? We can catch up to your sisters afterward."

"Is this some trick to get me alone?"

"Possibly."

Though getting her alone had its merits, he now noticed her weary look, and her slow steps had them lagging behind the rest of the company.

"Ladies," he called after her sisters, "we're resting here under the trees."

Dante seemed happy to have the two beautiful ladies on his arms all to himself. With a nod in Richard's direction, Dante wheeled them back around on the path and continued on. Abby gave him a long look over her shoulder and narrowed her eyes.

Richard led his wife over to a pair of tall trees so they could sit in the shade. Releasing the tie on her bonnet, Emma sat in the shade of a large oak, twirling the flower he'd given her between her fingers. She tossed her bonnet aside, lay back with a sigh on the grass, and closed her eyes. Her hands were folded over her ribs, her legs curled to the side and hidden under the swath of light yellow silk she wore.

Hiking up his trousers at the knee, he sat next to her, one knee bent for his arm to rest upon. He tossed his hat in the general direction of his wife's and stared down at her reclined form. Unable, and unwilling, to resist touching her soft skin, he ran the back of one finger down her rosy cheek. She gave a soft sigh, and her eyes cracked open to watch him.

"What were you doing last night that you didn't sleep?"

She covered her mouth on a yawn. "Went to bed much later than I planned."

"You're evading my question."

"I know." Her eyes now seemed sharp as a leopard eyeing her potential mate. "Tell me something . . . Would most men be as patient with their wives as you have been?"

He shrugged. "I can't say with any certainty that I've done anything right this past week. Not where you're concerned." It was an honest answer.

She took a long inhalation and turned her head away from him to look at the branches of the tree above them.

She stretched her hands above her head. The strain of her breasts against the stripes of her dress was torture to him. "What would you do if I gave you admittance to my room tonight?"

"I'd come."

Was it possible that he'd won her over after a week of following her around like some pathetic puppy starved for attention?

"Will everything change once you get what you came here for? Will you leave for London when I'm with child?"

He considered her questions carefully. It hadn't been a matter of coming home and starting a family. But there was the matter of his business, old and new.

"I can make no promises, Emma. All I know is I won't be leaving London for any stretch of time in the near future. My business now not only brings me home, but also keeps me home."

Emma stared at him with those impenetrable green eyes of hers for so long, he was sure she'd change her mind.

"I propose a deal," she said.

Women always made deals that benefited them. He nodded for her to continue, despite the unease worming around in his mind.

"You made a suggestion that I've been thinking about a great deal." She worried her lip. "This decision wasn't easy for me. But perhaps, if I am not with child by the time you leave, we should petition for a divorce."

"Do you have someone else in mind for marriage?" He hated to ask, but had to know. God help him if she did. He'd kill the man, whoever he was. Richard didn't care if that man was a bloody duke.

"No." There was nothing in her gaze to suggest she lied. "I just don't wish to spend the next twelve years alone. Your father was a wonderful companion for a girl who knew nothing of the world, and then my sisters were there for me when he passed away. But Abby will hopefully be married soon, and Grace won't be by my side forever."

"I can't see myself traveling farther than London."

Besides, he wanted to be present in his child's life. Though he hadn't gotten along with his father, the old man had always been there. Nagging, nagging, nagging to do what was right for his position, but the old man had still been a constant in his life. His mother, too, had always been there for him when she was alive.

"If I were to agree to petition for divorce should our

arrangement not be to your liking, you'd admit me to your bedchamber?"

"Yes." No artifice tainted her voice.

"A divorce would ruin you, Emma. You'd be shunned from society." He pushed his hand through his hair in frustration. How could she want that for herself? "Have you thought how you would live?"

Her fingers stretched out into the grass, toying with the green blades. Did she not want him in her life after all their years apart? He scratched at his jaw. It was a possibility, and that sudden realization sat like a rock in his stomach.

"The only thing I know with certainty is that I can't continue to live as I am."

"Divorce would do neither of us any favors. I want more time before you make a decision, Emma. Give me two months."

"If you stay for two months, the time is yours." He knew she mulled over her answer. "If you leave before then we will petition for divorce."

"I don't plan on leaving, Emma."

She looked at him in disbelief. He supposed he'd never given her reason to believe otherwise.

He didn't know a great deal about divorce, only that it was a long, tedious process. He nodded his agreement to her demand, knowing he would do everything within his power to change his wife's mind.

Unwilling to resist touching her since she'd agreed to let him in her bedchamber, he rubbed his thumb down the center of her lips, parting them. Not one protest passed her lips. He picked up the discarded flower she'd set on the grass beside her, and ran it over her cheek and lips in a feather-like caress.

He leaned in close to her face, his actions full of

suggestion. He scanned the area around them. They were quite alone.

"We can start now," he suggested

The hitch in her breath was palpable enough to make his heart beat faster in anticipation.

"We shouldn't."

Tossing the flower to the side, he lowered his lips to hers. He just wanted a small taste of what his wife offered. Her lips were soft, full. Running his tongue along the length of her upper lip, he tasted the sweet remnants of peaches before pulling at it and then releasing her.

She returned the kiss, lick for lick, nibble for nibble. His hand had found its way to her silk-covered breast, his fingers rubbing across the slightest distention of her nipple.

The last thing he wanted to do was stop. But if he didn't, they'd be here for the greater part of the afternoon and with decidedly fewer clothes on.

He stared down at her. Her pupils were dilated, the green eaten up by a blazing black. With a groan that had everything to do with denying his need to have her, he reluctantly got to his feet and offered her a hand.

"We should go back to the house before we're missed."

She placed her gloved hand in his and let him pull her to her feet. He released her, knowing if he didn't he'd let himself be led around by his prick.

"Before we go, I have something for you." He pulled out the envelope he'd kept in his breast pocket. "This arrived yesterday." He handed it over, watching her expression carefully.

Her brows furrowed as she took the letter and flipped it over to see the seal. There was nothing in her expression to suggest she wished the letter to remain a secret.

"Why are you only giving it to me now?"

He shrugged and took her arm. "Forgot I had it."

He was expecting a more telling reaction from her. Maybe a blush when she read the letter, or a hitch in her breath at seeing who it was from. Maybe she'd practiced hiding any revealing actions toward her lovers?

She leaned on his arm in silence, while he burned with a million questions about tonight and the nights thereafter. He asked none of the questions on his mind. It wasn't the right time.

Before they could enter the French doors to the study, Emma pulled him to a stop. "Ten o'clock sharp, Richard."

She didn't wait for a response, just opened the door and walked toward her sisters, muttering something about setting up an early luncheon.

A knock came at the adjoining door between their bedchambers at precisely ten o'clock. Her maid stood up from where she was turning down the bedding, and stared at her mistress. Emma nodded, indicating that she could leave.

The only hint the maid was gone was a draft that picked up loose tendrils of hair to feather against Emma's cheek and forehead where she stood in the middle of her room. Her bare toes curled into the carpet.

"Come in," she called out.

She hadn't locked the door between their rooms. She'd not refuse him now. She'd thought long and hard about taking this next step.

Richard pushed the door open and stood framed in the entry. He made an impressive figure with his shirt untucked from his trousers, his hair tousled as though he'd just run his hands through it. His expression was smug, maybe even a little victorious for winning entrance to her bed. Not that it had been a competition in holding out.

Her decision had not been made lightly. There was a great risk in all this; the possibility that she'd lose her heart to him again. The only reason she'd allowed this interaction was because she desired him. Desired to know the feel of a man holding her, taking her, loving her body. But what would accepting him mean to her art?

She closed her eyes and banished the thoughts. She'd been over this a hundred times. She had made her decision.

She waited for him to say something, or do something. The silence was so palpable between them, she held her breath so as not to break the growing tension. Unable to meet his gaze, she looked at her bed. There was a lone oil lamp in the room, letting off just enough light that they could see each other. He walked toward her, leaving the door between their rooms open.

"Good evening, wife."

"Good evening."

His touch was light on her shoulder, and he gave it a squeeze as if she needed reassurance. He was herding her closer to the bed with small steps. Before she knew it, she was sitting on the edge. The bed dipped down near her hip with his weight. His hand pulled the edge of her nightgown high up on her thighs. His hands were rough where they stroked along her legs.

Everything was moving along too fast.

"Relax, Emma. I'm not so much a stranger now, am I?"

She responded in a choked whisper, "Nervous."

*Nervous* didn't even come close to describing how she felt with her husband touching her so intimately. She'd imagined and dreamed of this so many times. Never actually thought it would come to fruition.

Curling her hands into fists at her sides, she tried to be

less stiff under his touch. She scooted up higher on the bed. He followed; his hands caressed all the bare skin he revealed while hitching up her chemise. The edge of the material tickled her flesh the higher it was raised.

What if she wanted more from him than simple intimacy? Oh, she knew she wanted more than this. She wanted a husband who loved her, who would never leave her. She wanted her art, and yes, she wanted him. But she daren't think she could have it all. His sole goal was an heir. Her greatest desire was to have children.

Her heart sped up with her thoughts. Her breathing rushed out of her and her palms started to sweat where they were clenched.

The back of his hand grazed her left breast through the linen, giving her something to focus on aside from her trepidation. The tip peaked and she could feel gooseflesh rise everywhere he stroked. Did he know that he was igniting an inferno of latent need?

He gave a soft chuckle. "I promise to be gentle."

She'd rather he not show her such a kindness. She would rather him not care. The more time they spent together, the closer she would become to him. It was inevitable. It meant that she would have to live through the heartbreak of him leaving her all over again.

Why did the hunger for more have to unfurl in her belly? Need started to drown her doubts.

Richard stilled and was quiet for some moments. The silence didn't help her unease.

"Should I stop?" he asked.

She loosened her hands and curled her fingers into the soft bedding, the tension slowly draining from her body. She shook her head. God help her, the last thing she wanted to do was stop. She wanted him here—she'd debated it and thought it through too many sleepless nights to have him leave now.

"I feel decidedly underdressed," she said.

He grinned and sat up on his knees to pull his shirt over his head. "Easily fixed."

With a deep inhalation, she focused on the speckling of coarse hair over his muscled chest, and the line of dark hair that led downward to his thick erection straining against the front of his black trousers.

Her breath caught at the sight. She hadn't been prepared for that. She'd never seen him naked before, never really seen any man naked. Tonight, everything would change. She forced her gaze away from the tantalizing sight and back to his lust-filled gaze.

"More interested now?"

He leaned forward, slid his hands beneath her rear, and pulled her down the bed. She liked being held by him, and being closer to him. Shyness was forgotten as she reached up to press her palms to his face; he kissed the inside of one hand, then the other.

He stared down at her for a long moment. Did he plan to kiss her? She'd never been properly kissed by him.

Not even on their wedding day. That was when her heart had first splintered and her childish hopes had been tossed to the wind like the rose petals thrown after their wedding. Brides were supposed to be kissed, loved, cherished. She was none of those things.

She closed her eyes, and waited. Finally, he pressed his mouth to hers. She tasted tooth powder, smelled the bay soap he'd washed with, and the deeper scent of sweat that added to the elixir of their first real brushing of lips. It was slow. Methodical. They explored and tasted of each other, his tongue sliding along hers. Her lips pulled at his between the sparring of their tongues. She moaned in protest when he pulled back.

Hands running the length of his back, she felt every firm ridge of sinew flexing and moving as he held himself above her body. She wanted to hold him here for an eternity. Never let him go. Crush herself against him and just stop thinking altogether.

The slide of her chemise over her flesh awakened her arousal from a long slumber. Every inch of her body felt as though it were burning up. She wanted to be naked against him. To rub against him flesh-to-flesh. Finally, he hiked up the offending material of her chemise. He looked down at her chest, his hands pressing and massaging into her flesh from waist to ribs to breast, pulling at the tight peak there with nimble fingers.

The way he stared down at her made her feel empowered.

"You're beautiful, Emma." He pulled gently at the dark pink tip of her breast, making the nipple stand taller.

"I want your hands all over me, Richard." She didn't know where the words came from, and she hardly recognized her own voice, it was so husky. But she was past the point of caring.

"Anywhere you want me." There was promise in his statement.

She watched his face carefully. He was like the cat in the creamery, lapping her up with his heated gaze.

A profound, inexplicable connection was made when their eyes clashed and they stared at each other in an unguarded moment. Everything felt exactly as it should be.

For now, everything felt right.

Emma was not a shy virgin on her wedding night. She was a grown woman, with a great deal of repressed desire. He was the only man she had ever wanted as an outlet. She wanted this. Had always wanted him even after their disastrous wedding night. And he was hers . . . for as long as he stayed.

He pushed his trousers down over his hips, shucked them off, and tossed them to the floor. She had to bite her lip to keep from whimpering at the sight of his manhood jutting out proudly between them. He cupped himself, pulling the skin back from the smooth head. She must have made some strangled sound because he released himself and rubbed his hand over the coarse hair at her center.

Fingers separating the folds of her womanhood, he pressed them to her core and let out a groan. "God, you're wet." Two fingers thrust up into her so suddenly she squeaked in surprise. "So damn wet."

He pulled his fingers out and painted the dampness over and around her nipple. Her breath left her in a rush when he leaned over her and sucked the firm tip deep into his mouth and groaned against her breast. She didn't know what to do with her hands so she threaded them through his hair and held him close. He was all unbridled heat above her.

He pushed her legs apart with his knees. The rough hairs on his legs brushed against her intimately.

"Do you know how sweet you taste?" he asked. "I want to fuck your pretty cunny with my mouth and thrust my tongue deep inside you."

Her eyes widened. Her mouth went dry. Did husbands and wives normally share this type of familiarity? Despite the bluntness of his words, she wanted to hear more wickedness leave his tongue.

Whatever he saw in her eyes made him still above her. "Wrap your legs around my waist, Emma."

She did as told, then his mouth was on hers again,

his tongue searching out hers. There was a franticness to his pace that made her heart race, that made her feel more daring than she ought to.

She locked her ankles at his spine as he heaved forward. He pushed her up a good inch on the bed as he seated himself within her body. There was pressure between her legs, but the uncomfortable sensation ebbed and that feeling she'd been waiting for started to unfurl in her body like a maelstrom being unleashed and given free rein. It was the exact same feeling that had bombarded her when she was with her husband in the cottage and again when he'd placed the sweetest, most fleeting kiss upon her lips earlier today. She closed her eyes and ground her pelvis up into his, wanting him deeper, wanting so much more.

She wished she knew how to put words to what she wanted.

He palmed her breast, squeezing her ever so slightly, making her arch off the bed.

"Richard . . ." She did not know why she whispered his name.

His mouth found hers and she bit his lip when he pulled out and then thrust back into her body. He didn't seem to mind her force and returned the gesture. They were locked in such a tight embrace she didn't know how he pulled in and out of her body, only that she didn't ever want it to stop. She tilted her pelvis up, wanting him to fill her deeper. His thrusts were hard, firm, so delicious.

She moaned, she whimpered, it was embarrassing to have so little control over her body as he made her feel. Feel everything she'd only dreamed of and imagined before now.

The grip he had on her rear tightened, and he stilled

above her. His breath rasped in and out fast next to her ear as he emptied his seed within her pulsing womb. The thickness lodged between her thighs seemed to throb for long moments.

She didn't want this to end. He'd leave her now. Just as he'd left her on their wedding night. She choked back a sob and closed her eyes against the tears threatening at the surface. Now was not the time to fall apart emotionally.

"Are you all right?" he asked.

"Yes," she mumbled and swallowed back her anxiety.

He rolled off her and flopped on the bed so they were shoulder-to-shoulder. She turned her head toward him, listening to his breathing slow as she pulled down her chemise, trying to make out his features in the dim room. She wanted to touch the shadowed outline of his face but didn't feel she could be so bold. What would she have to do to keep him here tonight?

She should have never allowed him admittance into her life, into her heart. She was still in love with her husband. What a fool she was. What a stupid fool.

His finger traced the lacy edge of the linen covering her shoulder. She shivered. He was all heat and solidity next to her, and she wanted him to wrap himself around her again. To touch and taste at her. To make her warm when she felt so cold inside. Before she could voice her wants, he was off the bed, leaving her chilled even in the heated summer air.

"Does this time suit you for tomorrow evening?"

"Yes," she responded numbly. Was he really leaving it at that? Had he not felt the depth of their connection? Had there been nothing sacred in the passion they'd just shared?

The door clicked shut behind his retreating form.

Pulling the sheet up around her shoulders, she reached

out to touch the impression he'd left in the blankets next to her.

Would he still be at Mansfield Hall come morning?

Not exactly what he'd planned.

He wanted to talk to her. Wanted to spend the evening inside her, around her, any way he could have her. But he hadn't a clue as to what he was supposed to say or do with her. He'd never spent the night with a woman. Never made idle conversation after taking his pleasure in her body.

That brought his thoughts right back around to the feel of her body. It was softer than he remembered. Filled out and womanly. Her breasts were plump and firm beneath the very proper night rail she'd worn.

Bloody hell, he should have stayed for another round. He was still hard as a goddamn poker. Wrapping his hand around his prick, he stood with his back to the door and stroked over the sticky length. Her wetness. His sperm. He wanted to suck at her breasts again, put his mouth in places that would shock her. He stroked his thick length harder. She'd been full of fire. His hand moved faster. Then he released another torrent of seed. His head fell back against the door, his hand milking his pulsing cock.

Shit.

He'd not taken his hand to himself since his school days.

Tomorrow night he would take it slower. Strip her down and explore every inch of her body. Taste every inch of her skin. Why had he left? She'd been so full of passion. He wanted that, didn't he?

Confound him!

His wife was not a simple creature to figure out.

# Chapter 9

*You consume my every thought.*

Emma scooped more eggs onto her plate, took another sliver of ham and sat next to Grace with a heavy sigh.

Grace put her fork down and turned to her. "What are you sighing over?"

"Hmm . . . I'm sighing?"

"Yes, like a woman completely smitten."

"Don't be silly."

Grace laughed. "You spent the night with your husband. I didn't think you'd give in to him so easily. Not after only a week."

"You shouldn't say such things." Emma turned and looked at the door, hoping no one lingered close by. "Anyone can happen by."

"When else am I going to be able to bring up the matter? I want to know all the details."

"I can't share any such thing with you." Grace stared at her, disbelievingly. "If you must know, I spent some time with him." With a whisper, she added, "Last night."

Her sister sat back with a harrumph and crossed her arms in a knowing smirk. "I knew it!"

"He didn't stay the night," Emma cut in.

"You probably told him to leave."

"I did no such thing." Uncomfortable talking about this, Emma fidgeted with the lace edge of the tablecloth. "We . . . he . . . he didn't stay long afterward."

"I may not have cared for Howard's attentions when we were married, but he often spent the night," Grace confided as she leaned forward and took Emma's hand. Emma squeezed Grace's fingers and sat back in the chair, shaking her head resolutely.

"I don't want to know your thoughts on this, Grace."

"Why not?" Her bottom lip pouted out as she absently pushed food around on her plate.

"Because, truth be told, I felt inept afterward." Oh, dear. Not what she'd meant to say at all. Her sister needn't know Emma's incompetence where her husband was concerned. She worried her lip and stuttered out, "I look forward to the day I'm with child."

"He didn't offer you your own pleasure, did he?"

Emma's silence must have been answer enough.

Fork clanking against the dish, Grace's fist pounded against the table, marking her words. "If I knew him better, I'd tell him what a selfish blackguard he is to worry about a good rub off for himself but not to worry about fulfilling the needs of his wife."

Emma choked on her eggs and picked up her glass of water to help wash it down. "Promise me you'll not say a word about this to anyone."

"Your secret is safe with me. But that won't stop me from showing my displeasure toward your husband. For heaven's sake, we saw him in a bawdy house, surely he knows how to make his lady scream."

Closing her eyes, Emma took a deep breath and pushed the remainder of her breakfast away from her, unable to take another bite. "The breakfast parlor is the wrong place for this conversation." Not that she wanted to discuss this at all.

"I know exactly what you need, Emma. You need to embrace yourself more. Do something completely unlike you, and something completely *naughty*." Grace's eyes narrowed, a mischievous smile lifting one side of her mouth.

Emma scrunched up her nose in distaste. "I'm perfectly content as I am."

"That sounds suspiciously like a challenge. And look, here comes Abby, in time for a little wager."

Emma looked at her youngest sister, hoping that Abby could read the pleading for help in her eyes.

"Oh, I do love a good bet. I always win. What is it I'll be winning today?" Abby was no help at all.

A smile brightened Grace's face. "I've suggested to Emma that she embrace her wilder side. Do something she'd never dare to do."

Abby laughed. Not a small laugh, either, but gales of it. She put her plate down on the side table when she was forced to clutch a hand to her side. "I have a cramp. It's cruel to make me laugh like this before I've had anything to eat." Abby straightened as her laughter quieted. "She'll not step outside the lines of propriety."

"You two are being decidedly cruel. I like my life exactly as it is. Why would I want to change who I am?" Emma tossed her napkin to the table. She wouldn't stand for this treatment. "Besides, what of my art? It's more daring than many a lady would care for."

Grace nibbled on her tea biscuit. "This has nothing to do with your paintings. I swear, even when we discuss your portraits you blush like a virgin on her wedding night."

Abby chuckled. "Grace, I'm willing to throw your

pearl earrings back into the pot if we can get Emma to do something scandalous by our measure."

"I'll not participate in anything that could hurt our reputations." That should set them straight. Or so Emma hoped.

"Hmm." Grace tapped at her lip in thought. "We will have to be discreet."

"Do share your thoughts." Abby sat across from them at the breakfast table, her plate full of eggs, kippers, and toast, with a large dollop of strawberry jam on the side. She took a napkin and flicked it open before settling it on her lap.

"We wouldn't want Emma to balk at the slightest hint of wickedness." Grace leaned forward on her elbows. "I suggest we make a list this afternoon."

"I do have fun," Emma protested and frowned at both her sisters in turn.

She painted every day. Her sisters knew how much she loved doing that. They had even seen her more risqué works. Most people of the ton would probably think she had a few nuts rolling around in her head to even think of painting such scandalous nudes.

"The things you do could hardly be construed as fun." Grace arched one brow at her. "Besides, this will take your mind off Waverly."

"She's right, Em." Abby pointed a fork full of scrambled eggs at Grace. "And I know how we can draw up the bet. We can wager on when Emma is most likely to withdraw from our planned escapades."

"And if I complete all your challenges, what then?" Emma pushed her chair away from the table. "You two have far more to gain. While the idea has its merits, you're sure to make the challenge too difficult for me to complete."

"Very true," Grace said easily. "What if we promised our undivided attention and time for you to paint or charcoal a portrait of your choosing?"

Emma had asked Grace on many occasions to model for her. Her sister had cried off because—well, because she'd have to disrobe for the types of pictures Emma planned. Having a new subject to paint was an opportunity to spur her creativity. Of course, she couldn't paint Abby till she was safely married.

"You're brilliant, Grace." Abby grinned. "I couldn't for the life of me think what she'd want from us, but that is perfect."

To prove her sisters wrong—and to win their undivided attention for the type of painting she wished to compose—she'd allow them this contest. And they were right: It would provide a distraction to the Waverly situation.

"I accept your challenge." How bad could it really be? "Am I invited to know what will be on the list?"

"Of course not," her sisters said in unison, then laughed at their timing.

"It's hardly fair for you to know all the challenges," Grace clarified. "You could pick and choose what to accomplish. Then where would that leave us in our wager? I do want my pearl earrings back."

"I doubt you'll win, Grace."

"You shouldn't be boastful, Abby," Grace responded. "It's always possible Emma will win, and we'll both be sitting for scandalous portraits."

"How many items are going to be on this list?" Emma should have asked for clarification on that before saying yes, but it was too late now.

"Good question." Abby tapped her finger on her lip in contemplation. "What if we agreed on not more than six?"

Six was too many challenges she could potentially fail at. "I could hardly name more than three things you might have me do."

"Fine," Grace said as she stood from the table. "Three it is. I even know the first challenge. I'm going to go prepare the list before the afternoon is upon us."

Abby took her jam-covered toast and followed Grace out of the breakfast parlor. "I'll join you."

Had she made a mistake by taking on this challenge? Surely not. She'd have two models by the end of it. Of course, she knew now to hide her sisters' likenesses when she painted. How she wished she'd been smart enough to do so with her first painting.

"Mr. Lioni. Fancy that I should find you wandering around in the cellar." Grace ducked her head so he wouldn't see the surprise lighting her expression. It was a task not staring at the man. He was so very handsome with his casual way of dress. She loved a man of his size in shirtsleeves. It made him seem so unashamedly virile.

She continued down her path, hoping to grab the first bottle of wine she happened upon and stall her daydream of Mr. Lioni and his superb physique. But she wouldn't be rid of him so easy. Mr. Lioni fell into step behind her. An all-too-tempting and tantalizing presence.

"I'm familiarizing myself with the manor. It's easy enough to get lost if you're not keeping track of where you're going."

She loved his accent. She noticed that he spoke slowly, to pronounce his English words with precision. What was it about this man's accent that had her legs turning to jelly?

"Indeed." She quickened her steps because she was a blushing fool in his company and liable to stammer nonsense if she didn't focus on something aside from his wide shoulders and tanned, bare neck.

On second thought, he could prove useful this afternoon in bringing Asbury out to the orchard for Emma's first challenge. The one thing Abby and she had agreed upon was that they needed to reunite the married couple. All was not lost with Asbury and Emma. They were still young and could build a strong marriage if they put their past behind them.

As much as Grace wanted to be angry with Asbury for abandoning Emma, for making her live the life of a nun, she couldn't. She'd decided last night over dinner that she liked the way Asbury regarded his wife with a mixture of curiosity and admiration when he thought no one watched him. Ha! She'd seen the look in his eyes. He was trying to fix their marriage. Obvious as it was, Emma was blind to his attempts. Grace was not.

She must play this carefully because she didn't know if men discussed the business of women with each other. She wouldn't put it past them to do just that. "What are your plans for the day, Mr. Lioni?"

"Nothing of importance. It's been work and no play for too many months. This reprieve in the country is welcome."

She turned to face him. "How do you plan to amuse yourself while residing here?"

That was a mistake to ask. She got a good look at his knowing expression and tried not to smile in return. She failed even before she thought to paste any sort of aloof expression on her face.

Why not invite the flirtation?

Mr. Lioni's burly, imposing frame came a step closer. She held her ground, liking how small she felt in his presence. She was no weeping willow like her sisters.

She was plumper, taller, and darker in coloring, like her father had been.

"I can think of many things to amuse my time," he said in an intimate tone. She'd bet her finest jade hair combs that he could amuse her time quite nicely.

Her knees wobbled beneath her skirts. Had she not been leaning against the dark cabinetry that lined the room, she would have slid to the ground in a heap of overexcitement. He reached out toward her, fingering the edge of ribbon tied about her waist.

"You interest me more than you ought to." That purr was still in his voice.

He interested her, too. When they'd retired last night to the parlor, he had been rather forward and very clear in his interest. She hadn't spurned any of his attempts because it felt good to be courted and chased by a man. That couldn't be the right word for what they were doing. No, it was nothing so innocent as courting.

This was the start of a grand affair. She wasn't sure if she was ready for something of that nature, despite being a widow for two years. Maybe she was the marrying type as opposed to the casual-affair type. She doubted Mr. Lioni was looking for the first kind of attachment.

"This is fine for you?" he asked, slipping his finger under the ribbon and pulling her a fraction closer.

Eyes going wide, she looked over his shoulder to the dim interior of the cellar. There was no one to interrupt them. No servants to see her doing something she shouldn't. Where was her resolve to be good? To not cede to the temptation standing before her?

Oh, she'd never had such control over her desires.

How far was she willing to take this flirtation? Far enough to see where exactly it would lead? Being confined in the wine cellar alone with Mr. Lioni definitely seemed decadent, but it wouldn't do for her to throw caution to the wind.

"I won't say I'm not tempted." When had she become so bold with her words? This man was almost a complete stranger to her. "But it wouldn't be proper." Not that she cared to play the proper widow. Maybe she did, a little bit.

Instead of taking that step forward—a step she really, really wanted to take—Grace lifted his finger away from the ribbon at her waist and spun around to walk farther into the cellar. Aware that he watched, she trailed her fingers over the chestnut-colored wood shelves that housed hundreds of bottles of wine; she pulled two at random.

Bottles in hand, she headed back in the direction of the stairs, passing Mr. Lioni with a smile that dared him to follow. Despite the fact that she should keep a safe distance between her and him, he might be useful in luring Asbury to their planned afternoon escapade.

"Have you a fun afternoon planned?" he called after her.

With a sly look over her shoulder, she said, "Very fun, and I think you can do me a favor. Come to the kitchen. I need to find something to open these bottles." She raised them, one in each hand.

His smile—more a smirk, really—brightened as he walked toward her and took the wine from her hands. Was it her imagination, or had he caressed her hand a little longer than he needed to? Had he leaned in close to her and taken a long inhalation?

With a shrug, she started up the stairs, aware that he stared at the sway of her hips as they climbed the rounded staircase. It never hurt to exaggerate the wiles of a woman during a flirtation. For now, Grace had to concentrate on Emma. She was sure she could save her sister's marriage or at least push it in the right direction.

When her sister was taken care of this afternoon, maybe she'd indulge more in Mr. Lioni's company. She'd just have to keep her head about her and make sure the flirtation didn't turn into something she couldn't keep control of.

# Chapter 10

*Why won't you come home? What is it I've done wrong?*

This was a very bad idea. Emma hadn't been thinking clearly when agreeing to the charade her sisters had orchestrated. She did not want to do this right now. Not after the letter she'd received from Waverly shortly after their breakfast. Thank goodness she'd intercepted it before Richard had seen it.

"Why did you wait for my husband to arrive at Mansfield Hall before mandating these challenges?" Emma asked of Abby.

Emma pulled her shawl tighter around her shoulders and sat on the stone bench in the garden. She couldn't figure out what her sisters had planned. But she welcomed any distraction. She would forget about the letter till later.

Abby snorted. "We didn't intentionally time it that way. We've never had the opportunity before now, Em. We'll be away from prying eyes this afternoon."

Emma raised a questioning brow. She wasn't entirely convinced of that. "Where is Grace?"

"She's gathering together a few items." Abby looked

over Emma's shoulder. "Your ears must be burning, Grace. Em just asked what was taking you so long."

Grace winked at Abby, then held the wicker picnic basket in her hands aloft.

"Your big plans for this afternoon are to go on a picnic?" Emma rolled her eyes. Really, couldn't her sisters be more inventive than that?

"Hardly," Grace responded as she looped her arm through Abby's. "We needed to procure a few items to help you achieve your first task."

"When will you enlighten me?" Emma asked.

"Soon." Abby took Emma's arm, tugging her along the cobbled path.

"Don't you think you should tell me what we're doing?" Both sisters turned to her and raised one brow each. "What if I don't agree to the challenge?"

"A valid point." Grace tugged them toward the apple orchard. They could easily get lost amongst the tidy rows of trees. She put the basket on the grass and took a blanket from inside and set it out on the ground. "We'll only reveal the dare after we've had a bottle of wine."

"Our great plan for the day is to drink a bottle of wine?" Emma snorted in disbelief. "Grace, I didn't know you took to such habits."

"It's only to help loosen your inhibitions," Abby chimed in, taking the bottle from the basket. "I think Brown stuck the cork back in too far, Grace. I can't get it out."

"Mr. Lioni opened the wine for me." Grace blushed a pretty shade of red at the mention of the visiting gentleman. "He promises to keep our secret."

"Sneaking wine in the middle of the day is hardly secret-worthy." Abby wedged the bottle between her legs and yanked at the cork with both hands. Without so much as spilling a drop on her white dress, she pulled it free with a pop.

Taking the glasses from the basket, Abby poured out the ruby liquid to the brims. When she was done, she set the empty wine bottle back in the basket and raised her glass. "I think we should have our first sip as a hearty cheers to our sister for allowing us to dare her."

"I agree." Grace raised her glass and clinked it against Abby's.

"Why do I have this sinking feeling that I'll live to regret this?" Emma made a toast with her sisters and took a small sip of the dry wine. "When will the big reveal be, then?"

"Well," Grace started, fanning her skirts around her so they covered her stretched-out legs. "We've decided that you need to climb a tree."

Emma laughed and sat down between her sisters. She had to hand her glass off to Abby in fear of spilling the red liquid over their white quilt. "You can't be serious. That is the funniest thing I've heard in ages." She took a gulp of air and tried to calm her breathing. It didn't work. It was so preposterous. Gales of mirth flowed from her, but her sisters sat stoically next to her, expressions steady and filled with amusement.

"We are serious." Abby took a long swallow from her wine and passed Emma's back to her.

"We figured it better to start small. We already agreed that the tasks shouldn't be impossible to accomplish," Grace reminded her.

"Why would you want me to climb a tree?" Emma looked at the trees around them.

"Because you never did when we were children." Grace shrugged. "You should live life to the fullest. Whenever else will you have a chance?"

"I agree. You want to enjoy the simpler things in life before you are too old for such tasks," Abby added.

Emma narrowed her eyes and glared at her youngest sister.

She was not old.

"I hardly need wine to fortify me for this."

"No, you don't." Grace laughed. "We just thought it would be fun if we did this while slightly inebriated."

Emma looked over her sisters in bemusement. This really wasn't so bad. And it was a much better way to spend her afternoon as opposed to worrying about the contents of Waverly's letter. It was a reminder of his promise to call on her again; a reminder that her painting wouldn't remain his secret alone for long.

Climbing a tree would pass the time. Nothing more. Well, it did seem fun and a more than amusing way to spend their afternoon together. It was also a good way to avoid her husband. She didn't know how she would face him after last night.

"You hardly needed a wager to make me do this." Emma stood on the quilt, eyeing the selection of twenty-foot apple trees around them. "Which one shall it be?"

Abby grabbed her hand and hauled her back down to the makeshift picnic they'd set up. "No, you don't seem to understand. You will have to take off your shoes and stockings. This is why we have the wine fortification."

"Abby and I plan to participate." Grace took another swill of the claret.

Emma scrunched up her face as she took another drink of her wine. She had never acquired a taste for wine or spirits of any sort, but the more she drank, the better it started to seem.

"Is there water?" Emma asked.

"That would be cheating," Abby said. "No, we'll have our toast, then strip out of our unmentionables so it's easier to climb the trees."

To Emma's astonishment, Grace procured another bottle of wine from the basket.

"I guess you didn't think to bring any food to snack on. It's all wine in that basket, isn't it?"

"Indeed it is." Abby hiked up her skirts to untie her leather kid shoes. "You should do as I am, Emma. You wouldn't want your younger sisters to shame you in a little tree climbing."

Tipping up her glass, Emma downed the rest of the contents. She was a tad light-headed, and doubted she needed another glass to help her partially disrobe. She was not shy with her sisters. They were all women here. Reaching under her skirts she found the laces at the side of her boots and pulled them off.

"I do believe you will both lose this wager. This is hardly something I wouldn't have done had you ever bothered to ask."

"And I think the wine is already speaking for itself." Grace hiccupped and pushed another full glass into Emma's hand. It was filled to the top again. "Looks like we will polish off two bottles amongst us."

"Goodness, what will the household think of us when we arrive stumbling back in their midst?" Emma giggled. Oh, dear, she must be quite far gone, because she *never* giggled.

"It's not as if it'll matter to us at that point." Abby hiked her skirts up even higher to release the garter on her hose and roll them down. "I suggest you do the same. You won't get a good grip with your feet otherwise."

Emma slid her hands under the multitude of her skirts to release her garters. Silly of them to intoxicate themselves for such a cause. But now that she was tipsy she didn't much mind. It lent a certain euphoria to the experience.

"You do realize I'm one step closer to winning this challenge?" she pointed out.

"One can never tell the final outcome until the task at hand is completed." Grace stood from the quilt and walked over to the nearest tree and latched her hands around the lowest resting branch. Wedging her bare toes into a curve near the base of the trunk, she hauled herself up. "I'm sure I only did this once growing up. It'll be quite fun to see if I can still manage a good climb. Come along. I don't want to be the only one in a tree."

"I'm simply strategizing," Emma stated.

Tucking her stockings into her boots, Emma decided on the tree next to Grace's chosen one. It had a low-hanging branch that was easy to wrap her hands around. She hadn't thought climbing trees hard until she actually put herself to the task. She levered her foot into a dark, scaly knot and tried to pull herself up. Her grip around the bark wasn't tight enough, and she slipped off the tree and back to the ground. At least she landed on her feet and not her rump.

Hands on her waist, Emma looked up at the imposing task her sisters had set forth. Surely, the wine she'd gulped down wasn't helping the situation. Standing up on her toes, she wrapped her arms around the fattest of the lower branches. Problem was, she wasn't strong enough to lift herself from the ground.

"You have to use your legs to kick you up once you have a hold on the branch, Emma." Abby was already sitting on the heavy hanging branch of her chosen tree, directly across from them.

"That is precisely what I tried to do," she called back.

Determined not to fail at the very first task she'd

been given, Emma set her foot against a little ledge and pushed up. She managed to haul herself so her stomach lay over the lower branch of the tree. Thankfully, it was wide enough to support her weight.

Throwing her leg over one side, she twisted her skirts to rest on either side of the branch and sat up. It seemed natural to give a great hoot as she sat there with a leg on either side of the heavy branch. She was far too impressed by her accomplishment.

"Excellent work." Grace had already made it halfway up her tree, and it looked as though she'd tied her skirts around her hips so they wouldn't impede her progress. "All you have to do is keep pulling yourself up. The hardest part is over."

"Easy for you to say. I've never had need to climb a tree before. It would be a great deal easier if we were wearing trousers."

"Oh, I'm so glad you mentioned that. You'll need trousers for your next challenge. But I'll say no more in fear of ruining it," Abby teased. "Grace, when can we reveal the next test?"

Emma looked over to Grace. Her sister had evidently made it as high as she could go. Her arm was wrapped around the sturdy trunk shooting up through the center, and her legs hung over the branch she sat upon, swinging back and forth. Quite scandalous, if Emma did say so. They were all quite wicked, and it felt great to not have a care in the world.

"Maybe tomorrow. And I must say," Grace said, "this is the most fun I've had in far too long. I didn't think it would be this easy to climb a tree."

Emma looked up into the blooming branches of her apple tree. She'd only made it to the first branch. The wind moved the higher branches in its gentle hold.

Varying shades of green leaves danced in place, small apples held fast to where they'd budded from flowers.

"Tell me I've passed the undertaking of tree climbing. I fear I will grow dizzy should I climb any higher." She stared down to the neatly cropped grass lining the orchard. It looked a great deal farther away than she remembered on first spying the ground from atop this perch. "I'm quite content to sit right on this branch and never move again."

"Aren't you even going to try, Em? Look how high I've made it, and my branches are thinner and scarcer than yours," Abby gloated at her accomplishment.

Emma picked an undergrown apple from the branch above her head and tossed it in her sister's direction. She had terrible aim. It veered off to the far left and didn't even hit Abby's tree.

Both her sisters laughed in tandem.

"Don't make me laugh when I'm so high off the ground," Abby said.

Rolling her eyes, Emma finally gave in to the need to laugh along with them. "Fine. I cede the competition of best tree climber to you, Abby. And let it be said, neither of you told me I had to climb all the way to the top. You just said I had to climb a tree. So I've passed the task you have set forth."

She looked over to Abby, who hadn't had more than one glass of wine. Their youngest sister was probably the only one not feeling the effects of the alcohol.

"A shame that you've made it this far and won't attempt to go farther." Abby climbed back down to a lower, sturdier branch. "I've climbed plenty of trees to know that there's nothing as fun as looking down on the world from atop the highest perch."

Grace was already at the bottom of her tree wiping

her hands on her skirts and untying the swath of material to settle it back over her legs. "You have passed one of the challenges. I'm happy to say, we've made the other two tasks quite a bit more difficult to accomplish. Come on down, unless you've changed your mind and do plan on soaring right to the top."

Emma looked down at her sisters. They both stood on the solid, unmoving green grass. Her vision was a bit blurry, an aftereffect from the wine. "The ground looks rather far away. I'm liable to turn my ankle should I jump."

"Emma," Grace said in a stern voice, "if you don't come down on your own, I'll have to call your husband to come rescue you."

"Don't do that." Emma groaned her embarrassment. "I should die of shame for being perched in a tree half drunk and half naked."

"I think we should have put more wine in her," Abby murmured.

What were her sisters planning, aside from scaling trees in the apple orchard? Emma stared down at the exposed roots of the tree. It couldn't be more than five or six feet from the ground; maybe she could wrap her legs around the trunk and slide down. Oh, she was definitely tipsy to think up something so imprudent as that. She wanted to lean forward and hug the branch she was on until the spinning behind her eyes subsided.

"I might just stay up here for a bit longer."

Grace snickered as she looked off into the distance. "Why, I do believe I see your husband walking this way with Mr. Lioni."

Emma's eyes snapped wide open. "Oh, no. Do hide, Grace. I don't want him to see me up here."

Both sisters ignored her, waving to the two gentlemen walking between the rows of trees. Emma stared after them, and could make out her husband's black hat bobbing closer as if it floated all on its own. A shame the branch in front of her covered everything else from view.

"Asbury, you've impeccable timing." Grace's voice was teasing, the laughter evident. Emma watched her sisters curtsy to the approaching men. Hadn't Grace promised to be furious at Richard on her behalf?

"It seems that Em has gotten herself into a bit of a pickle." Abby looked up at her, grinning nearly ear-to-ear. "She's like the cat that can't figure out how to get down from the tree once it's found a pretty place to watch the birds."

Her husband came into view then, removing his hat as he tipped his head back to look at her. A twinkle of amusement lit his eyes.

"Good day, husband." She tried pulling her legs up higher so her bare shins and ankles couldn't be seen from below. She didn't want to know what else he could see beneath her skirts. The movement unsettled her balance. She slapped her hands out and held tightly to the branch between her thighs.

"What a sight you make, wife. I do believe the whole county will see what pretty calves you have."

She gasped and, on instinct and in a fit of temper, grabbed another tiny malformed apple and chucked it at her husband. He ducked away just before it could hit its mark. There was satisfaction in knowing it hit him squarely on the shoulder. Not bad considering she'd been aiming for his head. His hand came up to cover his smile too late.

"It would do you good to recall we are in mixed company," she hissed. Were the words slightly slurred? She hiccupped. Oh, dear, now he'd know she wasn't her normal self.

Richard looked to the makeshift picnic they'd set up earlier, then back to her with one eyebrow raised. "You are a little more cheeky than usual. Do I have the empty bottles of wine to thank?"

"You odious, impossible man." Her sisters were bent at the waist. They laughed so hard tears streaked their faces. "I'm glad you are all laughing at my expense," she shouted loud enough they could hear over their own tittering.

"Oh, Em, don't be such a spoilsport." Abby wheezed for breath before she continued, "It's all in good fun."

"It was fun until this one"—she pointed at her husband, who still expressed great amusement at her predicament—"came along. Mr. Lioni, if you could please show my husband how a true gentleman acts and turn about."

She waved her finger in example. Fortunately, Mr. Lioni complied, but not before she saw the grin stretched across his face. And he couldn't hide the rapid rise and fall of his chest as he laughed silently along with her sisters.

Later on she might find this funny. Right now, she was straddled over a tree branch with her husband looking up her skirts, and he didn't even try to hide the fact that he was doing just that. She looked down at him, her lips pinched and eyes narrowed. Didn't matter, since he was staring at her dangling foot.

"Will you help me down?"

Finally he made eye contact with her. "I do like you just this way." Then he was looking back at her bare legs. "You should do this more often."

He was no help. Instead of arguing further, she pulled one of her legs over the branch—surely giving him a clear view of her lack of underthings—and without further ado launched herself toward her husband.

He had the good grace to catch her at the very least. But they catapulted to the ground, his hat rolling away. He grunted with the impact of their fall. She tried to scramble up from his lap. His hand had somehow found its way under her skirts and around her bare thigh. He squeezed her, moved that hand up to her rump, and had the nerve to pat her bottom.

"I think I need to get you out of the bedroom more often if this is the result." He whispered it so the others wouldn't hear.

She gaped at him in shock and finally scuttled off his lap and to her feet. Her skirts had twisted every which way, so she set herself to fixing them and dusted out the particles of tree bark that were speckled all over her. Better doing that than meeting his gaze when her face was flaming with heat. The man knew how to make her blush.

"I can see my wife home." Richard stood up and dusted his hat off.

As if on cue, her sisters and Mr. Lioni grabbed up the bottles and other picnic items. They left her standing there alone with Richard.

"Wait," she yelled, "you've got my shoes."

"Don't worry." Richard plucked a piece of grass from her hair. "I'll carry you should your dainty feet grow tired."

She picked up her bonnet and tied it under her chin with more force than necessary. "You are impossible."

His smile only grew bigger with the pronouncement.

The way was grassy enough that the hike wouldn't bother her feet. She focused on picking out the tree bits burrowed into her bodice. When she raised her head, she was no longer able to make out the forms of her sisters.

It was clear to her then: Her sisters had planned this.

Why would they do this to her? Especially after everything she'd unwittingly revealed to Grace this morning. She must better guard her tongue. She should never have divulged so much.

She should have trusted her instincts earlier when she'd questioned her sisters' motives. She struck out on her path, uncaring whether Richard followed or not.

"I've done nothing to warrant your anger."

She spun on her heels and glared at her smirking husband. "I'm not angry, simply annoyed with how my day has turned out." Because her sisters were traitors of the first order. How dare they abandon her here with her husband.

"Then I wish we had found you earlier."

Emma pressed her hand to her temple, feeling the beginnings of a megrim. One caused more by embarrassment at her situation than by the effects of the wine.

Richard's nimble hands brushed her fingers aside, and he massaged her temples. She didn't dare push him away. She wanted to groan at his welcome touch, lean in to him for support.

Perhaps she should take him up on his offer to carry her home. That way, she could make an innocent exploration of the hardness beneath her fingers. Her hands were already balanced on his shoulders, kneading into the muscle. He was so solid beneath her touch. She sucked in her bottom lip and raised her eyes high enough to see the sensuous outline of Richard's lips.

She wasn't brave enough to raise her mouth to his and brush their lips together. Definitely not brave enough to wrap her hands around the back of his neck and pull him nearer.

Richard crowded in closer as though he had heard her thoughts.

"That feels nice, Emma." He pushed her bonnet back

on her head and kissed her forehead. His thumbs rotated around her temples, soothing the ache away.

It occurred to her that she'd never have acted so forward, allowed him to act this way, if not for her drunken bout with her sisters. The massaging slowed; Richard's big, warm hands slid down over her shoulders, and his arms wrapped around her lower back so he could crush their bodies together.

"I won't take advantage of you. I want you lucid for everything we do. Tell me to stop, if that's what you want."

Whatever was he talking about? Ask him to stop holding her? Highly doubtful she'd ask him to move away. She wanted more. She wanted . . . she didn't know what she wanted.

Just the heat of his body sent a sliver of anticipation coursing through her limbs and heart. Her headache was gone. Or it so happened she couldn't focus on that particular pain with all the other sensations tingling throughout her body. She was especially warm where his hand clasped at her back. His fingers massaged the tender spot right at the tail of her spine.

The backs of her skirts were slowly raised; the afternoon air kissed her bare shins, then the back of her knees. This didn't seem like the right thing to do in the full light of day. Outdoors. Strange how her hands were not the only thing wrapped around his neck. She had snaked her arms around him, too.

His body hunched over hers, forcing her body to arch back. He was kissing the pulse pounding so strongly in her neck. So delicious a feeling. It wasn't simply left at kissing, either. He bit at her, licked at her. Made awful animal noises come from her throat and caused her fingers to curl through his hair to keep his mouth at her neck. She never wanted him to stop doing that. She could get lost in Richard's arms, if she allowed it.

She wanted to allow it. She wanted him to press himself tighter to her, around her. Inside her.

It was as though her body knew it couldn't let him get away. When the cool breeze around them touched her thighs, she let out a squeak of protest. Reality had intruded despite the sweet sensual awareness buzzing through her body. It was as though her limbs were also intoxicated, wobbly and relaxed to the point of tiredness.

She pushed at his shoulders, a silent declaration for him to release her. A shame her mind had started to climb out of the fog induced by the alcohol. A shame she hadn't gotten past the point of thinking altogether—if such a thing were possible. The last thing she should do was allow this kind of familiarity between them. He already owned her in the evenings, body and soul. She'd not relinquish her days to him as well. That alone belonged to her. It felt like the only thing she had control over.

He raised his mouth away from her neck with a groan of objection. She could feel the clenching and unclenching of his fists at her rear before her skirts, inch by slow inch, lowered, and he finally let her go. Every time he touched her, she felt like she lost a little more of herself to him.

"Sorry," she said, unsure why that word seemed important to mutter.

"No need to apologize. I promised to stop." He picked up his hat. She wanted to see his expression after her refusal. Wanted to know if he was disappointed that they'd stopped.

Instead of asking, always a coward with her feelings where her husband was concerned, she bit her lip and looked over his shoulder when he straightened and dusted off his hat once again.

Hat back atop his head, he proffered his arm. "Shall we head home?"

"Yes," she answered.

Their sides brushed against each other with every step; her breast rubbed the side of his arm. Absently, he stroked his thumb over the inside of her wrist. These small touches were taking away the barriers she'd worked so many years to build against this man. Walls built around her hurt feelings at his abandonment. Walls in place for protecting herself from future hurt.

"Why were you in a tree?"

"It's a rather long story." Opening the line of communication made everything less awkward.

"I believe we have enough of a walk for a 'long story.'"

"I'd rather talk of something less embarrassing."

He rubbed affectionately at her hand tucked along the length of his forearm. She smiled up at him. Liking that he touched her and didn't seem to realize he was doing so.

"You can't leave a man hanging in the balance."

"Had you come two minutes earlier, it wasn't simply a matter of my being up in a tree but all three of us."

Richard let out a hearty chuckle. "We'll save that story for our dotage."

That put a pause in her step. She'd assumed when he told her his plans of staying on at Mansfield Hall, it wouldn't last longer than getting her with child. Could she hope for something more permanent from him? She didn't—couldn't—dare hope that. It would lead to too much disappointment.

Him leaving on their wedding night had killed her faith in happily ever afters, dashed away her childish dreams and replaced them with the reality of what to expect in a marriage not based on a love match. He'd been kind to her during their courting period, too, and then it was as though none of it had mattered once their fates were sealed in matrimony.

She'd never been capable of expecting anything different all those years ago. She'd been so young. Married one year after her mother's death. Papa had wanted her settled before he kicked the bucket, as he always said.

"Do you really mean that?"

Richard's eyes narrowed in question. "Mean what? That we can save the story for another day?"

"For our dotage. Do you mean that as an expression, or in truth?"

He rubbed at his jaw thoughtfully. "I don't know why I said that."

Disappointment unfurled in her limbs.

The manor was in sight now. Both her sisters and Mr. Lioni were nowhere in view. And she was anxious to quit Richard's company.

"What of tonight, Emma?" Richard pulled her short of the French doors on the back terrace.

This was a question worth mulling. She didn't answer right away as she looked up at him. His expression was hard to read. Closed off. Why his request held a note of desperation interested her.

"I will expect you at ten."

Emma couldn't be more grateful that her sisters had locked themselves away in another part of the house on their return. The bigger question remained as to where her husband had gone off to. She'd not lower herself to ask the servants his whereabouts. That might make it look as though she was trying to hide something. Even though she was trying to hide something. She just prayed Richard didn't come looking for her.

"Shall I bring in refreshments, madam?" Brown asked.

"No, His Grace won't be staying long."

Not for more than a few minutes. She doubted her husband would be thrilled to see the other man in his home. But Nathan's—the Duke of Vane's—timing was also perfect.

She had a task for him. One she could trust with no other.

Nathan burst through the parlor door. "What are you about, making me wait in the hall, Em?"

She stood at his entrance and nodded for Brown to leave. Nathan came forward, kissed each of her cheeks, and then lifted her hands to his mouth to give them the same treatment. She hadn't seen him in three months. Although they made a point to correspond at least a couple times a month. His dark brown hair was windblown, as though he rode in on his horse without his hat on. His masculine, handsome face was etched in worry.

"What are you doing in this part of the country?" she asked.

"I was at a house party in the next county. When my man of affairs brought me your letter, I left shortly thereafter."

She had more news to give to her dearest friend. "I was going to send another missive today."

She looked to the door, nervous her husband would break into the room at any moment.

"Are you expecting someone else?"

She shook her head. "I'm being rude. Come sit with me."

"What's wrong, Emma?" His hand grasped hers as he took a seat next to her on the settee. "Your hands are freezing."

"I need to discuss a delicate matter with you."

She didn't want to talk about this with her husband quite yet. Their relationship was too new. Too fragile. Nathan, on the other hand, could help her correct a sudden problem.

"I've run into a problem with Waverly." Emma let out a shaky breath. This wasn't easy to talk about, but who else could she reveal her secrets to?

"Tell me you haven't taken that bastard to your bed, Em. I'll put a bullet between his bloody eyes."

Nathan well knew what Waverly wanted from her. It shouldn't surprise her that he'd figured that out.

"You know me better than that."

"And you know it is my everlasting desire to keep you as my own." His tone softened.

"There is nothing to be had between us, either." This banter was a usual course for them.

Nathan waved off the comment, wanting her to continue to the heart of her problem. "What kind of situation do you have with Waverly?"

She procured the letter she'd received from him this morning. "His demands are clear. He wants me to become his . . . mistress." The words tasted like thickly set trifle on her tongue. "He was cryptic when we spoke last. Said he would use me to his benefit."

The sparkle of amusement left Nathan's eyes. "The bastard won't get away with this, Em." He held the letter between his hands and made no move to open it.

She chewed at her lower lip. "I didn't mention this in my last letter, but it seems he's acquired one of my *self-portraits*."

The duke stood from the settee and paced in front of her, raking his hands jerkily through his hair. "He didn't get it through me."

"I wasn't suggesting it was the one I gave you. I

know how much you value that painting. He's acquired the other, and is threatening to reveal it to everyone. While I've never cared about my standing in society, I don't want to ruin Abby's chances of marrying."

"He'll prove nothing. I'll come forward and say I know the artist, deny it's you if I must."

Emma shook her head. If only it were so easy. "You know it's an obvious likeness." She'd been too young and too stupid to hide her identity when she painted it.

His open hand slapped down against the mantel. "Shit, Em. You should have let me take it off your hands years ago."

"It can't be changed now. I find it strange that he would go to such drastic lengths to secure me as a lover."

"Damnably." Nathan turned and faced her, concern etching his expression and thinning his lips. "What did he say when he visited?"

"It's all in the letter." She massaged her temples. The wine had finally caught up with her. "Unfortunately, he's not my only problem. My husband is here. At Mansfield Hall. I don't want him to know anything about this."

"Richard is here?" Nathan's voice was laced with skepticism.

She nodded her head in the affirmative.

His eyes narrowed in question. "Does he know I'm here?"

"No, and I don't want him to." Emma pulled at the edges of her sleeves, in her nervousness over the situation. "Just take the letter and leave, Nathan. I don't want a confrontation between you two."

He didn't argue with her. But he also didn't make any move to leave.

He held the letter aloft. "Hiding the evidence?"

"Yes, if you must know." Her husband couldn't know about her art. Not like this. "All I want is for you to buy that picture from Waverly. I don't know how you'll do it, but I trust you to get it back. I'll pay whatever he wants. I haven't spent any of my funds from the paintings I've sold."

"If I buy it, Em, it's mine. I won't take your money for something I should never have let leave my hands. You can trust me not to share it with the world, but it's mine."

She understood that. She stood from the low settee and offered her hand. Nathan pulled her into a hug, and ran his hand down the length of her back. It was nothing more than a comforting gesture between two friends.

Nathan's chin rested atop her head. "You should tell him."

"Tell me what, exactly?" Richard's voice was sharp as a sword cutting down the enemy.

Emma pulled away from Nathan quickly. She pasted a smile on her face and turned to face her husband. The door was shut behind him, probably so the servants wouldn't hear whatever he was about to say. He wasn't looking at her. Nathan was the target for his evident anger.

"You filthy swine." Richard stormed into the room. "You come into my home and put your hands on my wife."

Nathan stood firm. "See it any way you like, Asbury. At least I've been here for her for the past ten years."

"You bloody bastard!" Menace like she'd never before witnessed bulked up Richard's frame. His bearing was threatening.

She stepped forward and put a hand against his chest in the hope of stalling him. She felt the tension strumming along his body. The anger was palpable and volatile. "How dare you insult my guest," she snapped.

"Your guest," Richard said sardonically to her, then his full attention swung back to the duke. "Get the hell out of my house, Vane. If I see you here again . . ." Richard shook his head. "I can't promise I won't pound you into the bloody ground."

"You can try."

Emma turned to the duke, speechless at how to handle the situation.

Nathan bowed to her. "My lady." Straightening, he glared back at Richard. "This is far from over."

"Believe me, I know."

As angry as she was, she thought both men were overreacting.

"You're both insufferable."

And because she could do nothing about them puffing out their chests and butting heads like deer in rut, she left them in the parlor glaring at each other. If it came to fisticuffs between them . . . well, it was not her fault. She well knew she'd have to explain herself to Richard later, but she'd not do it when she could practically feel a firestorm blazing from him.

# Chapter 11

*I'm ashamed to say I hate you. I hate what you've turned our lives into. I hate that I'm nothing to you.*

This time when the knock came at the adjoining bedchamber door, Emma was surprised. Richard had not been at the dinner table tonight. Did he come to find out more about the duke? Or did he wish to spend the night with her?

"Come in," she called. She had still prepared herself for him tonight and climbed into bed to stop nervously pacing the floor. She sighed. She was always hoping for more, wasn't she?

The door opened, a relief of candlelight revealing the frame of her husband, so strong and imposing as he stood in the doorway. The word *virile* came to mind. Her breath caught and her heart beat a little faster. She'd probably take the smallest crumbs of affection if she couldn't have everything she wanted. What a pathetic creature she was. Especially after his treatment of her earlier. And his accusations. She shouldn't want anything from him.

She patted the empty space near the edge of the mattress, beckoning him closer. She needed to feel his heat, his strength, close to her.

"I thought maybe you'd forgo your visit tonight," she said without emotion.

Eyebrow raised, he sauntered closer on bare feet. Instead of sitting, he stared down at her with an expression she could make neither head nor tails of. What was his mood tonight? Was he still angry? Or was everything forgotten from earlier?

"Wasn't I clear that you needed to cut off all contact with your lovers?"

"Nathan and I are not lovers." It was the wrong thing to say. To use the duke's Christian name. Richard's lips thinned, and his jaw visibly clenched.

She turned her head away and waited for him to reprimand her. Even though she was the innocent party here. She knew that most people, catching her in an embrace with Nathan, would assume them to be lovers. It wasn't really Richard's fault for thinking the worst.

As though he heard her thoughts, he said, "You've sung this song before, assuring me there have been no lovers. I never expected you to live like a nun, Emma. I was gone a long time. What I did expect was for you to obey me as my wife when I asked you to cut off all threads to your paramours."

Was that the reason he used to justify his affairs over the years? Loneliness? The desperate want of another's touch? It was his own damn fault he never came back to her.

"I shouldn't have to explain myself, Richard. Nathan was the only friend I had when I was introduced to society. He befriended an awkward young woman when no one else would talk to the wife of a man heavily involved in trade."

"A friend does not embrace you as Vane did."

Perhaps not. But hers and Vane's friendship was different from most. Yes, she'd given him a nude of her likeness years ago. The gesture had been more about his love of beautiful paintings—it was a small token for his kindness and friendship over the years. It was a most unusual gift but somehow fitting for their most unusual friendship.

Richard tilted her chin up so he could see into her eyes. A flicker of excitement shivered down the length of her body, puckering her nipples at his simple, light touch. There had never been any other man for her except her husband. It had always been just him. She'd never admit such a weakness to him, though.

"I plan on spending the evening with you, wife."

He tossed her covers aside, letting out a rush of air from his lungs as he stared down at her form. She'd left the ties loose on the chemise so he could see the plumpness of her breast pressed against the thin material.

"Very pretty," he said hoarsely.

She automatically covered her chest with one arm, more to shield the evidence of her arousal than for modesty's sake. Lifting the edge of her chemise, he ran his knuckles over her knee and thigh. She closed her eyes and basked in the gentle touch.

"I'd prefer it if you greeted me without a stitch on."

She scooted up the bed when he knelt next to her. Putting her back to the headboard. His attempt to pull her closer failed when she pushed his hand away.

"You are always accusing me of awful things, then trying to seduce me. You should make up your mind on how you feel." She folded her legs under her. "I'm not some nightingale you can treat so cruelly."

"This isn't cruelty. This is my home, Emma. When I walk into my parlor I should not see you in another man's arms. As for the seduction, I'm a man, which means I generally have one thing on my mind." In demonstration of this, Richard ran his knuckle over the firm tip of her breast. "What I'm doing is considered fun. You do want to enjoy this, don't you?"

Of course she wanted to enjoy this. She did enjoy this. Instead of giving truth to his words, she said, "There is no fun to be had." Not while he teased her and in the next breath accused her of adultery. Not when he only graced her bed in the hope of an heir.

"Ah, is that what you think?" He reached for her ankle and pulled it out from under her slowly. She let him slide her beneath him. How could she refuse him when she wanted to hold him tight along her body and feel his weight heavy upon her breast? His hands spreading her thighs, and massaging at her breasts?

"I must be more diligent in educating you in these matters." His tone was teasing.

"Will you escape me when you're finished? Like you did last night?" She slid her bottom toward the edge of the bed. Regretfully, his hold on her foot fell away with the move.

Richard wrapped his arms around her waist and pulled her back tight along the length of his body. It was the warmth she'd been desperate to feel moments ago.

"I'm not the one trying to escape, Emma."

She froze in his arms. How true that was. Simple fact of the matter was that she didn't know what she wanted from him. One minute she needed him to hold her, the next she wanted to hide from him. Resisting him was near impossible. She'd not deny him tonight. She'd not run.

The heat of his chest against her back aroused her senses. He rolled her onto the bed and pressed his weight atop her. Trapped. Willingly. He watched her with his intent gaze, one hand reaching forward to pull a chunk of her hair forward. Her head tilted in the direction of his hand.

Running his fingers through the curls, he did nothing more than stare at the golden lock he had captured. He liked whatever it was he saw, she knew, because his eyes were half-lidded, his breathing a little faster. The bulge pressed to her thigh full of want.

Tipping her chin back, he ran his knuckles all the way down her throat, then up. He didn't do this once, but continuously. The pulse at the base of her neck thumped faster. The tenderness of the moment made her shiver despite the warmth of the room and the heat of his body. His hand trailed low enough to brush over the distended tip of her breast before moving back up to her neck. When his lips pressed against her erratic pulse, a light tingling traveled the length of her body.

Should she be ashamed that it felt so good to be touched and kissed like this? Ashamed that she wished her husband would do this to her more often? Steal the moments in the light of day if he must?

He nudged out her left knee with his hand; then his legs were between hers, making sure they stayed open. She wouldn't pretend modesty now. This was exactly where she wanted him.

He loosened his trousers and pushed them down his lean hips. She stretched her arms out to help divest him of his clothes. The feel of his strong thighs beneath her fingers sent a thrill of excitement coursing through her whole body and a rush of fluid to her core. She felt the deep pulse of need between her thighs and wanted him to press himself inside to ease it, but she held back, wanting to touch and explore his form. To learn his body as well as he had learned hers.

She half sat up on the pillows that were supporting her and reached around his back to run her hands over the firm, sinewy globes of his buttocks. Her husband was a well-formed man. Painting him would be no hardship for her eyes or her hands. She wasn't ready to touch the thick, heavy flesh jutting out in front of her. The crown was smooth-looking and the skin covering it slowly eased back the longer she stared.

Looking up to her husband, she wet her lips. What would he do if she kissed the flush tip of his manhood?

"God, Emma. You'll be the death of me."

His hands were rough as he grasped her hips, slid her down the bed, and positioned himself above her, rotating his pelvis, teasing the tip of his cock against her wet folds.

Breath hitched by his sudden action, she reached out her hands and grasped onto his straining forearms, arching her body up to meet his. One of his hands reached between their bodies and cupped her breast, his middle and forefingers lightly pinching her nipple through the cambric chemise.

Suddenly the gentleness was gone from his touch as he grasped her hip tightly. She reveled in the fact that she could do that to him. Make him lose a little bit of control. Make him need this as badly as she did.

He pushed forward so quickly she lost her breath on a moan. He was up to the hilt, groaning against her throat, kissing it every now and again and giving her that familiar thrill of pleasure she was beginning to crave in her gut, in her mons.

She was always so fucking wet. He'd meant to go slower tonight. Draw out their evening so there wasn't any awkward silence afterward when they lay together. But the second her fluids moistened the tip of his cock, he was a man starved for her body. He thrust forward in a need for more.

He wanted to laze about here all night and see how much wetter he could make her. Feel the small pressures of her sheath around his prick till he came. Her breath caught the moment he'd pressed his lips to her neck. He was quickly learning what pleasured his lady wife: She liked it when he touched her throat. Her breasts, too. God, he'd never get enough of their firm roundness.

He pressed his lips to her nape again with a deep groan. Her pulse beat furiously beneath, and he couldn't resist taking a small lick and scraping his teeth along the thumping vein. Her skin tasted like the floral body cream she wore, a little bitter against his tongue, but under that he tasted the saltiness of her perspiration just breaking the surface. The room smelled of sex; the sweetest smell in all the world. A heady, perfect mixture to his senses.

The texture of her skin was smooth and soft. He lowered his hand to cup her breast again. She stiffened a little beneath him when he tore the opening of her chemise to touch her bare flesh this time. He needed to get the damn thing off her. He wanted the press of her breasts against his chest. Slickness of sweat to build and aid the slide of their bodies the longer he fucked her.

Cursing himself for his hurry, he knelt between her legs and held her waist between his hands to guide her body along his rigid length.

His eyes feasted on the short, crisp hairs covering her womanhood. With one hand, he spread the lips of her sex open to see her pink flesh ride along his cock. His thumb rotated over the swollen red nub. What he'd give to suck that bit of flesh into his mouth and tickle it with his tongue.

Her body was tense as a cello bow with his each driving push into her body. She was close. He unsheathed himself long enough to wet her clitoris with the slickness covering his prick before slamming back into her. Thumb pressed and rotating against her swollen nub, he rode her harder.

Pulling her hips higher off the bed, he grasped her buttocks tight and ground their bodies together. He leaned over her to taste her skin, sucking on the pearly tip of her titty through the linen.

There was no holding back. Her body was so damn sweet, so damn perfect his balls drew up tight against his body and he exploded in her.

Well, shit.

He ground into her cunny and rode out his release. When the pumping finally ceded, he realized that she was tense beneath him.

"What's wrong?" he asked.

She took a great many minutes to answer his question. So long he wondered what in hell he'd done wrong, aside from finishing before her.

Finally, she replied, "Nothing."

"Don't lie to me."

"I'm not. You're just different tonight. I'm sorry. I must be doing something wrong." There were tears in her voice. Unfamiliar with causing tears in a woman through acts of congress, he stroked her leg as he would a skittish mare.

"I want you to find release."

Afraid he'd frighten her with any bold words of exactly what he wanted to do to her, he said no more. If he could excite her to a fever pitch, maybe she would relax in his company.

He held himself over her body, keeping most of his weight from crushing her. He was not willing to move from the warm haven between her legs. For Christ's sake, her inner muscles still milked at his cock.

They were far from done. If he left, her thoughts would be free to wander, and he'd give her no reason to think or compare him to any other man—namely the duke. So help him God, he'd kill the blighter the next time he dared to touch his wife.

He was a little shocked to realize he wanted to spend the night in his wife's company. He'd never spent a night with any woman. The women he'd enjoyed in the past had been nothing to him but a means to an end. To be counted amongst Emma's friends meant more to him now than anything, including his business.

The knife wound to his side must have addled his brain. He'd never been the sentimental type, and here he was sprouting sweet platitudes while he thought about Emma.

Truth of the matter was, he did want more. Sometime in the last few days, he'd decided he wanted his wife all to himself. Maybe it was his near-death experience. Or was it part of growing older? Quite possibly it was seeing his wife in the arms of another man that sparked this added possessiveness, this desire he had to own her.

Why had he wasted twelve years? Had he been less cowardly as a youth, she might be happier and more willing to receive his attentions now. Had he contacted her even once during their marriage, she might be warmer toward him. His own bloody fault she was at odds with him. He excelled at ruining good people.

He didn't like where his thoughts were going. He pulled out of her body. Lying on his back, he stared up at the blackness the canopy created. The taper on the candle was burning out and giving off less and less light. His breath had long ago calmed so he could hear her fidgeting with the ribbons on her torn chemise. He should have torn the damn thing off so he could suck the tips of her breasts into his mouth. His prick reacted to the thought. Filling out and ready for another round with his pretty wife. He ignored the desire to act on that thought, for now. There were things that needed to be said between them.

"I haven't done well by you, have I?"

He needed to hear the truth from her lips.

Rolling back to his side, he rested his head in his hand. The curtains remained open, but what little moonlight shone through did nothing to illuminate the still form of his wife. The rise and fall of her chest was so minimal that he almost reached his hand out to make sure she hadn't fallen into a deep slumber.

"I don't necessarily see," she answered, "how you could have done me wrong."

"Who knows what my point is." He flopped back down on the bed, staring up at nothing as thoughts tumbled over in his mind. Would she ask him to leave now that he'd finished having her? "Do you hate me? Hate what I did to you?"

She sighed and put one hand between them on the bed. "We were so young when we married. When you left, I thought you disliked the idea of marriage. I was barely a woman, for heaven's sake. A mere child, really."

"What did you think after a year? After five years, even, of not hearing from me? You couldn't have remained indifferent. I don't think anyone could."

He rested his hand over hers. Needing to touch her.

"*Hate* is too strong a word," she said truthfully. "*Angry* would have been more apt to how I felt. At first, I didn't understand what I had done wrong. Nor what I could do to make you come back. Then I grew up, and I understood the unfair predicament you'd been put in by marrying me, and me you. I was angry for a long time."

The greater question was if she was still angry after all these years. "There was nothing you could have done to make me stay. As you said, we were both young when we took our vows."

She sat up, pulling a pillow into her lap, to cover her bare legs, he thought. He stayed where he was. Watching her. He studied her pale skin in the dim light, the white night rail she wore as a shield, her beautiful golden locks of hair tumbled all about her shoulders and arms like Helen of Troy come to life. This wife of his could probably fell a whole army of men with her shy yet vivid beauty.

She'd tucked her legs under her. The bedding beneath him pulled tight as she tried to tug them higher. He wasn't willing to give them to her just yet. He wanted to get a visual fill of his wife. He had a lot of time to make up for. Starting now.

"Why discuss this now?"

"Does my presence in your bedchamber distress you so much?" He knew it for the truth without having to ask the question.

"No." There was a waver in her voice, belying her answer. "Did you run off so you could live the grand adventure?"

"Some would say that."

"Was it worth it?" She paused, her finger tracing the piping on the pillow. "I mean . . . would you change what you did or do the same thing all over again?"

"Hard to say. Some say you are doomed to make the same mistakes if given a second chance."

They both grew quiet. The only sounds to be heard were the odd creaks in the old house.

Emma gave a great yawn, barely covering it in time. It was an obvious hint that he should take his leave. He didn't much want to go. Would she welcome him in her bed overnight? He'd never spent the night with a woman. He'd never had need to.

He should do that with his wife, wanted to do that, because she was different from any other woman he'd made use of over the years. Not that he could explain that to her. And not that it was about making use of her. There was something more between them. Indefinable, but more.

The awkwardness of their after-moment was enough to convince him he needed to leave. She'd not welcome further advances. Maybe tomorrow night he could demand more from her. He pulled himself up and stretched his feet down to the soft-carpeted floor. Hating that he'd been so quick about reaching his finale without so much as a care for hers. Part of him insisted that wouldn't be the case if he stayed.

Glancing over his shoulder, he saw that her eyes were half-lidded with tiredness. Maybe the yawn hadn't been feigned.

Her sleepy gaze locked with his. "Will you be staying this time?"

Shame he knew her meaning had nothing to do with sleeping in her bed. It was not an invitation to stay, but a question on whether he'd travel abroad again. Were his adventures in trade really over? The answer to that was simple. His life in the opium trade was over. Though future business dealings wouldn't take him far from England, he knew his life in trade was far from over.

Perhaps if his father hadn't been so damn insistent on him taking a seat in the House of Lords next to him, he'd have stayed. Time could not go backward, so he'd never know.

All Richard knew was that the answer he gave his wife was the truth. "I plan to stay."

# Chapter 12

*I feel old, yet young in the sense that I have no life experience. A woman but not really fully a woman. A sad predicament.*

Emma set her brush down in the bowl of turpentine and looked to the tall clock. It was still fairly early in the morning. Richard would be searching for her soon. It was usually near midmorning that he found her. She definitely didn't want Richard searching her out in her private sanctuary. This was the last place she could just be herself. A refuge of sorts where she could forget everything that was going wrong in her life.

Questions flitted across her mind. When would she hear news from Nathan about her painting? Would Waverly do anything rash before the painting could again be safely hidden? How had the man even come by that canvas? It had been sold abroad to a collector more than eight years ago. Nathan was always so careful about whom he sold her works to.

She wiped the excess liquid from her detailing brush and set that down on the easel.

Staring back at her most risqué piece to date, she

brushed a rag over the still-wet paint to blot out some of the mistakes in the lineaments of her form. The light was too strong in the background; it needed more shadows, more fading, more detail to her figure. The lady stretched out on a gold-and-green brocade divan, her supple, naked body on full display. She'd paint in a sheer white shawl to cover the middle section of her naked body this time, and leave the breasts completely exposed.

The eyes of the lithe lady stared back at her in silent mockery. They said: *You wish you were free like me; you wish you could act without a care in the world, just as I do.* Emma thumbed over the facial features and decided right then she'd paint her facing away from the viewer, and wiped the wet mess into her apron. Tossing a cloth cover over the piece, she set a larger canvas atop with a serene landscape painted on it. She'd finish the painting tomorrow; hopefully she'd be sending this parcel to Nathan by week's end.

Sitting down with a heavy sigh, she cleaned her hands with the sponge and a tiny bit of turpentine, making sure she scraped out all the paint underneath her nails.

How was she going to face her husband after last night? She'd wanted him a second time, before their conversation had turned so serious. Goodness, the world would have thought her a wanton, a harlot. Come to think of it, she was starting to act more like one of the women in her paintings than the proper Countess of Asbury she'd schooled herself to be.

Placing her cool hands to her flaming cheeks for a moment, she tried to clear her mind of the intimacies she'd partaken in with Richard. She hadn't expected their time together to be so raw, so untamed. She hadn't wanted it to mean so much to her. What would it take to make Richard stay on with her? What would it take to make their marriage really work this time around? Ha! Her thoughts swayed toward a positive outcome.

She couldn't forget that him staying might mean the end of her painting. She wasn't ready to give up her only passion. Couldn't give it up.

Needing to focus on something else, she cleaned the painting area, tucked her apron away, and covered the powders she used in mixing paint colors. Perhaps if she pretended that nothing had happened, that they hadn't connected so deeply on an intimate level, her husband would remain quiet on the topic. She doubted she'd be that lucky. He'd use her desires against her; she was sure of that.

She wanted something more from the intimate relations they'd had thus far, but didn't know what "more" entailed. She couldn't think of this right now. Her husband seemed to consume more and more of her thoughts. That was not acceptable.

She had to go and see her sisters. Forget her problems for the time being and just spend the rest of the summer in her sisters' company. They could keep her mind from straying in directions it had no right to go.

"We're going to dress in trousers and roll down a hill like ten-year-old boys?" Emma asked.

Both sisters reddened at the comparison. Then Abby smirked and held the bundled stack of clothes toward her. "We even adjusted the size so they'd fit properly."

"We'll stay on the manor property. No one will see us. No one needs to know but us." Grace's mouth screwed up on one side in a grin.

Emma started shaking her head back and forth immediately. "You're lying, Grace. You always make that face, like you've sucked on a sour lemon, when you tell a fib."

Grace ducked her head, walked over to the bed to toss down her stack of clothes, and started to undress. "Of course we won't tell a soul what we've done. It's to be our little secret."

"Em . . ." Abby pushed forward, making her take the bundle of material. "We are doing the dare right along with you. You won't give up so early on in the game, will you?"

Abby had a point. It was too early to give up in this contest of theirs. She'd been resolute about completing every task from the start. She also wanted to avoid her husband again today. She didn't know what to make of last night.

"Fine, but I hope you have hats and jackets we can hide our figures beneath."

Abby sat on the edge of the bed and pinched up her face in thought. "I didn't think to procure those items when we were adjusting the trousers."

Grace turned around, a winning smile on her face. "Never fear. I'll retrieve something after we're dressed."

Emma looked down to her stack of clothes and pulled the twine that held it together. Setting the clothes out on the bed, she looked over them carefully. The shirt looked rather large and she lifted it in front of her. Abby was already loosening the buttons at the back of Emma's gown.

It was a silly challenge. There was no reason she couldn't do it. When she completed this, she would be one task away from winning a sitting from her sisters. Stripped down to their underclothes, they set about getting dressed in the menswear.

"I do say, I've never wanted to wear trousers in all my days." Grace was tucking her shirt in, looking down at her stocking feet. "But it's kind of freeing."

Emma looked down at her form, then back over to

Grace, who had been shaped as a true woman with her heavy bosom and wide hips. Grace looked positively indecent with the way the material of her trousers and shirt hugged her every curve.

"I'm not sure I'd be comfortable in trousers. No wonder men don't want us dressing this way. They can see far too much." Abby was staring over at Grace when she said that. "Good Lord, this is more scandalous than I originally thought." Though Abby seemed more excited than shocked.

"It is," Grace agreed. "Stay here, I'll go and retrieve some jackets."

"Where from?" Abby asked. "Someone might see you dressed as you are. I should go. No one will think me anything but a boy since I don't quite fill out the clothes as you do."

"No one will see me. Mr. Lioni is of a size that will suit our needs. I saw him walking the gardens earlier. I'll just steal into his room. He'll never even know I was there."

Emma grabbed Grace's hand as she made to leave. "What if he should catch you?"

"I'll say we left something of Abby's behind. Unless," Grace's eyes sparked with mischief, "you want to go into your husband's chambers and take his jackets."

"I say we throw a cloak about us. It'll be sufficient enough to disguise us."

"No, the challenge specifically calls for us dressing as men. You'll have to wear a jacket." Abby's grin was smug. Her sisters were enjoying this far too much.

"We should go with you, Grace," Emma offered. Not that she wanted to traipse around the house like they were.

"Admit it, Em, it's rather fabulous sneaking around like this," Abby chided.

Her sister was right. It was liberating for some reason. "I admit it. It is fun in the sense that we know we should not be doing this. Not because it's wicked, but because it's completely ridiculous."

Grace shook her head, laughing. "I don't think we can explain all three of us being in Mr. Lioni's room. I don't mind going. I'll be quick."

"Fine, but if you are caught, Grace, I—I'll not be happy." A shame that was the best thing Emma could come up with.

Grace chuckled softly as she slid quietly from her bedchamber and went to procure the necessary items for their escapades.

How was it she couldn't find any jackets? She'd been through his dressing room and was now sorting through stacks of clothes in the wardrobe. Aha! Finally, her fingers brushed over a fine wool frock coat.

"Seeing you thus, *cara*, gives me the greatest pleasure."

Grace shot upward and smacked the back of her head off a low-hanging shelf. "Ouch." Dropping the two jackets she'd managed to find to the floor, she clutched and pressed at the top of her throbbing head simultaneously.

Mr. Lioni rushed forward, pushed her hands away, and pulled her head down so to inspect the spot she'd been rubbing at.

"I did not mean for this to happen. I walked in, and your lovely derriere was enticing my wicked tongue." His hands were warm and gentle as he parted her hair in his examination. "Not even a bump. Maybe this is a good thing to happen because now you are in my arms."

She raised her head and looked at him. His dark brown eyes stared intently back at her. His lips were full, the bottom one more so than the top, just perfectly sculpted like that of a stone statue. His shoulders were wide, his height only a few inches taller than her five-foot, ten-inch frame. Mr. Lioni was a very masculine presence and the epitome of what she liked in a man. Whenever he was near to her, she wanted to tumble him into the nearest bed and see what else was manly about him.

Goodness, her thoughts were starting to burn her ears.

"*Cara mia,* I am going to kiss you—to change that look of confusion on your face to one of delight."

She swallowed against the lump in her throat. Unable to answer him, she simply nodded yes.

Taking her chin between his thumb and forefinger, he lowered his mouth to hers but did not press their lips together. What was he waiting for? She wanted to feel his mouth crushed to hers with a desperation that stole the breath right out of her lungs.

Slanting his mouth over hers, he said, "I have this desire to make you mine, *tesorina.*"

The words were like a rumbling purr and had her closing her eyes and swaying forward. Her hand pressed against his chest. She ran her fingers over the fine, firm muscle beneath his shirt. Oh dear, he was so impressively hard all over.

Tilting her head back, she slanted her mouth beneath his and pressed forward. His hands were wrapped about her waist, one of them kneading the top of her rump. Right in that moment, she decided she loved wearing trousers. There was so much more to feel; the contours and strength of his thighs, the rigid length of his manhood pressed tight to her stomach, the warmth of his body, and the rapid beating of his heart next to her breast.

His tongue swept around hers. Hers wrapped around his. He tasted of mint leaves. What did she taste like to him? She could have basked and taken more of what he offered, but not today.

Or at least not right now, she silently amended.

Her sisters would worry that she'd been caught and come looking for her if she didn't return. But she liked being caught very much by Mr. Lioni. Hadn't she promised she would enjoy a flirtation and no more? Oh, that simply wouldn't do. Being in his room, in his arms, must have put some sort of spell over her.

"This has been most interesting, to say the least," she started to say, and then realized he would want an explanation for why she was in his assigned room.

It didn't help matters that she'd dropped the two jackets she'd managed to procure. There was nothing to do but sidestep his path and head for the closed door. He caught her hand before she made it more than two paces, spun her back around, and planted his lips over hers again.

This time the kiss was a swift wrestle of lips and tongue, and it was he who stopped the heated licking and tonguing. When he released her, she swayed on the spot. He caught her up against his taller frame. His impressive, welcoming larger body encircled her. It was so nice to feel small next to a man. Rarely, with her height and plumpness, did she have that opportunity.

"You cannot escape me so easily. I would like an explanation as to why you are here."

She looked back over her shoulder to the jackets lying in a pile on the floor, and then down to her front. Hopefully indicating her state of dress without saying anything.

"If all women looked as good in menswear as you, I declare they should all dress just like this."

She smiled at his teasing and ducked her head. She was a little embarrassed to be found this way, but at the same time relieved that they could stop posturing with each other and start the affair that was inevitable between them. What was wrong with her? She'd talked herself out of not having an affair with him. This wasn't good. Not at all.

Now that she'd voiced it to herself, though, she could not deny herself this man. She'd played the role of wife to an elderly husband. She'd never had an affair with the younger men who danced attendance upon her. It hadn't felt right to betray her husband that way. He was always so kind to her.

But he was almost two years in the ground. Mr. Lioni was very alive, very interested, and she couldn't help but be attracted to his suave act. She was sure he was quite the lady's man. She'd have to keep her emotions from carrying her away. Have to keep from expecting more from this man than an affair.

"Stay for a while," he said. "It's still quite early in the morning. No one will notice your absence for a couple of hours."

The mention of a couple of hours and not a few moments was enough to make most women swoon. Goodness. She wanted this man.

"And lock ourselves in here for those hours?" she asked. Of course that was exactly what he meant by such a bold and wonderful suggestion. How she wished she could accept.

"Why else would I ask? I've a need to taste your skin. It's so cruel to tease a man like this, no?" His gaze raked over her tight-fitting trousers and gaping shirt as if he were already touching her.

Was it awful of her that she liked teasing him? His accent had thickened in the last few moments of their conversation. It had taken every ounce of resolve in her not to melt at his words. How desperate she was to know what Mr. Lioni was like in bed. It was a startling revelation.

What she was about to suggest was more daring than anything she'd uttered in all her life. "My sisters wait for me now. That being said, I would like to take you up on this offer later. Much later." Did he understand what *much later* implied? That she wanted nothing more than to spend the whole night with him.

"I will be counting the minutes, *cara*. Tonight is so very far away, though. Let me have a small taste to get me through the afternoon."

She retrieved the jackets and held the material between them. If he started kissing her again, it might not stop there. She'd let him have more than a small taste later.

"Might I take these?" she asked. "If you want to know what they're for, you can come out to the grazing hills on the north side of the property. Not more than a twenty-minute hike. But come with Asbury. It's nothing more than a silly adventure my sisters and I have planned."

He nodded his approval. "Is this something that will make the evening all the sweeter to wait for?"

"I can't say, for that'll depend entirely upon you." Then without any hesitation, and with a sudden reversal of the shyness she'd felt only minutes ago, she stood up on her toes and kissed him on the mouth. A sweet kiss with closed mouths this time. They could save the more intense version for tonight.

# Chapter 13

*For so many years I've needed nothing more than your companionship. I am slowly realizing I need to move on from that want.*

Richard watched the three Hallaways wander away from the house from his vantage point in his wife's bedchamber. All of them wore tan-colored trousers and shirtsleeves—like any ordinary man out for a stroll in the country, in a style of a few decades past. Although there was nothing ordinary in how they appeared. Had they pilfered from the old chests of clothes in the attic? Reaching down, he adjusted the burgeoned swell of his cock. What a state his wife put him in—more like *kept* him in.

He'd come to her room hoping to ask her on a walk around the grounds. Instead, he'd looked out the window when the room had turned up empty, and discovered her acting the hoyden as she had yesterday in the apple orchard.

He dropped the curtain back in place and strode from the room. Time to confront his wife. And find out what tricks the sisters were up to. He couldn't imagine this was how they normally spent their summers—partaking in childish pastimes. Not that he minded. It showed him a different side of his wife, one she seemed so bent on hiding from him.

Meeting Brown in the hall, he asked for his horse to be saddled, then waited in the drive for the blue roan to be brought around. Mounting, he turned the tall beast toward the hills and pastures that flanked the north side of the property. There were sheep here and there, lolling under the odd patch of trees that offered up shade during the heat of early afternoon. It took him less than a quarter hour to find them. He doubted they'd seen his approach since he came around the back of the property.

Seemed Dante had beaten him here. The man stood silently by in a grove of tall birches, hat tipped forward, arms crossed. Rounding toward the trees, Richard dismounted next to his business partner.

"What brings you here?" he asked.

Dante did little more than grunt and nod toward the women. "Came to see what all the commotion was."

Richard turned to the sound of their tittering and giggles. They were quite loud, their voices carrying upward on the light, hot breeze. "Have they seen you standing up here yet?"

"I doubt it. They're too occupied with themselves." Why was he getting such cryptic answers from Dante? What interest did he have in the women's doings? Richard looked down the slope, watching the girls lie about in the grass at ease. He had a feeling he'd ruin their tête-à-tête once he made an appearance.

"And you're standing here watching out for their welfare?"

Dante raised his head and stared him straight in the eye. "Something of that nature." Dante pushed off the trunk of the tree. "Shall we interrupt their morning fun?"

"Yes, I think we should."

Taking the horse's reins, he walked down the sloping hill. Emma's blonde curls bounced as she turned to face their approach. The bright smile faded from her face, but still twinkled in her eyes. He hated that he had that effect on her. As though he sapped the fun out of everything. Perhaps she was embarrassed about last night.

She had a smear of dirt across her right cheek, and her hair was littered with bits of grass. Grace's and Abby's appearances didn't fare much better. But it wasn't them who managed to catch his fancy.

"Oh, no, you don't." Abby stood up, her hands on her hips as she glared at them. "You can't come down here unless you do it in the same fashion we did."

Grace snorted and brushed the grass and dirt from her knees with vigorous strokes. "Don't bother." She waved off the suggestion. "We should get back, anyway."

Richard put out his hand for his wife to take. She stared at it, then looked at his expressionless face. She didn't refuse him. Taking it, she stood quickly, wiped her dirty hands down the side of her trousers and looked at him as though daring him to say something about her current state of dress.

Her hips looked snug in the garment. He wanted to grasp them in his hands and stare at every part of her feminine body enhanced by the tight-fitting material. He could make out the press of her breasts where the shirt seemed to mold against her body. If he moved it, he wondered if he'd get a glimpse of her breasts through the dip in the front. It didn't appear that she wore anything underneath the cambric. And just like that he was hard as stone in his trousers. It was a damnable effect his wife had on him.

Trailing his gaze up to hers, he was met with a frown. So she'd taken notice of what he'd been mesmerized by. It was not as though he could help himself, not with all her feminine attributes on display.

Looking over his shoulder, he could see Dante walking with the other women back to the manor. They weren't waiting for them. "They'll hardly miss us. Would you like to go for a ride?"

"You've only brought one horse."

"We'll just go down to the river. Won't be too much of a task for Odin here." He affectionately rubbed his hand over the horse's neck. Odin gave an approving snort.

Without giving his wife a second chance to say no, he swung himself into the saddle, leaned forward to get a good hold of the back of her trousers, and lifted her up to sit in front of him. Modesty dictated she keep her legs to one side, but if she was bold enough to wander around in the day wearing men's clothes, there was no reason for her to insist on sitting sidesaddle. He also wanted the sweet cheeks of her rear cushioning his cock.

"Face forward so you're straddled over the saddle like I am."

She turned to look at him over her shoulder. He thought she'd argue, but quick as her gaze had ensnared him, she broke it and turned about as he asked. Her back bounced against his chest with the horse's every step. She must not realize what holding her seat near his groin was doing to his anatomy. He'd be hard-pressed not to come in this position.

Attempting to distract himself, he asked, "What is it you and your sisters are trying to accomplish today?"

"Only a dare." Her voice was a little high in pitch. Nervous, he'd guess. Or aroused by their position?

"A dare to do what?"

"Just something amongst us sisters." Her answer was cryptic. He was going to enjoy uncovering all his wife's secrets.

"You can't leave me in suspense. This is two days in a row that I've found you in a strangely compromising position. Not that I mind."

"I'm beginning to believe they want you to catch me doing what they deem improper activities for a lady of my standing."

"I would never have known what you were up to if I hadn't sought you out in your bedchamber this morning."

"What was it you wanted?"

Her fingers stretched out, and she stroked Odin's thick mane of hair. The horse tossed his head in appreciation of his wife's touch, and he walked with more spring in his step. What Richard would give to have his wife caressing him like that.

Whatever question she'd asked was forgotten. Her rear rubbed over his groin with their every bounce in the seat. He was sure the minx did it on purpose.

As fast as the thought came, his body responded to her teasing. There was no way to hide the fact that she aroused him, either. Not that he wanted to hide it. She'd definitely felt the thickened length of him at her backside where she sat atop his thighs. He moved his hand to grasp her hip, massaging her there, unable to help himself from touching her.

Her breath caught—his first hint that she was aware of his current state of mind. Then her body seemed to stiffen.

"Don't do that," he whispered into her ear, then flicked it with his tongue for good measure. She jumped in surprise at the motion. "Relax, sweet wife. I just want to give you a little pleasure."

Her gasp turned into a slight moan and her body seemed to liquefy and ease into his. Taking the reins in one hand, he trailed his hand around her middle and cupped her unbound breast. He thrust his pelvis into her backside a little firmer. Had she been wearing skirts, he would have been tempted to push them up, free his cock, and slide into her body right there in the saddle.

The river wasn't more than a hundred paces off. When they arrived would she turn all prim and proper again? Or could he take her on the ground?

Pulling the shirt from the band of her trousers, he slid his hand over the bare skin of her stomach and lower down the front to feel the moist thatch of curls. He could no more stop himself than he could temper his own lust. The evidence of her desire coated his fingers. She could not hide the fact that he'd excited her. He knew she was aroused, maybe not at the fever pitch he was riding, but enough that her own cream had readied her passage for the kind of stimulation he had in mind.

All the air seemed to rush from her lungs as he dipped his hands into the plump petals of her mound. Tightening his thighs around the horse, he brought Odin to a stop. Richard dropped the reins so he could wrap his other arm around Emma. He needed to touch her bare flesh. What was this need to always be touching her? He wished he could explain the compulsion.

Hand sliding under the shirt he'd untucked, he rubbed his palm over the soft skin of her belly, the underside of her breast, then squeezed the firm mound. He bit at her earlobe, sucking the fleshy end into his mouth as he massaged her breast, rubbing his fingers over the distended nipple every now and again.

"I want to take you right here, Emma. Want you riding my cockstand in the saddle."

His hand rotated faster over the engorged bud of her sex. Her fluids drenched his fingers. He wanted to lick the cream from them, then lower his mouth to that warm, sweet spot of her body and lap it up like a man who had long thirsted.

The cadence of her breathing was uneven. She was so close to finding release. He felt it in her increased lubricity, in the gentle rocking of her hips, and in the thrust of her pretty titty against his hand.

His thighs must have tightened further around the barrel of the horse, for Odin sidestepped, causing Emma to pull forward on the saddle with a startled cry—a sound torn between pleasure and surprise—and dislodged his hand.

Odin whinnied his disapproval at their movements, but carried them forward at a steady gait. Richard didn't want to stop. He couldn't. Since her shirt was already pulled from the trousers, he raised the material high on her back, leaned forward, and nibbled the length of her spine that he could reach with his mouth and tongue.

Her hand came around to pull the shirt back in place, then she sat right on his stiff cock and crossed her arms over her breasts.

"We can't do this here. Please, turn the horse around."

"Let me take you down to the river. We'll have privacy there."

She let out a ragged breath, stalling as though she wasn't sure how she wanted to answer him. "We should head back."

Had he really made no headway with her last night? Or even now? He was sure he had. He closed his eyes and gathered the tethered threads of his control. They could finish this tonight.

"As my lady wills it," he said through gritted teeth.

Richard led the horse back to the stables. His wife, cool as ever, tucked in her shirt when he handed her down to the ground and said not a word thereafter.

He didn't touch her again after his botched attempt. Not because he was sure she'd refuse him, but because he doubted he'd stop a second time. Not when it was clear she'd enjoyed the liberties he'd taken. Later. She would be his later. He only needed to bide his time till evening arrived.

"I wasn't sure you'd come," Dante said as the door shut behind Grace.

There was a shy tilt to her head. Her fingers fidgeted with the ribbon that cinched around her waist to keep the robe from revealing what she wore beneath.

He'd been thinking of her too often since he'd arrived here. Asbury might just kill him for taking advantage of his sister-in-law. But it had been too long since he'd had the company of a woman. Would have been better for him had he found the company of a willing woman at a local tavern because he was liable to show her a rougher side of a man's desires than she was used to, being that she was gently bred.

Problem was, he wanted Grace. She wasn't the kind of woman a man dallied with, either. He knew that. Knew that she was the marrying kind. Told himself he should avoid her for that reason. He needed to go home once the business was sold, find a nice Italian woman who was as lusty as him, and have a large brood of children to fill his home.

Still, he wanted Grace.

"I almost didn't come." Her voice was husky. Wanton. Just how he liked to hear it.

He stepped forward and took her hands in his so she'd not be able to fidget anymore. "I am glad you changed your mind." He massaged the tips of her fingers and then kissed them. "Put your hands on my shoulders."

She did. He reached down and pulled the pink satin

ribbon tied at her waist. Her robe slid open to reveal a lace negligee that was anything but lady-like. He groaned at what was revealed and slid his hand around her satin-covered waist to the small of her back so he could pull her closer. She rolled her shoulders till the robe slid from the high perch. It caught at her elbows since her hands were currently occupied kneading into his scalp and neck.

"I want your lips on me," she pleaded, a note of desperation tainting her voice. She was a wanton, simply put. There was nothing that could please him more. She'd make a perfect lusty wife.

What else was a man to do but act on instinct alone with a willing woman in his arms?

Leaning down, he caressed the seam of her mouth with his tongue. She opened almost immediately to his seeking touch. Their tongues tangled together, teeth nipped at lips, and groans filled with need replaced the silence in his room. He couldn't wait to get her hot body wrapped around his as he pumped into her. He'd wanted her the moment he'd seen the lush beauty rubbing at the back of her neck outside his assigned chamber. He'd wanted to take her up against the wall that very day.

The few pins that had held her dark hair back had long since tumbled to the floor. Satiny waves fell forward over her shoulder and ran near to the middle of her back. He broke away from the kiss. Watching her lust-hazed eyes and flushed cheeks, he stepped back and pulled his shirt over his head. She seemed frozen to the spot as she gazed upon him.

"Drop your robe."

It slid off her body with a soft swish. Lace lined the front of the peach-colored negligee; he could see her big breasts right through it, the berry-ripened nipples hard and ready for his mouth to suckle.

Tiny straps of satin wrapped around her shoulders to hold up the delicate material of her nightwear. He pushed them off each shoulder and reveled as the satiny material slipped down her body. He took his time not to tear it as he slid it over her breasts. It caught and pooled at her hips. Dante didn't care. He'd hike the flimsy material over her head after he had a taste of her.

Her breasts were firm, round, and even larger than he'd thought. Pressing both hands to them, he tested their weight, and brought his mouth down to one of the dark red nipples. He sucked it into his mouth deeply, then released it with a pop. He gave the other breast the same attention. She arched toward him in complete supplication.

He nodded in the direction of the bed. "Sit," he ordered.

She walked over, not bothering to cover her charms, and stood by his high bed. He made quick work of his trousers and stood for her inspection. Sucking in her bottom lip, she hummed her approval. He was not a small man in any sense of the word. By her expression alone, he knew she approved of what she saw.

As he approached, she put her delicate hands out to his chest and stopped him. "I have nothing to prevent a child. Will you be able to pull out?"

She visibly swallowed with the question. Was she embarrassed to ask such a thing? He was not the type of man to leave bastards from one end of the world to the other. Though any baby put in her womb would not be made a bastard, he decided. When he made up his mind, he made it up quickly.

"You are safe with me," he promised. Tonight he'd pull out. After tonight . . . he'd worry about that when they arrived there.

She gave a nod and sat on the edge of his bed. He

thought she'd lie back; instead she set her knees apart, planted her feet on the protruding platform of the bed, and pulled him into the vee of her body. "Then I shall trust you on your word. Now kiss me again and fill my body with that glorious instrument of pleasure."

No sense dallying at that point. Testing her with his fingers, he spread her sheath's wetness and then plunged himself into her more-than-splendid core.

Closing the door to her painting room, Emma leaned against the molding for a moment. Her breathing was rough, coming at an excited pitch. Should she greet her husband in her room as she normally did? She had this strange desire to meet him in his room or maybe even surprise him somewhere else in the house. How would she convince him to stay the whole evening with her?

Should she touch him as he touched her? Could she be so bold? Yes, she wanted to be and would be that daring.

What he'd done to her this afternoon had made her crave his touch for the remainder of the day. She'd been so close to peaking, to exploding under his determined touch. Then the horse had shifted under them, and she'd been embarrassed about what she'd done with her husband out in the open. Tonight, she vowed, would be different. There would be no holding back.

She rang for fresh water once in her chamber. It wouldn't do to greet her husband smelling of turpentine and oil paint.

Her maid was helping her tie the night rail at her back when her husband entered her bedchamber. She raised a brow at his discourteous entry. He was early. Did he miss her as she missed him?

"Leave us, Francine."

Emma didn't watch the maid leave. Her gaze was drawn to her husband's naked torso. She wanted to trace every line of muscle clearly defined there. He wore nothing more than his trousers, the bulge of his hardened member evident beneath. Had he remained in a state of need all afternoon just as she had? She looked him over leisurely, absorbing the wholly masculine sight he presented.

She wanted to touch him. To feel the bulge of his cock in her hands.

She focused on stilling her nervous, shaking hands. Swallowing hard, she took a step toward him. He wore a lopsided grin that said he knew what effect he had on her.

"Shall we stand here all night, sweetling?"

She snapped out of her daze and shook her head. "About this afternoon . . ." Darn it, she wasn't planning to bring that up.

"Yes, this afternoon was simply a taste for what will happen this evening." He walked toward her, pinched her chin between his finger and thumb. He raised one brow and asked, "Shall I do it again?"

Her breath caught. The stark determination to seduce her as he had earlier was clear in his coffee-colored eyes. It made her legs turn to jelly. She rested her hands upon his chest for balance, for her legs weren't going to hold her up much longer. He took that as an invitation to sweep her off her feet and carry her to the bed.

There were too many candles glowing tonight. Her room was blazing with light. For some reason, that made her more nervous for what she planned.

"The candles—"

"Stay lit. I will see every part of you tonight."

She swallowed any other words of objection and turned her head away as he removed his trousers. Clutching the soft quilt beneath her fists, she focused on his half grin and waited for him to join her on the bed.

She wanted this. More than anything she'd ever wanted before, she wanted to prove to this man she was a worthy partner in their marriage. Prove that she was worth keeping.

To her surprise, he didn't join her immediately. Instead he trailed one strong hand from her shin to her thigh, over her hip, and around her stomach, drawing little circles there, making the nerves confined to her jittery stomach bloom out to the rest of her limbs.

She felt slightly intoxicated by his touch: Her head set to spinning; her heart felt as though it would pound right out of her chest; and she was sure that a great deal of wetness slicked her thighs at the vee of her body. Good Lord, her husband was doing things to her body that she wasn't used to, drawing reactions from her that she didn't quite understand. He was distracting her from her purpose.

"Richard," she pleaded for no other reason than wanting him to lie next to her long enough for her to catch her breath. To gather back her senses that seemed to have fled.

"Shh, let me do this. I find I'm completely enthralled by your beauty."

She clamped her mouth shut. She needn't rush this. She had plenty of time to explore him.

The bed was set high off the floor so she had a clear view of his pectorals. She could see the wound at his side. It seemed mostly healed, a puckered red scar that sliced over his rib cage. It made him look dangerous.

Some naughty whisper in her mind dared her to reach out and touch the hair on his chest, to see what it would feel like under her fingertips. She watched his jaw tighten as her fingers brushed through the coarse hair. His eyes closed as she moved her hand higher to his neck, her fingers pressing into his strong muscles, feeling their resistance and the latent strength lurking beneath the surface.

She had the urge to kiss her husband. She loved it when he kissed her, but she wanted to initiate it this time. Unsure how it happened, nor inclined to question what put her body in motion, she found herself before him on her knees, her thumb pressing into the center of his bottom lip, pulling it down the slightest bit.

She leaned minutely forward, her thumb still between their lips when she pressed her mouth to his for the most fleeting kiss, like the flutter of a hummingbird's wings against a flower petal.

Richard pulled her arm down from between their bodies, leaving their lips with nothing between them. One of his arms wrapped around her lower back, the other pushing through her locks of hair and holding her head still as he looked into her eyes. The brown of his gaze seemed to flicker and sparkle in ecstasy.

"Is that what you desire? Just a kiss?"

His words snapped her out of her daze and she attempted to pull away from the embrace. He wouldn't let her go. In fact, his hold seemed tighter, almost unrelenting.

"I never said that was a bad thing, my darling wife."

His lips connected with hers again, only this time the union was less chaste than her approach had been. He pulled her upper lip first, then moved to pull her lower lip as his tongue swept out to stroke over the smarting his nips caused.

She moaned into his mouth and wound her arms around his shoulders to pull him closer. Close enough that her upper body pressed against his. Her breasts crushed between them. His hand dropped from where he had been kneading into her lower back, and both his hands came up to cup her face with a tenderness that made her want to swoon in pleasure.

She would fall apart if he left her again. She knew that with a clarity that drew tears to the surface of her eyes; thank goodness they did not fall.

Despite her desire to remain an independent woman, despite her desire to hide away in her painting tower without the need of another, she knew she was fooling herself. She would never be complete without this man at her side, always and forever.

Their tongues seemed to meld together as they tasted of each other. It felt natural to kiss her husband like this, with all the pent-up desires she'd harbored for him over the years. Every feeling, every emotion seemed to pour out of her as she warred with his lips and tongue. He was not unaffected by their kiss; he groaned for every one of her mewls, his pelvis rotated forward in a rhythm all its own. The jut of his manhood on her stomach didn't so much frighten her as rouse her curiosity.

She pulled away long enough to say, "I ache so badly for you, Richard."

"I ache too, darling," he whispered over her lips.

His hands fell away from her face to gather the material of her night rail in his hands. He held it at her hips and stalled. "Lie back on the bed."

She complied and didn't have to question his intentions once he knelt on the bed between her open thighs. His manhood stood straight out from his groin and curved thickly toward his navel, the slit at the tip moist with fluid. Good Lord, he was a well-endowed man.

She must have made some sound of distress, because he was cooing sweet platitudes about how much he wanted and needed her. He pushed her thighs farther apart and pressed the head of his instrument inside, groaning so deeply in his chest it almost sounded like a growl of frustration.

His arms strained on either side of her. The cords of muscle flexing and moving awed her as he held himself still as a leopard waiting for its chance to strike. Raising her hands to his face, she beckoned his mouth closer so she could kiss him again. She liked kissing her husband. A great deal.

As his lips connected with hers, his manhood thrust fully forward inside her body. She released his mouth long enough to let out a surprised groan, and arched the upper half of her body off the bed and closer to his warmth. His lips found her neck.

He wasn't as gentle this time with his kisses. He bit at her, trailing his teeth and tongue over her life vein, then higher to her earlobe. Nibbling on the end wasn't the last of his exploration; he stuck his tongue right in her ear and licked around the shell before moving back down her neck. Goodness gracious, she loved the feeling it evoked. The shivery, tickling delight it created.

Pressing her hands into his back, careful to avoid his side where his half-healed wound was, she kneaded into his flesh, massaging the length in slow, teasing touches. His skin was smooth and firm. Hot to the touch.

Pulling out, he pressed his lips against her breasts. Licking and nipping at them in turn. Then over her ribs, the soft curve of her stomach. His teeth were sharp at her hip. Where was her resolve to touch him tonight? To inflame his desires as much as he did hers?

Rolling to his side, he rose up on one elbow and looked down at her, that mischievous grin of his sparkling in his eyes. One of his hands grasped her core with determined fingers. The other pushed out her legs, exposing everything to his gaze.

She failed to breathe as he looked her over in blatant approval.

Fingers rotating around her sheath, slicking her mound, he pressed inward in the same thrusting pattern his penis made. His thumb flicked over the little bud at the apex of her womanhood. It offered up the most exhilarating pleasure she'd ever felt in her life. She was still sensitive from their foray this afternoon. Needy. The sensations were inexplicable. Words failed her.

"Kiss me," he demanded in a gruff voice.

With his imploring tone, she forgot to be embarrassed by what he was doing to her body and turned her face to his. This kiss was sweeter, softer, and so much slower than the others they'd shared, but just as carnally explicit in implication. His tongue dipped into her when his finger thrust up inside her sheath. When his finger circled the entrance of her cunny, his tongue traced the seam of her lips. Her whole body took on a faint buzz from his ministrations. From his every touch.

The firm demand of his hard member pushed into her thigh. She thought he'd stop the sweet sensations he was playing out on her body and fill her again, but he didn't. He seemed quite content to carry on with his hand pressing and circling her bud.

She'd never felt a pleasure more beautiful. So perfect it nearly brought tears to her eyes. Her pelvis pushed up against his hand, rotating of its own accord, desperate to feel these sensations to the fullest. To finally find release under his titillating touch.

It was like rolling down the hill earlier today with her sisters. Her insides were all scrambled and excited. Her body felt as though it would never touch the ground. Her whole being felt suspended in the midst of nothingness and then she was crashing into a throbbing, mind-numbing release that seemed to split her body apart like a firecracker going off. All the sparks exploding surreally around her, all her nerve endings feeling as though they couldn't be expounded upon any further.

She bit into Richard's lower lip, her voice mute though she felt like she was screaming. Her heart stopped for the merest second before the full force of its pounding rang deafeningly in her ears.

Her whole body throbbed from the inside out, centering where her husband had massaged her bud, where it felt like that part of her body had a heartbeat of its own.

Her breath was coming so fast, her mouth so dry, she couldn't find any words, any sound to utter.

"Now, that is the kind of reaction I like," Richard said, with a smugness so common to his character. Then he positioned himself above her. "Wrap your legs around my hips," he demanded in a guttural tone.

So taxed of energy, she could do only partially as he asked, tightening her thighs around his hips. His weight came down on her then, one hand grasping her bare buttocks and squeezing as he pushed into her body with more vigor than he'd ever displayed before.

He was hammering into her so hard and fast they inched up the bed with each hard slam. She wasn't sure if the sounds she made came from the enjoyment of the act, or because he forced the breath out of her lungs with each upward plunge into her body. Her fingers flexed into the flesh of his back, molding the sinew beneath her hands.

Hands now clasping her hips, he held himself inert above her, breathing hard, his forehead sweaty as it pressed to hers.

"I could fuck you nonstop for a whole day," he groaned.

His movements took on a new measure of speed, as

though he wanted to push farther up inside her than possible. He swore a much cruder word than she'd ever heard him utter before as he worked himself inside her. Her pelvis thrust up to meet each of his shoves. Her hands couldn't hold on tight enough to his sweat-slickened skin. She'd never get enough of her husband. Never get enough of this feeling of breathlessness that he made her yearn for more of.

Then she felt his seed spilling into her with each subsequent plunge of his manhood. It seemed to go on infinitely, long enough that she felt a rush of fluid seep from her core and slide between the cheeks of her buttocks.

When he stopped spurting inside her, he fell atop her, his body clammy with sweat under her exploring fingers. She hoped her touch felt soothing, relaxing. He seemed replete enough as it was, but she'd not be able to spend too much time under his heavy weight. His member slid from her core and he rolled over to lie beside her.

To her everlasting surprise, he didn't leave. He pushed her to her side, and pulled her close to his chest, arm wrapped around her middle, finger flicking and rolling at her nipple as their breaths evened out.

Would he stay the night? Indulge in her once again as she wanted to indulge in him?

# Chapter 14

*In my heart, I know there is no hope of your return. Why can't I move on? Forget?*

After receiving the letter from Waverly, she hadn't expected him to call on her at home. Her maid had knocked on her door just past breakfast. Emma had rushed down to the parlor in fear of Richard finding another man calling on her. She couldn't deal with another barrage of accusations. Her relationship with her husband was growing. She'd not chance ruining that.

Waverly relaxed in a chair, ankle crossed over his knee as if he had every right to make himself feel at home in her house. He did not stand on her entrance. Which was well enough; she didn't want to pay him any polite kindnesses, either.

His clothes were rumpled, as though he'd slept in them. His shirtsleeves were rolled up, waistcoat wrinkled and improperly buttoned, his hair unwashed and greasy. Stubble lined his angular jaw . . . Was the man fraying around the edges? Or was this just overindulgence from the night before?

She cleared her throat. "I made it clear you weren't

invited here. I'd rather not make a scene by having the servants physically remove you."

"Touché, darling." He swirled a glass of amber liquid. "Touché."

Obviously, he also thought he could help himself to the decanter. She changed her mind about her husband finding her in the company of another man; she wished Richard would walk in. But then, Richard still didn't know anything about her paintings. And of course, she couldn't trust that Waverly wouldn't state his reason for being here.

Hands clasped tightly in front of her, she gave him a stern glare. "What do you want, Waverly?"

"To chat." Stupid man that he was, he shot her his snake smile. He was goading her, pricking at her ire intentionally. She'd not give in to his cruelties so easily this time.

"I find that hard to believe. You've set out to blackmail me. Not something a *friend* would do."

"Ah, but you've assured me we are no longer friends." He drank the rest of the liquor in his glass and set it on the floor since there wasn't a table nearby. "Perhaps you'd like to come and sit on my knee." He patted his hand to the place he wanted her to sit. "We could play it very differently that way."

The blackguard! She would not show her discomfort at this whole situation.

"Why are you doing this? We were friends."

"We were never friends, love. You were a means to an end. I've just needed to move things along a little faster after an unexpected turn in events."

What was he talking about?

Waverly stood from the chair and prowled closer to her, eyeing her as though she were potential prey. She held her ground and tilted her chin up to meet his gaze defiantly.

"Never understood your devotion to your marriage. Had you fallen for my charm early on, we'd never have come to this pass in our relationship. Things would be entirely different."

"I do not understand what you mean." Emma crossed her arms in annoyance. "How did you obtain the painting?"

He laughed. A horrid, awful crowing sound. "Would you believe I received a letter from Vane yesterday evening? Blighter thought to purchase a painting that he heard was in my safekeeping."

His fingers reached out and caressed the length of her arm. She could not hold back the shiver of revulsion that ran the length of her body from his touch. "Tell me, sweet, sweet Emma, was that painting for your lover? Did you paint it for Vane?"

She didn't flinch at the accusation. Most would think precisely that.

Waverly didn't deserve the truth: She'd painted it for herself.

That painting had been done at a transition in her life. A time when she realized she was no longer a girl but a grown woman. A woman with her own desires, her own needs to accomplish something for herself. The painting had been a bitter reminder of what she was missing in life. With its creation came the consciousness that she was like the trapped creatures she painted—that society only saw a shell of who she was, not the real woman beneath the polite facade of a countess.

How dare Waverly take that away from her! How dare he!

"What is it you wish to accomplish by revealing that

painting to the world?" She dared to take a step closer. She would not be cowed by him. "Ruin me if you will. I care not what society thinks. You are wasting your time trying to expose me as the artist."

"I could not care less what society thinks of you, dear."

His hands grasped onto her arms, the force bruising. Trying to dislodge his hold, she was yanked against his lanky frame. She turned her face away so he couldn't force a kiss on her. Never again would she give him that opportunity.

"You think mighty highly of yourself. You've always put yourself on a pedestal. The ice-cold, untouchable Countess of Asbury." He shook her when she refused to look at him. "I know your secrets. Secrets I'm sure you want hidden. Otherwise, everyone would know about your little pastime, wouldn't they? I guarantee your husband hasn't a clue what you do in your spare time."

The mention of her husband had uneasiness creeping into her mind. What did her husband have to do with Waverly? Emma wanted to ask Waverly, but didn't dare—he'd only tell her lies. She pinched her lips together and held herself rigid in his grasp.

The stubble on his face scratched her cheek and neck. He licked the length of her neck. She jerked her head farther away from him, a sound of distress passing her lips. His hold on her arms only tightened. The last time she pushed him away he'd become more aggressive. Unpredictable. She would not allow that to happen again.

"I don't care if you expose me," she hissed.

That was a complete lie. But what else was she supposed to say when he threatened her? She had to believe that Vane would retrieve the painting by any means necessary. Waverly would be out of her life once and for all.

"If you don't release me and leave, Waverly, I *will* call the servants and have you removed."

He chuckled against her throat, the sound low and intimidating. He jerked the sleeves of her gown down, tearing the material and exposing her from her shoulders to the top swell of her breasts. "And what if they should find you in a compromising position?"

The way he held onto the torn material left her immobile. She could not pull from his hold. Could not raise her hands to push him away. She had underestimated this man's daring. This man's lack of restraint once his rage hit its peak.

"I don't care." She spat the words in his face, finally daring to meet his eyes. It was a mistake. She'd known it would be. But she was running out of options to stop Waverly from doing something horrible.

His hands grasped the edge of her gown at the sides of her breasts and made to tear it right off her body. She squeezed her arms tight. Not allowing the material to budge.

"It's to be like that, is it?" Waverly said.

She just needed an unguarded moment to make her escape. She daren't call the servants. It was too late for that option.

"Let. Me. Go!" she whispered.

Waverly laughed, cruelly.

Emma was yanked back—away from Waverly—so fast she lost her footing and fell onto her rear. All the air rushed from her lungs with the impact to the floor. When next she looked up, Waverly was sprawled on his back, holding his bloody face and laughing maniacally.

She gathered up the material at the front of her ruined dress and looked at the man who stood beside her.

Her husband. Tears leaked down the side of her face. Silent tears because there were no hysterics, no sobbing. She couldn't bring herself to speak. To apologize. Beyond Richard, she saw Mr. Lioni. Grace tripped into the room behind him.

The sight did not help quell her tears. They flowed more freely. More abundantly.

Consternation lined her husband's expression. Mr. Lioni was tense. His actions defensive. Waverly pushed up onto his feet. Swaying where he stood. His right cheek was split open where her husband had hit him. Blood ran down the side of his face, splattered across the white collar of his shirt.

"Why, hallo, Grace." Waverly snickered. "Come to renew our *friendship,* too?"

Mr. Lioni stepped in front of Grace, his fists clenched at his sides, his stance strong and menacing. Even the muscles seemed to strain in his neck as he visibly tightened his jaw and clenched his mouth shut, his lips a tight, thin line radiating anger.

Richard shook with rage. To think what could have happened had he arrived a few minutes later. Had he not heard the commotion . . .

His fists tightened at his sides. He was ready to strike down Waverly again if need be. How dare that man accost his wife!

Emma was visibly distraught, her color almost waxen and her hands shaking where she clutched the torn material of her gown.

Grace came to his wife's side, wrapped her arm around Emma's shoulders, and helped her stand. He should be the one looking after his wife. But he couldn't. Not with Waverly in his home. The man needed lessons in how to treat a woman.

His eyes met his wife's. He'd talk with her later. Find out how she knew Waverly and find out why Waverly had been pawing at her. The man looked ready to rape her. Had been about to, had he not . . .

He was going to kill Waverly.

When the women exited the room, Richard breathed a sigh of relief. Waverly wasn't a steady man. This was a fact he'd known for many years. A long bout with opium smoking had ruined Waverly's mind, and filled it with paranoia and madness.

"Why are you here, Waverly?"

Waverly sneered. "Unfinished business with that pretty wife of yours."

Richard took a menacing step forward. He'd beat the man into the ground for such slander. His wife had no business with Waverly. End of story.

"My wife is no longer here. As I see it, you now have unfinished business with me."

Waverly eyed Richard's midsection, approximately where the knife had bitten into his side. The glance told Richard one thing: There was no question as to who had arranged the love slice that had nearly taken Richard's life.

Waverly was the mesmerized asp waiting for the shift in music to come out of his trance. Waiting for the moment to strike down anyone unlucky enough to get in his way. That had been a good quality in the man years ago when they'd initially taken up trade in a cutthroat business. One never knew what side of the knife you'd get with Waverly.

"Do stop posturing, Asbury. You've stolen the business out from under me. You had no right." His mad gaze turned to Dante, his eye twitching on the side of his face that was swelling up. Waverly stood on unsteady feet. "I want our old empire back."

"You signed the papers releasing your rights in trust for fair value," Richard pointed out.

"You caught me unaware. You knew damn well what you were doing to me."

Yes, he'd known what he'd done to Waverly. He had no regrets. Especially since it seemed his old friend had tried to have him killed and then tried to hurt his wife.

"What were you doing here with my wife?"

Waverly rubbed at his temple and shook his head like a dog come in from the rain. "Headaches come and go these days. Strange thing. What was I thinking, now? Hmm . . ." As though he had flipped some mental switch in his mind, he turned into a different man. His eyes appeared foggy, all lucidity gone.

"Your pretty wife. She owes me something. Mayhap you should ask her what she's been up to while you've been away." Waverly chuckled, obviously thinking himself clever. "She's a most interesting woman. More interesting than the plump one."

Dante took a step forward. His lips were tight, nostrils flared; the throbbing vein in his temple indicated he was liable to strangle Waverly at any moment. Richard shook his head and intervened. "Whether he deserves it or not, you cannot kill a lord of the realm, no matter your social standing in Italy." He cared not that Waverly heard the threat. It took a lot of control not to lash out at the man himself.

"You"—Dante pointed at Waverly—"I let live because I remember a time when your mind was intact."

"This is the last time I'll ask, Waverly. Clearly state your business with my wife." Richard's patience was growing thin.

"You know, I previously set my eyes on the dark-haired one. She's a widow. Fair game, don't you think?" Did Waverly babble as a way to avoid answering the question? "But your wife, on the other hand . . . she's a pretty piece. Full of passion, if you catch my drift."

"Stick to your own wastrel, half-drunkard kind," Dante growled.

"Feeling a bit defensive, aren't you, Dante? Have you a vested interest where the dark beauty is concerned? Or have you had a taste of Richard's wife, too?"

It took everything in Richard's willpower not to pummel the man. He had no idea why he held back. Waverly had it coming to him.

Dante cracked his knuckles. "I'm happy to show you the error of your thoughts."

"We're done, Waverly. We might have spent our formative years together as the best of chaps, but those days died the day you stopped bothering to pick yourself up and out of the harlot-filled opium dens you made a home of. Do you even realize you'll never be quite sane again?"

Waverly clucked his tongue and shook his head as though he were about to scold a child. "Don't sound so glum, Richard. I'm quite content with how things turned out. I'm of sounder mind than you're willing to give me credit for."

They could go back and forth with this banter all day.

"You'll have your funds from the sale. Piss them down the gutter if you so wish it."

"I don't care about the funds. The two of you have pulled the rug out from beneath my feet. I was more than willing to continue on as we were. We owned that part of the world."

"You are too busy living in an opium haze to see the new dangers we were facing. Unlike you, we have a care for our futures. Feel free to watch yours roll farther down into murk. Your life has long been worthless."

Dante uncrossed his arms and looked down his great Roman nose at Waverly, as though the man were no more than a pestilent insect.

A shame they couldn't squash the irritation as easily as squishing a bug.

"We're done," Richard announced.

"Trying to scare me off, are you?" Waverly wobbled where he stood, his hands visibly shaking. Waverly waved them away when they stepped forward to grab him should he fall over. "Bugger off. Happens from time to time. I don't need no one's help. Especially from you two. We were all friends. Now you've gone and ruined everything."

"You ruined it yourself." Dante grabbed the other man's arm and manhandled him to the double doors.

Once in the hall, Richard beckoned over the butler. "Tell the stable hand to have the horses harnessed and the carriage ready to go in ten minutes."

"It'll get done in less time than that, my lord." The man plodded quickly off. He must have sensed the unease congesting the air with their unwelcome visitor.

"You think you're sending me off packing." Waverly tittered. "Not so easy, never so easy."

"I've known you for eight years. Six of those years you've been a useless appendage to our company and our reputation. I've no compunction in shooting you square between the eyes, you damn blackguard," Dante said matter-of-factly.

"Spoken like a true gypsy heathen, you great brown bastard."

Dante was on Waverly before Richard could react. The bigger man's hands wrapped about Waverly's neck, strangling the breath out of the lesser man. The sick man's only reaction was to choke out more laughter, as though this were a great lot of fun.

"Let off, Dante." Richard made no move to intervene. "He's not worth the hassle he'll cause in the end."

"I'm more blue-blooded than this shitpot," Dante spat.

"Now is not the time to prove that fact." Richard watched as Dante's white-knuckled grip slackened from his assailant's neck. Waverly did not cease that maniacal laughter. The man truly was on edge, or over it as it were.

"See, you won't kill me." Waverly straightened his waistcoat, even though it couldn't be made to look better. "Haven't got it in you."

"Shut that prattle-brained mouth of yours before I do what he can't," Richard shot back.

"Just like old times, I say. Never could agree on much 'cept wenching and turning a profit."

"You lost the ability to turn a ha'penny into quid when you ceased to pull yourself out of the gutter," Richard said.

"Always so prickly—" Waverly didn't have a chance to finish his sentence. Richard had had enough. He brought his fist down on the other man's temple. The momentum of the punch aided by Richard's fury had Waverly slumping to the floor like a pile of dirty rags.

"That was for my wife, you prick."

Dante said not a word as he hoisted Waverly up and over his shoulder.

"What do you want to do with him?" Dante wasn't the slightest bit disturbed that Richard had knocked Waverly unconscious to get his mouth to stop running off.

"Put him in the carriage. We'll send him to his estate." Why he showed any restraint in dealing with Waverly was a mystery. "We've washed our hands of him."

"Will the sisters be better off in London?" Dante asked suddenly.

"We might want to send Abby and Grace somewhere else."

Richard watched Dante's reaction closely. Whatever it was the man felt for the middle sister, he kept it under wraps because there was no betraying expression when he suggested removing the women to a different location. Waverly was now a threat. The women would be safer elsewhere.

Or maybe not, in light of this afternoon's events.

"They should stay together," Dante finally said.

Richard nodded. "London it is."

"We can leave in a few days, then. Send letters ahead to arrange extra men for the town house."

Dante meant to hire mercenaries. People who would strike down an assailant or enemy first, think about the consequences later. A safe move for the women. Probably for him and Dante, as well.

The carriage rolled to a stop in front of the manor. Dante climbed the carriage steps and flopped Waverly down on the leather seats. Richard sent two of his more burly servants to help clear out the trash when they arrived at Waverly's estate.

# Chapter 15

*I've been longer without you than with you. There never was going to be more than this, was there?*

There she was, sitting pretty in the parlor. Alone. Richard watched his wife from the open door, not quite ready to interrupt her solitude. She'd changed from the tattered pink dress to a soft buttercream yellow. Her hair was half up, half down.

What did it say about him that he enjoyed watching her when she was unaware? She fidgeted with her hair, plucked at the bows on the sleeves of her dress. She reached forward and centered the tea tray on the table for the third time. Endearing traits if one were inclined to romanticism. He shook his head. He was not the romantic type.

His wife was never supposed to mean anything to him. He wasn't supposed to want anything other than her pregnant and unable to petition for a divorce. When had that goal changed? Hell, he didn't know what his purpose in this marriage was anymore.

What was he going to say to her? How should he broach the subject of what had happened? There was no way that Waverly had ever been a lover of hers. It wasn't possible. No, she'd never shared herself with Waverly. She'd refused the other man and it had been then that Waverly had turned on her.

He straightened his cuffs, pulled down his vest, and stepped into the room.

On hearing his entry, she stood. "I had Brown send up some treats and tea." She paused. "How long have you been standing there?"

"Not long."

He sat on the sofa next to her. She took that as a cue to pour the tea. She handed him a dainty, vine-painted teacup on a matching saucer, which he promptly set in front of him on the oak table. He didn't want tea. His wife loaded a dish full of sandwiches, a few sweetmeats, and passed it to him. She remained quiet as she served him. She didn't meet his gaze, just kept her hands busy. Her mind focused on the task at hand.

He needed to assure her that he wouldn't let that snake, Waverly, within ten feet of her. Maybe that would settle her nerves? Make her more at ease.

"What did you do with Waverly?" Her voice was cool, but he heard the tempered anger edging it. He could hardly blame her. Better for her to be angry than distraught, he supposed.

"Sent him home." She didn't actually care, did she? He snapped his mouth shut before he could make a caustic remark. He was edgy this afternoon. He had no right to bark at his wife.

Her chin rose up defiantly as though she was waiting for a scolding from him. That was not something he would do. Waverly's actions hadn't been her fault.

Chewing the cucumber sandwich, he thought carefully on his words. Emma picked at the edge of one of her sandwiches, uninterested. He looked at the mantel clock and checked the hour. He faced his wife again. Words escaped him.

Setting his dish of sandwiches next to his untouched tea, he stood and walked over to the window and looked down to the maze of flowers that filled the grounds. Grace was pruning the rosebushes. Yanking out long stems. Anger radiated off her.

He adjusted his necktie and found the courage to ask, "What is Waverly to you, Emma? Do you realize what he would have done?"

"He was overwrought. I would have eventually calmed him."

Was she so naïve to think that? He smacked his hand against the frame around the window. There was no question in Richard's mind that Waverly would have raped her. He wanted to shake some sense into her.

"Don't fool yourself in that matter, Emma."

The chink of her teacup on the saucer made the room feel deathly silent and uncomfortable. "What is your association to Waverly? He never mentioned knowing you."

"He was once a business partner."

"Business partner?"

Did he imagine it, or did *business partner* roll over his wife's tongue as though the words tasted sour? He tried for patience, went so far as to close his eyes, stretch his neck, and crack his knuckles before facing his wife.

"Yes, a business partner. Do you want to know what type of man Waverly really is?"

No response.

"Or what I've done with my life since we married?"

Still no response.

"It's not a discussion fit for delicate ears, so perhaps not."

She stood from the settee. Her chest puffed out like a swan angered by his mere presence, and likely to nip at him if he didn't calm her ruffled feathers quickly.

"I'm not some flower that will wilt at the first hint of rain."

"No. You appear to be stronger than that. Why is it that you ask after Waverly as if he were a longtime friend? As if he didn't attempt to rape you."

"I didn't know how to handle him! I wasn't expecting him to be so forceful," she shouted, then promptly clapped her hand over her mouth.

At least she was showing some sort of emotion over the whole ordeal. He didn't like her holding everything in. If she was angry, she should shout at him. If she was upset, she should cry. Whatever it was she felt, she should express it.

She flopped back down on the sofa, the fight suddenly gone from her. "Are you really going to tell me what you've done for the past ten years? Where you've been?"

"No grand, noble adventure, I assure you. No, much worse, I'm afraid."

"Your profession doesn't bother me, Richard. I don't care what's bandied about with you dirtying your hands in trade. Had you been around at any point in our marriage, you would know that I take little stock in what people disapprove of."

He stepped away from the window and loosened the buttons on his vest. He hated the fripperies men had to wear to fit into London society. "People like Waverly on the whole are worse than me, but you can judge me for yourself. Regardless, Waverly is not the kind of person you want for a friend. He can't be trusted."

She said nothing in reply, didn't even nod in agreement. Though her eyes were wide, probably in wonderment at what he could possibly impart. If only she could understand what he'd done, really understand the depravity he'd sunk to in the name of profit.

"I'm a scoundrel of the worst sort," he said. "My investments and my business in the opium empire have always been about exploiting weaknesses in human nature. Waverly and I set out to make a fortune off the backs of others. It was at the cost of others' lives that we achieved that goal. We took advantage of those who couldn't say no to an addiction that slowly destroyed their lives."

Richard loosened his necktie and placed it on the side table. Divesting himself of the fripperies he'd always despised. He wasn't really a gentleman, was he? Would a gentleman commit the crimes against humanity that he had committed?

"We were destroyers of men, women, and even children. I consciously knew that our actions weren't morally just. I think Waverly knew that on some level. There is but one difference between Waverly and me."

He stalled, closed his eyes, and took a deep breath.

"Waverly became reliant on the drug that we were selling. I watched him closely. Day after day his sane mind dissipated into madness. Maybe that makes me a stronger man for not succumbing to the vice we traded in. I don't really know." He sat heavily on the sofa. The opposite end of her in case she was disgusted by him. "The only thing I know with any certainty is that there is no turning back for Waverly. He'll never be well. Might put on a good show, but he's not safe."

For so many years, he'd been foolish to believe the world was at his fingertips. It never had been. Try for godliness and the devil was waiting around the corner to smite you down. He shook his head. He felt the vein at his temple throbbing in unison with his heartbeat, and massaged at his head. What would she think of him now?

After today's episode with Waverly, she must understand that the man was dangerous. To be avoided at all costs. He had to trust that she would do the right thing in this.

When she didn't leave him there to stew in his own pity, Richard held his hand out to her. "Come here, Emma."

He needed to be sensitive to her needs right now. She'd faced the devil that was Waverly and had barely escaped. She needed comfort. An assurance that Waverly would not get another chance to hurt her.

She looked at his proffered hand. The hesitation was evident in the way she curled her fingers around her locket and the way she fisted her other hand in her lap. He watched half stunned, half thankful when she slid closer to him on the daisy-patterned sofa. She set about smoothing out her skirts. It was the first time he realized that the action was a nervous habit of hers. It calmed him to understand such a small thing.

He was doomed to want more from his lady wife. Doomed to be there at her beck and call. Because, for the life of him, he doubted he could walk away from her now. All because she hadn't left at his admission. Yes, she'd stayed when he'd told her how horrible a man he really was. Had been. No more, though.

"I've known Waverly for a year. I did count him among my friends." She met his gaze, her eyes sad.

It was good to hear the truth coming from her. Made him feel worthy of her, somehow.

"Promise me you'll avoid the man. His mind isn't right."

*That bloody bastard,* Richard thought. He knew what the man was up to, why he had courted Emma in this dangerous game. All the puzzle pieces were starting to click together at an alarming rate. It was obvious that Waverly wanted the business back. Wanted his old life back, a life that could never bring peace of mind but only more misery. Seemed Waverly's morals in harming innocent bystanders hadn't changed one whit.

"He was always so cordial, so kind. It's hard to believe what he did today."

It wasn't a hard truth for Richard to swallow. Emma, in Waverly's mind, was a pawn to be tossed aside once an opportunity presented itself to further his goals. Richard would take special care to guard his wife. She'd not be used for that madman's nefarious plans to stop the sale of the business.

"He wears the helmet of a chivalrous knight well. It would do you and your sisters good to remember that he is the proverbial wolf in sheep's wool. Despite the armor he wears for polite society, he eventually lashes out. I don't want it to be at you three."

"None of us plans to speak to him again," Emma assured him as she plucked at a loose stitch on her belled sleeve.

He placed his hand over hers to stop her fidgeting. "I tried to help him before he left the business. It ate at me to watch a good man squander a perfectly good life."

Emma shook her head and traced the lines of his fingers since his hand was in her lap. "Waverly is a grown man, Richard. I know better than anyone that it's impossible to sway a determined man from his chosen path."

Richard leaned forward, elbows on knees, placing his head in his hands. It always came back to him leaving her. He doubted it was her intention to remind him of that major transgression in their marriage, but it would always be there, wedged as a bitter reminder that he had valued another kind of life more. One that hadn't included a wife.

Instead of dwelling on what could not be changed between them, he continued, "Waverly was a good man, but that was a long time ago. I always felt as though I should have done something more." Yet Waverly hadn't been a man bent on self-destruction until the unexpected death of the woman he'd been courting.

"In suggesting such, you assume all men are created equal." His wife was the welcome voice of reason. "We all have our faults, Richard. It's a part of human nature. Perhaps those faults are more prevalent in some. It is my opinion that Waverly could no more conquer his vice than a drunk could mend his ways by entering a tavern when he's sworn off spirits."

"I don't doubt your words."

He sighed and leaned back against the sofa, a pillow tucked behind his back. He did not want to sit here and think of all he'd done wrong in his life. He hadn't come in here to do that. He should be focused on his wife.

Turning to look at Emma, he asked, "Are you really as calm inside as you seem on the outside? Waverly hasn't caused any lasting damage, has he?"

She stopped fidgeting with the ribbon on her sleeve and looked him in the eye. No subterfuge, no lie evident. "I'm stronger than I appear."

Was she really? Had his abandonment made her stronger, or did she hide herself from the world behind an impenetrable shell so those around her never saw her pain? What a conundrum she was. An enigma he was determined to figure out.

"We leave for London in a few days, Emma. You, your sisters, me, and Dante."

"Why?" Her brows were drawn tight.

"I don't trust Waverly. I don't trust him not to come back and try something more damaging next time."

"You really think he'll come back?"

"I know he will."

Richard took a deep breath. What a thorn Waverly had become. Didn't matter. They'd have guards stationed at the house once they arrived in Town; letters had already been sent ahead to hire the necessary hands. His wife would never be accosted in that manner again.

She didn't disagree with him. Didn't tell him no. He was happy for that. Happy that she trusted him in this matter.

"Come closer, Emma."

Did she sense the shift in his mood? That the self-pity was gone from him? Without argument, she took his hand and scooted close enough that their thighs pressed together, even through the swaths of silk she wore. When she didn't pull her hand away, he threaded his fingers through hers.

He stared at their joined hands, marveling at the contrast of her softness with his roughness. Her paleness to his sun-darkened skin. Her fingers were thin, delicate, and unadorned. He should remedy that. A small token for their newfound arrangement. For his newfound adoration of her.

Trailing his hand over the row of tiny, round pearls lined up her spine, he found it hard to resist the lure they represented. He wanted to push the buttons loose of the ribbon-edged hoops. He trailed his knuckle over them again.

Her hand squeezed his tightly in return. Did she feel sorry for him? Pity his sullen mood? He didn't care. He just wanted her. Needed her, in fact.

"Tell me to stop."

Instead of responding, Emma released her grip on his hand and turned her back so he could release the buttons. Not one to waste an opportunity freely given, he slid the buttons free and pushed the lightweight material from her shoulders.

He plucked at the crisscrossed lacing at her back as though it were a stringed instrument. "I've locked the door." Did she understand what he implied? What he wanted of her? He was a selfish bastard to demand anything of her right now.

She nodded in understanding as she pulled off the shirt he'd unbuttoned. The white chemise dipped low in the back and front with a frilled-scallop design. He pressed his lips to the exposed part of her shoulder. He saw that her hands were wrapped about the locket dangling from her throat, just beneath her breasts.

More than anything, he wanted her to feel comfortable in his presence. He knew that she was anything but that right now. He didn't want her fluttering out of the room like a canary escaping the claws of a cat.

"Sentimental value to that locket?" He asked because this wasn't the first time he'd seen her wear it. Because he wanted to know what his wife held so near to her heart.

"Portraits of my sisters."

He grinned. He should have guessed. The three of them seemed very close.

Her chemise was tucked neatly beneath her off-white corset; the edge of the busk was lined with a soft pink French lace.

He had her profile. The fan of her lashes lay against her cheek; her teeth were visible where she bit at her lower lip.

Setting his hands on her hips, he asked, "Do you mind me touching you?"

Lids fluttering open, her head turned and her dark green eyes stared down at him in half question, half arousal. She released the locket she grasped and whispered, "No."

With his forehead pressed to her shoulder he took a deep breath, filling his lungs with the gentle lavender scent of her underclothes. He didn't want her to reject his advances, and that forced him to remain calm, to try to fight the blood rampaging through his body and rushing straight to his groin.

"You make me want you so fiercely, Emma. I'm liable to frighten you away before I can do any of the things I want."

She reached around and placed her palm to his cheek. "I haven't asked you to stop."

"God, Emma. Had I known this attraction existed between us . . ." He couldn't tell her that he doubted he would have stayed away. He wasn't ready to tell her that. Wasn't quite ready to admit that to himself yet.

He patted his lap in invitation. Not that he expected her to come so easily. "Come, darling. Have a seat on my knee so I can at least see you."

She stood and turned so she could sit as he requested. Her nose wrinkled up and a furrow creased her brows. He raised her chin with his hand and took in her confused expression.

"Waverly suggested I sit on his lap. I much prefer that suggestion coming from you."

"I'm sorry. I didn't know." He brushed a curl that had fallen forward from the corner of her eye. "What would you do if I kissed you?"

An innocent, hypothetical question he had no intention of waiting for because his mouth met hers in a gentle pecking of lips. She didn't push away or ask him to stop.

"I like that," she said, her voice hoarse. He liked that he was the cause of her breathlessness.

"I can't help myself. You're so soft. I want to touch you everywhere."

He covered her breast with one hand, stroking the nipple back and forth until it pebbled beneath the chemise above the lace-frilled edge of the corset.

She stilled his hand with her own. God, he wanted to lift that breast free of the corset and suck the hardened tip into his mouth. Instead, he pulled the next closest thing with his teeth—her earlobe—flicking over it with his tongue.

"I want to do very wicked things to you, Emma."

"I want you to do very wicked things to me."

He released her ear and looked at her. She blushed a pretty shade of pink; the color spread over her chest, up her neck, and even turned the shells of her ears crimson.

Running his thumb over her cheek, he ran the back of his hand down her neck and caressed her bosom where it was pushed up.

"I'd like to thoroughly scandalize you."

"Your intention is to make me blush, isn't it?"

"Sometimes. You blush prettily. For instance"—he took the pearled tip of her breast between his middle and index fingers and gently rolled it—"when I do this, your ears turn pink."

"How else should I react?"

"Exactly as you're doing. All blushing and beautiful. But I don't think you're willing to explore this any further, are you?"

She stalled before answering. "This evening would be better suited for this."

"Just the answer I wanted to hear."

"I should find my sisters. They might wonder where

I've disappeared to. Grace was worried to leave me alone."

"I'm positive they know you're with me. Perhaps we should retire early tonight. Have dinner brought to our rooms?"

She raised an eyebrow. "Everyone will know why."

"There you go blushing again. It doesn't matter what they think. We are husband and wife. We are also lucky to find ourselves hopelessly attracted to each other."

But it was more than that. So much more than lust. He'd explore that thought in further detail later. Much later.

"I won't be presentable in anyone's company if you keep talking in this lewd fashion."

She pulled away from him, a frown creasing her pretty brow.

She retrieved her bodice from the floor. He stayed where he was, sprawled on the sofa, taking in the view. She was positively delicious with her rump in the air begging for his attention.

Unable to resist his wife when he was sporting an erection that wasn't going to go away even with the help of his hand, he got to his feet and wrapped his arms around her. A groan escaped from deep in his throat. It amazed him how much he wanted her. He held her tight so she had nowhere to go. Nowhere to escape.

He pressed his face into her hair. It smelled flowery, but not so strong that it was sickening. Inhaling deeper of the light scent, he released her and set himself to the task of putting all the pearl buttons to rights.

"Won't your sisters have found something else to occupy their time?"

He didn't want to say his good-byes yet. What he wanted right now, more than anything, was to spend the afternoon with her. Alone.

"Abby tends to be cuddled up in the library after lunch. Grace might be anywhere. I usually find her in the gardens. She has a fondness for flowers."

"And what is it you like to do in the afternoons?"

She seemed stunned that he would care enough to ask such a question. "This and that, I suppose." She stalled on saying more. "It varies from day to day."

His wife had a secret. He liked a little mystery. Trying to hide his amusement, he asked, "What does *this and that* usually entail?"

"Sometimes I'll pick up a book or go for a walk. Sometimes I cut flowers for the house with Grace. Or I'll paint, or visit some of the tenants, depending on the weather."

So she was a painter. He'd not thought to ask her that even though he'd seen her drawing on a number of occasions.

"My wife has a hobby she's trying to be secretive about." He trailed the blunt tip of his forefinger around the high collar of her dress. She squirmed away at the ticklish touch. "I like what I'm uncovering in your character."

"It's nothing. Amateur, really."

"Sounds intriguing, my ever-modest wife. Now that you're all done up, why don't we venture to your painting room?"

"There's nothing much to see there."

"I'll be the judge of that." Picking up his discarded vest, he headed to the door grasping his wife's hand because he was sure she wouldn't move from the parlor otherwise.

"You're blushing again, wife."

# Chapter 16

*I don't know if you are alive or dead.*

Making their way from the parlor, Emma headed to the central part of the house and turned up a narrow set of stairs that led to her painting room. The room had originally been designed as a playroom for children. Or at least that was what she assumed since it was situated next to the nursery. There were plenty of rooms to paint in, in the house, but none so airy and pretty as this uppermost chamber.

Richard still held her hand in his grasp. She liked the attention and closeness that was blooming between them. But it probably wouldn't last beyond the day. She knew what her husband was doing. He was distracting her from Waverly. She should be thankful, but she didn't need him to distract her. She was perfectly fine. In fact, she'd stopped crying the second her sister had wrapped her arms around her shoulders and ushered her away from Waverly.

Turning the handle on the door, she pushed it open and stood to the side to let Richard pass. Stained glass high on the west window toned the room in gold and rose hues from the sunlight. A row of windows flanked both the north and south walls, allowing natural light to filter in during the day.

He stared back at her with a raised eyebrow. "So here lies the hobby my wife so enjoys. Does everyone know about this but me?"

"I don't share my paintings with many. It's mostly a private affair." Which was true of the paintings he would be privy to see.

Richard flipped through some animal portraits she'd painted. They were mediocre at best, and she told her husband so. "Not my best."

"I think you have quite a talent. Do you like painting animals?"

"No." She stepped farther into the room and shut the door behind her. "I prefer landscapes to animals. There are so many beautiful sights to behold at Mansfield Hall." She'd show him those soon enough. At hand, there was a stack of flowers she'd painted; also much better than the animals she'd tried her hand at. "I've done some floral arrangements for variety."

Pulling a sheet away from the tall stack of canvases leaning against a wooden table where she had scatterings of color pigments, she uncovered a vase full of peonies in various shades of white, pink, and burgundy.

"What do you prefer? Your landscapes or flowers?"

He stood behind her, placed his hands over hers to flip forward the canvas and revealed another arrangement; this one of cut sunflowers arranged in a small blue vase.

The feel of his exhalations brushing against her neck made her want to lean back into him. Made her want to bask in the latent strength of his form. Mold his naked torso with her hands until the image was forever stamped upon her memory. She'd like to paint her husband the same way she painted women. Gloriously naked. Without shame. Without reason to hide.

"You have a fine eye for detail," he said over her shoulder. He stepped closer, the underside of his arm brushing the curve of her breast. "Show me your landscapes. Everything I uncover is more beautiful than the last."

Her breath caught, with the compliment to both her and her art, but she managed to stay focused on sharing a small part of herself with Richard.

"Oh, my landscapes aren't that wonderful."

Putting the stack to rights, she tossed the sheet back over the floral paintings. Walking over to an easel, she lifted the protective covering to reveal the pond she'd been sitting at, feeding bits of bread to the birds the first day her husband had paid any mind to her.

She wanted to repaint this one. Add geese into the still water, swans in the midst stealing away the majority of food. Change the oak to a weeping willow, the edges of its branches full of soft green leaves brushing the water's surface. She wanted to paint in lovers embracing on the water's edge.

She tore her gaze away from the painting. Her imagination was running wild.

"You are a talented artist, Emma. Which is your favorite to paint? The flowers were by far the most vivid."

Her breath caught at his question. No, he wouldn't, couldn't know she painted nudes. "Portraits," she stuttered out. "I enjoy portraits most. I haven't painted many," she lied easily. "Most are still in charcoal and lead."

Of course, there was a nude portrait beneath the landscape she'd just shown him. That wasn't something she'd dare share with him. She should finish it and send it off to her buyer, before Richard could ever find it.

She was being a ninny. It was hidden. He'd never

find it among the hundreds of other paintings in this room.

"Show me your sketches. I'm rather intrigued."

Her cheeks heated with the compliment. Why was she so flattered?

He stood directly behind her again. Was it her imagination or did he intentionally crowd her whenever she moved away? Stepping around him, she turned back to her painting table. A swan-shaped weight held down her most recent drawings. Thank goodness the one she'd started of her husband was hidden in her bedroom wardrobe.

"I always do a sketch before I paint. None of these are on canvas yet."

Turning back to her husband, she held out the stack of portraits she'd done of the servants. He didn't take them. Only looked down at them.

She looked away from his knowing gaze and to the charcoal sketches in her hand. What would he think if he knew the truth of her paintings? Knew that she made a mint on the erotic pieces she'd painted over the years. What would he do if he knew there were two nudes out in the world of her? And one in Waverly's hands?

He could never know. Which meant his staying couldn't be permanent.

She turned away from her husband and set the papers down. He wasn't interested in seeing them, just in spending the afternoon with her.

"Should we take to the grounds? Maybe walk in the gardens?" She set herself to putting her lead sticks in a box, cleaning up her worktable. She needed a distraction because she didn't know what she was supposed to do or say.

"I don't wish to take a constitutional. What's set you aflutter?"

She faced him again. "I figured you'd had enough of this stuffy old room. Why don't we adjourn to the library or back to the parlor?"

He took a couple of steps toward her, set his arms on the worktable blocking her escape, and leaned in close. The heat of his body started a jittery feeling in the pit of her stomach. Couldn't she throw propriety out the window for the moment and seize what she wanted most? Her husband.

"I like it in here. I like the company even more." That gleam in his eyes told her he was thinking what she was. "If we go back downstairs, we will continue where we left off."

"And if we stay up here?" she asked.

Picking up one of her curls, he pulled it forward and twined it around his fist. He was forever touching her hair, and she liked that slight show of possessiveness from him.

"Don't you already know the answer to that?"

She did. Why hadn't she just given herself to him in the parlor as she'd so badly wanted to? Letting her hair fall to curve over her breast, he leaned over her and pushed the pigments, lead sticks, and papers back on the worktable. Picking her up by the waist, he sat her on the edge. She bit her lip as she studied him. He hadn't bothered to put his necktie back on. The top three buttons on his shirt were undone, revealing a few strands of hair on his chest.

"Do you want me to stop?" He pushed the mass of her skirts up to reveal her stocking-covered legs.

"No." That made him pause, his hands on either of her knees, spreading them wide as he stepped into the vee of her body.

Because her nerves were on edge, she couldn't seem to ask him what she wanted. So she reached for his trousers instead. She was finally taking the initiative with her sexual desires, and that scared her for some reason. It seemed more frightening than anything else she'd done in her life.

She'd only ever allowed herself to be brave with her paintings. Everything else in her life had to be orderly, reserved, proper, and befitting her role as countess.

Richard's eyes were half closed, his breathing heavy as she pushed his trousers down his hips. She stopped to take in the size of his manhood, studied the way it pushed out the linen of his underthings. A gasp welled in her throat, and his eyes snapped to hers, sharp as ever.

She felt confined by the corset, and wished she'd thought to strip out of her clothes. Wished her husband had thought to strip her bare. They stared at each other for what felt like an infinite amount of time. Each lost in the moment.

Spreading the slit of her drawers wide, he pressed his fingers into her sheath. The world exploded into a kaleidoscope of color. She slid forward to push him farther inside her body. She kept her feet firm on the edge of the table to hold her body still so she could just feel. Unable to delay their connection any longer, she set her feet on Richard's hips, pushed down his smalls, and pulled him in tight between her thighs.

It was a shame to lose the feel of his fingers inside her. Richard had a clever way in which his finger made her convulse and cream. He brought the fingers he had had inside her to her lips and smeared the wetness there. She froze at the strange slick touch. Then she pulled his head toward hers so she could kiss him. Tongue flicking out, he tasted of the cream he'd wiped there before assaulting her tongue with his.

His hands had worked their way under her skirts and pulled her buttocks right to the very edge of the table.

She kept her legs firm about his waist and moaned into his mouth as he slid silkily into her body. He groaned.

Threading her fingers in his thick hair, she held him fiercely against her. She didn't want to lose his warmth. The only thing she wanted to remember about today was the embrace of her husband. The rapture he filled her heart with.

Richard tried to shrug her hands free of his hair. She held on tighter, biting at his lips in her desperation to feel more. She wanted to forget everything except him.

"Damn it, Emma, let go for a moment."

"No."

It was the only word she could get out before his assault took on new strength, his body pounding heavy and throbbing into her. Every thrust of his pelvis was a branding of his ownership of her body. She didn't care. She wanted everything he offered.

Her tailbone smacked hard against the wooden table. When she tried to move away from meeting the cruel impact, Richard growled at her to hold still. With a break at their lips, she leaned back to watch his expression. His face was tense, his eyes locked on hers. She gave him a smug smile.

Slowly, she ran her finger over his bottom lip. "I want more."

"Give me a minute, woman," he gritted out. "I'll not have my crisis so soon."

He had stopped moving within her. She didn't like that one bit. She wanted him fierce and rough. She lay back on the table, hands grasping the far edge for leverage, and ground her pelvis to his, rotating her hips in tight circles till she felt her orgasm building. Sweet agony. That was what this was.

"Sonofabitch," he hissed. Lifting her from the table, her ankles still locked at his spine, he brought them both to the floor, her on her back, him held poised above her as he pulled his stiff rod from her body. "I'm going to go off if you keep doing that."

"I don't mind."

She reached beneath her skirts and toyed with the edge of her stocking. His eyes fixed on the tantalizing sight. When had she become so daring? She trailed her finger higher, drawing little circles on her thigh. Closer and closer to her goal.

"I married a veritable vixen." His grin was devilish. "Put your hands above your head."

She raised one brow at the request. Why should she stop? It was obvious what touching herself did to him. She wondered what would happen if she dipped her finger into her core like he did whenever they were about to make love.

He yanked one of the linen coverings from a small set of paintings on the floor and tore off a thin strip of cotton. Pulling her hand away from its final destination, he wrapped the material around her wrists and knotted them together.

She tried to pull away and was unsuccessful. She didn't really want to escape. This was a new side to her husband, too. He'd always been so careful with her in the bedroom. Did his needs run as dark as hers?

"What are you doing?" she asked huskily.

"Teaching you a lesson in manners. No hands, darling, not till you can behave."

"I am behaving. You're taking advantage of me now that you've strung me up."

"Am I now?" He chuckled.

She tugged at the knots to see if she could pull them loose. She couldn't. Then she didn't care, because his fingers were working their magic, pushing up hard into her body. She arched her head back and moaned. Her pelvis pushed closer, wanting so much more than his fingers.

"I want to feel you inside me, Richard."

His hand drove hard against her center. Then he was on her, his hardness filling her sheath as she arched up toward him. His lips brushed hers teasingly, then nipped at her neck. His motions in and out of her body felt so fluid, so perfect.

She couldn't remain idle beneath him. She needed to hold him. As she threw her bound wrists around the back of his neck, Richard tsked.

"As much as I like this wilder side, you forget who's in charge." He forced her hands above her head once again.

He pulled his cock out and teased her clitoris with the head. His hand squeezed her thigh with every slide against her body. "You like me fucking your folds, rubbing your swollen pearl, don't you?"

She couldn't form a response. Her reactions were answer enough. She wanted him to rub her harder. Faster. She was getting closer and closer to that blissful oblivion she craved. He backed off when she felt the first tingling awareness of her orgasm, stretching out the moment for them both. She wanted her hands free so she could dig her fingers into his backside and urge him on.

Finally, when he let her have her crisis, she screamed for him to take her harder. Something crashed to the floor. She didn't care. The whole world could tumble down around them and she would not care.

He slammed into her body, taking and plundering and branding. Her body convulsed around his as he gave in to his own release with a shout, his seed pumping into her with each hard plunge. Her arms were around his shoulders again, holding him close as their tongues warred for supremacy. His body rotated heavily into hers, setting off another orgasm. She ground her body hard against his in desperation for more.

His mouth was next to her ear, shushing her, kissing her. His hands smoothed her sweat-slicked hair away from her temples. "Are you back with me?" he asked.

She nodded and lifted her head from the floor to press a sweet kiss to his lips. He indulged her, holding their bodies tight together in the after-moment.

Reality suddenly flooded her conscience. How embarrassing that she'd just allowed her husband to do this to her, and here of all places. What must he think of her? She'd practically demanded his advances. Thrown herself at him like a common harlot.

Pulling away from her, he sat on his haunches and tucked his softened member away so he could do up his trousers again. Something jabbed into her back. A painting? She went to reach down and move the offending object before she realized she was still trussed up like a winter goose.

She brought her hands forward, nearly shoving them under Richard's nose so he'd untie her.

"What if I like you just like this?"

"You can't be serious. Please, Richard."

She pushed herself up with her elbow and looked around. The stacks of drawings and pencils on her worktable had been pushed to the floor. Paintings were toppled over. Her work easel was empty.

Her work easel was empty!

*The nude.*

Still as a rabbit that's caught the scent of a fox, she looked around frantically while Richard unbound her wrists. Setting eyes on the nude, she breathed a sigh of relief to see it lay facedown. Maybe if she didn't make a big deal about the state of her painting room, Richard might not notice the destruction they'd caused in their need.

She needed to clear him out of here.

"In our haste, we toppled over a lot of paintings," he noted absently. "I'll help you set it to rights. Make sure nothing was damaged."

Why did he have to care! "I'll see to it later."

"I was part of the problem." He placed the strip of material he held on top of the table. "I'll help you set it back up."

"No, don't. Just take me to bed." Did she sound desperate to leave her painting room? She hoped not.

Richard turned to her. "Emma. I didn't mean for this to happen. I'm surprised you let me so much as touch you after what happened."

"I told you, I'm stronger than you give me credit for," she mumbled.

He picked up the pencils that had rolled to the floor and set them back on the table. He straightened the paintings around the base of the table while she straightened her skirts and stood up on wobbly legs. He picked up the large landscape that had hidden her nude, leaning it against the wall.

Hoping he wouldn't see her nervousness, she reached for the nude. She didn't make it in time. He was already there, picking it up and nearly setting it down on the table to be forgotten. She knew the moment he figured out what the picture was, because he stopped midstep and turned back around to face her. She saw a flicker of confusion in his eyes.

Then his expression closed off, completely unreadable as he looked up to her. "What have we here?"

There was no anger there. Not yet, anyway. Surely that would come soon. She hated that she couldn't read his face. Didn't have an inkling as to what thoughts flitted across his mind on the discovery.

Her secret was out. What would he think of her? What would he do? Would he demand she stop? She needn't tell him that she sold the paintings. He must have read the guilt in her eyes, because when she reached for the small canvas, his grasp was firm.

"Did you paint this, Emma?"

She took a deep breath and stared back at him. "I did. Now, if you'll please give it back to me, I'll put it where it belongs."

"Hidden amongst the more mundane. Is that how you operate?"

"You shouldn't have been in here. I'm sorry you found it." Emma reached for Richard's hand, but he stepped away from her. "Please, we'll go. There's no need to mention it again."

"I'm not sorry I found it. Had it been the male form you were painting I might be angrier. But this . . . it almost looks like you." He turned, put it under direct sunlight, and peered closer at the figure in the painting. "You've blotted out her face. Good God, Emma, the body is of a likeness to yours. Why in hell would you paint nudes of yourself?"

"I don't expect you to understand," she huffed out. "And it's not me. There are a great many differences between me and her."

She grasped it tighter and tried wrenching it out of his possession. He let it go and crossed his arms over his chest, giving her a long assessing glare.

"Are there more?"

She stalled too long to make the lie believable. Richard's eyes were already moving to the stacks of paintings set around the room. She knew without a doubt that he'd go through every last one of them before the night was through.

"This is the only one."

"Why do I doubt you?" He started on the stack he'd just neatened. He would find nothing, of course, not even a sketch in rough form. Thank God she had burned those.

"You can look through all the paintings. I promise there are no more."

Richard frowned. "Then where are they?"

"There are no more."

"The waver of your voice tells me you lie. Don't lie to me, Emma. Where are the rest? I want them in my hands now!" Richard flipped through another stack of paintings on the floor. "I'll not have anyone else looking at them."

"I can't give them to you when I don't have them."

"Tell me you haven't given them to someone." He scratched his head in thought. "Are you painting these for a lover?"

"I don't have a lover." What was his obsession with her having a lover? The very idea infuriated her. "I've sold them." She wished she'd tempered her tongue. Wished her anger hadn't given him that much information.

He set his hand out on the table, as though it were the only thing holding him upright at the moment. "Why the hell would you sell nudes strikingly similar to your own form?"

"Can't you hear me?" She stamped her foot to the floor and clenched her fists at her side. "That is not me."

"To whom did you sell them?" He wasn't quite yelling at her, but his voice was firmer than she'd ever heard it. He was being completely unreasonable.

"I have a buyer in Town. I see him once a year for the exchange."

Was she going to be able to keep track of all her lies?

"How many are there? I don't want you to fib on the number, Emma. I want to know exactly how many nudes exist."

She pinched her lips together. He would not listen to reason, would not hear anything she was telling him. The image was not her—the only similarity was in the woman's slender form. What harm could he do now that the paintings were sold? She didn't even know who had purchased them. Hadn't wanted to know, because she trusted Nathan to handle the business end of the transaction with discretion.

"Answer me, Emma."

"Thirty."

Anger flared in his eyes.

She lowered her head and stared at the painted lady mocking her. They were always mocking her, saying their life was not ever going to be a life she could enjoy for herself. Wasn't that the reason she had painted them? To escape into a world that would never exist for her.

"Thirty-one, if you include this piece."

Two of them were of her. Oh, God, what would Richard do with that truth? That secret was safe. It had to be. Nathan would come through for her.

Emma shoved the picture back into his hands. There was no room for weaknesses right now. She must be strong. She must hold her ground.

Really, was it so shocking for a woman to paint and sell nudes? Or was it just unacceptable for her to do so as the Countess of Asbury? She'd painted nudes for nine years now; she wasn't about to stop because her husband couldn't see the true beauty in her art.

"Take a long look at it, Richard. When you come to your senses and can see the image as it really is, then I expect an apology."

She stormed out of her painting room and went to her private chambers. She didn't care if it looked like she was hiding from him. Her emotions were running high. Simply put, she didn't want to see anyone right now.

Especially her husband.

# *Chapter 17*

*I wonder if I would have discovered the real me, had you stayed?*

"It pleases me to see you," Dante said as he turned to her, tossing his necktie on the bed. "I thought maybe you wouldn't come again."

Grace stood with her back to the door, fingers fidgeting at the decorative ribbon about her waist. "I didn't think you'd welcome me after my association with . . . with our unwanted guest."

"Waverly always proved a shrewd business partner. His facility in life was to be a charmer of the worst sort. I wouldn't doubt it if he had orchestrated his acquaintance with you quite intentionally." Dante ran a hand through his hair. "*Cara,* you must promise to stay away from him."

"I realized his intentions toward me long before he showed up here." How she wished she hadn't been so stupid with Waverly. "I came to see you because I don't want you to think me a loose woman. I never . . . that is to say, the things you and I did are not things I do with any man."

Not only did she know she blushed, but her ears were hot, and she was sure her whole face was crimson with shame. She didn't like this feeling at all.

"Waverly has long been unwell." He walked toward her, his hands in front of him, palms facing her. With a desperation unlike her, she wanted to take his hands, but dared not. Not till she knew how he felt about her.

"You never need to hide yourself from me," Dante finished.

It had never been her intention to hide from him. She took a calming breath and hoped the heat in her face and neck had cooled. She would be brave. She would not shy away from this man who had come to mean so much to her in so short a time.

"Can I come to you?" he asked.

Why was he asking her when he rounded in on her regardless? One slow step at a time. Could she be hopeful that he still wanted her? Her heart stuttered and stopped. Stuttered and stopped.

Her palms were sweating, so she rubbed them against her dress. "Why aren't you questioning my past relationship with Waverly?"

"Although the thought of you with another angers me, I'm not going to stop pursuing *our* relationship. I want you so badly, *cara*. I can't even think straight when you're around."

She saw the truth of his statement reflected in his eyes. His face was all seriousness: brows furrowed in concern, his lips a smooth even line. There wasn't a twitch to be had in his face as he regarded her evenly.

She would not have him thinking less of her, because that was what she feared most right now. "I just wanted you to know I was never intimate with Waverly," she blurted out.

"This information makes me an even happier man."

Standing in front of her, he chucked her under the chin. "Your past is yours. We all make mistakes, hmm?"

She nodded. "Do you mean that?"

"I do."

She raised one hand and brushed the back of it over his shirt, touching him so lightly she didn't even feel his firm muscle beneath. She wanted to take more, touch more, but dared not. She was so confused.

"You are wearing too many clothes, *cara*." Her eyes snapped up and met his again. "It is an unusually warm night. I think we should undress so we are more comfortable."

Reaching around her back, where it pressed to the door, he clicked over the lock.

Her heart beat faster in her breast with the obvious insinuation. Not that she hadn't hoped for this to happen. It was just that she thought he wouldn't want anything to do with her. Hands raised, she put them on either side of his face and felt his evening stubble. She wanted to scratch up against him like a cat starved for attention. Like a cat in heat.

"You want me to stay?"

He gave one of his slow grins. A twinkle of mischief was evident in his expression. "The things I want to do every time I see you. Stay the night with me."

Going up on the tips of her slippered feet, she whispered, "Only if you make me cry out your name, Dante."

"I will make you scream my name, *cara*." Dante took her mouth in a ferocious kiss that she felt all the way down to her curling toes. Goodness, they'd gone from a slow seduction to an erotic coupling.

His hands were at her back, caressing her and releasing buttons at the same time. She fumbled with his shirt, pulling it from his trousers, up over his smooth chest, then finally over his head. When the sleeves caught at his wrist, he ripped the decorative clips right out of the cuffs. She released the ties on her corset, loosening the strings enough to release the clasps in front.

Dante stared down at her bosom like a man starved. "I could live a happy man right here."

Grace untied her skirts and pushed them from her hips. She couldn't seem to get undressed fast enough.

"Take off my trousers." His voice was hoarse. The material made it as far as his knees before he was hitching her legs over his hips and pressing up into her body in one long, smooth thrust.

"Glorious. So glorious." He pressed his forehead to hers. "You are sweet heaven."

Her head fell back against the door, her arms wrapped tightly around his shoulders so he could bury his face into the plumpness of her breasts.

Did this mean there was something more between them? She bit her lip and swallowed the question for later. It felt so good—right—having him inside her body. It was as though he owned her body.

"You make me hot," he said, biting and sucking at her breasts. "Like a young man who gets hard at the first sight of a beautiful woman."

She pulled his face back up to hers and speckled kisses over his hair-roughened face, his nose, the corner of his lips. She couldn't stop kissing him.

"Lock your ankles around me. I'm going to walk you over to the bed."

There was no way he could carry her weight like that. She did the opposite of his request and tried to set her feet down on the floor.

He caught her leg up again before she could escape and pulled away from the wall so quickly she was forced to do his bidding.

"You needn't carry me," she yelped in surprise.

"I don't want to leave your body. That would be a crime." He teasingly patted her buttocks, then stroked and squeezed it. "You clench around my cock so sweetly, *tesorina*. Besides, you are light."

"You're addled to think that." But she was giggling like a young girl who had just received her first compliment.

"Maybe addled only where you are concerned. Pull off the chemise." His hands clasped tight at her buttocks to steady her while he kicked off his trousers. "You are not going to be able to leave this room when we are done. I'm going to tire us both so much we can't walk."

"I like how you think." She leaned in close to him, sucked at his bottom lip, and gave it a loving bite before releasing him. "But what if someone comes looking for us? We haven't even made it past the dinner hour."

"We'll ring for dinner soon, and tell the servant we are indisposed."

She gasped at the bold suggestion. "The serving staff will think I'm a great hussy."

"I will say I am having dinner with my affianced."

Dante stopped walking and held her tight, never letting her fall. He was grinning.

"Do you mean it?"

"*Cara,* I would not say something if I didn't mean it. We are already in a compromising position." He demonstrated how compromising by pulling out of her body near to the tip of his instrument, then shoved himself back in. "You must become my wife now."

How could she respond to that? She wanted to run away with him. Yes, preferably as man and wife. She'd known that since their first time together.

"We've known each other for so short a time." She

nibbled at her lower lip. Unsure about everything. Did he mean it?

"This does not matter. I'm a grown man of thirty-five, you a decade younger." He kissed her sweetly on the mouth. "I've never asked another woman for her hand in marriage. So this is not something I ask lightly. Say yes."

"Oh, Dante." She returned his kiss enthusiastically. "Yes, I will be your wife. I want that more than anything."

"Good," he said.

Then she was falling backward onto the bed, his firm, hard body following. After that, she didn't think any more. Couldn't think except to call out his name when he pleasured her and gave her two orgasms before he had his release. Then he kissed the whole of her body, not leaving a single inch untouched before climbing between her legs again—that was when she screamed his name. She hoped no one else in this wing of the house heard their impassioned cries. She didn't really care, though, because she was going to be Mrs. Lioni.

The very rational part of Richard's mind told him that the painting was not his wife's body and likeness. There was no birthmark covering the right hip on the woman in the picture. There was a roundness to the stomach that his wife did not possess. The woman's thighs were thicker, fleshier, and the hair of the woman was a darker blonde than that of his wife's. He could argue that the breasts were similar, the pale pink nipples identical in coloring to Emma's, though hers turned dark red in the height of passion unlike the vixen stretched so wantonly across the divan in this picture.

He still planned to purchase back every single nude she had painted over the years. If it were ever revealed that Emma painted golden-haired Venuses and amorous Aphrodites for the gentlemen in society, she'd be closed to all social circles in Town. Not that he cared what society thought.

His foolish, adorable wife was going to keep him on his toes. Tucking the canvas under his arm, Richard left her painting room. He had left no canvas unturned. He had to make sure there were no more paintings in here, no sketches of a lusty nature. It had taken him some hours to complete the task.

He stopped outside Dante's room on hearing a breathy moan. His brow furrowed, and his hand went to the door latch. It might be his house, and he expected a certain level of respect toward his guest and his wife's sisters, but he couldn't demand Dante keep his hands to himself. He was almost positive who his friend spent the evening with.

Grace was a grown woman. A widow, Richard reminded himself. And she was in Dante's room, not the other way around. With a shrug, he eased away from the door and walked the remainder of the hall to his bedchamber.

Setting the painting on his bureau, he stared at it. While he did not have an eye for art, he could see that this one was something that could easily be coveted by any man who considered himself a connoisseur of the female form.

It was not an amateur painting. It was at least a hundred times more detailed and real than the landscapes and flowers Emma had shown him earlier. Thirty paintings of this nature existed somewhere in England. Hell, they could be anywhere on the Continent for all he knew.

Emma took a late dinner in her room that night. She pushed around the asparagus on her plate. She didn't have an appetite. Not after the fight with her husband. Just when she thought everything was coming together in their relationship, everything fell apart at the seams.

Her fork fell to the plate with a clank.

She wasn't angry with her dim-witted husband anymore. Perhaps she should be, but her temper was usually short-lived. There was comfort in knowing he couldn't do anything about her sold paintings. He would simmer over the evening and be his cool, calm self by morning. She was sure of that.

She wondered if he planned to come to her room later. She frowned. She shouldn't want that. In fact, she'd refuse him at the door. Lock him out as she had the first night he'd arrived at the manor.

She'd given in to him so easily. It wasn't fair for him to walk back in her life and take the reins right out of her hands. In the matter of days, she'd lost herself. It had taken years for her to build her confidence. And he took all that away in a single day.

What if she just left? Went to London and let the infernal man chase her down if he truly cared to mend their marriage. If he didn't, then she'd have to hope that she wasn't pregnant. She could not be tied to a man for the rest of her days and be alone. How would she survive without his companionship now that she'd tasted of it so thoroughly?

There was at least fifty thousand pounds sitting in a trust fund originally set up for her extra pin money. She'd not spent a single cent from the sales of her nudes. What if she left Mansfield Hall? Forgot about London altogether and moved to the wilds of Scotland?

She pushed away her plate and slouched back in the chair. That didn't sound much more appealing, either.

She brooded as though her life was at an end because her secret had been revealed.

Her art would remain a constant in her life. The same could not be said for her husband. He would eventually leave again. She would continue to sell her paintings and squirrel away the money. If they did divorce, she'd need that money to find a little cottage somewhere. To live as an independent woman.

As she stood from the writing table where she'd taken her dinner, the door to her private sitting room flew open.

Richard strolled in without a care for invading her private space.

"Good evening, Emma."

She inclined her head as she gathered her courage to face her husband so soon after their fight.

Richard narrowed his eyes to the lone lamp lit on her table. "Why is it so dark in here?"

"I was in a black mood. Gothic lighting seemed fitting." She folded the napkin she was holding and placed it on the table. "Why are you here?"

"I wanted to discuss the disagreement we had earlier."

Her brows rose, and she tapped her foot impatiently, waiting for him to continue.

He stepped fully into the room, leaving the door wide open. Behind him, the last rays of sun shaded her bedchamber in tones of orange and gold.

"I realize now that my assessment of the situation might have been rash."

"Rash?" Why was it that he made her want to strike out at something? "Really, Richard, your reaction was far more than rash. You assume you can take control of my life after being away for the better part of it."

"I'm not here to fight about this." Richard yanked on the bottom of his vest and stood taller.

That was not something she expected to hear from him. Why was he here, then?

She sat in one of the chairs arranged neatly around the hearth, giving her husband her back. "I have things I need to attend to. I would appreciate it if you'll make your speech and leave me to my own devices."

She turned her head so she could watch him from the corner of her eye. Richard put his back to the silk-papered wall and crossed his arms over his chest.

"What of our night together?"

She couldn't help the snort that left her mouth, or the subsequent laugh at his nerve to suggest they continue their night as planned. As though nothing significant had happened between them. If he wanted to control her life, he was in for a surprise. She had vowed never to let a man rule her actions or her heart ever again. She'd been foolish enough to let Richard back into her life at all. Had she been thinking with her head instead of her heart, she would have pressed the issue of divorce.

Her hand curled around the cushion by her thigh. "To assume I would accept your advances is pure arrogance."

A small part of her cried out in denial at refusing her husband now; she tamped that need down in her mind, locking it away with all the other emotions she'd been forced to ignore for so many years.

The attraction she felt toward her husband, the desire to have him in her life and in her bed, would subside if she just ignored it. She'd gone twelve years without him already. She could last long enough to get a divorce.

Infernal man. How vexing this day had turned out. She should be focused on her anger—not her attraction. He had accused her of adultery, and indecency with the paintings. Yet during their marriage, he was allowed to do exactly as he pleased. That infuriated her.

He gave one of his slow, easy smiles that made her

heart skip a beat and then speed up. Did he know the effect he had on her? Was he trying to provoke her? She turned away from his smug expression.

"I came to ask you about the buyer for your art. Now that we've both had time to think and calm ourselves, have you thought about telling me who he is?"

She shook her head and stared at her lap. He'd never forget her art, would he? She'd never reveal the duke's involvement as her buyer. Nathan could always be counted on for his discretion. Though, for some reason, she didn't doubt Richard's ability to ferret out who the buyer was. Even so, until that time arose, she need not worry about it.

"I will find out whether you tell me or not, Emma."

Her head snapped up. The light was fading fast behind Richard, and she wished she could see his expression more clearly. She wanted to walk over to him and push him off balance—to wipe that grin clean off his face. Her irritation was getting the better of her.

Taking a deep breath, she focused elsewhere. "Then you don't need me to answer the question."

He stalked forward. All the humor was gone from his face as he grasped her arms and lifted her to her feet so she couldn't avoid his sharp gaze. Unlike Waverly, he did not hurt her where he held her arms. He was careful but firm in his resolve.

"You do neither of us any favors with your contrary attitude. You may refuse to answer my questions now, but what will you do once I know the name of your buyer?" His grip loosened, but he didn't release her. "He cannot be saved from my wrath indefinitely."

Emma pulled herself out of his hold. "I have done nothing wrong. Not once, in all the years we were married, have I done anything untoward. I don't see why you care."

"Because I do, damn it!" He brushed his hand through his hair in frustration. "You cannot brush the matter of your paintings under the carpet as if the topic has no bearing on our lives. You've done something that will harm our future. Harm the future of our children. I intend to buy all the paintings, Emma."

"That's not possible."

It wasn't that she wanted to be contrary in this. Not in the least. But there was no way to find all the paintings. Half remained with her buyer, those that were of his mistress's likeness; the other half had been sold to anonymous bidders. She did not know their identities. She very much doubted the duke would reveal the purchasers' names simply because Richard demanded the information.

It didn't matter. No one would connect her signature to that of the Countess of Asbury. She'd been careful with her initials. They remained, even today, as discreet letters: an *E* for her first name, and a *C* for her middle. Nothing more or less to give away her real identity. She hadn't wanted to be associated with something so . . . wickedly enterprising.

"You are wrong on that count, my dear. I most certainly can track down every last canvas." His jaw tensed; the vein at his temple visibly throbbed. She hadn't wanted to tell him about any of this. But she needed to make him see reason.

"You don't understand how impossible a task that will be. My buyer privately auctions the pieces."

Richard walked away from his wife. He stopped at the wall, pressed his hands flat against the surface and took a deep breath to calm the rage goading his temper. Auctioned. The bloody pieces were auctioned.

His wife tried his patience. Laughed at his sense of

dignity. Cared naught for anything he tried to correct to start them on the right foot toward a better future, a better marriage. Goddamn her. Goddamn him!

His head dropped forward between his arms, and he stared blindly at the parquet floor. What was wrong with trying to cover up the fact that she painted indecent pictures? Why shouldn't he feel obligated to track down every last one of them whether they were in England, Scotland, or some other place on the Continent?

He'd go to the farthest reaches of the world for her in this matter. He didn't care to question why that was. Though he felt it was his duty as her husband. His duty to any children they had. This wasn't any different from the loyalty he shared with his friends. She just so happened to be the first woman he'd given any loyalty to. The first woman he'd ever really cared about.

*The first woman he had ever cared about.*

He wanted to laugh at his own stupidity. Sometime in the past week he'd started to care about Emma. That had definitely not been planned.

He hadn't come in here to yell at her. To argue with her, or to fight with her. In fact, the moment he'd seen her all laced up tight and wearing all those damn layers of clothes, treating him as cool as ever, he'd wanted to undress her. Lay her out and taste every inch of her creamy white skin and burn away the icy facade she wore like a second skin. He wanted her wild and wanton, as she had been in the painting room. He wanted his adorable, warm, caring wife back.

If he could turn back the clocks to this afternoon, he would. He almost wished he'd never discovered her secret.

He spun around and glared at her. There was a stubborn tilt to her chin, her hands clenched firmly together in anger. She had the nerve to stand up to him. That should make him furious, but it didn't. It made him want to laugh at his stupidity all over again.

No one else had ever bothered to defy him. He was the Earl of Asbury, one of the richest men in England. When she challenged him, it made him bloody hard and wanting to be inside her silken warmth to prove his dominance at least over her body, if not in their marriage.

"For God's sake, Emma. Let me make something in our marriage right." He shouldn't have revealed that much to her. He hastened to correct what he meant. "You are the Countess of Asbury."

He shoved his hands in his jacket's pockets so he wasn't tempted to shake her, and then kiss her senseless and forget the whole nonsense of her paintings.

"As the Countess of Asbury," he continued, "you cannot risk your reputation or that of our future children by painting such scenes."

It angered him that some other man was experiencing the untamed beauty in those pictures. Probably getting a good rub off with the erotic images he could only imagine since he'd seen just the one.

"Perhaps you can enlighten me as to how anyone is supposed to find out." One of her brows quirked up.

"Your buyer could let it slip." Someone would want to know who was painting such images. They might already know that she was the artist.

"He won't." Her steadfast determination that her secrets were safe bothered him to no end.

"You don't know that."

"Richard," she said softly. "I do know that. I don't know what to do to make you believe me."

"Emma," he said with a calm he did not feel, but felt he owed after his irrational behavior. "I'm through arguing. Whether you like it or not, I will purchase them back by any means necessary. Continue to paint them if you must." He meant that. He'd not take away the one secret he'd flushed out of her. "I know you won't stop. I don't expect you to stop. But I will not allow other men to enjoy your art."

She scrunched up her brow and stared back at him distrustfully. "You've always been a man of your own mind." Was that disappointment he heard in her voice?

"Am I forgiven, then?" It was imperative for some reason that she didn't dislike him. Not after all the inroads he'd made this past week. Not with all the feelings he was developing for his wife.

He held his hand out to her. An invitation. A truce. Who knew what it was; he certainly didn't. She looked from his hand to his eyes but did not step forward. He dropped his hand away.

"The hour is late," she said. "We . . . that is to say, *you* should retire in your chamber this evening, while I retire in mine."

Of course she wouldn't invite him to her bed. Not tonight, maybe not tomorrow night. It was probably for the better. He was still acting an ass no matter that he thought through his words before he uttered them. He didn't deserve to spend any time in her bed.

He inclined his head. "Until tomorrow."

"Indeed."

He wondered what she'd do if he kissed her senseless. He stepped forward, grasped her hand and pulled her into his arms. The supple feel of her breasts had him groaning with the contact. The warmth he felt where his hands wrapped and held onto her lower back had him tightening his hold. None of those stolen touches was as fulfilling as the soft give of her lips beneath his. Nor as satisfying as the dulcet moan she released into his mouth as her lips parted.

It was a shame that the kiss had to come to an end at all. He pulled his mouth away from hers and stared into her clear green gaze. Placing his hands on either side of her face, Richard kissed her forehead before leaving her.

# Chapter 18

*I weary of my lonely life. But it is an existence I've created all my own.*

Abby was in the drawing room, writing out a letter, when Emma went downstairs for tea in the morning. It looked like she'd been writing for some hours, since the sides of her fingers were stained an indigo blue from the ink.

"Good morning." She smiled at her sister's back, since Abby didn't immediately turn at her approach. "To whom do you pen a note? It looks to be a veritable novel."

Her sister looked at her with a mischievous glint in her eyes. Then it quickly changed to surprise.

What was her sister up to?

"I'm afraid I can't tell a tale to save my life. No great novels will be forthcoming from me." Abby gathered up the pages and folded them before tucking them inside the pocket on her dress. "It's a letter to a friend."

If Emma didn't know her sister better, she'd ask if the friend was a gentleman. Abby'd had her coming out on her nineteenth birthday when she was out of her mourning weeds for their father. It had only taken Abby six months to decide she did not want to be a part of the marriage mart. Her younger sister had declared all the men to be fortune hunters, and that she was the farthest thing from being an heiress, and therefore she would never marry.

That hadn't stopped Emma and Grace from dragging their youngest sister back to Town every season in the hope that a gentleman would offer for marriage.

Whatever Abby was up to, she wouldn't reveal anything until she was ready.

Emma took a seat on the green twill sofa and poured herself a cup of tea. "Will you sit with me?"

Abby picked up her teacup from the writing desk and plopped herself down in a chair across from her. "I've missed you since your husband's been back. You seem preoccupied with him."

"I hadn't realized." Was Abby resentful of the time Emma had been spending with her husband? She hoped not. "He's discovered my passion for painting."

Emma kept her voice even, as though it didn't matter, even though it did matter a great deal. After a sleepless night, she couldn't stop thinking what lengths her husband might go to find her buyer. At least Richard couldn't intimidate the duke.

The clink of Abby's cup hitting the saucer was the only sound to be had for a good minute. Emma waited for her sister to realize the full truth behind those words.

"You mean *the* paintings we are currently wagering on sitting for?"

"The very ones."

"Oh, no, Emma." Abby got up to set her cup on the tea trolley and then sat next to her on the sofa. "What has he said about them?"

"That he wishes to buy them all back."

"He can't. You don't know where they are." Her sister's clear green eyes widened. "Or do you?"

She could not tell her sister a half-truth. Despite the fact that it would be better for Abby to know nothing, Emma said, "I know where half of them are. The other half is anyone's guess."

The one thing she would never reveal to her sisters was that Nathan had been the one to purchase the majority of them.

"He was quite put out with me yesterday. I can only hope the night has given him time to reconcile his opinion of me and my art."

Abby took Emma's hands in her own as a way of comfort. Emma appreciated the gesture. She felt a little off balance today, and the moral support of her sister would go far.

"Emma, if anything, he's just shocked to find his very proper wife indulging in something completely out of character from what society might expect of you. You've presented such a pristine image of yourself over the years that no one would suspect such a thing."

"I'm worried about what lengths he'll go in finding the truth of my buyer's identity."

"I don't see why you don't tell him." Abby put her arm over Emma's shoulder. "Unless Richard has forbidden you to paint?"

"At first he said I was to cease, that I was to give him all the paintings of that nature. Then he decided it would be better for him to track them all down so no one knew my dirty little secret." He hadn't said quite that, but it had certainly been implied.

"I'm so sorry."

Emma absently played with her locket. "He's going to find out sooner or later."

"I wish I had words of wisdom to offer you."

"I think I just needed to tell someone. It's unfair of him to come back into my life and pretend he hasn't ignored me for a dozen years. Pretend he can have the final say in my day-to-day activities." Emma let out a long exasperated sigh. "I have to warn my buyer."

She didn't want to reveal her contact for so many reasons. Her husband already thought the worst of her. Assumed the duke was a lover of hers. What a mess this was. What a worse mess it could become. It always seemed things got worse before they got better.

"Would you like to go for a walk?" Abby was already standing from the sofa, offering Emma a hand up. "It might help clear your mind."

"Fresh air will probably do me good." Emma joined her sister.

"We have another challenge for you today, Em. That is, if you are up to the task. I'll understand if you aren't."

She had completely forgotten about the wager, with everything else going on in her life. It would help her focus on something other than her husband. She should indulge this one last time. Emma opened the French doors that led to the gardens. A wall of heat met their approach to the outdoors. It was only ten in the morning, and already the day was stifling hot.

"What is to be the challenge today?"

Abby mulled at her bottom lip. "A swim."

"A swim?" Emma laughed and sat under the large oak that shaded a bench. "You can't be serious. Where?"

"At the pond." Abby pulled her thin shawl off and set it beside them. "Don't look so worried. I shouldn't have told you. I thought it would take your mind off your husband."

"Cheer me up by announcing we'll take a dip in the pond?" Emma shook her head. "I'll freeze within a minute."

"Since when do we leave you to do the tasks alone? Grace and I plan to join you. We'll freeze together and laugh about it later."

"But the pond? The last time we swam together, a snapping turtle bit me." Emma shivered. She didn't like any animals that made their homes in ponds.

"The pond is fairly shallow, and you can see the bottom. It'll be fine. Besides, we haven't had a decent swim since we were children."

Yes, and all because of an ugly little turtle with a very sharp beak.

"It'll be fun," Abby insisted. "We'll wait till the sun has had a chance to warm the water before we go. It's the perfect day for it."

Emma wiped a damp curl from her temple. She had to agree, it was the perfect day to cool off in some water. Maybe a swim wouldn't be so bad. "I can't believe I'm even considering this."

Abby laughed as she fanned herself with her hand.

Emma stood from the bench and tugged Abby along with her, their arms linked. "We should go find Grace."

"We're going to freeze." Emma wrapped her arms around herself. The very thought of dunking her toes in the pond had her teeth chattering even though she was wiping sweat away that had formed at her temples under the shade of her hat.

"I brought plenty of blankets to wrap ourselves in afterward," Grace said. "It'll be fun."

Despite Abby's earlier words, she'd not taken to the task with them. She'd had an urgent post to write to a friend. Emma was inclined to believe that perhaps the men would be joining them, as they had for the last two challenges.

"When do the men plan to make an appearance?" she asked.

Grace seemed startled by the question. "Whatever do you mean?"

"I've noticed with every task you and Abby set forth, my husband has been there to see me completely unlike myself. I wonder when he and Mr. Lioni will just so happen to be walking by today."

"I don't know. I haven't ever invited Richard along for our excursions."

Emma raised a brow at her sister, then went back to folding her skirts on the grass beside her. "I'm disinclined to believe you. It might remain that you haven't invited Richard. Have you invited Mr. Lioni?"

Her sister blushed. A rare occurrence. Not unless she wanted to hide something.

"Grace." Emma reached out for her sister, settling a hand on either shoulder to stop Grace from turning away from her. "Tell me you haven't fallen for Mr. Lioni."

Grace looked away.

"Oh, no, Grace. He won't stay on forever. Why would you do this to yourself?"

"I don't know. It just happened. Dante is different from other men." Green eyes met green eyes.

"You're on a first-name basis with him?" Emma's jaw dropped. "Tell me you haven't . . ."

The look her sister gave her was one of pure guilt, like being caught stealing cookies from the kitchen. Emma released her hold on Grace and covered her own mouth, too late to stop the gasp of shock that escaped.

Grace crossed her arms over her bosom. "Emma, I'm a grown woman. Don't you dare reprimand me in matters of the heart. We enjoy each other's company. We—"

"Then why do you argue as though you have to?"

"I won't be judged by you, Emma. I could never live as you have. Alone in this monstrous house." Grace threw out her arms to encompass the land around them. "Without any callers, without a care whether or not you have the company of a man. I don't understand how you live that way."

"You should be ashamed of yourself. How dare you compare my situation to yours." Emma pulled the hat from her head and tossed it toward their neatly folded clothes. "Abby doesn't know, does she?"

"It's not as if I plan to tell the whole world I've taken a lover."

Emma pinched her eyes shut and rubbed at them. It wasn't fair to judge her sister. They were in the privacy of Mansfield Hall.

Grace stood and walked to the edge of the water. Her hair was piled high on her head so it wouldn't get wet. Emma had done the same. They both sported their unmentionables and short camisoles. All their other clothes were stacked on the grassy bank for when they came out of the water.

"I wasn't going to say anything. But I don't want you to think poorly of me . . ."

"It's not that. I just worry."

Grace turned to her as she stepped into the water. "You needn't. Dante and I planned to make an announcement of our betrothal over dinner tonight. We're to be married soon."

Emma stumbled on a rock. She caught herself before she fell into the water. Her sister caught her arm.

"I know it seems sudden. But I fear I've fallen in love."

Emma stared back at Grace. Was Grace afraid that

her sisters would reject the idea? Think her foolish? This was a great deal different from a simple affair. "I will stand beside you in your decision. I won't judge the suddenness of your betrothal. I hope you realize other people will assume you are marrying because you're with child."

"I don't care what they think." Grace turned away, focusing on the water in front of them instead of meeting her gaze. "Once they see us together they will know it is a love match."

Was it possible to fall in love with someone inside of two weeks? Emma had once thought herself in love with Richard. But that had been different. She had been just a girl then. She hadn't known any better, didn't really understand the concept of love when she'd hung on Richard's every word during their courtship. Now that she was more mature and knew herself better, she wasn't so sure that what she felt for her husband was love. A need for companionship did not equate to love in her books.

"I'm happy for you, Grace." She hugged her sister. "What exactly does marrying immediately mean? Will you go somewhere to marry within the next week?"

"No. We'll have the banns read. I've convinced him to stay in London."

Grace walked farther out into the water. Emma followed, going so far as her knees. It wasn't as cold as she thought it would be. The heat of the day had helped to warm the water considerably.

"I'm sorry I got upset," Emma apologized. "I've not been myself this week. I'm going to miss you if you move to Italy."

"And I'll miss you. But we'll still see each other. I think we'll only spend half our time there, and half here." Grace gave her a small smile. "Please don't tell Abby I told you. She'll be displeased that you knew before her."

"I won't say a word."

"The water isn't too bad. It's tepid," Grace said. That would probably change the deeper they waded in.

"What is the purpose of this challenge, Grace? You never did explain that to me. We used to do this all the time when we were children."

Grace leaned back and swam a few hand spans out into the water. "Join me, and I'll tell you."

Sinking into the water up to her waist, Emma then submerged her body beneath the surface and swam toward her sister. "Grace, despite the fact that the water is lukewarm, I'm starting to shiver. You don't plan to stay in here long, do you?"

"Not at all. The men will join us shortly."

"I knew it!" She sent a rush of water toward her sister. Grace swam out of the way before she could be splashed. "Grace, this isn't funny. They are going to see us half naked in the full light of day. You have taken this too far."

"It doesn't matter that they see us half naked, Emma. It is nothing they haven't seen from either of us before." Grace had the nerve to let out a full-throttled laugh from deep in her lungs. "This is the wager Abby and I decided on. You can't change it. Well, you can. You can back out now and lose your chance to have us sit for you."

"You are decidedly cruel." Emma scrunched up her nose at her sister. "Why bother to involve my husband at all?"

"You'll thank me for this one day. I promise you that much." Grace wasn't going to answer her. "Your husband, on the other hand, may thank me today. Maybe when he realizes you aren't wearing nearly enough clothes, because he's scowling something fierce and striding here at double the speed he was before he'd spotted your golden curls bobbing along in the water."

"What is the meaning of this, Emma? Are you trying to catch your death?"

Before she turned to Richard's voice, Emma glared at her sister through narrowed eyes and hissed under her breath, "I will not end the challenge so easily, but you will pay for this, Grace!"

Grace swam closer, close enough to whisper, "The second part of the challenge, and the reason Abby isn't here, is that you have to convince your husband to come into the water by any means necessary. I do believe you have your work cut out for you; he looks positively furious."

Turning in the water, Emma pasted a fake smile on her face as she met her husband's glare. Why couldn't he be as carefree and uncaring as his friend? Mr. Lioni sat on the lawn with his knees up, elbows resting on them, twirling a long piece of grass between his fingers. He wasn't watching her, though. His attention was arrested by Grace.

"*Cara,* is this an invitation to join you?" Dante unlaced his boots.

"I do believe it is." Grace tittered.

"Emma, what is the meaning of this?" Richard drew her attention back to him.

She stood on the silty bottom of the pond, since she was only chest-deep in the water.

"Grace and I are simply remembering our childhood. We felt like a swim. It's so dreadfully hot today that the idea was perfect."

For some odd reason, she wanted to convince Richard to join her for a swim. To put behind their evening of disagreement.

"Why don't you join us?" she called out, swimming into deeper water. "Mr. Lioni has no shame in doing so."

Richard crossed his arms over his chest and walked down to the edge of the pond. "And freeze half to death?"

Emma swam closer to him, sure that a devil whispered in her ear to do something she'd never dared dream of doing before now. "You could try catching me. I'll keep you warm."

Mr. Lioni laughed and stripped out of his clothes. "Your wife is a firecracker."

"It'll be fun," she assured Richard. She was determined to get him into the water.

Though the water wasn't getting any warmer the deeper out she swam, she had a few ideas in how she could warm up. Richard was scowling at her now and remained unmoving. She swam a little closer.

Mr. Lioni lumbered into the water. He paid her no mind. His focus seemed intent on Grace, who was swimming farther out into the water, laughing so hard that Emma wasn't sure how her sister stayed afloat. Mr. Lioni used firm, sure strokes to swim after Grace.

Emma looked back to Richard and decided to give a better enticement to lure him in faster. Not that she needed to; he had worked his boots off. But half the fun in this dare was in teasing her husband. So she stood from the water, revealing her drenched camisole. It stuck to every curve. Richard growled something foul as he yanked his shirt from his trousers, with renewed fervor.

He pointed an accusing finger at her. "Stare at another man like that again, Emma, and I'll be tempted to put you over my lap."

She'd barely glanced at Mr. Lioni. Was he jealous? The very thought was enough to make her heart leap right up into her throat. She stifled a gasp.

"You wouldn't dare," she said in mock surprise.

"Test me again and you'll find out."

She pouted out her bottom lip. "I'm an artist. The male form has always fascinated me." None so much as his. Not that she'd tell him that when she enjoyed the possessiveness he displayed.

"I hadn't had the opportunity to properly explore a man's shape until you came back to the manor. Now I have two fine specimens at my fingertips," she teased.

"I plan on fishing you out of there and taking you back to the house. There, I will demonstrate just how serious I am about taking you over my knee."

Under the full impact of the sun, his complexion was golden. The hair on his chest speckled the space between his pectorals in a small matting of deep brown. There was another trail that went from his navel and led into his smalls. Richard's body was well toned, his muscles subtler than Mr. Lioni's. Despite their size difference, she didn't doubt the men were equal in strength.

Richard still stood on the edge of the bank, glowering at her.

He obviously needed more temptation then her simply standing there in a drenched chemise to draw him into the water. Feeling more brazen then she'd ever felt in her life, she curled her fingers under the short camisole and pulled it over her head. With a crooked smile, she threw the wet material at her husband.

"Are you joining me? Or do you plan to stand there all day, like a surly bear?"

He caught the damp material, stared at it and dropped it. The tips of her breasts had beaded the moment she'd stepped into the chilly water, and he was staring at their distended, darkened tips. He growled something unintelligible, then pulled off his smalls.

She gasped. "Richard, what do you think you're doing?"

"Chasing my wife out of a bloody cold pond."

"Why are you removing all your clothes?"

"Perhaps I'm stripping so you can enjoy the male physique in all its grandeur."

By *grandeur* he must mean the state in which he now was—quite aroused. She could hardly swallow, her mouth was so dry. His instrument stood erect from his body, the skin pulled back from the purplish head. He was a beautiful sight. His testicles were drawn up in a sac that had to be as big as her closed fist.

She had put him in that state.

Tossing his smalls up on the bank, he came forward. Tempting as it was to let him catch her—she had missed being in his arms last night—she didn't want to make this too easy for him. She swam as fast as she could, deeper into the water. He needed no time to adjust to the temperature of the water and was already swimming after her. He was as determined to catch her as Mr. Lioni had been to catch Grace.

His hand slid over her calf and down her ankle. With a laugh, she managed to kick out of his reach. An adept swimmer, she decided to evade him by ducking fully under the surface of the water, turning about, and swimming in the direction she'd come from.

Before she could make her quick escape, his arm snaked around her waist and pulled her back above the surface of the water. She swiped her hair from her face. Richard held her to his chest, kicking out with his legs to bring them to shallower water.

"Did you really think I'd let you get away?"

"Does it matter now that you've caught me?" Her voice was husky. Filled with so much need.

She couldn't help but smile at his dark, serious gaze and set her hands on his shoulders for balance. Did he really think she'd be frightened off by his scowl? She put her feet to the rocky bottom of the pond. He still held her waist. She felt the firm, welcome intrusion of his manhood against her navel.

"Do I at least get a kiss for catching you?"

His head was already descending toward hers. Their lips were wet and cool to the touch from being in the water. She pulled her mouth away from his after the first innocent stroke of mouth on mouth. She wasn't ready to pull her body away, though. He was warm when everything around her was suddenly cold. He was solid when everything else moved and felt unsteady.

Instead of swimming away, she wrapped her legs about his waist and let him hold her weightless body against his. It was a sensually erotic position. She couldn't help but spread her fingers through his still-dry hair. The thick waves stuck to her damp fingers, so she grasped his hair tighter.

Lifting her mouth to his, she said, "Where are Grace and Mr. Lioni? I don't think I could bear to know they watched us."

"They swam toward the reeds, behind the willow that shades this side of the pond. They've been gone since before I stripped out of my clothes."

"So, we're all alone?"

"All alone." His hand lowered to cup her buttocks.

"I shouldn't be giving you this privilege. There is still a lot to discuss about yesterday."

"There is," he agreed. "Let it wait till tonight."

He hitched her up higher on his body, the crest of his manhood pressed at her core where he'd slipped through the slit in her drawers. She wanted to slide over the thick length lodged there, wanted to forget they were in broad daylight indulging in something so completely sinful she should be ashamed of her reckless behavior.

With temptation in reach, she did everything her mind was telling her not to do: She pressed down till the head of his cock was wedged within her. Richard's grip tightened on either cheek of her buttocks.

"This isn't the best place for this," she groaned out low.

"I'm not inclined to move elsewhere now that I have you where I want you."

She laughed, feeling giddier by the moment.

His hand skimmed up her back with a firm touch. "Have you ladies been indulging in some wine this afternoon?"

"None." Which made her wonder what exactly had come over her. It wasn't like her to behave this way. "How did you know I would be at the pond?"

His hand fisted around her hair, which had fallen from the knot she'd tied it in when she'd ducked under the water. Richard kissed her forehead. Kissed her lips. Lust was reflected in his gaze when he pulled away and stared back at her. Then he thrust right up into her core until they were pelvis-to-pelvis. He didn't move within her, just held her tightly to his body.

"There was a note included with my luncheon." Leaning forward, his tongue flicked against her ear. "Said to meet you at the pond." He sucked the lobe of her ear in his mouth. "I had to investigate, of course."

She hated that she couldn't find it in her to be angry with Grace for lying to her. Not with her husband doing wicked things to her. Making her feel wicked in return.

"What if Grace and Mr. Lioni come back?"

With only one side of his lip lifting with his smile,

Richard looked quite devilish. "They won't be back anytime soon."

"What if Abby should find us? Or the servants?"

"The pond is secluded on the property. We are surrounded by trees on two sides, hills to the north, and the apple orchard to the south."

He must have understood her concern, because he was walking toward the shade of the weeping willow where the branches caressed the surface of the water. How he walked there with such ease when she was sheathed around him she couldn't guess; didn't in fact care to guess when he was doing such pleasurable things to her body.

There was a patch of grass between the trunk of the willow and the pond. Richard made his way in that direction, holding her weight easily as they cleared the water. He pressed her back to the rough bark, his hands holding her rear.

"Is this uncomfortable?" he asked.

"Doesn't matter. I don't want to go anywhere else."

She didn't even care if she scraped her back a little. She wanted to feel more. To feel him thrust hard inside her. To make her forget that she was ever angry with him.

She let out a squeak when he shoved up inside her and her back scraped along the tree. Spinning their positions around, he brought them to the ground with her in his lap.

"Richard? I . . ."

She bit her lip. What did she want to say? That she was in love with her husband? No, those words needed to stay buried. Her feelings needed to stay buried. Any utterance that she was in love was liable to make him leave sooner than he planned.

He grasped her hips tight and slammed their bodies

together. She bit her lip hard. How easily he made her forget everything but him.

Emma made him forget every intention he had. Made him want to luxuriate in the moment like a sated sunbathing cat whenever she was around. There was nothing better than the pleasure he found inside her body.

He played with her breasts, pressing and massaging them as he sucked one nipple into his mouth, rolling his tongue over the pearled tips. He buried his face between their sweet softness, then squeezed them together so he could lick at both nipples, groaning against them as she rose and fell, riding his cock without any shyness. He lowered his hand between their bodies to rub at her swollen clitoris, stroking and circling it with an unyielding touch.

Her arms wrapped around his head to hold him to her breasts, even though he had no intention of letting up on them. She had the most perfect breasts. He could play with them all day.

He could feel the rapid beat of her heart, or was that his heart pounding in his chest? She peaked then, her sheath flexing around his straining cock. Milking him tight as a fist pumping his rod. A rush of warm cream coated him with her climax and he released his seed in the next thrust, in the next breath. He was sure he shouted out something, but whatever it was it was muffled because he was gently biting at her breasts.

She stilled above him, their hot damp bodies sticking sweetly together. He had no intention of moving. Ever. He wasn't even losing his firmness inside her after spilling his sperm. Testament enough that he couldn't get enough of his wife. Some way, somehow, she'd completely beguiled him.

He wrapped his hands around her back, pressing his fingers along the delicate line of her spine. Her breathing was still ragged, almost frantic. Her damp, hot skin roused his need, damn well nearly held it hostage. Her soft breasts pressed into his cheek. He rolled his face over them.

"We should right ourselves," she said breathlessly.

"I think we should stay here. Like this."

"We couldn't."

She tried to rise from his lap. He refused to let her up and held her hips tight in his grasp. He was not ready to release her. Not ready to go back to arguing about her damn paintings. He just wanted to stay like this. Without a care. He wanted to be alone with her and forget everything else that hung in the balance.

The only sounds to be heard were the crickets that had started to chirp again, the birds that sang above them, and the soothing rustle of leaves in the hot breeze.

"We should indeed. It's just the two of us. No one to interrupt us." He rolled his tongue around her nipple. "I'm clay in your hands, and you don't even know it, do you?"

"You aren't."

Her finger traced little circles over his shoulder. It wasn't difficult to understand what she was getting at. He didn't want to think of anything but the two of them. He wanted nothing more than to forget civilization and spend the day wrapped around his wife in sweet oblivion.

He pressed his lips to hers. His tongue ran along the seam. Her tongue shyly met his. He pulled away to say, "Stay with me, Emma. I need you again."

"Shouldn't we be standing ten feet apart glaring at each other instead of indulging in this base behavior?" Her words were said teasingly.

"I like this base behavior. Your cunt is still milking my cock. You can't honestly want to stop."

"You talk so crudely to me." Her lashes lowered, her cheeks darkened.

He stroked his thumb over her cheek.

"You do look pretty when you're blushing. Say something naughty. Repeat my words for me." He thrust up into her with a groan.

"I can't," she answered.

"Yes, you can."

"It wouldn't be lady-like."

"Just this once. Say cock. Say you like my cock thrusting into your core."

Had he known it was possible for her to turn completely red he'd have suggested she speak ribald words to him long before now.

Emma shook her head and sucked in her bottom lip.

Grasping the back of her neck, he pulled her closer so he could nibble on her kiss-swollen lips. "You'll say it one day. The idea of you uttering wicked words makes me want to fuck you senseless."

He smiled against her mouth when she jerked away at his choice in words.

Lifting her from his lap, he stood her in front of his face. He wanted to taste her. To see that part of herself she usually kept hidden. Finding the ties on her pantalets, he pulled them down her legs.

She grasped his hand before he could lift her calf free of the material on one side.

"What are you about?" she asked.

"I'm of a mind to taste you." He sucked and licked her thigh in demonstration for what he planned to do.

When her pantalets fell to the ground, he stared at the golden thatch of hair between her thighs. It was a few shades darker than the curls about her face, but still blonde. Tasting a woman was something he'd never done before. Never wanted to do. Everything was different with his wife.

He placed a kiss against the short coarse hair.

"You can't do that." She tried to yank up the damp material that had fallen around one of her ankles.

Grasping her buttocks, he pulled her closer. With his free hand, he stroked the lips at her core, separating them with his thumb before parting the petals of her sex. The folds were pink like a tea rose in bloom.

"Richard, stop."

Instead of explaining what he planned to do, he gave her a last warning before he stuck his tongue between the folds. "Put your hands on the tree for support."

"Whatever for?"

Sucking one lip of her sex into his mouth, then the next, he dipped his tongue down through the saturated folds until he found the swollen nub of her clitoris.

Her hands slapped hard against the tree behind his back. Her body swayed a little closer. "Oh, goodness gracious."

Then she gave over to him. Her legs spread marginally, allowing him to press his face into her cunny harder. He stuck his tongue inside her sheath and fucked her that way for a few strokes before sucking at her clitoris again.

"I can't hold myself up."

With a growl, he let her go long enough to stand away from the tree and tumble her down onto a soft patch of grass. He didn't like interruptions. Not at all. He wanted to taste and fuck her to his heart's content. Until neither of them could walk.

He pushed her legs apart with his shoulders and licked at her core. Her thighs squeezed around his head, her pelvis thrust against his mouth, then she was coming.

Before she could stop convulsing from the pleasure he gave her, he climbed atop her body and shoved his cock deep into her sheath, right up to the cods.

Bracing himself on his elbows, he watched Emma's face. She made eye contact with him and they stared at each other while his pace increased. His crisis was coming on fast. When his seed pumped out of him for a second time, he traced the seam of her lips with his tongue until he was finally sated. Her legs still clung tight around his hips.

The fact that she didn't want to get up made him grin.

"And what is it you plan on doing for the remainder of the afternoon, wife?"

She grinned up at him. "You."

# Chapter 19

*Here I sit, penning another letter. Time changes us all, but some habits cannot be broken.*

Grace sat to Mr. Lioni's right when dinner was served. She was positively glowing. Emma had kept her word that she'd not tell a soul. She hadn't even mentioned a word to her husband this afternoon when they'd talked after he'd done such wicked things to her. And outside where anyone could have seen them!

Oh, dear, that thought had her blushing. She reached for her glass of water and took a healthy gulp, hoping it would calm her flush. Richard stared knowingly at her. His fingers steepled in front of his mouth so she couldn't see the smirk he doubtlessly sported.

Her whole body ached, but she wanted to hide in her room with him for at least a few days. To do every wicked thing running through her mind. To even taste him as he had tasted her.

She arched her brows at him and looked down to her plate to cut off a piece of fish. She couldn't focus on dinner if she stared at him all evening.

When was Grace planning to say something? That would provide a wonderful distraction.

Everyone seemed unusually quiet at the table. Abby was absently pushing her food around on her plate. Mr. Lioni was sliding sly glances at Grace as though the rest in attendance couldn't see them acting like infatuated lovers. Richard was sipping at his wine, watching her over the rim as he swirled around the contents in his glass. He'd finished eating some time ago. She supposed he'd worked up a healthy appetite after being engaged in excessive sport all afternoon.

Emma cleared her throat and turned to Abby to break the spell her husband held over her. "How did you spend your afternoon?"

"Sent off my letter." Abby pushed around a green bean on her plate. "My friend wants me to stay with her for a while. She's due to have her first baby any day now. She's asked me to be there for the delivery."

"That's not something unmarried women usually tend to, Abby," Grace said.

"True," Abby continued, "but she's very alone out in Northumberland."

"You plan to travel there on your own?" Emma asked incredulously.

Her sister couldn't be serious. Abby had never traveled alone. She'd never been separated from her elder sisters. What would they do without her around? What of all their plans to find Abby a husband?

"You can't leave yet, Abby," Grace said. "You have to be here for the wedding."

"Wedding?" Abby's head snapped up and she stared at Grace. At least Abby had stopped playing with her food. "What wedding?"

Richard stared at Mr. Lioni with a frown, but Mr. Lioni only had eyes for Grace.

"We're to be wed once the banns are read." Grace positively beamed as she looked to her fiancé. "We planned to make a formal announcement over refreshments in the drawing room."

Mr. Lioni leaned close to Grace and kissed her cheek.

Emma sighed. What would it be like to be so in love that you displayed it to the world around you? She looked back to her husband. He was watching Mr. Lioni, one brow quirked in question. He put his wine on the table and crossed his arms over his chest as he leaned back in the chair.

"You're getting married?" Abby frowned, not looking the least bit thrilled with the news. "You should have told me, Grace! I've already sent my post off, telling my friend I'd be on the road in less than a week."

"Can't you send another letter explaining the situation? I can't have my wedding without you here, Abby."

Abby pushed her plate away from her and tossed her napkin on the table. "It's too late. If I don't leave by the end of the week, I'll not make it in time for the child."

"You mean baby," Emma corrected.

"Yes." Abby patted her lips with her napkin and didn't meet her sisters' eyes. "Of course."

Emma didn't like this situation in the least. Why was Abby so adamant about leaving them? She'd been content for so many years traveling between her sisters' homes, back and forth from London to the country.

Grace looked near ready to cry.

Before that happened, Emma said, "It's fine, Grace. I'll stand in for both of us. You'll have so much excitement around you that you'll not notice Abby's absence."

Then she shot her youngest sister a look full of upset. How dare Abby take this moment of happiness away from Grace. Couldn't Abby be happy for someone else at least once in her life? Never had she acted more the spoiled child than she did now.

"I believe dinner has concluded," Richard said as he stood from the table.

He came around to Emma's side and leaned close to her ear, whispering, "I will give you a moment with your sisters. I'll see you in your room later."

Of course he'd not kiss her with everyone in the room. Their relationship wasn't one of love, but one out of the necessity to create an heir.

"Ladies," Richard announced, "I bid you a good night."

He must have indicated to Mr. Lioni that the sisters needed some time alone, because the other man pushed out his chair and stood from the table, bidding first Grace a good evening, then her and Abby.

As soon as the door closed behind the men, Emma turned to Abby and asked, "How is it you decided on this before mentioning anything to either of us?"

"I wasn't aware I needed your permission." Abby tossed her napkin on the table.

"You don't." Grace stood and came around to their side of the table. She pulled out the chair next to Abby and sat down. "But didn't you take a moment to think that this was a monumental decision? Or that you might want the support and opinions of your sisters?"

"The reason I didn't tell you before I sent the letter was because I didn't want you to persuade me to stay." Abby looked down and stared at her entwined fingers. Unwilling to meet either of their eyes, it seemed.

Placing her elbow on the table, Grace put her cheek in her palm and stared at their youngest sister with something akin to hurt. Emma couldn't blame Grace. She also felt hurt by her sister's sudden desire to leave them behind.

"I didn't intend," Abby said in a rush, "to miss your upcoming nuptials. After such a short acquaintance, the last think I expected was for you to marry so . . . hastily."

"I didn't plan for everything to happen so fast, either." Grace took one of Abby's hands in her own. "Is there some other reason you want to escape us so suddenly?"

"You'd catch me out rather quickly if I dared to lie. With your husband home, Emma, you'll have less time for me . . ." Abby sat back in her chair and looked from Grace to Emma. "Less time for both of us. I think our summer of leisure was over the moment Richard came home. Grace, I'm sorry about my rotten timing. I just think it's time I struck out on my own. I feel so trapped here. Like I'm missing something that I'll regret later. I need to do this."

"I empathize with that feeling," Emma said in complete understanding. It still wasn't right for her sister to leave them like this. "Do you need to leave by week's end?"

Abby nodded yes. "That doesn't mean I can't visit you later on. It's not as though we'll never see each other again. I need to do this—for myself. To see what the world has to offer without the support of my sisters along the way. Some things we have to do for ourselves."

Grace wiped tears from her eyes. "I'll miss you dreadfully. I think I miss you already." Grace wrapped her arms around their baby sister and gave her a fierce hug.

"Oh, do stop crying," Abby complained. "You'll make me follow suit."

"It serves you right, Abby, for springing this on us so suddenly." Emma wrapped her arms around both her sisters and gave them the tightest squeeze she could muster. "Come along, we'll spend the evening together, and help you make a list of all the things you'll need for your trip." Emma wiped at her damp eyes and led their entourage upstairs.

"I insist you take my best footman with you, Abby," Grace said, "You'll need someone with you should you get robbed."

"You make it sound so dangerous," Abby teased with a laugh.

"It's liable to be. You'll be near the Scottish border. Who's to say what types of ruffians are out that way," Emma said.

Abby smiled. "I'm not so worried."

Emma sat on the edge of her bed in complete dishabille. Seemed senseless at this point to play at false modesty when her husband had seen her in every way without her clothes on. The clock hadn't even chimed in at half nine when the door opened. She had suspected he would come early.

"To what do I owe to your lack of timidity?"

Richard wore trousers. He had no shirt on. She had to look at the door frame beside his bared arm so she wasn't caught studying his physique. She really should still be mad at him. Too many things had changed in her life today. And in her sisters' lives. Would things ever change for the better between her and Richard?

"Our foray in the parlor . . . the tour of my painting room . . . our swim in the pond. Other things we did at the pond. Need I go on?" Motioning with her hand, she indicated his half-dressed form. "Were you busy this evening?" She hadn't seen him after supper.

"Dante and I wanted to see if Waverly was still in residence at his estate. We made some inquiries."

"I would think after yesterday that he'd stay away permanently. Are you worried he'll come back?"

"There's that too-trusting nature of yours again." Richard shook his head in disapproval. "Waverly's bound to make another appearance. I'm sorry you and your sisters ever had to be in his company."

"The only thing I'm surprised about was his ability to trick us into thinking him a friend."

Emma had never made such a bad judgment of someone before.

"He's clever when he needs to be. It would have been no hardship to fool everyone around him. For short bursts of time, at any rate."

Richard walked toward her, like a lion tracking a gazelle separated from the herd. For some reason she knew it was imperative to hold her ground, sure and steady, though inside she wanted to dash across the room and out of his reach. She knew what he was about, what he planned to do. Seduce her into not thinking clearly.

She desperately wanted to know what Richard's intentions were for their future. If a baby did not grow in her belly from their unions, would he leave? If she wasn't pregnant, would they still petition for a divorce? Did she have it in her to make such a permanent break from Richard? She wasn't sure she was strong enough to do that. Strong enough to hold herself together when he left again.

What a foolish woman she was. She was letting her heart rule her better judgment. This could only end badly for her. She didn't trust the feelings running rampant in her mind. They were all conflicting and confusing.

So focused was she on her own thoughts, she didn't realize how close Richard was until he dropped to his knees between her thighs. There was nothing lascivious, nothing mischievous about his intentions if his calm presence was anything to go by.

Wrapping his arms around her waist, he did nothing

more than put his head in her lap and sigh. She didn't know how to handle her husband. He was usually more playful and teasing, and when he wasn't those things, he was demanding and far too domineering. Never did he act as though he needed her for any sort of compassionate embrace. Setting her hands on his shoulders, she rubbed them soothingly, venturing higher to run her fingers through his dark hair and massage his scalp.

"That feels good, Emma." His voice was muffled since he spoke into her lap.

"Is there something I can do for you?"

"This. I like this. No one has ever let me hold them for a while. Not that I've ever wanted to hold just anyone."

He pulled her in tighter to his body, putting her so close to the edge of the mattress that she'd have fallen to the floor had Richard not been holding her in place. She liked to be needed by her husband. Liked that she could simply hold him if he needed that kind of comfort from her. He'd never needed her in any capacity before this. Not as a true wife, a lover, or a friend. He'd never seemed to need her—really need her—before now. Before tonight.

Then he pulled her from the bed to sit astride his thighs. Her hands still threaded lightly through his hair, allowing her to keep her husband close.

What a horrible place she had put herself in. She was irrevocably in love with her husband. It would tear her apart from the inside out when they parted ways.

Richard's dark eyes focused on her, their faces inches apart. He didn't apologize for his actions or the lust radiating from his body. Tension bunched the muscles of his thighs and arms as he held her.

She should ask him about their future. Ask him about his plans. Would he tell her he still didn't know? His answer was likely to wrench at her heart. She would wait. Wait to see if she was pregnant.

"I must confess," she said. "I always thought that our intimacies would never change from our first night together."

"Who led you to believe such a lie?"

"It's what I always believed." She dropped her gaze to his chest, and stared at the dark coarse hair, and traced her fingers through it.

"You must have thought me a veritable fiend. Rutting for my own pleasure, without a care for yours."

"I don't think you a monster, Richard." She circled her finger around his nipple; it was so tiny compared to hers. He closed his eyes, hands tightening around her back. "Simply a man with desires."

"I was angry the day we were married. I knew I'd hurt you, but didn't know how to comfort you."

"Angry because you had to marry me?" she ventured.

He shook his head. "With my father. You were too young. I felt like a monster having to take your innocence."

"The only parent to blame was my father. He insisted we marry because he thought he'd be dead before the year was out. He didn't want me to go into another year of mourning after my mother's death. I think he was afraid you'd find another woman to marry in London."

His fingers were drawing lazy patterns on her bare hip, under her shirt. "We always did have that in common. Crazy fathers."

"Your father wasn't so bad. He was very kind to me over the years." Emma ran her fingers through the hair between his pectorals. It was too tempting to ignore any longer.

Hands moving from her hips, Richard brushed the sides of her unbound breasts. His hands roamed over the back of her shoulder blades, then higher till his hands rested on her scalp. His fingers tangled through her hair.

Her lips parted to ask him something, anything to break the silence. He pulled her head closer to his. The slide of his tongue against hers set her body afire. She liked kissing her husband; she liked doing things a countess probably ought not do. Instead of worrying, she hesitantly explored his tongue with her own. The taste of whiskey was faint in his mouth.

She would have kept exploring him like this if he hadn't pushed his groin up into hers. She tried to scramble off his lap at the rough scratch of his trousers against her very naked womanhood.

"Stay with me like this," he whispered between heated kisses. "Let me make love to you this way. Right here. Right now. Clothes on, lights burning bright, everything as it is. Just let me have everything of you tonight."

She settled back into his lap with the soothing, pleading tone in his voice. Biting her lip, she looked him in the eye. His gaze was expectant. As though he couldn't bear for her to reject this small concession.

If she did this, she knew without a doubt that there would be no turning back to the proper marriage she'd always envisioned. This would change things between them. Not that the games they'd played at yesterday and this afternoon hadn't put her on this path to begin with. But something about this seemed different.

"Only if you kiss me like that again. I love when you kiss me that way."

When he smiled back at her, all the tired lines around his eyes smoothed out. "I will do so much more if you'll trust me. Permit me leave to pleasure you in all the ways I can think of." He demonstrated his desire by running his hands up the sides of her thighs, slipping them around to grab her bare buttocks. "No pantalets. I like this wild side I've brought out in you."

She could do no more than blush at the praise. His smile brightened, and he pulled her in tight to his hardened groin.

"Do you feel how badly I need you?"

Eyes wide, she clutched at his arms, which flexed strong and masculine beneath her hands. She wanted to stroke the corded strength, shade it in charcoals on a piece of paper. Run her fingers along each and every line until it was memorized.

She couldn't continue on this path with her husband. It was dangerous. For her. He was slowly destroying her from the inside out. Meddling with her heart for his own purpose.

"Tell me what you want of me, Richard."

"Nothing more than to give us both pleasure."

Of course that was all he wanted. He didn't want her heart, even though she'd torn hers out of her chest and handed it to him still pumping and full of life. She might as well throw it down in the dirt for all he cared.

She closed her eyes. She could play the same game he played. She could enjoy the newfound intimacy they shared.

"Will you pleasure me in kisses?" She wanted to ask for explicit details, but her tongue stuck to the roof of her mouth, refusing to give voice to the questions she had.

"Just trust me. Can you do that?"

"I did this afternoon. I have so previously. I could do no less now."

As though he couldn't help himself, his hands kneaded into her backside, fingers inching closer to her wet core.

She was sure she'd remained drenched for him the whole of the day. His finger slid along her slit.

"God, Emma. I love that you're always ready for me. I've been negligent where you're concerned. If there is one thing I can promise it's that my inattention stops now."

That was a tall promise to make.

And she didn't believe him for one second.

Pulling his hands away from her core, he brought them around to release the buttons on his trousers. He fiddled with his smalls till she felt the smooth warm flesh of his cock resting against her lower stomach. She wanted him inside her body. She craved him.

He pulled her rear in closer with one hand. The other hand spread her nether lips over the base of his cock.

"What are you doing?"

"Relieving some of the pressure. How does that feel?"

"Different," she replied without hesitation. Though she was too embarrassed to elaborate—to tell him that she wished him to stand so she could learn his body by sight, by touch.

"Remove your nightshirt, darling."

Looking toward the windows, she saw the curtains were pulled away from the glass to reveal an orange-and-red-toned evening sky. The sun was mere minutes from fully setting, and she was baring herself to her husband without a care. She liked this new Emma she'd grown into.

"I've been craving another sight of you since we arrived back at the manor." He rocked her body along his, the dampness at her core slicking over the firm ridge wedged between the lips of her sex. So thick and so demanding it nearly had her mouth watering to taste it. To taste him.

"It's only been a few hours since we were at the pond." It felt good doing this. Different, but the way she was stretched out over him, the way her nub was stimulated, had her breath coming faster.

"Too long . . . Remove your night rail." He helped her by hitching it over her waist.

Gathering up the linen of her nightclothes, she pulled it over her head and set it aside without delay. What did he think as he inspected her body? Did he like what he saw? Afraid to see the answer in his eyes, she focused on his chest again, feeling the muscle as she moved her hands higher so she could mold them around his shoulders and biceps.

"What are you thinking so hard about?" she asked.

At his sharp intake of breath, her eyes snapped up to his. He no longer stared at her face but studied her breasts.

"You are beautiful, Emma."

He lifted one of her breasts in his hand and ran his knuckles over the areola and nipple. It immediately formed into a hard point. She was afraid to look down and watch his ministrations. Afraid of how her body reacted to his touch.

"Is it sensitive when I touch you here?"

She nodded. So sensitive, she sometimes didn't know if she liked his touch or not. The tingly, anxious feeling skittering across her flesh told her just how pleasurable it was.

"You're so damned soft I can't stop touching you here. I'm going to suck on these pretty titties. Suck them till you're writhing against me."

At her gasp, he picked her up by the waist and sheathed himself within her body. He sucked the tip of her breast deep into his mouth, and held her hips inert as he rotated in slow sensuous circles against her pelvis. Releasing her breast, he swore crudely, then heaved upward.

"Bloody hell, I could stay here for an eternity."

He held her shoulders tight, pulling her in close as he jerked up into her body. He only stroked up into her for a few blissful thrusts, then he lifted her from his body and set her on the edge of the bed again.

He stood before her, his privates exposed where he'd undone his trousers, and in plain sight. She swallowed. She wanted nothing more than to lick that part of him.

"Don't seem so shocked."

Scooting up the bed, she looked for the nearest pillow to toss at him. She wasn't quick enough to grab one before Richard clasped his hand around her ankle, slowly pulling her back down the bed and closer to him.

He kicked off his trousers, then knelt on the bed, his manhood sticking out hard from his body. What a curious thing it was. She watched it as it bobbed all on its own.

Breath hitched, she looked back up and met her husband's gaze.

"When you look at me like that, it makes me harder. Do you want to touch me, Emma?" He wrapped his hand around himself, pulled the skin fully from the tip of his instrument to reveal a smooth rounded head.

Good Lord. She'd never seen it in such clear detail before. Never been given the opportunity. Now that the occasion was here, she didn't know quite how to handle it.

Walking to her across the bed on his knees, he stroked his hand over the straining length.

"Touch me, Emma."

She shook her head no. How could she do that? What would he think of her if she acted so forward? He didn't ease up on the grip he had on his cock.

He lowered his head and curled his tongue around

her nipple, which immediately firmed at his cool wet touch. "I want to see you do wicked things to me . . . to yourself."

"Isn't this the reason men have mistresses?"

As soon as the words were out she wanted to snatch them back.

Richard lifted his head from her tender breast. "Never suggest such a thing again. I might not have remained pure during the course of our marriage, but I never understood the need to shower any woman with riches and affection."

She pressed her lips together, refusing to form any sort of rebuttal. Of course he didn't need to shower a woman with anything.

Her expression must have shown her dissatisfaction, for he quickly amended, "No woman other than one's wife, that is."

"How very practical of you," she said drolly.

"I think most might think me more frugal than practical, dear wife."

"Have you never kept a mistress?" She sucked in her bottom lip. Did she really want to know the truth? Would he even give her the truth? "When I saw you in London, with that woman . . . I thought that was just how you spent your evenings."

It made her sound jealous. And she was jealous of the other woman. It was a question pulled from deep within her heart. She needed to know, even if she didn't like the answer she received. What would he make of it? Would he even give her an honest answer?

"No mistress," he said simply.

She was thinking too hard. Richard didn't want her thinking at all. He supposed he should be thankful that she'd welcomed him back into her bed. They still needed to discuss the procuring of her art, but that could be done later. Much later.

She had a lot of questions she wanted answered. He understood that. And tried to be patient, even though he was hard as a damn poker again. Instead of continuing their conversation, he lowered his mouth to her breast and suckled the soft flesh into his mouth. Her hand came around and clasped his head.

His tongue curled around the pert, firm tip and sucked deeper. That had her back arching off the bed. Rolling her to her side, he hitched her leg over his hip so he could rub his cock between her slick folds, sliding it over her nub. God, he wanted inside her again. Wanted her to suck his cock so he could watch himself fuck her throat. Wanted to fuck her pretty titties, too. Good God, what had come over him?

It was too soon to ask for that. She'd probably faint dead away if he suggested such things.

Her fingers were tight in his hair, her thigh tight around his hip. What was it about her that made him act like a horny, insatiable youth? Rolling her to her back, he spread her thighs wide, reared back, and entered her tight sheath. He inched in slowly, loving the feel of her gripping and pulling him in with the flexing muscles of her core.

He looked at her glassy-eyed expression as he seated himself up to his cods. He kissed her nose, her forehead, her cheeks, and finally her mouth. Rotating at her core, making sure the lips of her sex spread farther open with the movement, he pressed his body tight against hers to stimulate her clitoris. His hands were tangled with hers above her head. He didn't want to let go. It offered some strange intimacy, handholding during their lovemaking.

When had it become more than intercourse with his

wife? And he was calling it lovemaking now? But his wife was different from any other woman he'd had. He was glad for that. Glad that coming home to his wife had made him feel like a whole man again. He'd been a monster for far too long.

Quite possibly, he was in love with his wife. That was something he would have to explore another time. Before he could make an ass of himself and utter any of those condemning words, he lowered his mouth to hers. Their tongues explored, twisted, and melded as he pounded into her body with renewed enthusiasm.

Emma's breath mingled with his. His with hers. Her ankles were locked about his backside, and she arched against him. She broke from their kiss to let out a moan. Her sweet breasts squished between them. Their bodies were slick from their exertions, and the smell of sex was like an aphrodisiac perfuming the air.

Shaking off the hold he had on her hands, she pressed her fingers into his shoulders and held onto him tightly. Her pelvis thrust up with his every downward stroke. She screamed her release, her fingers biting into his flesh to keep him from going anywhere. Hell, he wasn't going anywhere. Moving up on his knees, he grasped her hips and pounded into her body until he finally went over the edge with her. He jerked above her till the last drop of semen pumped out of his body.

He held her body arched off the bed, pressed his lips to her slick, salty skin, and licked a line all the way up her abdomen, between her ribs, stopping between her breasts. She was breathing heavily, her chest rising and falling fast. No faster than his, he realized. Goddamn, he didn't want to move. Didn't want to leave her body.

He managed not to collapse atop her and had enough sense to get them both under the sheets before they fell asleep. Pulling her up against his body, he threw an arm over her and held on to one of her breasts. His cock was half stiff where it pressed into her buttocks and lower back. He'd make love to her again later. Right now her breathing had petered off to a steady even rhythm.

He'd tired his wife out. The thought made his lips lift in a grin.

This silence was nice. He just wished he could stop thinking altogether and sleep next to her. What was this attraction he had to her? Did he plan to make her more permanent in his life? To give their marriage a real chance?

The more he thought about it, the more he wanted it. This was definitely a surprising outcome to his trip to the country.

There would be no divorce. He'd not give her up so she could find another man to spend her life with. He'd be the only damn man in her life once he scared the duke off for good and found the damn buyer of her paintings.

She'd have to get used to him being around. Or perhaps he could court her, as he'd never really done when they were young. Shower her with attention. Make her forget about ever wanting a divorce. He could be charming when he wanted to. And he did want to be just that. For her, anyway.

And once she was pregnant, there would be no escaping their marriage. Not for either of them.

Emma pressed back into his body, her heat and soft curves a welcome intrusion to his thoughts. This was how they were meant to spend their nights. He didn't plan to sleep outside her bed again.

Smoothing back the curls from her forehead, he kissed her temple. She didn't stir, so he didn't pester her anymore despite the erection straining between her back and his stomach. A few hours' sleep should be sufficient rest for her. Then he'd start their lovemaking all over again.

# Chapter 20

*If ever our paths cross again, what will you make of me?*

"I wonder if I should leave ahead of you for London? Your sister's plans have thrown a wrench in ours."

Emma looked up from the sketch of Abby she'd been filling out. Her youngest sister had sat for her for an hour earlier in the day. Enough time for her to get down a rough outline so she could paint it later.

Richard had been reading a paper at his desk as she concentrated on her work.

"You're so anxious to leave?"

The taste of bitter disappointment bled into her words. Her reaction had been very telling of how she felt about her husband deserting her. Did he know he owned her body and soul? That the slightest change in their arrangement—no matter how temporary—would destroy her? What a fool she was for allowing this attraction to bloom into something more for her.

He grinned like a cat that had caught and swallowed the canary on its first swipe. Yes, he knew she didn't want him to leave her. Hadn't everything she'd done and revealed over the weeks proven that?

He didn't say anything for some minutes. Then he put down his paper, leaned back in his chair, and scrutinized her.

There was only the two of them in the library this afternoon. Grace had cried off with a headache, and Mr. Lioni was nowhere to be found. Emma was inclined to believe the two were together. Abby was in her room packing. There was no one to interrupt them, yet they were ten feet apart from each other.

"I didn't mean it as though I were abandoning you." Richard stood, straightening his vest as he walked over to her and sat beside her on the sofa. "We have an agreement that will take us to the end of September."

Ah, yes. The agreement.

Too many weeks to become further entangled in her feelings with a man who had no intention of staying with her. Who had no intentions of falling so stupidly in love with her as she had with him. A very small part of her had hoped he might change his mind. That he would stay on with her for the rest of their days. What a foolish dreamer she was.

She pursed her lips as she wrapped her charcoals in a cloth. She could not concentrate on her drawing with her husband sitting so close to her.

"You're having fun at me. It's not kind."

"But you're rather adorable when you're piqued."

Richard rubbed the back of his knuckle over the gathered pleats on the short sleeve of her day dress.

She shivered with the contact. Her eyes closed briefly as she felt the warmth of him seeping through the fine material. What would happen if she revealed the depth of her feelings? Would he leave sooner? Would he stay on longer to humor her? Could he possibly return those feelings?

"It's a great likeness of Abby," he said. "Will you show her?"

Wiping her hands on her apron she'd donned to protect her dress, she leaned forward to set the sketchpad and charcoals down on the table. "Not till it's painted. And you've changed the topic."

"I merely redirected it."

He took her hand in his, turning it over to study the dark stains from the charcoal.

"You seem flushed, Emma. Should I call for lemonade?"

She pulled her hand away and wiped it on her apron. So he knew what he did to her . . . how he made her feel whenever he touched her. Instead of giving him the satisfaction of an answer, she glared at him. The second he had taken a seat so close to her, she knew what he was about. What he wanted.

Damn her for wanting it, too.

"When we're in Town, we should visit the music hall. Maybe do some shopping," he said absently. As though going about Town with her was an everyday occurrence. "I have invitations to a few private dinner parties I've yet to accept. Would that please you, Emma?"

There was a great buzzing in her head. She swore her heart swelled so much in her chest that it would burst right through her breast. This reaction shouldn't take her by surprise. He didn't want to divorce her. He wanted to keep her happy long enough to get her pregnant—that much was obvious.

"That would be nice," she finally muttered. More than nice, to be in his company for a few nights. Her eyes grew misty at the thought of him caring enough to show her around Town.

To distract him from that embarrassing fact, she mustered as much calm as she could and untied the apron she wore. She lifted it over her head. Taking her time to fold the apron, she set it on the chair beside her.

When she turned back to her husband, his right eyebrow was raised.

Words clogged in her throat with the emotion welling up in her. He wasn't going to abandon her once they were in London.

She leaned in close and kissed him full on the mouth. It was a clumsy attempt and she pulled back just as quickly as she'd collided with his lips, but Richard's hand was strong and firm on her back to keep her from moving too far away.

Leaning forward again, she took her time in meeting his lips. She splayed her hands over both sides of his smooth face, lingering with her lips over his, and closed her eyes. Pecking softly at first, then growing bolder by tasting first the top lip, then the lower with her own parted mouth. This was what she would miss most when he left. Kissing him. She loved everything about kissing him.

He broke away. "I see that you approve wholeheartedly of the plan."

He reached around to lift her over his lap, one leg on either side of his thighs, her skirts fanned around them. His hands found their way beneath all the silk and lace, landing on her cotton-covered thigh.

"I should tease you more often if it gets you on my lap so easily. You're a darling creature."

One of his hands reached under her skirts and around to her bottom. He squeezed her left buttock before sliding his hand forward, closer to the vee of her body.

"The door isn't locked," she said. But she made no move to get off his lap. She really wanted to continue.

So much so that she tilted back so his hand was closer to where she wanted him to rub her.

"We're decently clothed."

She gave a short laugh. They wouldn't be decently clothed for much longer.

His fingers moved back and forth over the spot she needed touched between her thighs. There was no need to rouse her passions; they were already blazing inside her, the evidence of that wetting his fingers through the material of her pantalets.

What a wicked man her husband was.

Bearing down on his hand harder, she silently demanded more from him. Truly vixenish behavior, if she did say so herself. "You've accomplished what you set out to do. You've scandalized me."

"Hardly, Emma. You still hold back."

She sat down on his hand, stopping the sweet caress that was driving her to distraction. She ran her forefinger over his parted mouth. Her tongue darted out to wet her upper lip. She wanted to taste him.

His tongue shot out to taste, then suck her finger into his mouth.

"You make me want to be very wicked, Richard. Make me want to do and say such naughty things."

His hand moved closer to its goal even though she was crushing his hand. He still managed to slip his finger through the slit of her drawers and into her pulsing sheath.

His head dropped back to the sofa, his eyes closed on a groan. "Always so damn wet. I want to suck all the cream from you and then fuck you senseless."

He pressed his finger deeper inside her. Pulling one of his hands out from under her skirts, he massaged and kneaded her breast.

"No boning in your stays today." He squeezed a little

tighter around her breast since there was less to impede his searching hand.

Instead of the soreness she'd felt on waking this morning, her breasts felt swollen with need.

"I was tender from everything we did last night."

She couldn't say aloud that her breasts were suffering so sweetly from his overfondling. Was such a thing even possible? It must be. Not that fondling was the only thing he'd done to them, and to the rest of her.

"I'll be gentler." He kissed the exposed part of her bosom. "I'm going to unbutton your bodice. I want to see more. Need to."

Emma looked over the edge of the rose-chintz sofa to the door. It was closed, but did have a habit of creaking whenever it was opened. Still, she wasn't sure she could be so scandalous as to allow him to do such a thing, in the middle of the day and in so public a room.

She couldn't look at her husband as his face was pressed into her breasts. "It seems risky."

His teeth grazed the flesh before he pulled away. "But you want to."

She looked back down into his intense gaze. His pupils were dilated from his rising passions. Aside from his firm manhood pressing into her, she could tell how badly he needed her by the stark longing reflected in his deep brown eyes.

Lowering her mouth to his, she whispered, "Yes." Then she angled her mouth to take possession of his lips and tongue. How she loved his lips, his mouth, his tongue, his taste.

There was no other word she could use to describe what she was doing except devouring, consuming his very essence. She wasn't afraid to taste from him as he did of her.

The hidden eyelets down the front of her bodice were

loosened quickly. The warmth of Richard's hands seeped through her cotton corset and chemise when he wrapped them around her rib cage. His hands brushed the undersides of her breasts. Tantalizing. Teasing. A promise of what was to come.

She placed her hands over his and moved them higher. She moaned into his mouth when his hands finally covered her breasts and squeezed them closer together. She wanted to be touched the same way he had touched her last night. She ached for his touch.

Would she ache for it when he left? She shut her thoughts down, refusing to think about that. Not till the time came.

He cut off their kiss with a primitive growl. "You tempt me beyond reason, woman."

"I don't know what's come over me."

Which was the complete truth.

It definitely wasn't like her to climb atop her husband and grind the center of their bodies together. The dew from her body was intensifying with every movement against the iron-hard part of him she wanted lodged deep inside her body.

Never in her wildest dreams did she expect to find this passion, this fervor of the flesh.

"You're my very own woodland nymph. All beautiful and glowing with need as you rub off on me. I want to take you." Richard's face nuzzled into the swell of her bosom where he'd pulled down the front of her chemise. "God, let me have you, Emma. I'll not survive the day with this cockstand. It's not going to go away unless I come."

"I want to, but what if—"

"They'll turn right back around." He was already releasing the buttons on his trousers. "We'll look as if we're embracing, nothing more."

Taking a deep breath, she stared into his eyes. When he moved his hands away, indicating his trousers were undone, Emma reached beneath her skirts and wrapped her hand around the root of his member. The skin was smooth and soft, a contrast with the firmness of his penis. She gave it a light squeeze. Richard drove into her hold with a groan.

Her fingers curled around the heavy sac beneath his rod. She rolled the marbles in her palm, then the skin tightened up, and he thrust into the great volume of her skirts. She ran her hand up his length and stopped at the head. The slit at the top was wet with his own fluids. She drew circles over that part of him, spreading his juices.

"Need you now, Emma." There was desperation infused in his hoarse voice.

Spreading the slit in her drawers, she slid the smooth tip of his instrument through her feminine fluids. She impaled herself on his great steely length easily. They were both motionless once he was up to the hilt in her. She felt a heavy pulse between her legs. A little heartbeat throbbing at her core. He flexed his cock within her.

She contracted her inside muscles around him, as though she were squeezing his manhood with her hands. It felt so good to have him in her body.

The room was quiet around them, their breaths both ragged even though neither of them moved.

"Stretch your back, love. Enough to lift your breasts above the corset."

She did as he asked, looking down at what was revealed in doing so. The tips of her breasts were firm and a little redder than normal. A rather animalistic—dare she say, feral—gleam came into his eyes as he stared at her.

How wanton she must look, scandalously undressed

and in complete disarray. Did she look thoroughly seduced to her husband? She imagined she did. It made her feel empowered somehow. On top of the world in the moment. Or at least on top of her husband.

She needed more, wanted to feel more, and pressed one breast to his mouth so he'd suckle it in deep. He did not disappoint, though he was gentler than usual. He didn't nibble down and graze his teeth against that most tender part of her. He used only his tongue and lips as he played with the sensitive flesh.

He pushed his thumb against her nub and rubbed against it with each downward stroke of her pelvis atop his. Their rhythm was slow and easy, as though they could indulge all afternoon.

Her fingers curled around the edge of the sofa, and she threw her head back so her breasts could be licked and sucked by her husband with greater ease.

"So damn beautiful," he murmured.

Wrapping her arms around his head, she held him tight to her heart as he laved at her exposed flesh. This was as close to her heart as she could allow him. She pinched her eyes shut and concentrated on her husband. A lone tear had escaped, but would dry long before Richard ever saw the physical manifestation of the emotional distress he caused her.

His hands clasped her hips tighter as he increased their pace. She met him eagerly. Thrust for thrust, shove for shove.

Finally he let her set the final pace. His hands tangled in her loose hair and pulled her face close to his. They stared at each other in a silent moment, their bodies still heaving together, their mouths open to take in deeper breaths, and she thought for a moment she saw the same feelings she harbored lurking beneath his gaze. Could he feel the same as she? Did he have any love for her?

He shut his eyes before she could decipher the emotion she had seen. He pulled her that final fraction closer. Kissing each other to muffle their cries of passion, they both came in a deluge of ecstasy.

She slumped atop him. Unwilling to move even though they should right themselves. She held her arms tight around his head and shoulders. His hand smoothed over her back, in a soothing, ceaseless caress.

Dare she hope he felt the same things she felt? Dare she imagine a life with him always and forever?

She was oversentimental because of the moment of passion they'd just shared. She closed her eyes and held him tighter. Afraid that if she let him go now, the moment would forever be gone. Their future forever gone.

He said nothing in the aftermath of their lovemaking. Didn't ask her to move even after their breathing had evened out.

He just kept at his touch along her spine. Up and down, up and down, until she swore she could fall asleep in his arms. It was a false security.

In two days' time they'd travel to London.

She'd have her menses shortly thereafter and she'd know if he was going to leave her. There would be no passionate embraces during that time. No scandalous rendezvous in the parlor.

He would either wait patiently . . . or fulfill his lusty needs elsewhere. It hadn't escaped her notice that he was a man with daily needs. If he found the arms of another, she'd not accept him back into her bed, or back into her heart. She'd take the money in her trust and leave for good.

# Chapter 21

*It has taken an age for my confidence to grow. I don't think I could bear it if you came home now.*

"What are we going to do without you?" Grace asked Abby as they hugged.

It was hard for Emma to watch her baby sister leave them. To strike out on her own. But this was obviously something their sister needed to do.

Emma's hands tightened around her shawl. The train was scheduled to leave in ten minutes. It was too soon.

"You have to promise to write weekly." Emma pointed her finger in reproach.

It would be strange without Abby's company.

Abby rolled her eyes. "Stop fussing. You are only going to make me cry more."

"Well," Grace said, "it serves you right. Leaving us without any warning. I still say you shouldn't be staying on with this friend. It's not right. If word were to get back to London of what you were doing, your suitors might drop off."

"What suitors? No one cares about me. I'm nothing

but a poor relation to two of England's wealthiest women."

"Aside from the money you will come into on your twenty-fifth birthday, you know we've set aside money for you to settle on a decent marriage," Emma said.

What else was Emma supposed to do with the money she'd saved from her paintings? She received more pin money than she knew what to do with; add to that the small fortune in selling her paintings and she was indeed a wealthy woman.

Come to think of it, she could support Abby and herself for the rest of their days on that money. It was a thought to file away for a later date.

The first whistle of the train screeched around them, making Emma jump a little. Their time was drawing to a close too soon. Tears prickled at her eyes.

"Come, give your oldest sister a hug good-bye." Emma wrapped her arms around Abby.

"I'll miss you dreadfully," Abby whispered.

"And I you. If you are bored, or not ready to do what you've set out to do, you know you can come home straightaway."

Abby pulled away and gave her a smile. "I know."

Abby kissed them both on the cheeks and climbed aboard the train with the help of the attendant. Grace stood beside Emma, wrapping her arm around her waist, and waved at their sister. Once Abby took her seat at the window, she opened it.

"I love you both," she shouted over the crank of the wheels.

"We love you, too," Emma called back.

Grace's waves grew in enthusiasm as tears slid down her cheeks.

Emma waved at Abby and clutched her free hand to

the locket about her neck. Is this what it felt like for mothers sending off their daughters?

"Write to us every day," Grace bellowed as the steam engines roared to life on the train.

"Only if you promise to tell me all about London when I come back."

The train started rolling on the track.

Abby leaned over from her seat and stuck her head and shoulders out of the window. "I love you two," she hollered back.

"She would have married sooner or later." Emma grasped Grace's gloved hand in her own. "We would have had to let her go eventually."

"I don't much like this feeling of letting her go," Grace confided.

"Neither do I."

"I had hoped to have a little longer with her." Grace put her head on Emma's shoulder and sighed. "We're all going our own way so suddenly. I never expected this. For things to change so fast in our lives. For us to part so quickly."

Emma couldn't agree more. She wrapped her arm around Grace's shoulders and turned them in the direction of the carriage. They had no time to waste. They were leaving for London come sunrise and there was a lot of packing to do. A wedding to plan for, and a husband she still needed to figure out.

Richard pulled a stack of letters from the desk drawer. The ones he'd tossed in there on his first day home after he went through his father's things.

Releasing the twine that bound them, he placed the unopened envelopes on the top of the desk and studied them. There were a dozen of them, but none of them were addressed. An elegant scroll indicating his wife's name was written on the back of each lavender parchment. Could these be letters between lovers? Correspondence between Emma and her buyer? Or could the letters merely be kind words and messages between friends? If any of those were the case, then why were they all undelivered?

His desire to better understand his wife far outweighed the fact that what he was about to do was a violation of her privacy. Picking up the letter opener, he tested its weight in his hand. Emma would be livid if she found out.

Still, he slid the point under the edge of the envelope and sliced it open. Pulling out the neatly folded paper and flattening it on the desk, he read it:

*Dearest Husband,*

*I am but a slave to the feelings that bombard me every time I pen another letter. Six years of loneliness, and I still harbor a desire for your company. I am incomplete and long for something more. The fact of the matter remains . . . you consume my every thought. Yet, you don't deserve that kind of devotion . . .*

Richard put the missive down without finishing it and sliced another envelope open. It was dated four years ago:

*Dearest Husband,*

*I feel like Sleeping Beauty, forever asleep with the waking world continuing on without me fully aware. Only there is no prince to wake me from this slumber, this half-life. This melancholy only burrows deeper into my heart when I write these letters. I should stop. I should burn this before*

*I have the opportunity to sign it. I should burn them all. Hopeless dreams is all they represent . . .*

Pushing the chair away from the desk, he pulled open the drawer where he'd found the pretty pile of letters, his heart racing as he did so. Inside, there were the letters he'd read through near the front of the drawer, a few quills, blotters, pencils, and paper. He tugged the drawer farther out, almost toppling it to the floor when it ran out of track to hold it up.

His heart nearly stopped with what was revealed.

Of course there were more. He wished that weren't the case.

Removing the remainder of the letters from the drawer, he set them on the desk and pulled the twine free.

Richard thumbed one open, uncaring that he ruined the envelope. He untied another of the neat stacks, and tore open that envelope, too. All addressed to him as *Dearest Husband.*

All of them.

He shook his head. There wasn't a man less worthy of that salutation than him. Why the hell did she give a damn about him? Why? Hadn't he proven that he was an ass over the years?

He shoved at the papers on the desk, and they fluttered away from him. Some fell over the edge and to the floor. He stood and paced the carpeted floor.

What should he do with this revelation? Should he confront his wife? Not once in twelve years had he written her a letter, sent her word, or even sent her a gift. He didn't deserve this kind of loyalty from her. He didn't want it. He should have left well enough alone.

Goddamn her. He'd never given her a reason to give him any heartfelt words.

Richard rubbed at his chest as he continued to pace.

The likelihood that she had ever indulged in an affair diminished in his mind. Not that it still wasn't a possibility. After all, he had caught Vane and Emma embracing. But it seemed unlikely after this recent discovery.

Smacking his hand down on the mantel, Richard loosened his necktie.

His wife had longed for something more. Something he hadn't been willing to give her. Not when they'd first married. He didn't deserve sincere words.

He needed to talk to her.

And say what?

That he'd violated her secrets when he had no right?

Now that he knew what thoughts she harbored, it changed things. He didn't know how or what, but their relationship wouldn't be the same anymore.

He resumed pacing the room.

A soft knock came at the door shortly before Emma entered. Their eyes connected. Richard didn't know what to say. There was a lump in his throat that he couldn't swallow or talk past. He wasn't ready to face his wife. He had to think, had to decide what this new information meant to him. He couldn't do that with her here.

Was he angry with her for not sending them? Upset? He had no answers right now. All he knew was that she had needed him when she wrote those letters, and he'd never been there for her. Had never wanted to be there for her.

"You should have sent them." His words came out a hoarse whisper.

Her gaze flicked in the direction the letters had been scattered. Emma's breath caught visibly in her lungs on an inhalation. The moment she took in the evidence of what he'd done, she rushed toward the papers and fell to her knees.

Gathering the letters up with shaking hands, she

crushed them to her breast and looked at him with watery eyes.

"You had no right!"

Richard walked back to his desk and stacked up all the letters he'd torn open. Then he knelt next to her and focused on picking up the few unopened envelopes that had toppled over the edge. Better to focus on that then the betrayal he'd glimpsed so raw in her gaze.

Emma's tears streaked down her face.

He put his finger to her left cheek and caught one of the tears before it could roll any farther. She didn't look up at him.

"You should have sent them," he repeated.

Not that he knew what he would have done with the letters ten years ago. Hell, he wasn't sure he would have known what to do with them two years ago. Would he have come home sooner? Would he have written back? A few weeks ago, the answer to those questions would have been simple. He would have said it changed nothing. Now . . . it changed everything.

Despite that, he liked to think that he'd have responded to her letters had she ever bothered to send them. Wished he could say that he and his wife might have found some common ground and maybe even become friends over the years.

But she'd never sent the letters.

And he'd never bothered to write one.

They were like complete strangers to each other.

"These were private."

Emma ripped the letters out of his hands and held them close to her heart. As though she could hide the deepest thoughts and desires that had been revealed to him in those letters.

It was too late for that now. He wouldn't let her take

back the knowledge he'd gained in the last hour of reading them. He couldn't bear not to know this truth.

He held his hands out to her. "Emma."

Would she continue to hide from him still? After everything he had learned about the inner workings and thoughts of his wife? He knew he had to do everything in his power to make sure she didn't bury this as easily as she thought she had buried the letters in the drawer. Her head was tipped down.

She didn't respond.

"Emma."

She stood quickly and wiped the back of her hand over her eyes. It did little to vanquish the deluge of tears that flowed down her face.

"You've taken something away from me by reading my private thoughts."

"I'm glad for it, Emma. How else was I ever to know anything about you?"

He took a small step in her direction. Careful that he didn't scare her off like a wounded animal. She hurt so deeply, he felt it more than saw the distress he'd caused in her.

When she tried to gather up the papers on the desk, he caught her hand to stall her progress. He wouldn't let her walk away so easily. He'd seen her heart bled out onto paper. Had seen the very essence of her kind soul in her written words.

She belonged to him. Had belonged to him the moment their fate had been sealed in trading vows. He had never understood just how precious she was. Not until this very moment.

"I'd rather know the true you."

She didn't pull away from him, so he threaded his fingers through hers.

Slowly, he took a step nearer to her. He raised his

hand and thumbed away the tears coating her face in a shiny, wet sheen. Her eyes shut with his gentle touch. The lashes were darkened to a brown. Droplets of tears spiked them out from her face.

She shook her head. "Don't do this to me, Richard."

"What am I doing?"

"Making me want things I can't ever have."

He wrapped his arms around her and pulled her into a hug. Her head rested against his chest, her face turned to the side.

Her hands clenched between them. She made no move to hold him tight against her.

True, he'd never given her any reason to think there was more between them than the convenience of producing an heir. He'd never given her a reason to think he might care for her.

He needed to give her a small truth. A reassurance. One to further seal her fate to his. Because he was a greedy enough bastard to want her all to himself.

"I'm afraid you'll have a hard time getting rid of me now."

Her fingers uncurled from the papers she held between their frantically beating hearts. As her head tipped back so she could look at him, a few of the loose sheaves of paper fluttered to their feet.

She searched his eyes for a few moments, her brows knitting. His hands were snug around her waist and back, so Richard lifted her till she was eye level with him. It was as if they both held their breath for fear of breaking the stillness. The only sound to be heard was the slide of papers between their bodies. Forgotten.

Her tears had dried up. Her trembling lips had stilled.

"I'm not leaving you, Emma. I refuse the very idea of a divorce."

"But . . ."

"There are no buts. You belong to me."

Then, before she could utter any more disagreements, he lowered his mouth to hers.

It was quite possible he had fallen in love with his wife.

No, he *had* fallen in love with her; he'd just been to thick-headed to realize that before today.

# Chapter 22

*It's our anniversary today. A bitter reminder that I mean nothing to you.*

Emma took her seat in the family box with the assistance of her husband. She'd never come to Her Majesty's Theater before. It was the place where gossip went from a kernel of truth to a full-grown weed of lies not easily plucked from the roots.

Never had she seen a need to flaunt the fact that her husband had run off to another continent. But Richard had insisted they do something grand for their first night in Town.

Things had changed between them overnight.

"Thank you," she said to Richard as he set her shawl on the back of the chair. He gave a slight squeeze at her shoulder before he took his own seat. "We could have gone for refreshments before we came up."

He slid his seat closer to hers and leaned in to whisper intimately in her ear. "But the fools that make up the aristocracy already have us on their tongue. Gossip and speculation are circulating this very moment." He took her hand between his. They were so warm, so comforting. "I intend to make up for my lack of consideration in the past."

She turned so they were nose-to-nose instead of mouth-to-ear. "If there is one thing I've learned over the years, it is that their opinions don't matter."

"They will matter when we have children. We'll play their game and stay a step ahead of them. You, my darling wife, will be sought after by every matron and party planner after tonight. Everyone will want your ear."

She had no desire to be wanted simply as good gossip fodder. Her husband didn't understand her in the least. She still would not care less what society thought of her when—if—she had children.

Sliding her hand from beneath her husband's, she opened the program for the evening's lineup of musical festivities. Bach cello concertos followed by England's very own Thaddeus de Burgh . . .

Nathan's brother.

Her breath caught in her throat. Surreptitiously, she raised her eyes to look at their surroundings. The Duke of Vane was nowhere to be found. At least not in any of the private boxes she glanced over. It was early yet, and Emma had a sinking feeling she'd have a run-in with the duke later in the evening.

Nathan was supportive of his brother's career in music. There wasn't a doubt in her mind the duke would be here. She folded her program and set it in her lap, gaze skimming over the crowd anxiously.

What would Richard say and do if he saw the duke again? It wasn't bound to be a friendly meeting. Suspicions would circulate among the crowd. Would bets be placed as to what her husband would do? What Nathan would do should her husband and supposed lover meet face-to-face under the watchful eye of the ton?

Eventually, Richard would come to see that she and

Nathan were nothing more than friends. Now was not that time. Not when their relationship was so new. And turning out to be everything she had always wanted.

"What's wrong?" Richard asked, almost as if sensing her unease.

Was she so obvious?

She gave a faint smile and replied, "Nothing is wrong. I was just thinking it's a shame Grace couldn't come with us tonight."

"She has a lot on her plate with the wedding three weeks away."

He lifted her hand to his lips and brushed a kiss against her satin-covered knuckles. Richard, the romantic, was a force to deal with. The whispers around them swelled. The crowd gathering in the music hall had certainly seen her husband's open adoration for her. Did he treat her that way because he knew everyone who was anyone watched them with keen interest?

She ducked her head, afraid to meet anyone's scrutinizing gaze. Though she liked his attention, she felt a twinge of embarrassment at him displaying it so openly.

"You shouldn't be so bold," she whispered.

"Why not? I'm enjoying the company of my wife on a beautiful summer evening. Parliament is setting up for the fall, and here I am, the infamous runaway earl fawning over his lovely wife."

Such sweet platitudes would make most women faint dead away. However, Emma had more sense than that. She flicked open her fan to cool the flush taking over her body.

"I don't want to be a curiosity."

"We're all a curiosity, darling. Now, can I convince you to raise your skirts?"

Her head whipped around, a sound of protest escaped her parted lips, and Richard quirked his brow suggestively.

"Richard," she hissed, flicking her fan faster.

If they hadn't had all eyes on them in the hall, she'd have smacked his hand away from her knee. She must act calm. Pasting what she hoped amounted to a smile on her face, she looked for any familiar faces in the crowd, ignoring her husband's ribald request.

He chuckled at her blatant determination to discount his naughty suggestion.

Her eyes alighted on the duke, who seated his mistress, Anna. He bowed in her direction when their eyes met. Nibbling at her bottom lip, she lowered her gaze, pretending not to have seen him. Would Richard notice the duke?

What if Nathan looked for her during the intermission?

She'd worry about it if the issue arose.

"I believe," Richard said, not withholding the distaste that seeped into his tone of voice, "that the Duke of Vane is trying to draw your attention."

She raised her eyes and stared across the theater, pretending disinterest.

"Yes, indeed."

Clutching her fan tight in her grasp, she closed it and squeezed it in her fist. Her body was as tight as a string on a violin about to snap.

The gaslights would dim soon enough. Then she could beg her husband to leave during the intermission. She did not want to deal with another confrontation between the two men.

Sizing the duke up from across the music hall wasn't an easy feat since the man was focused on Emma. The woman next to the duke must be his mistress. The dress she wore was too low-cut to declare her a lady; the red of her lips and rouge of her cheeks further attested to that fact.

His wife's odd behavior had Richard thinking she continued to lie about having an affair with the other man. The duke was known for throwing wild orgies that lasted weeks on end. If Emma was a friend of the duke's, chances of her attending those parties were pretty high.

His jaw clenched so hard his molars ground together. He didn't give a damn that it was illegal to kill your peers for a slight. Maybe he'd just beat the bloody pulp out of the libertine. He'd be damned if he'd stand by knowing his wife had had relations with that man. And then be witness to their *knowing* glances back and forth.

The gaslights were turned down, and a cello player took the stage for the opening number. Richard slouched back in his chair, his fingers tapping along the arm. He was good at waiting. They'd find refreshments during the intermission and hopefully run into the duke while doing so. Richard would have words with the man.

Richard took off his hat and ran a hand through his hair.

He'd get to the bottom of the duke's relationship with his wife before the night was through.

It was impossible to enjoy the performance of the cellist. He didn't even want to tease his wife. It wasn't that he was angry with her, more so with himself for leaving her open and vulnerable to the likes of a man like Vane.

When the final chords of the cello sounded and the lights came back up, he took his wife's hand and pulled her to the curtained exit. He said not a word. She didn't protest being manhandled, which he supposed was a sign she knew what he was about.

When they made it to the front foyer of the hall, where

champagne and lemonade were being distributed to the hot mass of attendees, he wheeled Emma around to face the crowd, keeping an eye out for the duke.

Emma pulled her hand out of his with a scowl on her face. "Richard, this isn't necessary."

"It absolutely is. I'll not be made a blockhead by my own wife."

Amazing how calm his voice was when he was anything but calm inside. He wanted to demand every detail of her relationship with Vane. Wanted to ask someone where the duke could be found so he could pummel the blighter into the floor.

His thoughts turned uglier by the minute. There was a word for it. Jealousy. Quite possible he was jealous of a man who'd spent time with his wife over the years, when he'd been off ruining the lives of innocent people.

The duke walked down the grand staircase that led up to the boxes, his harlot on his arm. Richard took Emma's hand in his and pulled her through the throng. Her lemonade sloshed over the rim of her glass, wetting her gloves. She covered up the mishap with a chuckle and hurried by his side, not that he gave her much choice.

Richard cut through the reeking swath of society and set his eyes upon the formidable height of the duke. The duke must have known something was afoot, because he bowed to Emma. "My lady, always a pleasure to be in your company."

The man had the audacity to take his wife's hand and kiss her knuckles. Straightening, the duke raised a disdainful brow at Richard. "Asbury."

Vane turned to his woman, patting her hand where it rested upon his arm. The ladybird was rather beautiful, her hair a shade darker than his wife's, her eyes a deep blue. The woman's curves were more pronounced than

Emma's. Somehow, she looked familiar. Had he met her somewhere before?

"Anna, sweetheart." The duke's words cut off Richard's observations. "Get us some refreshments."

She slipped away without another word or glance at her protector.

"We have many things to discuss, Duke."

Guests at the theater were starting to eye their party. He was making a scene and couldn't seem to help himself. His quick temper was ruining his carefully laid plans for their future. All because he was jealous of this pompous arse.

"No need to draw unwanted attention our way, Asbury. I would be happy to call on you at your residence."

"You'll not come anywhere near my wife." The words were too low to be heard by observers, which surprised him, because he was feeling anything but rational right now.

"I must apologize," Emma cut in with a stern, clipped voice. "My husband is not himself since he's been home. Traveling for so long and mingling with other cultures has made him unfit company for polite society."

She pulled her arm from Richard's and gave the duke a curtsy. "I will leave you gentlemen to talk. Anna will be looking for company, and I'm all too happy to oblige."

She looked about the room, then leaned close to Richard as if they were having intimate words. "Let their tongues wag, Richard. You ought to be ashamed of the way you're acting."

He ignored her parting barb and focused on the duke as Emma walked away. "You have put me in an awkward position, Vane."

"Only as awkward as you make it." The duke leaned

against the wall as though discussing someone else's wife was a conversation one normally partook in.

Then it hit Richard. Now that he'd thought on it, he knew where he'd seen the duke's mistress. He turned about the room to look for his wife and Vane's mistress. That woman bore a striking resemblance to the nude portrait Emma had painted. The duke most certainly knew of his wife's pastime.

Could this mean he'd found his wife's buyer? Could it be so easy as that? He still wondered if there was more to the relationship between Emma and the duke. He wondered to what extent the intimacy ran between them.

"You are a bad association for my wife."

"Is that supposed to convince me to cut off all ties I have to her?" the duke asked sardonically.

Richard looked his foe over. "How is it you befriended my wife?" He was feeling possessive, jealous to the extreme. It niggled that this man knew his wife better than he.

"A rather entertaining story. I ran Emma over a potted plant. Quite literally."

"You are no longer on a first-name basis with my wife."

The duke gave him a sly smile. "That'll be her choice. I've known her a good number of years. Many more than you've bothered to come around for. Our friendship goes back too many years to ignore."

"I've been married to her longer than you've known her," he felt the need to point out. "Her personal life is none of your concern."

"I never said it was. You, on the other hand, did."

"We are at an impasse." Richard felt like the pompous arse now.

He tried searching out his wife amongst the gathering without success.

"She and Anna will have found some private corner to talk," the duke said. "Anna, as I'm sure you noticed, is not the sort to mingle freely with the others in attendance."

"My wife shouldn't be consorting with her, either."

"I cannot stop your wife from befriending my mistress. As unusual as it is, it just is. Be careful that you don't insult my woman. I'll not have her slighted by your high-handed opinion."

The protectiveness the duke displayed for the harlot seemed to calm Richard's blood. The man wasn't in the running for his wife's affections. Hell, he didn't even know if he himself was in the running for her affections.

The champagne-colored feathers in Emma's hair danced like a ballerina on air as she and the ladybird approached. They had another gentleman with them. He looked like a younger version of Vane.

Emma took Richard's proffered arm.

"We found Teddy," the duke's mistress said.

"I came to pay my regards," the younger man said. "I should have known you'd be in the family box. Surprised you weren't *en masse*."

The duke gave a low throaty laugh and gave the man an affectionate embrace. Brothers perhaps? "This is a family affair. Teddy is being modest."

"He's sharp on the violin; a Beethoven in his own right," Anna chimed in.

"I'm sure you've guessed this is my brother, Thaddeus de Burgh, Viscount of Sheffield. Though he's liable to curse you for using his title. So unbecoming for a titled man to play the part of a starving violinist and composer."

Thaddeus seemed to redden with his brother's introduction.

The young man offered his hand hesitantly. Richard didn't think anything in taking it. Richard had met people from so many walks of life and varying cultures in his former trade that a handshake wasn't just for commoners.

"You must be the countess's husband," the young man said. "My brother speaks highly of her."

"A pleasure to make your acquaintance," he said stiffly. It was hard not to pinch his lips together in disapproval. Every tidbit of information he learned about the relationship between the duke and his wife irritated him further.

"My brother is recently back from Vienna. He trained with Mendelssohn and Schumann in Leipzig since he was a youth." The duke was obviously proud of his younger brother. His brother frowned and looked as though he wished to hide in the back room until he took to the stage.

"I'm eager to see his performance. I confess to not reading the whole program." Emma had likely been too distracted by the duke's presence. She turned to de Burgh. "Do you play your own composition tonight?"

"Yes, a jovial piece. Something to end the evening on a high note."

A bell chimed, indicating the intermission coming to a close. Richard took his wife's arm through his and bowed to the duke and his companion.

"It was good to catch up with you, Anna." Emma clasped the other woman's hand familiarly. "Please don't be a stranger. I couldn't bear staying in London for an extended period of time without having your company."

"I wouldn't dream of avoiding you."

After addressing Emma, the harlot turned to the duke with a look of complete adoration. Or was it respect and affection in her loving gaze that threw him off a step—

quite literally. Definitely not a look his wife had ever given him.

"We should return to our seats," Anna finished.

Richard made his bow. "We'll meet again in the near future. We have business to discuss."

The business of his wife's paintings.

Richard was so close to putting this nightmare to rest that he grinned.

"Absolutely." The duke nodded, caressing the arm of his mistress, and left for his box.

She might have had an affair with the man at one point in their long friendship, but he doubted she'd be friends with Vane's mistress had she still been having an affair with the man. He had misjudged his wife. Things were starting to become clearer. He hadn't necessarily come out of that conversation on top of the situation, but he'd correct that once he met with the duke privately.

Instead of leading Emma back to their box, he planted a firm, passionate kiss on her lips. She clasped onto his arms as he stroked his tongue into her mouth.

"What—"

Before she could speak another word he kissed her again. Gasps and the sharp whispers of the other guests sounded. Richard didn't care. It might put to rest the rumor of her affair with the duke. All he wanted was to get his wife home.

"He won't sell the paintings to you."

"I can be quite convincing."

"Vane is used to getting his own way."

"So am I." And with that he ushered her from the opera house and to his waiting carriage.

Emma was taking out the last of her pins and putting them in a small porcelain dish. She brushed her hair out at the vanity. She'd been content in ignoring him since her maid had left fifteen minutes ago. She knew her husband desired only one thing: for her to join him in bed. She'd not make this easy for him.

"It's always going to be about the paintings between us, isn't it?"

His fingers rubbed along his jaw. "Not necessarily."

"Why won't you let the topic rest then?"

"Because my wife's name is attached to indecent nudes."

"Why is it so important to stir up the waters where my paintings are concerned? You'll draw suspicion to us in ferreting them out."

Aside from the one painting Vane was having little success in purchasing from Waverly. She'd fished the details of the acquisition out of Anna when they were at the musicale. Waverly still refused to sell it. He refused to even see the duke about negotiating a price. This was not going as she had planned.

Richard leaned forward on the bed, putting his elbows on his knees and his head in his open palms to rub his eyes.

He then stood from the bed and made his way over to her, stripping out of his shirt and tossing it to the floor. When he was behind her, he took the brush from her hands and set himself to cleaning up the locks of hair that had tangled together. His actions were surprising and had her stomach fluttering in nervousness. They didn't generally share in this type of intimacy.

"What is it you plan to do—or maybe I should ask what have you done with the money?"

She frowned at him in the reflection of the mirror. "I'll answer your question if you'll answer mine."

He shrugged and separated her hair down the middle so he was brushing smaller sections. "The idea of what

I imagine men doing while ogling your work bothers me. Simple as that."

Emma turned around on the stool. The pieces of hair he held slid from his fingers as she tipped her head back to look up at him. He put his finger her under the chin and leaned forward to brush their lips together.

"Are you jealous?" she asked.

"Maybe a little."

Her heart sped up with the admission.

"Emma, do you realize those paintings serve one purpose for a man? They're likely purchased so the buyer can get a good rub off when he's alone."

"It's none of my business what they do once they've bought them."

He took her hands and had her stand before him. She wore a negligee of the finest thinnest silk tonight.

"The paintings all auctioned for over a thousand pounds."

"I can manage that amount of money. It won't break me to buy them all back."

"Well over a thousand pounds each."

He laughed, and kissed her. "You are a marvelous woman."

"Richard?" She wondered how that made her marvelous.

"A woman after my own heart. One who can match my ability in turning a profit. We are well matched, wife. Very well matched."

"I shouldn't tell you this, but I will: The duke purchased fifteen of those paintings because they are of Anna."

"Hence the reason he'll not sell them back to me."

"Yes."

He kissed her soundly on the mouth, his hands cupping either side of her face. "He can keep them, but I will find the other paintings. I will make it clear to the duke that I don't care if he wants a reminder of his mistress every time he turns around. Now tell me what it is you've done with the money."

"Nothing. It sits in a trust. I've not spent one ha'penny of it."

"It's the fact that you are doing something you shouldn't that provides the thrill, I daresay." He shook his head. "I still want the rest of your pictures for myself."

She raised her brow in question. "And whatever will you do when you are alone with them?"

"You see," he said, pushing her satin robe from her shoulders, "I've completely debauched you."

"Very true," she said, pouting out her lower lip and fanning her lashes at him. "But are you sure I haven't completely scandalized you?" She sank to her knees in front of him and proceeded to release the buttons on his trousers.

He looked down at her, mouth open in shock. "Emma?"

"Richard?"

She gave him a devilish smile as she yanked his trousers down over his hips. She had trouble pulling down his smalls, his erection strained so tightly against the material. Richard helped her by pressing the stiffness to his stomach.

It was much more intimidating at eye level. It had to be the same thickness as her wrist. It wouldn't be easy to do what she planned. But she'd not be stopped. She wet her lips with her tongue.

"What are you about?"

Instead of answering, she licked his cock from his sac all the way up to the tip. This would not be easy on her knees. He was simply too big. She stood and pressed her fingers into his torso, making him walk backward as she advanced.

She didn't know what came over her. She'd never dared to act so forward, so in control. She'd not hand over the reins now that she had them firmly in her grasp.

Richard stopped at the bed. Eyes feasting on her feminine wares. She stood still for his inspection. Savoring the moment. It was a powerful feeling being wanted so desperately by a man.

"I can see your mount of Venus tickling the material softly between your thighs. I wonder if I'll find it dewy." He licked his lips with the suggestion.

Her nipples peaked to firm points. Unbidden, a half moan, half squeak escaped her mouth at the naked desire in his perusal.

She wanted to press her naked body against his. Rubbing and sating their flesh with touch and taste. What a beautiful man he was. All sleek hardness, an athletic, lean build promising strength, stamina. Pleasure. So much pleasure.

She took another step toward him. The tip of her lace-covered breasts brushed against his bare chest. She resolved then that she'd put shyness on the shelf for the evening and learn her husband's body as he had learned hers: with her hands, her lips, her tongue.

With a light kiss to his mouth, she pushed him back on the bed. He pulled her down on top of him, refusing to release her mouth for a gentle sweeping of his tongue. His fingers were busy pulling the silk garment she wore up her legs, her buttocks, her back. He held it there in his fists waiting for her to decide what to do.

She broke the kiss so he could remove the negligee. Before he could take possession of her mouth again, she scooted slowly down on her knees so she could feast on his cock with her eyes and her mouth. She sucked the head of his instrument into her mouth, laving around it with her tongue.

The head of his cock emitted a pearly drop of semen. She ran her tongue over that slit, massaging it with the edge of her tongue and then flattening her tongue against the smooth skin and sucking him farther into her mouth.

A moan escaped her as she took him in deeper. Richard let out a groan and pressed his hand to her head, urging her on. Urging her to suck him in faster and deeper. She rode his length with her mouth, her hand fisting the base of his cock as she did so. Her fingers explored the soft skin it stroked, then she rolled the balls in his sac together. The sac tightened in her hold.

"Emma. Come off me."

She shook her head. She liked this too much to stop. He liked it, too, if the thrusting of his hips was anything to judge by.

"I'll not come in your mouth." He sat up and pulled her up off his cock.

She pouted out her bottom lip. He nipped at it. Flipping her to her back, he bit the side of her breast, sucked in her nipple, and thrust his fingers inside her core. She felt her own wetness coating her thighs.

His rod soon replaced his fingers and he rode her hard and fast. One of his hands wrapped around her hair, pulling it so tight in his fist that her head arched back. His other hand squeezed her buttock so hard she was sure she'd have an imprint of his hand there come morning.

She reached around to hold him close, grasping his buttocks. They flexed in her hands with each push forward into her sheath. She felt her orgasm. It was so close she grasped the cheeks of his rear tighter. She wanted him deeper.

"Harder. Oh, God, harder," she moaned.

Richard's mouth caught hers in a fierce kiss as he drove into her harder. Just as she'd begged.

Her body strained against his, needing to be closer, needing something more when finally she exploded. A spurt of fluid rushed from her; she felt it coating him and her thighs, dripping between her buttocks. He shouted out his release soon after. His weight did not fall down on her. He held himself above her, let go of her hair, and kissed her gently, tenderly on the mouth.

Pulling his cock from her body, he rolled to his side and gathered her close. She felt like she belonged in his arms. This felt right having him here, in her bed, beside her, holding her.

She had to bite her cheeks so she didn't utter any words she'd regret come morning. It was still too soon to tell him how she really felt. To tell him that she loved him. Had always loved him.

Her head rested on his arm, and she closed her eyes.

Richard tucked her hair behind her ear, kissed her temple, and said, "Good night, love."

She held that endearment close in her heart as she snuggled her rear closer to him. He had a tendency to use endearments with her. Whether he meant them or not, she couldn't be sure. But she'd cherish every one as if it were the most precious word uttered to her.

# Chapter 23

*How long is one expected to remain true to another person? How long is one expected to live a lonely existence?*

Emma had squirreled herself away in her study the moment Grace left to visit with a friend. Her husband had gone out with Dante a couple of hours ago to finalize some business arrangements, or so he had told her. She had a sneaking suspicion he headed over to the duke's house for a talk about the paintings.

It was imperative that Richard never find out about the two nudes she'd done of herself. Uncovering that lie would put a wall between her and Richard. She didn't know why she thought that, she just did. She'd have to send a note to Nathan, beg him to hide those paintings and ensure they were never leaked out into society.

Rubbing away a crumbling of charcoal on her newest sketch, she smoothed out some of the shadows on the paper. The picture she worked on was like a headless statue, the rendering similar to Richard's physique. She'd have to alter it when she was done so he wouldn't recognize it outright. Though she couldn't wait to see his expression when he realized it was him.

She smiled. What other man did she have at her disposal for such a thing? None. He'd grumble and posture with her when he discovered this. She wouldn't hide it from him.

The door creaked open behind her. Blowing the loose black from the picture's surface away, she cleared her throat. "Luncheon already, Brown?"

She turned around in the wide leather chair she'd pulled up to the worktable. Her skirts tangled around her legs as she tried to get out of the seat and put herself at a safe distance from Waverly. How had he gotten into her home? There had been guards stationed inside the front entrance since their arrival a couple of days ago.

"Where is Brown?"

Waverly shrugged and came farther into the room. "What have we here?" He slid the paper across the desk so he could study it. "How does your husband feel about you drawing naked men now?"

Emma squared her shoulders and stood as tall as she could. She had to put her nervous, trembling hands behind her back. *Show no weaknesses,* she reminded herself.

"How did you get in?" she asked, edging out of his reach and closer to the door.

"I have my ways."

Waverly balled up the picture she'd been working on and threw it to the floor.

His gaze met hers.

"If you need to speak with Richard, he will be home shortly."

She had no idea if that was the truth or not. What she did know was that she needed to put a safe distance between her and the intruder standing across from her.

He stood by the chair she'd vacated moments ago, his hand squeezing around the top edge.

"You know, Richard never said you were a pretty creature, not in all our years together. I was surprised to see him act so protective of you. He must not know your dirty secrets."

"He knows everything. You are not a threat."

"You are a means to an end, dear Emma. Nothing more than a means to an end."

Emma's skirts hit a table near the chaise longue. She nearly toppled over the table beside it to escape Waverly's reach. A chair crashed to the floor when she tried to grab it. The crystal ware she swept off the table next to the chair fell to the ground and bounced away with only a slight ringing noise. She scanned her periphery, afraid to take her eyes off Waverly. She needed something to throw, something breakable. She needed to make noise for anyone to come to her aid.

"Stop this," she shouted.

He rushed toward her and yanked at her arm painfully as he pulled her nearer. She tried to squirm from his grip, but Waverly's arms were wrapped solidly around her. She tried again to pull away from him. She could not loosen the man's forceful clutch as he turned her about so her back was to his chest. He pressed a cloth firmly over her mouth and nose.

She opened her mouth to scream, but no sound came out. She bit down on his hand, tasting the man's blood before she fell heavy as stone in his hold with a sharp smell stinging her nostrils. Her last thought was of Richard.

Richard's old business was now completely in the hands of Heyworth: the fleet of ships, the deeds for the shipping docks, the plantation in India. All of it was finally gone. The money had been split amongst him and his two business partners, which included Waverly.

Though Waverly hadn't been present for the final sign-off, he'd sent his man of business to take care of loose ends.

Richard had had his solicitor invest his funds into the rail. He wasn't surprised when Dante followed suit. The man had a reason to visit England often with his bride-to-be.

All said and done, they mounted their horses and wound their way through the city streets.

"I need a favor," Richard said.

He could trust Dante with his wife's secret. The man was steadfast and reliable. Had been for all the years Richard had worked with him.

"Something with Waverly?"

Richard shook his head. "I need to visit the Duke of Vane. He has something that belongs to me."

"And what is this thing that should belong to you?"

The cautious tone of voice Dante used made Richard wonder if his friend thought that *object* might be his wife. Definitely not the case after all that had happened between them. All they'd shared with each other. The last few nights in bed had been different. More tender. More about sharing each other than using each other for pleasure.

"My wife likes to create ribald paintings. The duke has been selling them for her. I plan to retrieve the ones still in his possession."

"Your wife asked this of you?"

No, it wasn't something Emma had asked for, but she'd thank him sometime in the future for the lengths he planned to go to retrieve the art. To make sure her secret remained just that . . . a secret. Dante chuckled when Richard made no response other than to scowl.

"My guess is that your wife does not want them back."

"I'm so easy to read?"

"Only where Lady Emma is concerned."

That was because he was besotted with his wife.

On arriving at the duke's residence, they were situated in a room better suited for a brothel. Large gilt mirrors hung on three of the gold-papered walls. A massive crystal chandelier hung down in the center of the room. Two rose-colored chaises and two deep red settees made up the sitting area. It was gaudy and overdone. What made the room, though, were the handfuls or so of paintings of the duke's mistress. All were nude, all in various erotic poses.

Dante walked around the periphery of the room and looked thoughtfully at each piece, thumb and forefinger rubbing at his jaw. Richard didn't care to study any of the art. But the longer he was made to wait, the more he'd come to the realization that the duke was rubbing in the fact that he was in possession of some of his wife's paintings.

Did Vane flaunt these paintings to everyone who came through the house? He doubted it. Despite the duke's long *relationship* with his mistress, it seemed she was nothing more than a pretty ornament.

When the door opened to the parlor, Vane came in with his mistress on his arm. She wore a navy dress so low-cut that he could see the pink of her areolas. Her blonde hair tumbled down her back in a riotous flow of curls. No embarrassment tainted her cheeks. No smile lifted her lips as she held her head high and licked her lips in sensual invitation.

Had she been trained to play the role of Venus? Was this inappropriately beautiful woman on the duke's arm part of the man's image? Richard almost pitied the woman.

Almost.

The duke twirled her away from him, so she lay reposed on one of the chaise longues, like a Greek goddess, they as supplicants to her every bidding.

Richard broke eye contact with the woman, and narrowed his gaze on the duke. Richard understood why the man's mistress was present. She provided a distraction to probably many a man. That tactic might have worked on him before he'd come home to his wife. Not now.

Richard sneered at the duke. "You know why I've come."

Vane raised his hand and motioned to the room around them. "You desire my mistress so much that you're willing to purchase all these paintings?"

The duke's expression remained aloof as he stood beside his mistress, his hand folded over her raised one.

Richard wasn't sure who was master and who was the slave in their relationship. Richard couldn't help but make the comparison to the ladybird being worshipped like Cleopatra on her sensual throne ready to order her disciple—the duke—to kiss an asp.

"My only desire," Richard replied, "is to protect my wife's reputation."

"Ah. Admirable as that is, her reputation is safe with me."

"When Emma's fate is not in my hands, but rests upon your word, you will understand why I hesitate to agree."

"A shame for you, then."

The duke's hand massaged his mistress's arm, then over to her bare shoulder. He fingered possessively at the deep sapphires strung about her neck like a collar.

Dante remained a silent presence. His expression unreadable as he walked around the room.

"You may not part with the pictures displayed here, but what of the pieces not in your possession?"

"You won't leave this alone if I don't throw you a scrap of control, will you?"

"I doubt I'll ever stop."

"I'll make a deal with you, Asbury."

Vane leaned over his mistress, his hand slipping into the front of her gown and over the woman's breast as he whispered something in her ear.

She stood fluidly, without glancing at the other men in the room. The kiss she placed on Vane's lips was anything but chaste. Not with Vane's hand grasping her buttocks and pulling her close so their tongues could tangle. She left the duke standing in the middle of the room like a prince blessed before a medieval game of jousting.

"I will make inquiries," the duke said finally. "It's the best I can offer."

Exactly what Richard wanted to hear.

"No price is too steep, Vane. I'll not play games with the future of my wife's reputation."

"It will take me a few months. The paintings have been spread far and wide."

"Fine." Richard stuck his hand out to shake on the deal. When Vane took his hand, Richard asked, "How many do you own?"

The duke grinned. "Sixteen are in my possession and will remain so. I'm in the process of acquiring one more for my collection."

Richard wondered why he'd sold one of his mistress's portraits to begin with. Unless it wasn't of the ladybird's likeness.

He released the duke's hand. Feeling uneasy about the deal he'd just made. Felt like a deal with the devil.

"Does anyone know or suspect who the artist might be?"

"No. They believe it to be Anna's work, which works for our purpose of keeping Emma's identity a secret."

That was fine with Richard.

Richard inclined his head before he left. "I'm staying in London. Let me know when you start to locate the pieces."

There was no reason to delay his trip home.

"Of course," the duke called out after him.

When he arrived home, he ran up the steps, eager to see his wife. But when he opened the door, it was to a living nightmare. The hired mercenary was sitting in a chair by the front door, a maid holding a cloth to the gash across his head, trying to staunch the blood oozing out.

Richard took the stairs three at a time. "Emma!" He needed to find her, make sure she was all right.

Throwing open his bedchamber door, he yelled again, "Emma!"

Did he really expect her to answer? He barged through the dressing room door next, then the guest rooms and the nursery. None held any sign of his wife. Charging back down the stairs, he threw open every door on the main floor. There was a small room of the back of the house where Emma had set up her paintings. He should have checked there first.

Slamming the door open so hard the handle jammed into the plaster when it met the wall, Richard rushed into the room. Chairs were toppled over. A crystal dish lay forgotten on the floor, a ball of paper crumpled up next to it. Emma's charcoals were scattered on the surface of a small worktable; a few lay broken on the hardwood floor.

The rage he felt in that moment knew no bounds. Waverly would hurt for this.

A plain figurine of the female form was close at hand. He picked it up, and then it lay splintered and shattered in the fireplace. His gaze locked upon the painting resting upon the marble mantel.

Emma's beautiful golden curls were pulled back from

her face, making the silky locks appear short. Her half-lidded green eyes looked on the observer in sensual bliss. One of her arms stretched behind her on a wall. In her fist she held a sheer white length of material, which fell softly against her porcelain skin as it wrapped around her arm like a lover's skin. It covered one ear, her flushed pink lips, and one breast. Her other hand fisted the sheer material over her mons, covering her feminine core.

Where had the painting come from? Had it been in Emma's keeping? Had someone brought it to her? Was it possible that this painting had been in Waverly's possession?

There was no note to answer his questions. No clues as to why it was here and Emma was not. There was nothing to help him find his wife.

Without a doubt in his mind, Richard knew Waverly had abducted Emma. Maybe he shouldn't be so quick to accuse the other man, but who else would take her? The room lay in shambles, evidence enough that she'd struggled against her captor.

Richard hadn't really known Waverly in the sense one would know a friend. Not now. So where would he take her?

A gasp sounded behind him. Grace stepped farther into the room, her eyes caught on the painting. Just as his had. He stood there frozen, like a great buffoon, unable to say or do anything to make this situation any better.

"That bastard," Grace cried. "What has he done with my sister?"

She pulled the painting down and held it to her breast so the exposed image of his wife was hidden.

Richard picked the balled paper up from the floor and unraveled it slowly so it didn't tear. Most of the black had smeared together, but he could make out the male form she'd been drawing. He crumpled the paper back up and closed his eyes.

He needed to remain calm if he were to find his wife. He needed to think rationally.

"Where does he stay when he's in Town, Grace?"

Richard opened his eyes and looked at her, surprised to see her glaring angrily about the room instead of crying in fear for Emma.

"There is his house in Grosvenor Square, but I don't think he's opened it up in all the years he's been in Town."

Grace looked back at Richard, her gaze so like her sister's, his breath caught.

It was a starting point. That was all that mattered.

When she awoke next her vision was swimming. Her limbs felt tingly and heavy; too heavy to lift. She had to find a way to get out of her captor's hands.

"Awake, are you? Can't deceive me."

His voice made gooseflesh rise on her skin. She opened her eyes to a dark room. Blotches of color spotted her vision so she closed her lids again. She was lying on a makeshift pallet on the floor. She could see the legs of chairs and couches level with her eyes. Why hadn't he tossed her on the furniture instead of pulling all the linens on the floor?

She couldn't smell anything since her nose tingled. Waverly was off to her left, not that she could be sure. Wouldn't be sure of anything until the fog dissipated from her head and the low buzzing in her ears cleared. She was nauseous, dizzy.

"Where have you brought me?" Her voice cracked; her tongue felt like a heavy, dry weight in her mouth.

The shuffling of feet rang like abbey bells in her ears. She wanted to be rid of the sound and went to cover her ears, but when she tried to lift her hands they were like a deadweight behind her back.

It took her some minutes to figure out that rope bound her wrists together.

"Now, now. Don't you be moving around too much. I don't want you throwing up on me." The high-pitched squeak of something being unscrewed rang in her head. "Take a sip, here."

A flask was tipped against her lips. The burning liquid was poured down her throat before she could protest. Half of it sputtered out when she started coughing against the fiery taste of gin. She turned her head away. Not wanting the spirits. She'd not stay lucid if he continued pouring that down her mouth.

"Not much longer. He'll come, you see—he's reliable in that sense. Whether he comes in time is another matter, isn't it?"

She wondered what he planned to do with her. Was he going to torture her? Kill her?

"Where are we?" she asked the dark figure hovering a foot away from her.

"My private residence. Don't you worry, no rats to come and nibble at your toes. Not a pleasant feeling, that."

She closed her eyes against the nausea the image of rats invoked. Colors danced behind her lids, causing a fresh wave of sickness to turn over in her belly. Her eyelids were heavy. So hard to open. She squinted, unable to focus on anything.

What had he done to her?

She must have groaned that aloud, because he said, "Chloroform is wearing off. You'll feel a bit fuzzy for a while."

"Why have you done this?" Tears started to slide down the side of her face.

"Not sure, really. Remembered clear as day before I went to collect you. For the life of me, can't recall the reason behind it now. Just knew it had to be done." Waverly tipped the flask back and took a loud gulp of the alcohol.

"Let me go, Waverly. I serve no purpose."

"But you do. See, you were supposed to be leverage to get Richard to stop the sale of our business."

So that had been his purpose. Blackmail her into becoming his unwilling lover and threaten to expose the affair should Richard go through with the sale. Thank God she hadn't fallen into his trap.

Emma rubbed her damp eyes into her upper arm. The room around her came into sharp focus one moment only to go dim and gray in the next. She couldn't die like this. She refused to die like this.

She had to think. She was at Waverly's residence. She'd never been here before. Hadn't thought he kept his London home open. Had someone seen him carry her in here? Chances were he'd covered her and anyone passing by would have thought her nothing but a doxy.

If his intention was to simply kill her, then why was she still alive? Did he plan to reveal her secret to the world now that it served him no purpose in blackmailing Richard?

Her head throbbed and she had to shut her eyes again to get rid of the stabbing pain in her temples. She twisted her hands behind her back, trying to loosen the rope that bound her.

If she could use her hands, she could find an object to hit him with and run. She only needed to get out into the street. Someone would help her in Grosvenor Square. She didn't care that in all probability, they would recognize her. All that mattered was finding help.

Her knuckles audibly cracked as she worked her left hand half free of the binding. Her wrist was burning where it rubbed against the rope; it felt like she'd stuck it in a fire to cook.

Waverly didn't seem to notice the sound. He sat heavily in a large chair she couldn't make out the details of. He leaned forward with his elbows resting on his knees, head hanging down, his flask held by loose fingers between his knees. Was the man letting his guard down?

Did he plan on killing her? If so, why hadn't he done so by now? That gave her hope that she would escape. Did Richard know she was gone? Taken against her will? She couldn't remember what damage had been left in her painting room. Hopefully there was substantial evidence that something had gone awry. Hopefully Richard knew she was in trouble.

A clock in the house chimed. She closed her eyes and counted the gongs.

One. Two. Three.

She pulled her hand free of the rope.

Four.

She flexed her hands, willing the tingling of sleep away.

Five.

Sliding one arm beneath her, careful not to move the rest of her body, she prepared to push herself up. She needed to make a dash for the door.

Six.

She was on her feet and running.

# Chapter 24

*Is it possible to love someone you don't know? To love them so much you can't fathom ever losing them, even if they aren't yours to lose?*

The house was silent. No servants about, no voices to indicate that his wife was actually here. Nonetheless, he prowled around the main floor as silently as he could. Peering into cracked doors instead of opening them in case they creaked.

When he looked into the drawing room, he saw his wife seated in a chair. Hands bound in front of her. The room was dim, and it was hard to make out her features, but she didn't seem too bad off. Better than what he'd imagined in the last hour. Her eyes were cloudy, not totally focused. Her lips trembled but there were no tears streaking down her face. Her skin was clear of any cuts, though there was a dark bruise on her cheek.

His fists clenched at his side. He'd hurt Waverly for hitting his wife. She had no part in Richard and Waverly's past. Why in God's name would the man do this to her?

His enemy leaned against the wall, close to his wife.

He probably wanted to be close to her in case she tried to escape. There was a pistol in his hand, pointed at the floor.

Richard pushed the door open with his foot and held his hands up to show he held no weapon.

"Fast thinking on your part, Asbury. Didn't think you'd be seeing your wife alive again. She's a feisty thing. Almost escaped me about ten minutes ago." Waverly shrugged. "Guess I'll just have to kill you together. It's almost romantic."

Richard made no comment. Waverly was a loose cannon that needed to be snuffed quickly of its firepower. "Let my wife leave, Adam."

He hadn't called the man by his birth name since they were children. Felt peculiar coming from his lips, but hopefully made its way to God's ears before anything dire could come of the current situation. He'd not be able to live with himself if his wife was hurt by his own idiocy in not dealing with Waverly sooner.

Not that he knew precisely how to deal with the madman.

He looked to his wife again. He wanted to take her into his arms and comfort her, assure her everything would be as it was before. He couldn't make a promise like that, though. Someone would be hurt today. Richard didn't care who it was, so long as it wasn't Emma.

"Ah, Richard. So nostalgic. I didn't mean to take this bit of muslin, but you forced my hand." The tip of Waverly's pistol caressed his wife's temple and cheek. The man's hands were shaking so badly, his wife was hard-pressed to keep still with the assault. Every time she jerked away, Waverly yanked her back in place by her hair.

Folding his hands behind his back, Richard stood before Waverly in as nonthreatening a pose as he could muster. He prided himself on being a patient man. This task would take more patience than he'd ever been forced to endure. More patience than any man should have to tolerate in a lifetime. But he could not react to any words Waverly chose to insult his wife with.

He was a learned man. Both in school and in life. Yet nothing in all his years had prepared him for dealing with a situation like this. It was damnably hard not to go to his wife, take her by force from Waverly, and damn the consequences of acting rashly. Richard tore his gaze away from Emma and stared only at Waverly, pretending he was unsurprised about the whole state of affairs.

"What is it you want, Waverly?" A miracle that his voice wasn't infused with all the worry and anger pumping through his blood; it was even, calm.

"Good question, that. Can't quite remember what it was I wanted from you. Just know it was something important."

"We can talk about this gentleman-to-gentleman. No need to involve the lady."

"Oh, no, no. You can't make me forget that I want her for something. She's important."

Emma tried to rise from the chair only to be pushed back into it.

Richard shook his head at her. He didn't want her risking her life. He would find a way to get her out of here.

She was trying very hard to remain quiet. Her lips trembled so fiercely she was biting down on the bottom one, but was unsuccessful in stopping its waver. Tears streaked her face, and sweat plastered her hair to parts of her forehead and cheeks.

"Let the lady go, and we can discuss this like gentlemen, Adam."

Richard dared to take a small step forward. Hopefully his movement would go unnoticed by his foe.

Waverly straightened, his expression suddenly calm. He pulled Emma to her feet and raised the pistol. Richard acted on instinct, and rushed forward to tackle the man, shouting to his wife, "Find help, Emma."

Something sharp pierced his shoulder. He rolled back on his heels. His arm felt numb and cold. Except where warm blood was dripping down his fingers to pool beneath him.

"Didn't mean to do that," Waverly mumbled, shaking his head.

Emma whimpered when she saw him. She pulled herself to her feet and looked as though she'd come to him. Seeing the look on his face, she stepped backward instead of forward. At least Waverly had his gun focused on Richard now.

The only escape for his wife so happened to be the door behind Richard. He wanted her out of this room. It was just a matter of getting her safely to the exit. He started inching into the room. Hoping Waverly would circle him and unwittingly give Emma a chance to escape.

Waverly scratched at his forehead with the muzzle of the pistol as though absently remembering something. "Do you remember when we set out to India?"

"I do." He took another step to the right. Waverly didn't budge.

"Remember what we promised each other?"

"It was a long time ago. Why don't you remind me?"

"That we'd make our riches in trade. That our fathers could both sit and stew in England while their misfit sons blackened their good names in trade."

"Yes, I remember."

"Should have never gone to China."

"You're probably right."

Richard took another small step in Waverly's direction. The man still didn't move. Emma had inched to the far wall, out of Waverly's hand reach, but not out of shooting range. His patience was starting to run thin. It was almost better to tackle Waverly again, and hope the gun went off without harming anyone.

The faint steps of the bobbies sounded in the background. Some of the tension released in his shoulders. Dante had brought someone to help them. Now if he could just get Emma out of the room, this whole farce could come to an end much quicker.

Waverly's head tilted to the side, a strange expression coming over his face. "Do you remember Ling Ma?" he asked suddenly.

A woman they knew years ago. That was when Waverly's addiction to opium had shown itself in all its ugliness. Waverly had taken a liking to Ling Ma, had professed his undying love—that he would bring her back to England and marry her, his father be damned.

She had died in an opium den next to Waverly. She had simply never woken up. That was when Waverly had turned to opium daily. That was when Richard had realized his friend was in trouble and that he had to intervene or lose him.

Waverly had been lost the night his ladylove had ceased to exist.

There was nothing Richard could have done. With Waverly bringing her into the conversation now, Richard realized his friend had always been a lost cause. Realized that Waverly had found and understood true love before Richard ever had. It was no wonder he'd never understood his friend's desire to ruin his life. Richard knew now that his life would cease to exist without Emma.

"She was a fine lady," he responded.

Was it possible that a ghost was the root of his old friend's madness? Richard hadn't realized, after eight years, that the man still longed to have that particular woman by his side. Hadn't understood it because Waverly had still indulged in intimacies with other women after Ling Ma's death.

A small fleet of men stood ready at the open door, Dante with them. Richard raised his hand to stop them from coming forward. To stop them from raising a weapon at Waverly: The man was still a loose cannon, and Richard would not risk harming one more hair on Emma's head.

"The finest of ladies, yes, yes. That she was." Waverly nodded in agreement with himself. "Told her we shouldn't go to the den that night. I wanted to take her someplace nice, buy her whatever she desired so we could make the journey back to England."

Richard hadn't known that. He looked to his wife; her shaking had subsided somewhat. If he had lost her as Waverly had lost Ling Ma, how would he react? He wouldn't be complete. He wouldn't feel at home in England. He'd probably not want anything that reminded him of her close by.

Why did he feel that way? Simple answer to that was that he loved her. More than he loved anything or anyone in all his life. He loved Emma.

"Selling the business is like saying good-bye to her. Didn't want to say good-bye to her eight years ago, don't want to say good-bye now."

Seeing an easy way to free his wife without incident, Richard said, "Adam . . . Emma is my Ling Ma. Let her leave. We can talk all night if you want. We can do whatever you want."

Would Emma understand the significance of his declaration? He hoped so.

Waverly looked over his shoulder at Emma. When he turned and faced Richard, his expression softened. As though Richard had finally gotten through to the man. Waverly motioned to the men standing in the door. "They're here to take me away, aren't they?"

Telling the truth would gain Richard nothing in this instance. Instead of answering the question, he said, "We can figure out everything if you'll put the gun down."

"Can't do that, I'm afraid. Can't do that at all. Means I can't find peace. Means it'll never end if I do."

"You're making little sense, my friend."

"Don't suppose you would understand." He sat on the floor and crossed his legs. "Tell your lady she is free to go."

Emma inched around the back of the room along the wall until she was at the door. She gave him a long, sad look before she was yanked through the doorway, finally out of sight. He breathed a sigh of relief, knowing she was safe.

"That's better, then. Much better. Wouldn't want her to see all the bad in life. She's innocent, that one. She's got that look in her eyes." Waverly scratched his chin with the end of the gun, shaking his head all the while.

Richard paused in seeing a change come over the man he used to call friend. There was some glimmer of hope that seemed out of place reflected in his eyes.

"Suppose this is how it always should have been," Waverly said with a sad tone in his voice.

Without any warning, Waverly put the tip of the gun in his mouth, and pulled the trigger. His head slumped forward and an oozing bloody mess squirted out the back of his head, then took to a slow discharge of blood so dark it looked black. His arm dropped lifelessly to his lap, the gun falling from his limp fingers and thumping harmlessly to the hardwood floor.

Richard rushed forward to feel for a pulse in the man's neck. There wasn't one. He couldn't say why he cared, especially after everything Waverly had put Emma through. But he did. It seemed so pointless for the man to kill himself so suddenly.

Dante was at his side, pulling his hand away, telling him he needed his shoulder looked after. He heard Emma yelling and then screaming at the guards in the hall to let her pass, demanding to see her husband.

Richard stood on shaky legs and was able to turn away from the motionless body on the floor before he dropped to his knees and threw up. He wiped his mouth on the sleeve of his frock coat. He knelt there for some time—motionless between the body and his own vomit. Hands grasped his elbows, bringing him to his feet. Richard stared at Dante. Numb. He walked mindless of where they were headed. He felt nothing. Heard nothing. Saw only death every time he blinked his eyes.

When he entered the hall, Emma wrapped her arms around his shoulders and squeezed him close. He shut his eyes and breathed in the familiar flowery scent of her hair. He was never going to let her go again. He pressed her against the wall and just held her. He hadn't the strength to move. Couldn't even find words to express what he felt.

She was his world. His life. And the thought of losing her . . .

He couldn't imagine it.

"Are you all right?" he asked. Everyone had left them alone in the hallway. Probably to give them some much-needed privacy.

"I'm fine, Richard. I just want to get you home and have a doctor look at your shoulder."

"It's just a scratch." He hugged her tighter. Afraid to let her go.

"It's not. You're bleeding all over me."

He didn't care. All that mattered was that his wife was in his arms again. He placed his hands on either side of her face and looked at her, searching her eyes for God knew what.

She made no comment to his strange study. Her arms were wrapped tight under his arms and around his back.

"I knew you'd come for me," she said tearfully.

He pressed his forehead to hers. "I almost lost you."

"You haven't lost me." A lone tear leaked out of the corner of her eye. He kissed it away, tongue sweeping up the salty drop.

He had come close to losing her. Too close.

"Let's go home, Emma."

The doctor shut the door as he left their bedchamber. Emma stood from the wooden chair she'd perched on the edge of for the whole of Richard's examination, and sat next to him on the bed. Richard was propped up against a multitude of pillows. His shoulder had been cleaned and wrapped to stave off any further bleeding.

He looked haggard. Exhausted from his ordeal tonight. And rightly so. His head rested back against the headboard, his eyes thin slits.

Emma wasn't sure how she should feel. How she should act toward her husband. So much seemed unspoken between them. Past pettiness no longer mattered, in light of everything that had transpired with Waverly. The paintings, the accusations, the silly fights they had had, they were nothing once death stared you in the face; nothing when death taunted and teased you, until you were ready to give up hope.

She pressed her head to his good shoulder. Richard wrapped his arm around her and gave her a tender squeeze before letting it drop back to the bed. She pressed her fingers to his stomach. The muscles flexed in surprise beneath her touch.

She wanted to touch him all over, to make sure he wasn't a figment of her imagination. Her hand spread out over his abdomen. He was warm and real beneath her. Alive. So alive.

She turned her face and pressed her lips to his collarbone. "I love you, Richard." She kissed him again. "I've loved you a long time." Those words had been burning in her gut all day.

He raised his hand to pat affectionately at her hair. She tilted her head back and gazed at him. Despite everything they'd been through today, a small smile lifted his lips.

"Why do you look so smug?"

"Because my wife is as smitten as me."

She raised herself up. "How can you joke at a time like this?"

"Only with you, Emma." He gathered her hands in his when she made to pull them away.

"And why is that?"

Richard brought her hands to his mouth and pressed a kiss against her curled fingers. "Because, despite everything we've been through and after everything I have witnessed with Waverly, I couldn't be a happier man."

"How can you say such a thing in light of such tragedy?" She turned her head away and stared at the lamp on the nightstand.

"The only thing worse than Waverly killing himself would have been losing you, Emma." He squeezed her hand. "And it was too close for comfort tonight. I might not have been able to live with myself had anything happened . . ." Richard paused and took a deep inhalation. "I can't deny I've lived a hard life. I've seen worse and even been the cause of worse than what Waverly showed us tonight."

"Do you regret everything you did?" She felt awful for asking such a question, and was surprised when he answered her.

"I do. More than you can know. But I can't change the past. The only thing I can do is move forward and hope I make better decisions in my future."

"What does this mean for us?"

Did she dare to hope they could have a life together? A marriage where they depended upon each other?

She held her breath as she waited for his answer.

"How do you feel about spending the rest of your days with me, wife?"

Her head whipped around and she gazed at her husband. There was no teasing in his voice. It was a genuine question.

"Are you still going to pursue my paintings?"

He shook his head. "The duke has offered to track them down. He will be the one pursuing them."

Clever answer. "No divorce, then?"

"No. No divorce. Just us. In London, at Mansfield Hall, I care not so long as you are with me."

"Is this a product of Waverly's death?"

"I never planned to give you up, Emma. I've grown to love you deeply these last few weeks. Waverly made my resolve to keep you resolute."

Tears prickled at her eyes with his admission. "I'd be happy to spend the rest of my days with you, husband."

He leaned in close and brushed his lips against hers. "There is one other thing we need to discuss."

Emma gave him a curious look.

"You forgot to tell me about one of your paintings. The one with *you* wearing no more than a white strip of silk."

"Oh." Emma flushed. He knew the truth, and she cared not how he found out. Going up on her knees, she placed her hands on either side of his face. Lowering her lips close to his, she said, "I do believe we have the rest of our days to uncover each other's secrets."

Read on for a sneak peek at the next breathtaking romance from Tiffany Clare

# *The Secret Desires of a Governess*

June 2011

St. Martin's Paperbacks

*1848*
*Northumbria*

Elliott Taylor Wright, the Earl of Brendall, stilled when he heard footsteps. A squelching wet sound drew nearer to his study. Definitely not a usual occurrence. He flicked his watch open: ten after nine. No one came up to the castle if they could help it.

Martha, his housekeeper, would be gone from the main house for the evening. She always made sure to put his son down at eight. That didn't mean it couldn't be Jacob wandering around, finding some sort of trouble while the hour was still early. If that were the case, the boy would find his bed before long.

Not worried about unwelcome guests, Elliott stood from his wide desk, papers scattered over the surface. He stretched his back, then rubbed his eyes.

He looked toward the door when another faint sound reached his ears. That was not his son; the tread was too heavy for a boy of eight years.

With the unlikelihood that the noise was his son . . . who could be wandering the castle? There was only a handful of servants, but they rarely spent time in the main house this late in the evening. They had everything they needed at the keep—another building on the castle grounds. They left him well enough alone once the day closed. As he preferred.

It *was* possible someone was looking for him. And if that were the case, they'd know where to find him.

Except . . . the noise continued right on past his study.

He walked over to the door, slid it open soundlessly, and peered down the dimly lit hall.

A figure in white turned left at the end of the long corridor. The mud-caked hem of her skirts snapped with the turn of her heel before she disappeared from sight.

Elliott stepped out of his study, shut the heavy door as silently as he had opened it, and followed the evening prowler. Padding quietly down the hall, he wondered when he should make his presence known. He was intrigued by the notion of having a trespasser.

She was a tiny thing, probably a good seven or eight inches shorter than he. Elliott studied her slender figure. Her hair was straggly and soaked right through; the pins had released a long braid to fall down to the middle of her back, and dripped a trail of rainwater down her skirts. He couldn't make out the color, but he guessed a light brown.

Wetness clung to her like a second skin, making the line of her underthings beneath the worsted muslin visible to the naked eye. Not an ideal material for the unreliable climate in Northumbria. Her shoulders were narrow. Her waist couldn't be more than what his two hands could wrap around.

Her skirt painted a muddy path along the hardwood floor with every step. The sloshing sound he'd heard earlier was still present. It must be coming from her waterlogged shoes. She carried a dripping shawl over one arm, a valise in her other hand.

She turned down another corridor. Did she not realize she was headed back to the entrance she'd come through?

With no desire to wander the halls of the great house all evening, and curious to know who she was, he called out to her.

"I see few visitors here, madam."

He set his shoulder against the darkly paneled wall and waited for her to face him.

She froze at his comment and turned with more grace than he thought possible in her sodden, bedraggled state. Raising her dainty chin, she narrowed her eyes, making tiny wrinkles form between her brows. Her features were clearer now that she stood next to a lit lamp on the wall.

She resembled a drowned rat.

"You!" She pointed a castigating finger at him.

He raised a questioning brow. Who did the little witch think she was?

"How is it you've found your way here?" he asked.

On closer inspection, she was deceptively nice to look upon. Her complexion was clear, freckles dotted across her nose and the upper portion of her cheeks. Her lips, he imagined, were full. Right now, though, she pinched them tightly together, either in anger or to keep her teeth from chattering since the edge of her lips held a tinge of blue. How long had she been standing out in the rain to come to this state? It occurred to him then that he should offer her the warmth of a fire before he sent her on her way.

"I walked," she spat like a feral cat.

He pinched his lips tightly together and swallowed his offer. It was then he noticed her eyes were as rich and clear a green as peridot, with the slightest hint of gold, and as fiery as her nature proved to be.

"I had to walk fifteen miles because no one arranged for a carriage. I couldn't even hire a coach to bring me this far."

He looked her over once more. Even though it was damaged from the rain, her dress was well-made and of a fine, expensive material. A lady would have traveled with a maid. A ladybird on the other hand . . .

Elliott crossed his arms over his wide chest at that thought. He watched her gaze flick to the open throat of his shirt, trailing lower to the exposed skin of his forearms where his shirt sleeves were rolled up. Then she met his gaze head-on, weariness making her lids heavy. She had traveled far by the looks of it.

"Madam, do you always address your betters in such a fashion?"

"How—how dare you speak to me thus. I'm here on your invitation!"

That gave him pause and he stood away from the wall. He hadn't invited a woman up to the castle for more years than he cared to count. When he wanted the company of a woman, he rode over to Alnwick, one of the larger townships. But he'd been too busy over the past few months to indulge in a good tumble.

Until she stuttered, "I–I'm the governess."

*The governess?*

Elliott forced himself to take a step away from her.

"You're the governess?" Disbelief and disappointment were evident in his voice.

"Yes . . . I put an advertisement in the *Northern Times* last month. I was asked to start immediately."

And she looked ready to hit him, whether from his briefly untoward behavior or her uncomfortable, bedraggled state was hard to determine.

Well, damn.